Backtrack

THE HAGGERTY MYSTERY NOVELS
BY BETSY BRANNON GREEN:

Hearts in Hiding

Until Proven Guilty

Above Suspicion

Silenced

Copycat

Poison

Double Cross

OTHER NOVELS
BY BETSY BRANNON GREEN:

Never Look Back

Don't Close Your Eyes

Foul Play

Backtrack

A NOVEL

BETSY BRANNON GREEN

Covenant Communications, Inc.

Cover image by Romilly Lockyer © Riser/Getty Images, Inc.

Cover design by Jessica A. Warner © 2007 by Covenant Communications, Inc.

Published by Covenant Communications, Inc.
American Fork, Utah

This is a work of fiction. The characters, names, incidents, places, and dialogue are products of the
author's imagination, and are not to be construed as real.

Printed in Canada
First Printing: May 2007

13 12 11 10 09 08 07   10 9 8 7 6 5 4 3 2 1

ISBN 978-1-59811-339-6

PROLOGUE

Scarlett Louise Stewart stood in the dressing room at the Circle of Love Bridal Shoppe in Atlanta, Georgia, and examined herself carefully from each direction. Since she was on a raised dais and the room had mirrors on every wall, nothing was hidden from her critical gaze. She started with her long, honey-blonde hair, which she had piled haphazardly on top of her head. Her hairdresser would do a much better job on her wedding day, but this helped to get the full effect of the pearls glistening at each ear and around her neck. They were old pearls that had belonged to her grandmother, which increased both their beauty and their value.

A slight turn to the right gave her an unobstructed view of her veil, which was fingertip-length—long enough to be dramatic, but short enough to be tasteful. Her train was also abbreviated, and the silk dress itself was free of distractions like lace and sequins. The subtle patina of the fabric caught the light as she turned. Lettie smiled. Perfect.

"Oh, Lettie, you're perfect," Mary Margaret concurred from a few feet away where Lettie's three bridesmaids were gathered.

Lettie smiled even though she knew it wasn't hard to get Mary Margaret's approval. "Thanks, but you have to say that."

"I mean it," Mary Margaret insisted. "In fact, I think you are the most beautiful woman in the *world*—and the luckiest." Mary Margaret used her fingers to itemize. "You're marrying an extremely handsome man, you're almost through with college, you have a wonderful condo right in the heart of Atlanta, and . . ."

"Whoa!" Lettie raised a gloved hand. "I've worked very hard to get what I have."

"No one's disputing that," Alexa, another bridesmaid, assured her. She turned to Mary Margaret. "Add *the hardest working woman in the world* to your list of Lettie's enviable attributes."

Lettie narrowed her eyes at Alexa, who had a tendency to be a little sarcastic. Then she addressed her third bridesmaid. "How do you think I look, Beth?"

Beth Middleton, who was a bride-to-be herself, nodded. "Like Mary Margaret said, you're perfect."

Lettie's gaze returned to Alexa, who could be counted on to tell the truth even if it hurt. "Well?"

"I can't say perfect," Alexa hedged. "But only because I don't believe there is such a thing. You're probably as close as anyone could get."

Lettie was satisfied with this response. "Good. Now, you all go out and tell Gray to come in."

Mary Margaret's hand flew up to her mouth. "Oh, we can't do that! You know it's bad luck if the groom sees the bride in her gown before the wedding!"

Lettie dismissed this with a wave. "I'm not superstitious, so go and get Gray."

Mary Margaret looked to Beth and Alexa for support. "Tell her not to do it!" she begged.

Beth tried. "Let's wait until your mother and Sister Grantland get back. We can ask them what they think before . . ."

Lettie cut her off. "It won't matter what they think." She turned to get a side view. "I want Gray to see me in this dress and that's that."

Mary Margaret opened her mouth to present another objection, but Lettie shook her head firmly. So, with a look of resignation, Mary Margaret followed Beth and Alexa out.

While waiting for Gray to arrive, Lettie smiled at her reflection. All her dreams were about to come true. Tears of happiness stung her eyes, and she blinked them back quickly before they could damage her perfect makeup. She heard the dressing room door open and lifted her head regally as she turned to give Gray the full effect.

He seemed affected all right. He closed the door behind him and then leaned against it as if he couldn't stand on his own.

Lettie had to control a smile. "So, what do you think?" she asked, turning a little to the right so he could see the way the light reflected off the expensive material.

"You're beautiful." The words were right, but the tone was wrong and Lettie frowned.

"I'm having my bridal portraits done at noon tomorrow," she told him. "Then we close on our condominium at four, and Mama wants to take us all out to dinner afterwards to celebrate." Gray seemed to be staring at a point over her shoulder, and she wasn't sure he was listening. "Gray, did you hear me?" she asked, fighting annoyance. It was his wedding too. Lettie and the mothers were doing all the work—it seemed like the least Gray could do was pay attention.

"I heard you," he replied vaguely.

She studied him through narrowed eyes. He'd only been home three weeks from his mission in San Juan, so his light brown hair was still too short, but he did have a nice tan. A four-sport letterman in high school, Gray had maintained a trim, athletic physique with daily exercise. But his eyes were Lettie's favorite feature, and as she thought of them, her frustration dissipated.

His eyes changed color depending on his mood. When he was giving a talk in church or working on his homework, they were dark green. Right after he scored a touchdown or hit a home run—or kissed her—they were a warm brown.

Stepping off the dais, she walked over to him. A tall girl herself, the top of her head fit just under his chin. She gave him a hug, careful not to crush her gown. Then she looked up into his eyes. She expected to see the passionate brown color but instead saw the deep green she associated with the serious side of his nature.

"Gray?"

"Oh, Lettie," he said, and the pain in his voice alarmed her. "I can't do this."

She pulled him tightly against her, all thoughts of the expensive dress forgotten. "Can't do what?"

"Get married," he whispered.

"You don't want to marry me?" she asked in confusion.

"I love you." The serious green eyes were shimmering with unshed tears. "But I can't get married this week."

"Why?" she forced past her terror-stiffened lips. Then she steeled herself for revelations of a grievous sin in his past or a fatal disease in his future.

"You remember I told you about Lowell Brooks, my trainer on my mission?"

This seemed like an odd segue, but Lettie nodded. Gray had told her all about Lowell Brooks in the first several letters he'd written her on his mission, and she knew he had called Lowell almost as soon as he'd gotten off the plane from Puerto Rico three weeks before. Since that phone conversation Gray had talked of little else besides Lowell and his plans to lead paying tourists on hikes through the woods. "Of course."

"I told you how he wants to start a business in the Great Smoky Mountains National Park?"

"Yes, a hundred times." Lettie didn't like the direction their conversation had taken and made no effort to hide her contempt for this business venture. "You don't seriously think there's a market for that, do you?"

"Yes, I do!" Gray insisted. "Lowell says that all kinds of folks want to take vacations in the mountains and are willing to pay for someone to rent them equipment and guide them along the trails." His eyes were changing to passionate brown, and Lettie's fear intensified. "But the best part is that he's been working hard to set everything up since he got home last year, and just this month he found a piece of land for sale near the Tennessee entrance to the park. It already has a building on it that we could use as our office. So all we'd have to do is put up a couple of equipment sheds and get some camping gear and we'd be set."

"Lowell wants you to help him buy land in Tennessee?" she repeated to be sure she hadn't misunderstood.

Gray nodded. "The owner is a friend of his father's and will sell it to us for a fraction of what it's worth."

"But you don't know anything about the Smoky Mountains!" Lettie pointed out. "How will you be able to lead people?"

He laughed. "Oh, that's no problem. Lowell knows that park like the back of his hand, and he'll teach me the ropes."

Trying hard not to panic, she said, "What about college?"

He shrugged. "I can sign up for some night and online courses. It will take me longer to finish, but that's not a priority for me at the moment. I can get a college degree anytime, but we can only buy this land now."

"What if you don't get any customers?" Lettie asked, grasping for anything that would make him see the foolishness of his plan.

"Lowell's already got people lined up through the end of the year. All he's waiting on is the go-ahead from me." He paused for a second before adding, "And my $10,000 start-up capital."

Now she understood. If Gray chose this path instead of the one she had plotted for him, they wouldn't be able to buy the condominium. Gray had some money left over in his mission fund, and his parents had gifted him the rest to make up the $10,000 down payment for their condo. She swallowed hard. She loved that condo, but she loved Gray more. So slowly she nodded her head.

"Okay. We won't buy the condo. We'll probably lose our earnest money, but we can deal with that. We'll start looking for an apartment, or a tree house—whatever is available near your new business. I'll find a job there and—"

"I can't ask you to do that," he interrupted. "You only have a few months left before you graduate."

"There's probably a college up there I can transfer to," she said without much enthusiasm.

He was shaking his head. "In order to build up the business, Lowell and I will have to dedicate our total attention to it for a year. We'll have to camp with our tour groups, so I'll be gone for long stretches of time. That's no way to start a marriage."

She stepped back when she saw that his eyes were green again. "It's not that you *can't* marry me. You just don't want to," she whispered, staring at him in shock. "You've chosen Lowell Brooks over *me!*"

"Lettie . . ." he began, but she held up a hand to stop him.

"So you're canceling the wedding at the last minute, even though we've sent out three hundred invitations and spent thousands of dollars?"

"I've been trying to find a way to tell you," he offered as an excuse.

"Well, you haven't been trying very hard!" Lettie was suddenly furious. How dare he imply that if she'd been listening more closely this confrontation could have been avoided.

"I told you all about Lowell and his plans . . ."

Later she would realize that there had been plenty of warning signs, but in the heat of the moment all she could see was his selfishness and deceit. "We've been planning this wedding for months— since before you even got home from your mission. If you didn't want to get married, all you had to do was say so!"

"I wanted to find the right place and time to explain," he said, and he did look miserable. If she hadn't been so mad at him, she might have felt sorry for him.

"And you decided that this was the perfect moment, with me standing here in my *wedding dress?*" She shook a handful of the gown for emphasis.

"I'm sorry," he whispered.

For the first time in her life Lettie felt pure hatred toward another human being. "You certainly are," she agreed. Then she lifted her silk skirts and ran from the dressing room before he could see the tears coursing down her cheeks.

CHAPTER 1

Five Years Later

Eugenia Atkins had just returned from her regular morning walk around her neighborhood in the town of Haggerty, Georgia, with her little dog, Lady, and was washing up the breakfast dishes when the doorbell rang. She dried her hands on a dishcloth and wondered aloud, "Who in the world that could be?"

Lady barked in response as they walked into the entryway. Eugenia pulled open the front door to find Reverend Watson Howard, affectionately referred to by his Methodist congregation as Brother Watty, and his wife, Barbara Jean, standing on the porch.

"Good morning!" Barbara Jean greeted. The preacher's wife was thin and stylish, and in her presence Eugenia always felt large and dowdy.

"Barbara Jean," Eugenia returned with less enthusiasm.

"Sorry to call so early," Brother Watty apologized. He was shorter than Eugenia, which doomed her to a bird's-eye view of his unfortunate comb-over. "Swan Glover is having surgery this morning, and we went to the hospital to pray with the family before she was anesthetized."

Eugenia averted her eyes from the little beads of sweat that were forming on his pink scalp. "That was nice of you."

"And on the way home we thought we'd take the opportunity to invite folks to our one-day revival," Barbara Jean continued his explanation. "Have you heard about it?"

Eugenia was annoyed by this question. "It's been on the sign in front of the Methodist church for a month now," she pointed out. "And you're running ads in the newspaper, on the radio, and on TV. I'd have to be blind and deaf not to know about it."

Barbara Jean frowned, but before she could comment, Brother Watty said, "Well, then, since you know about all the wonderful events we have planned, can we count on you to come and join with us in praising the Lord on Sunday?"

Eugenia was even more annoyed that they were putting her in a position of having to make explanations about decisions that she considered private. "You know I go to church with Kate and Mark—to help with their children."

Barbara Jean's eyes cut over to the Iversons' dark, empty house. "I thought Kate and Mark were gone."

"They're not gone," Eugenia corrected. "They're just in Atlanta so that Mark can receive some special training for his important new job with the FBI."

Barbara Jean sifted through all this information and grabbed hold of the tidbit that suited her purposes. "If they're in Atlanta, they're *gone,* and that means you can worship with us this weekend."

Eugenia was not about to be railroaded into anything by Barbara Jean Howard, so she said, "I'm not sure what obligations I have on Sunday, but I'll try to attend your meeting."

Refusing to be satisfied with this noncommittal response, Barbara Jean said, "I'm sure you'll agree that we should make room for the Lord in our lives!"

Eugenia narrowed her eyes at the other woman. "I do agree with that, but I can have the Lord in my life without attending your one-day revival. And if you ask me one more time, I'm going to say no."

Barbara Jean's nostrils flared, but before she could launch another verbal assault, Brother Watty stepped between the two women and flashed Eugenia a bright smile. "A guest preacher from Knoxville is speaking on Sunday, and he's supposed to be real entertaining."

Eugenia took pity on the man. "I'm sure he's very good, and I'll do my best to stop by."

Apparently deciding that this was the best he could hope for, Brother Watty took his wife by the arm and led her down the steps. The little sweat beads on his head glinted like diamonds in the early morning sunshine. "We hope to see you there," he called over his shoulder.

Eugenia waved good-bye and then waited until the preacher and his wife were out of sight before remarking to Lady, "Well, I'm not sure what to make of that."

The little dog barked and ran circles around her feet.

"Barbara Jean drives me crazy," Eugenia said as much to herself as to the dog. "But Brother Watty is nice, and I can't fault them for trying to get people to come to church. Now I've got to finish washing our breakfast dishes, and then we'll get ready for the Horticulture Society meeting."

Lady followed Eugenia back to the kitchen and settled quietly in her little dog bed. Eugenia just had time to get her hands wet again before the phone rang. It was Polly Kirby, her neighbor two houses down.

"Good morning, Eugenia!" Polly was always cheerful. "Did you hear that Jack and Beth Gamble are back in town?"

"No," Eugenia replied thoughtfully. "When they left after Christmas, Beth said they were going to stay in Atlanta until the end of the Senate session."

"Apparently Beth is going to a high school reunion, and Jack is going to keep the kids while she's gone. He decided it would be easier to do that here than at their place in Atlanta."

The thought of a helpless man in charge of two young children was irresistible to Eugenia. "I'll have to go by there on my way to the Horticulture Society meeting and offer him my assistance."

"You're so good," Polly approved. Then she moved on to the real purpose of her call—snooping. "Was that Brother Watty and Barbara Jean I saw leaving your house?"

"Yes." Eugenia decided to go ahead and divulge all she knew in hopes of getting rid of Polly sooner. "They were on their way home from visiting Swan Glover before her surgery and decided to invite folks to the one-day revival they're having on Sunday."

There was a brief pause, and then Polly said, "They didn't come by and invite me."

Eugenia frowned. That was odd. "Maybe they're only inviting Methodists," she ventured.

"What would be the point of having a revival if you only invite the people who come to your church already?" Polly asked.

"That's a good point," Eugenia had to admit.

"In fact, they didn't visit a single house on Maple Street besides yours," Polly continued. "At least not one I could see from my upstairs windows."

Ordinarily Eugenia would scold Polly for spying so shamelessly on the neighborhoods, but at the moment she was too confused to care. "I was the *only* person they visited?"

There was a little giggle from the other end of the phone line. "Yes, and I think I know why. I heard that you've become the subject of a religious contest."

Polly was often silly but rarely wrong. "A religious contest?" Eugenia repeated. "What is that?"

Polly was only too happy to explain. "Well, Mabel Reynolds told me that your determination to worship with the Mormons was discussed at the Quilt Club meeting yesterday. Apparently Barbara Jean said that the one-day revival was the perfect chance to win you back to the Methodist fold—since Kate and Mark are in Atlanta. That's when Jane Ann Ford announced that the reason you haven't been attending the Methodist church in the first place is because you're mad at Brother Watty, so even with the Iversons away, the Methodists didn't have a chance of winning you back."

"Humph," Eugenia said disparagingly. "I'm not mad at Brother Watty."

"I don't know how anyone could be mad at that sweet man," Polly agreed. "But Cornelia Blackwood told Barbara Jean that the Methodists should step aside and let the Baptists have a shot at you—before the Iversons come home and lure you irretrievably back to the Mormons."

"The very idea," Eugenia muttered.

"Barbara Jean and Cornelia argued for a while, and it finally ended in a challenge. Whoever can get you to attend services this Sunday wins."

Eugenia sighed. "I declare, if that's not the most ridiculous thing I've ever heard!"

"It explains why Brother Watty and Barbara Jean came to see you personally this morning," Polly remarked. "They are trying to get the edge on the competition."

"Surely no one would take such a challenge seriously," Eugenia began, but Polly interrupted her.

"Don't look now, but Cornelia and Brother Blackwood are coming up your sidewalk."

Eugenia disobeyed Polly and peered out the kitchen window. Sure enough, the Baptist preacher and his wife were headed right for her house.

Assuming Eugenia would want to be polite, Polly said, "I guess you need to hang up so you can invite them in."

"I'm not going to let them in!" Eugenia whispered into the phone. "I'm going to sit here quietly and pretend like no one is home."

"But they'll see your car in the driveway."

"That doesn't mean anything!" Eugenia hissed as she heard a knock at her door. "I walk places all the time."

"They'll know you're avoiding them," Polly predicted.

"But they won't be able to prove it," Eugenia returned with another covert glance outside.

"They'll just come back," Polly warned her.

"And I'll deal with them then, but one religious argument each morning is enough for me." The knocking subsided, and she asked Polly, "Are they leaving?"

"Yes," Polly confirmed. "They're almost to the corner."

"Thank heaven for that," Eugenia said with relief.

"You can't hide from both the Baptists and the Methodists until Sunday."

"I can try." Eugenia chewed her bottom lip. "I've never been the subject of a contest before, and I'm not sure how to feel about it."

"It should make you feel important," Polly said. "Think how honored the winning congregation will be!"

"And how mad the losers will be," Eugenia added. "Fortunately I have a few days to decide how I'm going to handle this. Right now I've got to hurry or I won't have time to visit the Gambles before the Horticulture Society meeting."

Polly giggled. "I'll see you there."

* * *

Mary Margaret McKenzie stood in front of the bathroom mirror in her apartment in Tifton, Georgia. She concentrated on applying her makeup and tried to ignore the pill bottles lined up on the side of the sink. There were pills to boost her blood pressure and pills to improve her immune system, pills to increase her appetite and pills to help her sleep. Shaking her head, she wondered how doctors could expect anyone who took so many pills to feel healthy. Just looking at all the little bottles made her sick.

When she was first diagnosed with cancer six months earlier, she'd been frightened yet hopeful. The doctors had explained at length all the treatments that were available and bragged about their success rates. Always an optimist, Mary Margaret was sure that she would eventually join the ranks of the newly healed. She had faced the surgeries and treatments with near enthusiasm. When the doctors told her she was in remission, she wasn't surprised. After all, that's what they had led her to expect.

Now her hair was growing back and, thanks to the chemo, she'd lost weight. But she lived in constant fear that the cancer would come back. Learning to face her own mortality was a humbling experience. Each day seemed so much more important now, and she was determined not to put off any of the things she wanted to accomplish in life.

Her eyes strayed into her bedroom and focused on the duffel bag stashed by the door. She'd been planning the reunion trip for weeks and felt strongly that she and her friends needed this time together.

Mary Margaret returned her gaze to the mirror and stared for a moment into her own solemn blue eyes. Then she bowed her head and prayed. *Please, Lord, show us how to help each other like we used to.*

Then she opened her eyes, swallowed a handful of pills, and headed for the door.

* * *

Beth Gamble sat at the kitchen table in her house in Haggerty, patiently coaxing her eighteen-month-old son, Hank, to eat his oatmeal. He was teething and hadn't slept much the night before. Consequently, Beth too was exhausted.

"Look, Hank, Chloe ate all her breakfast," Beth offered as encouragement.

Chloe looked up from the spelling words she was studying. "Come on, Hank. Eat that mush so Mom can quit talking about it. She's breaking my concentration."

"Mush," Hank repeated and stuck his hand directly into the bowl of oatmeal.

"Thanks," Beth told her stepdaughter. Then she removed the tray from Hank's highchair, accepting defeat. "Now you watch Hank while I get something to clean him up with."

Chloe sighed audibly as she reached out to hold Hank's gooey hand. "Hipolita never let Hank get this messy when she fed him."

Beth knew it was childish to let this mild criticism bother her, but she couldn't help it. "Well, Hipolita's gone, and you're stuck with me," she said more sharply than she'd intended.

Chloe's dark eyes widened with concern. "We're *glad* you're here."

Beth tore off a paper towel and walked back to the table. "I know. I'm having a little trouble learning to do things as well as Hipolita did. She was such a good housekeeper."

Chloe nodded. "Daddy says she was perfect."

Beth concentrated on wiping Hank's fingers, determined not to cry. Hipolita had been Jack's housekeeper long before he met Beth. Because of Hipolita's quiet competence, the large and busy household ran smoothly. But a couple of months ago Hipolita had announced that she was getting married and would be moving to Orlando. Since then nothing had been the same.

Jack had offered to hire a replacement. In fact, Beth found his persistent encouragement to do so almost insulting. Hipolita had been like a part of the family, so Beth never felt guilty about accepting her help. But now, if they hired a stranger, it would seem like she couldn't handle her job as wife and mother. So she had refused the offer, and Jack had finally stopped mentioning it.

Beth glanced around the kitchen. The dishwasher needed to be loaded, and it was time for Hank's bath. Jack was down to one clean shirt, so the laundry couldn't be postponed any longer. Hipolita had a knack for anticipating needs before they actually arose. Beth could never decide what to do first and always felt like she was running behind.

Careful to keep the discouragement from her voice, Beth lifted Hank onto her hip and asked Chloe, "Are you ready for me to test you on those spelling words?"

"Why don't you let me quiz Chloe on her spelling words," Jack suggested as he walked into the kitchen. Dressed for a day of working from home, he had on old jeans and a T-shirt. His longish dark hair was curling on the ends and tucked behind his ears, and his brilliant blue eyes were full of mischief. Beth sighed. The sight of him still took her breath away. Her gaze dropped to the armload of dress shirts he was carrying. "I'm headed to the dry cleaners, and Chloe can go with me and spell while we ride."

Beth eyed the shirts guiltily. "I was planning to do laundry today."

"I know." Jack kissed her first and then Hank. "But it's good politics to contribute to the local economy by giving the dry cleaners some business."

It was a kind and sensitive gesture, but if it made her feel like more of a failure. She was searching for a response when the intercom buzzed.

"We have company," Chloe announced unnecessarily as a voice spoke from the intercom.

"Beth? Jack? This is Eugenia Atkins. I heard you were in town and wanted to stop by and welcome you home."

"Talk about getting your day off to a bad start," Jack muttered.

Beth laughed. "I like Miss Eugenia."

He shrugged. "Me too—in small doses." He lowered his voice and whispered, "We could ignore her."

"That would be rude," Chloe pointed out.

"And she'd just come back," Beth added as she walked over to the intercom and pushed the TALK button. "Good morning, Miss Eugenia. I'll unlock the gate for you."

"And I'll head off to the dry cleaners," Jack said. "Come on, Chloe, and don't forget to bring your spelling words."

Hank reached his hands out and said, "Daddy."

"Do you want to go with us?" Jack asked the little boy.

"So, you're all deserting me?" Beth said as she passed the baby to Jack.

Jack shifted the shirts into one arm and secured Hank with the other. "You can't blame him for his sense of self-preservation."

Beth rolled her eyes and then followed the rest of her family outside. Jack was halfway across the driveway by the time Miss Eugenia's old Buick pulled to a stop beside the patio. Jack waved to their guest and then ushered the children into the garage.

Miss Eugenia climbed from the car wearing a purple and pink polyester dress, knee-high hose, and black orthopedic shoes. Lady was in a basket hooked over her arm.

With as much enthusiasm as she could muster, Beth said, "You're out early."

"Actually, I'm behind schedule," Miss Eugenia responded. "But when I heard you and your family were here in Haggerty, I had to come by."

Beth smiled. "Thanks."

Jack's SUV emerged from the garage, and Beth caught a brief glance of her children, strapped in safely, as Jack drove quickly away.

"Where was Jack off to in such a hurry?" Miss Eugenia asked.

"The dry cleaners," Beth explained. "Won't you come in?"

Miss Eugenia nodded. "I have a meeting at ten o'clock, but I can visit for a few minutes."

As they stepped inside, Beth saw Miss Eugenia look around the less-than-neat kitchen and was immediately defensive. "I haven't had a chance to clean up after breakfast yet."

Miss Eugenia waved this aside. "You know what they say, dishes and cobwebs will keep, but babies won't."

Beth frowned. "I've never heard anyone say that."

"It's a poem my mother used to recite," Miss Eugenia told her. Then she placed the dog basket on the floor and recited:

I hope that my child, looking back on today,
Remembers a mother who had time to play.
Children grow up while we're not looking.
There'll be years ahead for cleaning and cooking.
So cobwebs be quiet and dust go to sleep,
I'm rocking my baby, and babies don't keep.

Beth had to blink back tears, wondering how her children would remember her. Probably as completely incompetent.

"My mother was a wise woman," Miss Eugenia was saying. "She taught me that it's important to prioritize."

"I've been so overwhelmed ever since Hipolita left that I don't even have time to prioritize," Beth found herself confiding. "She kept everything in perfect order. It's all I can do to maintain minimum health department standards."

Miss Eugenia ignored the weak joke and scowled at the mention of the Gambles' former housekeeper. "I personally think you are much better off without Hipolita. She seemed very ill-tempered, and allowing her to spend too much time with the children would eventually have had an adverse effect."

Beth laughed. "Hipolita was wonderful with the kids. She's just a little reserved."

Miss Eugenia expressed her disagreement by saying, "Humph." Then she pushed Chloe's abandoned cereal bowl away from the edge of the table and added, "You really should consider finding a *cheerful* replacement for your housekeeper."

"You don't think that would make me seem lazy?" Beth asked.

"Heavens no!" Miss Eugenia replied. "Why would you say that?"

Beth shrugged. "I don't know. Cleaning and cooking is what wives do."

"Domestic skills aren't the only measure of a good wife," Miss Eugenia assured her. "I myself have never been overly fond of dusting and mopping. I'd rather be outside with my flowers."

"You do have a lovely garden," Beth complimented.

"Thank you," Miss Eugenia said graciously. "Besides, being a politician's wife has added pressures and responsibilities to your life—so it's only sensible for you to relieve yourself of things that someone else can easily do for you."

"Being the wife of a senator is the hardest thing I've ever done," Beth agreed.

Miss Eugenia leaned forward. "Doesn't it drive you crazy to see Jack and his policies criticized constantly on television and in the newspaper and even by your neighbors?"

Beth felt a completely unexpected kinship with Miss Eugenia. "Yes, that's the most difficult part for me. Of course, all those social gatherings with beautiful, accomplished people are no picnic either."

Miss Eugenia chuckled. "I don't envy you that." She reached down and stroked her little dog's head. "I'm surprised that Chloe is out of school. Surely Atlanta schools don't take their spring break this early."

"No, her spring break is still a couple of weeks away, but Jack has arranged for her to take tests and turn in assignments online."

Miss Eugenia shook her head. "I never thought I'd live to see the day when little children learn from a computer instead of a teacher."

"Technology is amazing," Beth agreed.

"If you get bored while you're here, I'd be glad to have you accompany me to my various club meetings. Right now I'm headed to a meeting of the Haggerty Horticulture Society. Willadene Maddox is the guest speaker. She's an amateur taxidermist, and she's going to display her collection of birds and squirrels."

Beth controlled a shudder. "As interesting as that sounds, I will have to decline. I'm leaving this morning on a camping trip to the Great Smoky Mountains National Park with three of my best friends from high school."

"I heard that you were attending a reunion," Miss Eugenia said. "But I didn't realize it was a camping trip."

Beth frowned. "How could you have heard that already? We only got in last night."

"And you met Louise Layton at the Piggly Wiggly," Miss Eugenia reminded her. "She shared the news with a few of her closest friends, and now everyone knows."

"The whole town?" Beth asked.

"Close enough," Miss Eugenia confirmed. "Never underestimate the communication capabilities of a small Southern town."

Beth shook her head in wonder. "I won't—ever again."

"Isn't the Great Smoky Mountains National Park in Tennessee?"

"Yes, ma'am," Beth confirmed. "And North Carolina."

"You're going quite a ways from home," Miss Eugenia remarked. "And camping way up in the mountains sounds dangerous."

Beth raised an eyebrow. "Do you think Jack would let me do anything dangerous?"

Miss Eugenia smiled. "No, I guess not."

"Actually, we may be stretching things to call it a 'camping' trip," Beth explained. "We will be in the mountains and some hiking is involved, but we'll have a guide. And we'll be staying in a lodge, not tents. I am a little nervous about leaving Jack and the kids, though," Beth admitted. "He's never handled them alone before."

"It will be good for Jack—make him appreciate you more," Miss Eugenia predicted. "And that's important for any marriage, even a happy one. Absence truly does make the heart grow fonder." A sad expression clouded Miss Eugenia's eyes. "I can tell you from personal experience that's true. It's been so long since I've seen Emily and little Charles, I barely remember what they look like."

"How long have the Iversons been gone?" Beth asked sympathetically.

"One week and five days," Miss Eugenia reported.

"Any news on when they'll be back?"

"When I talked to Kate last night, she said soon—whatever that means." Miss Eugenia stood and hooked Lady's basket over one arm. "Well, I'll get out of your way. Have fun on your trip, and tell Jack if he needs me while you're gone, all he has to do is call."

"Thanks. I'll tell him," Beth promised as she walked Miss Eugenia to the door.

Miss Eugenia had only been gone a few minutes when Jack and the kids returned.

"You were driving around the neighborhood, waiting for her to leave," Beth accused.

Jack deposited Hank in the playpen and told Chloe to go take her spelling test on the computer. Then he pulled Beth into his arms. "Is there a law against watching the spring flowers bloom?"

Beth rested her cheek against his chest. "If there was, you'd find a way around it."

He kissed the top of her head. "I'll take that as a compliment. What did Miss Eugenia want?"

"She misses Kate and Mark and their children," Beth murmured.

"Well, if she thinks we're going to fill the void, she's mistaken," Jack said firmly. "I can't have her practically living here the way she does at Kate and Mark's house."

Beth laughed. "How will you stop her?"

"I will electrify our security fence if I have to," he said, and she wasn't sure he was teasing. He sat down in a kitchen chair and settled her onto his lap. "Now let's quit talking about Miss Eugenia." He pulled her in and kissed her, ending all conversation.

A few minutes later she put her hands on his shoulders and pushed away. "We have to stop this," she said a little breathlessly. "Roberta will be here any minute."

"Roberta has seen us kiss a thousand times," he pointed out.

"And she's probably getting tired of it," Beth continued in mild resistance.

The back door opened and they both turned to see Roberta, Jack's secretary, walk in. "Cut the mushy stuff," she said by way of greeting. "It's time to get to work on your new campaign."

Beth frowned. "New campaign?"

Roberta gave Jack an impatient look. "You haven't told her?"

Beth struggled to keep her voice level as she addressed her husband. "Told me what?"

Jack pulled her a little closer and answered his secretary. "I'm about to tell her, but I was trying to soften her up first."

"Just tell her," Roberta advised. "If you soften her up any more she'll melt." Then Roberta exited the kitchen, presumably headed upstairs to Jack's home office.

Beth put her hands on Jack's cheeks and directed his gaze toward her. "Jack," she prompted.

He sighed. "Mr. Fuller wants to nominate me as the Republican candidate for governor."

Beth closed her eyes so he wouldn't be able to see the dread she felt and whispered, "Governor." Jack thrived on the pressure and publicity associated with his job as a state senator—but Beth hated it. And she resented Mr. Fuller, the president of the Georgia Republican Party, for continuing to interfere in their lives.

"So, what do you think about the prospect of being Georgia's first lady?" Jack asked.

Beth's lips felt numb, but she managed to say, "It's completely beyond imagination."

* * *

Mancil Bright dumped a shovelful of pebbles into the garden near the entrance to Bolivar City's water treatment facility. He smoothed out the rocks and then stood back to admire his work. The landscaping project was nearly complete, and it had turned out better than even he had expected.

Actually, they'd basically been finished two days before, and everyone working on the project knew that Mancil was stalling—

even Kenny Dobson, the guard who supervised the crew during their work-release excursions. But since all of them preferred spending their days outside the walls of the Hardeman County Correctional Facility, no one complained.

Mancil walked over to the crowning glory of his botanical design, a grouping of oleander bushes. He searched the plants quickly and removed a few withered pieces. He was adding them to the collection of dead leaves already in his pocket when Isaac Bass stepped up beside him. Isaac was one of Mancil's fellow inmates, a member of the landscaping crew, and the closest thing Mancil had to a friend inside Hardeman County Correctional.

"How much longer you think we can stretch out this job?" Isaac asked.

Mancil glanced over at Kenny. Once he was sure the guard wasn't listening, he said, "I figure this is our last day. There's a limit to the number of times we can move the same rocks around."

Isaac nodded. "This sure has been a good one, though. Nice weather, lots of room to work, and it turned out real pretty."

Mancil saw Kenny staring at them. "If you want the job to last until this evening you'd better get back to your spot and pretend to be smoothing out gravel."

Isaac chuckled softly. Then he moved away and went back to work.

* * *

Alexa Whitstone stood in the kitchen of her home in the suburbs of Tifton, Georgia, and stared at the letter in morbid fascination. She didn't need to read the words since they had been irrevocably committed to her memory. She'd found the letter in the mailbox a few weeks before, innocently mixed in with the usual collection of bills and junk mail. If she could go back to that moment—one that had seemed so ordinary but had actually been a turning point in her life—she would have thrown the letter away without opening it.

She relaxed her fingers and allowed the single sheet of expensive letterhead to fall onto the cluttered kitchen counter. Burying her face in her hands, she tried, once again, to figure out where she'd gone wrong.

Alexa and her husband, Brian, had been married for three years. They both had good jobs and worked hard, so they were able to afford most everything money could buy. They had a nice house in a new suburb of Tifton, they drove expensive cars, and they had even been talking about getting a condo at the beach. It seemed like they were on a path to lifelong happiness.

Then Brian started working late and traveling to Atlanta often. Eventually, he decided that commuting was too time consuming and announced that instead of buying a condo at the beach, they should buy one in Atlanta so he'd have a place to stay when work took him there. Alexa didn't mind too much about giving up the condo at the beach. Brian worked hard, and if a second home in Atlanta made things easier for him, she was willing to sacrifice.

Once they had the condo furnished, Brian was rarely home and always seemed distracted. She asked if there were problems at work, but he said things there were better than ever. She worried that he might have an undiagnosed health problem, but he said he felt great. She wondered if he was having some kind of emotional or spiritual crisis. But she never worried that he'd fallen out of love with her. Not until the letter came.

It wasn't even a personal letter. It had been typed and printed by a secretary, whose initials below the signature line proved that Brian hadn't even had the decency to keep Alexa's pain and humiliation private. In concise legal terminology, Brian had made it clear that he wanted their relationship to end.

Stunned, she'd called him and asked, somewhat hysterically, for an explanation. He'd said he was sorry, but there was really nothing to talk about. His mind was made up and only the legalities remained. She'd begged and pleaded for him to reconsider until he'd finally ended the call. After that he didn't answer the phone.

Remembering her pitiful behavior, Alexa shuddered. Then she opened her purse and extracted the bottle of Lortab she'd been prescribed several weeks earlier when she'd had some dental work done. She shook two tablets onto her palm and tossed them into her mouth. Then she returned the prescription bottle to her purse, nestling it beside the two identical bottles already there.

After her humiliating phone confrontation with Brian, she'd called the dentist and asked him to renew her prescription for the pain medication. Then she'd called a doctor she worked with in the hospital emergency room and asked him to call her in another prescription for the pain pills.

In a matter of minutes she'd arranged for enough medication to keep her numb for a month. And it was a comfort to know that if the pain finally became too much to bear, she could take all the pills at once and put an end to her misery once and for all.

CHAPTER 2

Lettie Stewart stepped off the elevator onto the hallowed ground of Tatum and Trent's executive suite and headed toward the dining room. She checked her appearance in one of several mirrors that lined the hallway, pleased to see that she didn't look as nervous as she felt. At this exact moment she should be picking up her friend Mary Margaret for their reunion trip to the mountains. But late last night Parker Reed, the office manager for Tatum and Trent, had called to say that her presence was required at the partners' weekly breakfast meeting.

Knowing that this was either very good or very bad, Lettie had been unable to sleep all night. She'd arranged for Mary Margaret to meet her at Tatum and Trent so that the breakfast meeting wouldn't throw them too far off schedule. Then, instead of dressing in a comfortable pair of jeans and leaving for her well-deserved vacation, she'd put on one of her prim and grim business suits and driven to the downtown high-rise that housed the prestigious investment firm where she worked.

When she reached the door of the dining room, she paused to tug her suit jacket into place. Then she knocked. Parker opened the door immediately, indicating that he'd been standing there waiting for her. He ushered her inside with a cheerful, "Hey, Lettie."

"Good morning, Parker," she returned.

"It certainly is," he agreed. He led her through a vestibule and into the small but elegant room where the partners were assembled around a large, linen-covered table. Lettie's mouth went dry.

"Welcome!" Mr. Trent greeted. He was short and had white hair and a friendly smile. People often underestimated him, giving Mr. Trent the advantage. Lettie was determined not to make that particular mistake.

"Thank you," Lettie said politely.

Mr. Tatum, the tall, solemn antithesis of his partner, stood and pulled out an empty chair beside him. "Please, join us for breakfast."

Lettie allowed Mr. Tatum to seat her, and Parker took the chair to her left.

"We're having my favorites today," Mr. Trent confided. "Eggs Benedict, cheese grits, and orange rolls."

Lettie wasn't the least bit hungry, but to be polite she put one of the tiny orange rolls on her plate. She had just popped it into her mouth when Mr. Tatum said, "I'm sure you're wondering why we summoned you here."

After swallowing the roll whole, Lettie nodded.

"We've been talking about you a great deal lately," Mr. Tatum continued. "All of us feel that the portfolio you developed for Blue Ribbon Coffee was stellar."

"Brilliant," Mr. Trent agreed.

"The average rate of return for your accounts is consistently high," Mr. Tatum said with no emotion whatsoever.

"You're a credit to the firm," Mr. Trent praised, and several other partners bobbed their heads in a show of solidarity.

Lettie couldn't help but be pleased. She worked hard, and it was gratifying to know that her efforts had been noticed. She took a sip of orange juice and said, "That's nice to hear."

"In fact, all the partners are impressed by you," Parker contributed. "Your work is always so complete and thorough."

She could have pointed out that anyone else could achieve the same results by working twice the required number of hours each week. But instead, she just smiled.

"And now it looks like your hard work has paid off," Mr. Trent told her. "We are prepared to offer you a junior partnership."

Lettie clasped her trembling hands in her lap. Although she had been working toward this for years, the timing of their announcement took her completely by surprise. "Wow. I can't believe it."

Parker laughed. "You'd better believe it. I have an order form right here requesting that the printers add your name to the company letterhead."

Mr. Trent stood and walked around to where she was seated. He extended his hand and said, "Congratulations!"

The handshake was more of a gentle hand-squeeze. "Thank you," Lettie replied.

Mr. Tatum waited until his partner was seated again before pointing out, "This is a historical moment for our firm. You are the first woman ever to make partner."

"I'm honored," Lettie said, and she was.

"And to celebrate, we're planning a reception," Mr. Trent added. "We'll invite influential people from the community."

"Because of the historical nature of your promotion, the reception will be something of a media event as well," Mr. Tatum said. "Good publicity for the firm."

"We've rented the banquet hall at the Marriott on Friday night," Parker said.

"Friday?" Lettie repeated.

"We want to make the announcement before it leaks out," Mr. Trent explained.

"But I'm going to be out of town for the rest of the week," Lettie said. They all stared back blankly, so she added, "I've had this vacation scheduled for months."

Parker leaned forward and whispered, "Who cares if it's been scheduled forever. You're being offered a *partnership*."

"And I appreciate that," Lettie whispered back. "But I'm supposed to be going on a reunion trip with my best friends from high school. One of them in particular has gone to a lot of effort to arrange it and . . ."

Parker waved her words aside and smiled brightly at the other partners. "The trip can be rescheduled. I'm sure your friends will understand."

After another moment of consideration, Lettie nodded.

Mr. Trent beamed at her. "Excellent. I'll leave the details of Friday's reception to you and Parker."

"We'll take care of it," Parker promised.

Mr. Trent waved toward the food. "Now, everyone enjoy your breakfast."

Lettie was too nervous to eat and finally asked if she could be excused.

"You don't like your food?" Mr. Tatum asked.

"Oh, no, it's delicious," she assured him, wishing that she'd been seated beside the more approachable Mr. Trent. "But I need to contact my friends and cancel my vacation."

Mr. Tatum nodded solemnly. "Very well."

Parker didn't look happy about her early departure, but he walked her out. Once they were in the hallway, he said, "They've offered you a chance of a lifetime. You could have shown a little more enthusiasm."

"I'm sorry," she told him. "It was just such a surprise, and I'm upset about having to cancel out on my friends at the last minute."

"I'll smooth things over for you." Parker turned back toward the door to the dining room.

She smiled. "Thanks."

"You can repay me by taking me to lunch," he said. "We can discuss the reception then."

"Okay," Lettie agreed. Then she hurried to the elevator.

When Lettie walked into her office, she put her purse under her desk and dialed Mary Margaret's home number. There was no answer, which meant her friend was already on her way with suitcases packed, anticipating the upcoming weekend trip.

Overwhelmed with guilt, Lettie stared out the window at the busy downtown street below. Becoming a partner at Tatum and Trent had been her goal since she accepted the job right out of college. She'd felt then that if she could reach that level of professional success, her life would have meaning. Now the partnership was within her grasp, but the fulfillment she'd been seeking for so long still eluded her.

Her depressing thoughts were interrupted by a hesitant knock on the office door, followed by Mary Margaret's soft voice saying, "Lettie?"

Lettie turned around to face her friend and break the news that their plans had to be changed. But when she saw Mary Margaret, she lost her train of thought.

"Mary Margaret! I barely recognize you!" Lettie cried as she walked over to hug her guest. Then she continued her examination. Mary Margaret had struggled with her weight for as long as Lettie could remember, but the woman who stood before her was trim and sporting a modern, short haircut. "What have you done to yourself?"

"I lost some weight," Mary Margaret responded.

"And cut your hair!" Lettie saw the uncertain look in her friend's eyes and quickly assured her, "I love it!"

Mary Margaret smiled, but she still seemed a little nervous. Lettie pointed at the chairs arranged in front of her desk. "Why don't we sit down? There's something I need to talk to you about."

"I need to tell you something too," Mary Margaret admitted with an anxious glance around the office. "But I was hoping we could do it on the way to pick up Alexa."

Feeling like the lowest of life-forms, Lettie said, "We've got time."

Mary Margaret sat down and Lettie took the chair across from her. Then, in an effort to delay the moment of truth, she suggested, "Why don't you go first?"

Mary Margaret cleared her throat. "I don't know how to tell you," she began with obvious reluctance. "There's no easy way to do it, and no matter what I say you're going to be so upset—even though you shouldn't be. Everything is fine now . . ."

Lettie tried to follow Mary Margaret's train of thought with growing alarm. "What is it? Tell me!"

Her friend took a deep breath and blurted out, "A few months ago I was diagnosed with ovarian cancer."

Tears of shock and pain sprang instantly to Lettie's eyes. "No!"

Mary Margaret leaned forward and collected Lettie into her arms. Lettie clung to her friend, feeling foolish. Mary Margaret was the one who was sick and needed comfort.

With effort she controlled her tears and sat up straight. "You're going to be okay, aren't you?"

"Of course!" Mary Margaret assured her. "The doctors were able to surgically remove the cancerous tissue, and then I had chemotherapy treatments as a precaution. I'm in remission, and I've never felt better in my life!"

Lettie's fear faded. "Why didn't you tell me sooner?"

"You're so busy—I didn't want to worry you," Mary Margaret explained.

The guilt returned. She was too busy for her friends. "I would have come," Lettie insisted.

Mary Margaret nodded. "I know."

Lettie stood and started pacing around the room. "I can't believe this happened to you!" she railed against things beyond her control. "It's not fair!"

"No," Mary Margaret agreed. "But then a lot of things in life aren't fair, and the experience wasn't all bad."

Lettie looked at her friend in amazement. "I don't know how you can be so positive."

Mary Margaret laughed. "I've gotten a lot of practice over the past few months. But realistically—none of us knows how much time we have left on earth. That's why I'm so glad we're taking this reunion trip."

Lettie was trying to formulate an adequate response when Parker stuck his head through the open door. "Oh, I didn't realize you had company," he said when he saw Mary Margaret.

Lettie considered her options quickly. A few minutes before, disappointing Mary Margaret had seemed heartless, but now it was unacceptable—regardless of the professional cost. "Will you excuse me for a minute?" she asked Mary Margaret. Her friend nodded and Lettie joined Parker in the hall.

After taking a deep breath, she said, "I'm sorry, Parker, but I can't cancel my vacation. Will you tell Mr. Tatum and Mr. Trent that the reception has to be postponed until next week, or would you prefer that I do it?"

Parker didn't even try to hide his irritation. "You're going to risk offending the senior partners for a vacation?"

She considered trying to explain, but Mary Margaret's medical problems were none of his business. "I'm just asking for a few days."

"Mr. Tatum and Mr. Trent will be disappointed," Parker said. "We've already reserved a room at the Marriott."

Lettie squared her shoulders. The firm and her promotion were important, but Mary Margaret mattered more. She wasn't going to let her down again. "I've made my decision."

He sighed. "Okay, I'll tell them." He started down the hall and then turned and gave her a reluctant smile. "Lucky for you I can put a positive spin on anything. By the time I get through listing all the reasons next week would be better for the reception, they'll be demanding that we change the date."

She smiled back. "Thanks, Parker."

Lettie took a deep breath and walked back into her office. Oddly, she felt better than she had in a long time. Maybe she needed this vacation more than she'd realized.

"Who was that?" Mary Margaret wanted to know.

"The office manager of this firm," Lettie replied as she reached down to pick up her purse.

"He's cute," Mary Margaret remarked.

Lettie looked up in surprise. "You think so?"

"Sure," Mary Margaret said. "Don't you?"

Lettie shrugged. "I never thought about it."

"He likes you," Mary Margaret added.

Lettie shook her head. "That's ridiculous. Now let's get out of here before we're interrupted again."

Once they were settled in Lettie's Honda and headed toward Alexa's house, Lettie said, "I'm glad you insisted on this reunion. It's been a long time since I've done something for fun." She glanced over at Mary Margaret. "What gave you the idea?"

"You're such a no-nonsense, logical person—this is probably going to sound silly to you."

Lettie wasn't particularly pleased with this description of herself. "Try me," she suggested.

"While I was going through my treatments, I'd have to lie in a cold room for hours, and I needed something compelling to occupy my mind."

Lettie felt a new wave of guilt as Mary Margaret continued.

"So I made up a list."

"What kind of list?" Lettie asked.

"A list of all the things I've never done, but want to."

"Such as . . ."

"Ride a horse, fly in a plane, climb a mountain, kiss a man." Mary Margaret looked at Lettie and smiled. "Get together with old friends for a weekend—things like that."

"The man-kissing goal is definitely the most interesting," Lettie teased. "Have you accomplished that?"

Mary Margaret shook her head. "No. But this weekend I'll fly in a plane, climb a mountain, and reunite with my old friends."

"That's what I call making progress," Lettie conceded.

"And in addition to helping me make headway on my to-do-before-I-die list, I'm hoping this trip will be beneficial to us all."

Lettie cut her eyes over at her friend. "Beneficial in what way? Do you have some ulterior motives?"

Mary Margaret smiled. "I'll admit to a couple."

"And they are?" Lettie prompted.

Mary Margaret twisted on the car seat so she could address Lettie more directly. "Beth is swamped in domesticity. Jack is a wonderful person, and I know she loves him, but the pressures of motherhood and being a politician's wife are wearing on her. She needs to get away for a few days."

"And you know this because?" Lettie prompted.

"Because I talk to her at least once a week."

The now-familiar sense of guilt reclaimed Lettie. If she'd kept track of Beth, she would have known she was struggling. Lettie hated to ask, but she forced herself. "What about Alexa?"

The smile left Mary Margaret's face. "I'm not sure what's wrong with her. She won't return my calls, and her mother says she hasn't been at church the last few weeks."

"So during this weekend trip you hope we can teach her better phone etiquette and rekindle her interest in religion?"

Mary Margaret shrugged. "If she's having problems, I want her to know she's not alone. When we were young we faced things together. We encouraged each other and shared our experiences— good and bad. I'd like for it to be that way again."

Lettie was skeptical about their ability to turn back the hands of time, but Mary Margaret would do it if anyone could. "I guess a couple of days in the mountains won't hurt any of us," Lettie allowed. Then she shot her friend a suspicious glance. "Now what's your plan for a hopeless man-hater like me?"

"You don't hate men," Mary Margaret said with confidence.

"Not all men," Lettie agreed. "Just one."

Mary Margaret met her gaze steadily, and Lettie had the uncomfortable feeling that her friend knew the truth. Lettie returned her eyes to the road.

"He hasn't married either," Mary Margaret said, causing Lettie's heart to pound.

"How do you know?"

"Because our guide for the trip is Lowell Brooks, and I asked him."

Lettie was horrified by this announcement. She put on her blinker and pulled her car to the side of the road. Then she gave Mary Margaret her full attention. "Why didn't you tell me that you booked our trip with Lowell Brooks?"

"Because I knew you'd refuse to go," Mary Margaret replied honestly.

"Well, withholding that information didn't work. I'm still going to refuse to go."

"Please, Lettie," Mary Margaret begged. "I promise that you won't be put in any kind of uncomfortable situation."

"You don't think that camping with Gray's missionary trainer and current business partner will be uncomfortable for me?"

"I don't see why it would be—if you're really over Gray like you claim."

Lettie searched for a response that wouldn't incriminate her or be an outright lie. Finally she gave up and said, "Lowell probably thinks you were checking on Gray's marital status for me! He probably thinks I'm still interested!"

Mary Margaret shook her head. "No, he thought *I* was interested in Gray."

Lettie assimilated this information and wondered if Mary Margaret had found a prospective boyfriend. "Are you?"

"No," Mary Margaret replied. "How could I be interested in the man you love?"

"I don't love Gray," Lettie denied emphatically. "And I don't want to see him again—ever."

"I knew you'd feel that way, so I took precautions," Mary Margaret assured her. "Gray doesn't even know we're coming, and Lowell said that Gray was scheduled to take another group out this morning. So he'll be gone by the time we arrive, and he won't be back until after we leave on Sunday."

Lettie felt some of the tension leave her shoulders. "I'll agree to go if you *promise* that you don't have some secret plan to make me face Gray."

"I don't," Mary Margaret pledged.

"I know you'd like to change what happened, but you can't—no one can. Do you understand?"

Mary Margaret nodded.

"My personal life is off-limits," Lettie reiterated.

"Okay."

Lettie knew she was protesting too much, but she couldn't help herself. "Gray Grantland is a painful part of my past. I may not be completely over him, but I'm certainly not interested in reviving a relationship with him."

"I said that I understand."

Lettie doubted that Mary Margaret could understand, since she'd never even had a boyfriend—much less a broken heart. But Lettie didn't challenge her. "By getting Beth to go on this trip you'll accomplish your goals for her, and I'll do whatever I can to help you with Alexa. But I'm going to hold you to your promise about me and Gray."

"You can trust me, Lettie."

Knowing that Mary Margaret would never lie, Lettie dropped the subject and returned her car to the road.

* * *

As Eugenia parked her old Buick in her driveway, she saw Polly coming down the sidewalk toward her. By the time Eugenia had opened the car door and removed Lady's basket, Polly was standing beside her. Polly pulled a lace handkerchief from the neckline of her loose-fitting, floral-print dress and dabbed at the perspiration that had formed along her hairline. "What did you think about Willadene and her collection of self-taxidermied animals?"

Eugenia frowned. "Honestly, I found it all kind of disturbing."

"She doesn't kill the animals," Polly pointed out. "She finds ones that have already died and preserves them."

"I know what she does," Eugenia replied. "And it's still disturbing."

"She takes her specimens to local schools, which is educational."

Eugenia wrinkled her nose. "She might be spreading diseases to hundreds of innocent schoolchildren. Imagine the kind of germs you could find on an animal carcass!"

"That's why she does the taxidermy," Polly defended the other woman. "To get rid of germs and fleas and such."

"Fleas," Eugenia muttered. "The very idea."

Polly fanned herself with the now damp hankie. "It's a little warm today."

Eugenia nodded. "And the humidity is high."

"Well, I guess I'd better get home and start on my cake."

Eugenia raised an eyebrow. "Cake?"

"For the cake-baking contest at the grand opening of the new Haggerty Senior Citizen Center tonight," Polly elaborated. "You remember."

Eugenia pursed her lips. "Oh, that."

"Are you coming?"

Eugenia shook her head. "You know how I feel about that senior center."

Polly nodded. "You think it's a waste of public funds, but the contest will be fun. You could make your mother's red velvet cake and win the grand prize."

"I only make my mother's red velvet cake on Christmas Eve."

"You could make an exception," Polly continued to plead. "It seems like you'd make an effort since Whit has been instrumental in establishing the senior center."

Whit Owens had graduated from high school with Eugenia and then left Haggerty to pursue a career in law. During the course of his life he'd married and divorced three women and fathered one child by each wife. When Whit's father died, Whit had returned to Haggerty to take over the family law practice. Eugenia rarely had the need for legal advice, so their paths hadn't crossed in a significant way until the previous summer, when Miss Geneva Mackey died and left Lady to Eugenia in her will. Since then, she and Whit had been good friends, although the rest of Haggerty was always trying to turn their friendship into a romance.

Polly interrupted Eugenia's thoughts by saying, "Statistics show that seniors who stay active live longer and healthier lives. Senior centers are a way for older people to socialize and support each other."

Eugenia was exasperated. "We don't need a senior center to have a place for old folks to gather. The entire town of Haggerty is a senior center! We socialize with each other at the gas station and the grocery store and church and all our club meetings."

Polly gave Eugenia a reproachful look as she turned toward her own house. "Well, we have one whether we need it or not. Let me know if you change your mind about going tonight." Polly had taken a few steps when she turned and asked, "Did you get a chance to go by and visit the Gambles before the horticulture meeting?"

"As a matter of fact, I did," Eugenia reported. "Beth's reunion is a camping trip to the Great Smoky Mountains National Park."

"Oh my." Polly fingered her handkerchief, which she had tucked back in the neckline of her dress. "I don't understand why anyone would want to sleep outdoors in the cold with bears and other vicious animals creeping around."

"If Jack's agreed to let Beth go, I'm sure it's perfectly safe," Eugenia said. "And if you run into the Blackwoods, tell them you have no idea where I am."

Polly frowned. "But, Eugenia, I *do* know where you are."

"Not for long you don't," Eugenia assured her. As soon as Polly was out of sight, she put Lady back into the car. "We'd better get out of here before Cornelia tracks me down," she told the little dog.

When they arrived at the law offices of Whit Owens, Eugenia breezed into the reception area and informed Whit's receptionist, Idella Babcock, that she wished to speak to the boss.

"My goodness, Eugenia," Idella replied with an annoyed look. "Whit has a business to run. You could have at least called first to see if he was busy."

"I'm sure he'll make time for me," Eugenia returned with confidence.

Then Idella spied Lady in the basket on Eugenia's arm. "And you could have left that little ball of pet dander home—you know I'm allergic!"

Eugenia clutched Lady's basket tighter and replied, "The sooner I see Whit, the sooner Lady and I will be gone."

Idella made a face in Eugenia's direction before pushing the intercom button on her telephone console. Then she sullenly notified Whit of Eugenia's presence.

Whit sounded pleased to have company. "Send her on back," he instructed his receptionist.

After giving Idella a smug smile, Eugenia and Lady proceeded down the hallway to Whit's office.

"To what do I owe this great honor?" Whit asked as he ushered them inside.

"We're hiding from Brother Blackwood and Cornelia," Eugenia told him honestly. "According to Polly, there's a contest between the Baptists and the Methodists to see who can get me to attend their church services on Sunday. I've had visits already this morning from Brother Watty and Barbara Jean and the Blackwoods. And the day is young!"

Whit laughed at her predicament. "If you've already visited with both our local religious leaders, why are you hiding from the Blackwoods now?"

"Well, I didn't actually talk to them," Eugenia admitted. "I sort of pretended not to be home."

Whit's eyebrows lifted. "Why would you do that?"

"Because I don't know where I'll go to church on Sunday, and I've decided to lay low until I make a decision."

"Well, whatever the reason for your visit, I'm glad you're here. I was just about to call you."

If Eugenia had been a few years younger, she might have blushed with pleasure at this comment. As it was, she merely said, "What were you going to call me about?"

"Well, you know that the senior citizen center is having its grand opening tonight?"

Most of Eugenia's happiness ebbed away. "Of course I know that. Polly has talked about little else for weeks."

"The Haggerty Chamber of Commerce, of which I am a proud member, has hired a professional activities director to run the center. She's arriving in town today, in time for the center's grand opening."

"What is a professional activities director?" Eugenia asked. "Is that a fancy way of saying 'babysitter for old people'?"

Whit laughed. "She's more than a babysitter. She's a registered nurse with references from several assisted living facilities across the country. We're fortunate that she was willing to take the job since it meant she had to relocate from LaGrange."

Eugenia was mildly intrigued. "How much does this job pay? Maybe I should have applied for it myself."

He laughed again. "The pay is good but not phenomenal. The hours are great, though, which was the selling point for Miss Sullivan. She only has to work for a couple of hours each evening."

"Exactly what kind of duties will she have?"

"Miss Sullivan is responsible for planning all of the activities for the center. I've looked at her proposed schedule and I think it's great. She's got a night for bingo and one for square dancing, and on

Saturday night they'll show a different movie every week. Doesn't that sound like fun?"

"About as much fun as a root canal," Eugenia muttered, and Lady barked in agreement.

Whit chuckled, and Eugenia noted that he seemed particularly jolly today. "Charlotte has planned a cake-baking contest for the grand opening tonight."

"Charlotte?" Eugenia repeated.

"I mean, Miss Sullivan," Whit stammered in obvious embarrassment.

"You've met her, then?"

Whit cleared his throat in an uncharacteristically nervous gesture. "No, but we've talked on the phone a few times."

Eugenia narrowed her eyes at him. "Polly was telling me about the contest. She's planning to participate."

"I'm so glad," Whit responded. "We haven't had time to publicize the contest as much as I would have liked, and I'm worried that there won't be many entries. I'd hate for Miss Sullivan to get off to a bad start." After a short pause, he added, "You're a mighty fine cook yourself."

"Are you asking me to make a cake for your contest?"

"I am!" Whit admitted with a smile. "And I was hoping you'd call around and ask other ladies you know to do the same. Your support could turn tonight from a disaster to a rousing success."

Eugenia didn't particularly want the senior center to be a success, rousing or otherwise. However, she did want to help Whit, so she said, "I believe you are overestimating my power in the community, but I'll do what I can."

"Thank you!" Whit said.

Eugenia gave him a stern look. "For the record, let me say that I think getting old people together on a regular basis is a bad idea."

Whit's eyes widened with surprise. "Why?"

"Seeing the decrepit condition we're all in and knowing it's just going to get worse is depressing," Eugenia told him. "But I'll bake a cake and come to your grand opening tonight because you've asked me to."

"And you'll make some phone calls to your friends?" Whit reminded her.

Eugenia nodded. "I suppose. Since you're forcing me to attend this debacle, I presume you're going to be a gentleman and pick me up?"

Whit looked embarrassed again. "Oh, I'd love to, Eugenia, but I promised Charlotte that I would come to the senior center right after work and help her make final preparations for the grand opening."

"I see," Eugenia said. "Well, how about taking Lady and me out to lunch at Haggerty Station then? You can protect me from any religious zealots who might be there."

Whit's cheeks turned pink. "I'm so sorry, but I'm meeting Charlotte there in fifteen minutes. She doesn't know anyone in town yet, and I wanted her to feel welcome. I'd invite you to come along, but my reservation is for two and you know how snippy Nettie gets when you change at the last minute."

"Of course," Eugenia said, although she'd never known Whit to be afraid of Nettie's foul moods before. In fact, he had always seemed to enjoy teasing the cranky restaurant owner.

"Well," Whit said as he rose from his chair. "It was nice of you to drop by."

Eugenia recognized her dismissal. She stood and carried Lady to the door. "I guess I'll see you tonight," she said over her shoulder.

"I'm looking forward to it." Whit shrugged on his suit coat, looking like an excited schoolboy.

With a sigh, Eugenia walked down the hall, past Idella and outside. "What do you make of *that?*" she asked Lady.

The little dog licked her face in response.

"Let's go home and make some phone calls," Eugenia said. "Then we can start on a red velvet cake. If I have to participate in this contest, you'd better believe I plan to win."

* * *

Jack walked into the bedroom where Beth was packing for her trip. "Chloe got a hundred on her spelling test, and now she and Hank are playing with Roberta—the world's most overpaid babysitter," he announced.

"Roberta does more than babysit," Beth replied. "She puts up with you."

"That's true." He sat on the edge of the bed, and after a few minutes of watching her put clothes in her suitcase, he said, "I can't believe I agreed to this."

She smiled over at him. "But you did."

"At Christmas it didn't seem like such a bad idea. Now I think I must have had a bout of temporary insanity."

She stopped packing and sat beside him. "This trip means a lot to Mary Margaret."

"I know," he said as he took her hand in his. "But we've never spent a night apart since we've been married."

She squeezed his fingers. "You'll survive."

"I'm not so sure."

She laughed.

"And the kids will miss you," he added.

"I'll miss them too, but I'll only be gone for a few days. And don't forget that both grandmothers and Miss Eugenia have all volunteered to come on a moment's notice."

"Talk about going from bad to worse," he muttered.

Beth brought his hand to her cheek. "If you really want me to stay, I'll call Mary Margaret and cancel."

He drew her close. "I really want you to stay," he whispered against her temple. "But I don't want you to cancel. I'm not quite *that* selfish."

Beth kissed his cheek. "Thank you." She stood and resumed her packing. "And according to Miss Eugenia, this brief separation will make our hearts grow fonder."

"Personally, I'm satisfied with our current level of fondness. But knowing you'll love me more when you get back might pull me through these days of loneliness."

Beth zipped the suitcase closed. "You'll be so busy with the kids you won't have time to miss me."

He picked up her bag and headed down the stairs. "I could never be that busy."

* * *

Gray Grantland pulled his pickup truck off the mountain road in front of the office building of Smoky Mountain Tours—the business he jointly owned with his friend and partner, Lowell Brooks. Since he was running late, he parked near the entrance in one of the spaces they usually reserved for customers. The cold wind sliced through his jacket as he walked up to the door and unlocked it.

It was only marginally warmer inside, which told Gray that Lowell hadn't been in yet that morning. After turning on the heat, Gray sat at his desk and began his daily routine. First he checked the most current weather reports on the Internet. The forecast called for a stationary cold front that was giving the southern regions unseasonably warm weather accompanied by severe thunderstorms. To the north, dry, frigid conditions were expected. Gray sighed. Apparently winter was going to show its face one last time before acquiescing to spring.

Satisfied that the trip he had planned with some of their regular customers was not in jeopardy, Gray opened the mail. There were two requests for guided hikes, and Gray walked over to the master calendar posted on the wall to see if the dates were clear. He made notations on the forms and should have gone straight back to his desk and called to confirm the trips, but instead his eyes dropped to the line Lowell had drawn across the next four days in bold red marker. He scowled.

The trip had been on the calendar for a long time, but Lowell had never given Gray any details about it. Gray had asked, at first out of idle curiosity. But when Lowell declined to divulge even the most minor detail, it became sort of a challenge. Now after weeks of fruitless interrogation, Lowell's refusal seemed more like an insult than a joke.

This mysterious behavior was completely out of character for the gregarious Lowell, who usually shared more than Gray wanted to know about both his profession and his personal life. The only explanation that made sense was that Lowell had a girlfriend.

Gray had always known that eventually Lowell would meet the right woman and fall in love. Apparently that day had come. If Lowell had shared his feelings, Gray would have been happy for his partner. But this exclusion from Lowell's life hurt.

Lettie came to his mind uninvited, and Gray wondered if she had moved on. Pushing the dark thoughts away, Gray went outside to load his truck for the day's hike. Thankfully he would be spared the awkwardness of being there when Lowell's true love arrived.

CHAPTER 3

Lettie parked her car in front of the two-story colonial in the upscale neighborhood where Alexa lived with her husband, Brian. Then she and Mary Margaret walked up the sidewalk and rang the doorbell. There was no response.

"Do you think she forgot?"

"I'm sure she didn't forget," Lettie said with more confidence than she felt. "Maybe she slept in. Didn't you say she works a lot of nights?"

Mary Margaret nodded. "Yes, she says the hospital pays night-shift nurses more, so that's what she requests."

Lettie rang the doorbell again. When there was still no response, she resorted to using her fist to pound on the shiny blue surface. Finally, Alexa jerked open the door. "What?" she demanded.

At a loss for words, Lettie studied her friend. Alexa had always been beautiful in a sharp, edgy sort of way. But the woman standing before her barely resembled the girl Lettie had known in high school. Alexa was wearing wrinkled hospital scrubs, and her stringy hair hadn't been washed in days. She looked pale, and there were dark circles under her eyes. Holding a hand up to shield her blood-shot eyes from the sun, Alexa returned Lettie's stare for a few seconds. Then she asked, "Is it Thursday already?"

Mary Margaret shot Lettie a concerned look before saying, "Yes, it's Thursday, Alexa. Are you ready to go?"

Alexa pushed a clump of dirty hair behind her ear with trembling fingers. "Uh, well, no—not really."

"Are you going to make us stand out here or are you going to let us in?" Lettie asked impatiently. After a brief hesitation, Alexa stepped aside and admitted her friends.

Lettie glanced around in dismay. If possible, the living room looked worse than Alexa. Take-out containers, old newspapers, and discarded clothing covered the floor and furniture. Lettie watched as Alexa closed the front door and drifted aimlessly in their direction.

"Where is Brian?" Lettie asked.

Alexa fingered a Wendy's napkin on the back of the couch. "Atlanta."

Lettie was relieved that Alexa's husband wasn't a party to this carnage. That meant there was a possibility that at least one participant in the marriage was still sane. She took Alexa by the arm and propelled her toward the bedroom. "I'll help you pack," she offered. Over her shoulder she suggested to Mary Margaret, "Could you get a garbage bag and pick up the trash at least? That way if Brian comes home while we're gone, he won't have rats for houseguests."

Mary Margaret nodded and headed for the kitchen. Lettie took a deep breath and joined Alexa in the bedroom. Alexa sat on the edge of the unmade bed, staring at the clothes strewn on the floor.

Lettie frowned. "What's wrong with you? Are you sick?"

"I had some dental work done recently, and the pain medication I have to take makes me groggy."

Lettie jerked open the closet and pulled out a duffel bag. "You may need a lower dosage. Have you talked to your primary care physician about it?"

Alexa closed her eyes. "No."

"Well, you should."

"I'm too tired to call anyone."

Slightly alarmed, Lettie put the duffel on the bed and asked, "When will Brian get back from Atlanta?"

Alexa shrugged. "I'm not sure."

Lettie considered this for a few seconds. Then she unzipped the bag. "We'll have plenty of time to talk during our trip. Right now we need to hurry."

"Right now I need to go back to sleep." Alexa leaned toward one of the pillows.

Lettie reached over and stopped her. "No you don't. You can sleep in the car. I'll pack while you take a shower."

Tears pooled in Alexa's eyes. "I'm too tired. I don't think I can go."

"Oh, you're going all right," Lettie informed her friend. "You may have drugged yourself into a stupor, but Mary Margaret's not going to pay the price for your mistakes."

Alexa blinked in confusion. "Mary Margaret?"

Lettie put her hands on Alexa's shoulders and shook gently. "Mary Margaret has put a lot of time and effort into this reunion trip, and I'm going to make sure she has all of us together for a weekend if I have to carry you on my back."

Alexa waved at the disaster area. "But I don't even have any clean clothes."

"Then I'll pack dirty ones," Lettie said grimly. "Now get in the shower. Our flight leaves in less than three hours, and we still have to pick up Beth."

When they emerged from the bedroom ten minutes later, Alexa was wearing jeans and a T-shirt. Her pale face was devoid of makeup, and her still-damp hair was pulled back in a severe ponytail. She had a duffel bag in one hand and was clutching her purse with the other.

"She's taking prescription drugs, and I think the dosage is too high," Lettie whispered to Mary Margaret. "Once we're in the mountains we'll figure out a way to get her to cut back."

Mary Margaret nodded. Then she asked, "Should we take these bags of trash with us?"

Lettie shook her head. "Brian can take them out to the dumpster when he gets home." She checked her watch and moved toward the front door. "We've wasted too much time here. Let's get going."

* * *

After leaving Whit's office, Eugenia and Lady stopped by the grocery store to pick up a few ingredients for a red velvet cake. Once they were back at home, Eugenia fed Lady first and then made herself a sandwich. In between bites she called several friends and invited them to the senior center's grand opening. Most of the conversations eventually worked themselves around to the subject of which church Eugenia would attend on Sunday. She was careful to be vague about her plans but made every effort to assure everyone that she wasn't mad at Brother Watty.

When her sandwich was gone and her first obligation to Whit complete, she assembled the ingredients of her mother's famous red velvet cake on the counter. She adjusted the settings on her ancient KitchenAid and opened the box that contained her collection of recipe cards. Her fingers shuffled deftly through the well-used cards in search of the one she needed. The recipe for the red velvet cake was written in her mother's handwriting on an old, yellowed card. When she reached the end of the box without success, Eugenia frowned.

"That's odd," she told Lady. "I guess my eyesight is going like everything else, and I just didn't see it." She started at the first and went through the cards again, more slowly this time. Once again she didn't find the card. "Well, I declare, this is annoying," she muttered. After removing the cards from the box, Eugenia examined each one individually. Finally she was forced to admit that her red velvet cake recipe card was missing.

"Now where in the world could that recipe card be?" Eugenia said as much to herself as to Lady. Then she reached for the phone and dialed her sister's number.

"Do you have my recipe card for red velvet cake?" she demanded without preamble.

"No," Annabelle replied. "I've never made a red velvet cake in my life. Why would I have your recipe card?"

Eugenia couldn't argue any of Annabelle's points, so she said, "Please look in your recipe box and see if my card for red velvet cake got mixed in with your recipe cards somehow."

Annabelle sighed audibly—as if Eugenia was the biggest inconvenience in the world. "Hold on just a minute."

Nearly five minutes had passed before Annabelle returned to the phone. "I do not have your red velvet recipe and . . ." She paused dramatically. "My recipe card for boiled custard is missing as well."

"Your boiled custard recipe card?" Eugenia repeated. "What does that have to do with anything?"

"What will I do if I can't find it?"

"Are you planning to make boiled custard right now?" Eugenia asked.

"Of course not," Annabelle replied as if Eugenia was also the most ridiculous person in the world. "But what will I do the next time I want to make banana pudding or homemade ice cream or . . ."

"I know which recipes call for boiled custard," Eugenia interrupted her sister. "What I don't understand is why you need the recipe card. I could make boiled custard with my eyes closed and one hand tied behind my back."

"It gives me a sense of security to see everything written down," Annabelle said. "You don't want to go to all the trouble of making a quart of boiled custard and then realize you've put in too much salt or something."

"Grab a pencil and listen closely while I recite it for you," Eugenia instructed. "First you put one cup of milk in a saucepan and scald it."

"You still scald the milk?" Annabelle interrupted.

"Of course I still scald the milk. It says to do so, right on that recipe card you've lost."

"I didn't lose anything," Annabelle assured her. "And I haven't scalded the milk for twenty-five years. However, my boiled custard tastes the same as yours, so obviously scalding is a waste of time."

Eugenia rolled her eyes and said a quick prayer for patience. "What's the point of having a recipe if you aren't going to follow it?" she asked.

"I can't talk to you," Annabelle replied impatiently. "I have to find that recipe card."

A split second later Eugenia was listening to the dial tone. She hung up the phone and pursed her lips. Although the conversation with Annabelle had been aggravating, it still had a silver lining. It gave Eugenia the idea of writing out the recipe for her mother's red velvet cake.

It only took a few minutes, and when she was done she was reasonably sure that she had it right. But unlike boiled custard, which Eugenia made regularly, the red velvet cake was made only once a year on Christmas Eve. So as she stared at what she had written, Eugenia wasn't completely confident of her ingredients and their specific amounts. If she had been making the cake for a group of friends, she wouldn't have worried. But since she was making it to win *Charlotte's* cake contest, it had to be perfect.

With a sigh, she called Polly. "Did I loan you the card with my mother's red velvet cake recipe on it?" she asked. If Polly had borrowed the recipe without permission for some inexplicable reason, this would give her a face-saving opportunity to return it.

"No," Polly responded.

"Well, do you have it written down anywhere?" Eugenia tried.

"No," Polly said again. "I have several recipes for red velvet cake in various cookbooks, but not your mother's."

Any recipe wouldn't do, so Eugenia thanked Polly for nothing and hung up. Lady walked over and nuzzled Eugenia's ankle. Eugenia recognized this as an attempt to cheer her up. Reaching down to pat the little dog, she said, "Since I only use this recipe at Christmastime, do you think it's possible that I packed it up with my holiday decorations?"

Lady cocked her head as if in contemplation, and Eugenia had to laugh.

"It won't hurt to check." With renewed optimism, she went to the back porch and dragged out all the boxes that contained anything even vaguely related to Christmas.

An hour later Annabelle walked through the back door. She surveyed the mess and shook her head. "You've never been much of a housekeeper, Eugenia, but things have definitely taken a turn for the worse."

Eugenia pushed an inflatable snowman out of the way so Annabelle could get inside. "I still can't find my recipe for red velvet cake,"

Eugenia admitted reluctantly. "I thought I might have packed it up with the Christmas decorations, but it's not here."

"I haven't found my recipe for boiled custard either, and now I've got a craving for banana pudding. So I've come to get you to write the recipe down for me. Maybe having it in your handwriting will be almost the same as having it in Mother's." Annabelle stepped carefully over the tangle of colored lights and artificial holly garland. "If you'd wind those up every year they wouldn't get into such a state."

"This year you can wind them up for me," Eugenia suggested.

"Why do you need the red velvet recipe?" Annabelle asked as she followed her sister into the kitchen. "Christmas Eve is months away."

Eugenia took a blank recipe card from her box and began writing the instructions for boiled custard. "I know when Christmas Eve is. I'm making a red velvet cake for the senior center's grand opening tonight."

Annabelle frowned. "I thought you were opposed to the senior center."

"I am," Eugenia confirmed. "But Whit's afraid that there will be a small turnout, so I promised to participate in the cake-baking contest. And if I'm going to participate, I want to win. I figured making a red velvet cake would be the best way to ensure that."

Annabelle nodded absently. "Your red velvet cake is unbeatable."

"I would have invited you and Derrick," Eugenia continued. "But I figured you were having dinner at the White House or something."

"I don't know why you'd think that. Derrick and I have only been invited to the White House once, and that was over a year ago. We don't have plans tonight and you know how much Derrick likes to bake. I'm sure he'll enter a cake in the contest as a favor to Whit."

"That's good then." Eugenia completed the recipe card and handed it to her sister. "And will you pick me up on your way?"

Annabelle's eyebrows shot up. "You're not riding with Whit?"

Eugenia tried to keep her voice neutral as she said, "No, he's got to be at the senior center early to help get things ready."

Annabelle frowned. "It's strange."

"What's strange about that?" Eugenia demanded defensively. "Whit is a member of the chamber of commerce, and since they hired Miss Sullivan to be the director for the senior center it's perfectly reasonable that Whit would want to help her set up."

Annabelle seemed surprised by this outburst. "I wasn't talking about Whit. I meant it's strange that we're *both* missing recipe cards. Don't you think so?"

Eugenia hadn't given it any thought, but upon consideration she nodded. "There's probably a reasonable explanation. Maybe we loaned them to someone and can't remember."

"There may be a reasonable explanation, but that's not it," Annabelle said. "You forget things, but I don't."

Eugenia was about to object to this insulting and erroneous statement, when a terrible thought occurred to her. "You know that Polly is collecting recipes for a sequel to that fund-raising cookbook, *Dishes from Sea to Shining Sea?*"

Annabelle nodded.

"Do you think she stole our recipe cards for the new cookbook?"

Eugenia expected Annabelle to defend Polly quickly and emphatically, but instead she seemed unsure. "Polly is very passionate about raising money to buy Bibles for the people of India. And she does love Mother's red velvet cake."

"*And* homemade ice cream made with boiled custard," Eugenia pointed out. "She's had access to both our recipe boxes."

"But if she wanted our recipes, why would she take the cards instead of just asking us for a copy?"

"Unless she thought we wouldn't want our mother's recipes published." Then a worse explanation occurred to Eugenia. "Or maybe in her old age Polly's become a kleptomaniac!"

"Don't be ridiculous," Annabelle scoffed.

"It's not ridiculous," Eugenia insisted. "It happens to people all the time. I saw a whole show about it on *Dr. Phil.*"

"Well, I guess we'll know when we get our copies of the cook-book," Annabelle said.

"I can't wait until next Christmas to find out!" Eugenia cried.

"Well, what are you going to do?"

"About Polly?" Eugenia asked.

"No, about the recipe for the cake you need to bake for tonight," Annabelle clarified.

"Oh, well, I wrote down what I think is the correct recipe. I guess I'll have to go by that. But if I didn't remember it right, I might not win." Eugenia glanced at the cookbooks that lined the top of her kitchen cupboards. "Is it possible that I stuck the recipe card in one of my cookbooks last Christmas . . . ?"

"There's one thing I can guarantee," Annabelle interrupted again. "You definitely won't win the contest if you never get your cake made. So abandon this futile, not to mention messy, search. Go with what you wrote down. You've made the cake enough times. I'm sure your instincts will guide you."

Eugenia sighed. "That probably is the best course of action."

Annabelle scrutinized her sister for a few seconds. "You're taking this recipe thing too hard," she said finally. "You don't seem like yourself."

"It's kind of lonely around here with the Iversons gone," Eugenia admitted, hoping to keep Annabelle from guessing that she was upset about Whit and his strange behavior.

"I'm glad you're going to this activity at the senior citizen center," Annabelle continued. "You need something else to think about besides your neighbors."

"Yes, that center has given me something new to think about," Eugenia murmured.

Annabelle seemed pleased. "Well good. Now I'd better get home so Derrick will have time to make a cake before tonight. What time does the grand opening start?"

"Six o'clock."

"We'll be here at 5:45," Annabelle said. Then she stepped over the shriveled snowman and out the back door.

* * *

A few minutes before noon, Mancil Bright put down his rake on the grass near the entrance to the water treatment plant. He dusted the traces of topsoil from his hands onto his prison coveralls and walked over to where the guard, Kenny Dobson, was reclining against a large shade tree.

"I'm ready for lunch," Mancil commented casually.

Kenny checked his watch and nodded. "Yep, it's getting to be that time."

"You want me to get the cooler out?" Mancil offered.

Kenny pushed away from the tree trunk. "Yeah, go ahead. I'll round up the boys."

Mancil smiled to himself after he was facing away from the guard. Manipulating Kenny was child's play. He crossed the lawn to the white prison van that transported them to their work-release job every day and opened the back door.

Mancil lifted the lid on the industrial-sized cooler the food services people packed their lunches in. Kenny's sack was easy to identify since it was larger than the others. Mancil glanced covertly behind him to be sure no one was close enough to observe his actions. Reassured, he reached into the left pocket of his coveralls and removed an old sandwich bag that contained the oleander leaves he'd been collecting over the past few days. They were dry and crumpled easily to a coarse powder. He stuck a hand into Kenny's lunch sack and removed one of the bologna sandwiches.

After folding back the waxed paper used to keep the sandwich fresh, he lifted the top slice of white bread. He sprinkled the oleander leaves onto the layer of pickle relish that topped the thick slab of bologna, and then he used his finger to press the leaves until they disappeared into the relish. He replaced the slice of bread and refolded the waxed paper, careful to retain the original creases. Then he returned the sandwich to Kenny's bag and lifted the cooler.

* * *

Eugenia had just finished repacking her Christmas decorations when Polly called.

"Did you find my mother's red velvet cake recipe?" Eugenia asked hopefully. If Polly was a kleptomaniac, she wouldn't hold it against her as long as the recipe card was returned.

"No," Polly disappointed her by answering. "But Eva Nell called from Haggerty Station, and would you like to guess who is sitting at a table near the front, bold as brass, eating lunch with another woman?"

"Whit?" Eugenia tried to sound disinterested.

"You knew?"

"Yes. The woman is Charlotte Sullivan, the new activities director for the senior center. Since Whit's a member of the chamber of commerce, he asked her to lunch so she'll feel welcome in Haggerty."

"And you don't mind if she has lunch with your boyfriend?" Polly verified.

"Whit's not my boyfriend. I keep telling people that. We're just friends, and I don't care who he takes out to lunch."

"I'm glad you're not upset," Polly said. "And from the way Eva Nell described them laughing and carrying on, I'm sure Miss Sullivan feels plenty welcome now."

"Whit can be entertaining," Eugenia acknowledged with a heavy heart. "Now I'm going to have to ask you to excuse me. If I don't get started on my cake it won't be ready for the contest tonight."

"I hope you win," Polly said.

"Thank you. Annabelle and Derrick are picking me up, so if you'd like to ride with us, be over here at 5:45."

"I'll be there," Polly promised.

Lady started barking as Eugenia hung up the phone. She leaned down to pick up the little dog. Lady was a very sensitive animal and was particularly attuned to Eugenia's moods. "I'm okay," she reassured Lady. "Now you go take a nap while I make the best red velvet cake ever." *Even without my mother's recipe card and even if I have lost Whit to this Charlotte Sullivan,* she thought to herself.

* * *

Alexa slept during the drive from Tifton to Haggerty, which suited Lettie fine. She had enough on her mind without having to deal with Alexa's drug-induced daze. But when they pulled up in front of the Gambles' house Alexa sat up straight and stretched.

"Feeling better?" Mary Margaret inquired.

"A little," Alexa replied around a yawn.

Lettie pushed the buzzer to announce their arrival. Beth's voice greeted them and then the security gate slid open. Lettie proceeded to the end of the long driveway, where Beth was waiting for them.

"How are you?" Beth demanded as Lettie climbed from the car.

"I'm good," Lettie said. "And you?"

Beth gave her a quick hug. "I'm fine."

Lettie smiled. "The real question is, are you ready to go? We're running behind schedule."

"I'm all ready." Beth pointed at a small suitcase by her feet in confirmation.

Lettie reached for the suitcase, hoping they could load Beth up and leave without anyone getting out of the car, but this turned out to be wishful thinking. Mary Margaret opened her door and hurried over to embrace Beth. "I've missed you!"

Lettie waited for the ever-observant Beth to mention Mary Margaret's weight loss and new haircut. But Beth ignored these huge changes in their friend's appearance and said merely, "I've missed you too."

So Beth already knew all about Mary Margaret's illness. She might be overwhelmed with motherhood, but Beth still made time for sick friends. Lettie opened the trunk of her car and shoved Beth's suitcase inside. "We'd better head to Albany if we want to make our plane."

"You have to come inside and see Jack and the kids before we leave," Beth insisted. "It will only take a minute."

"It's time for me to take my pain medicine anyway," Alexa said as she climbed out of the backseat. "Can I get a glass of water, Beth?"

"Of course." Beth laced her arm through Alexa's and led the way toward her house. "Why do you need pain medicine?"

"Dental work," Alexa replied briefly.

"And the pain medicine puts her into a near coma," Lettie informed Beth with a frown. "I think she needs to ease up on it."

"And when you get your license to practice medicine, I'll listen to your advice," Alexa said over her shoulder as she walked into the Gambles' house with Beth, followed closely by Mary Margaret. Left without much recourse, Lettie trailed behind her friends.

Beth's husband was nice, and the Gamble children were cute and not too obnoxious, but being exposed to marital bliss was never easy for Lettie. Not that she begrudged Beth her happiness, but at times like this she couldn't help but think of what might have been. And thoughts like that could only lead her to a place she'd rather not go.

Beth seemed to sense Lettie's discomfort, and their stay at the Gambles' house was mercifully short. Once they were on the road headed for Albany, Lettie took a deep breath and tried to relax. They had plenty of time to make it through security. Everything was going to be okay.

* * *

Mancil removed sack lunches from the big cooler and distributed them to the prisoners who were temporarily working as gardeners for the city of Bolivar. The men took seats in the shade and began to eat. Mancil left Kenny's sack in the cooler so the guard could get his own lunch whenever he was ready.

A few minutes later, Kenny joined them. After claiming his lunch, he closed the lid and deposited his considerable bulk on the cooler. "Looks like you're about done here," Kenny said as he unwrapped one of the bologna sandwiches.

Mancil tried not to stare as the guard took a big bite. "Yes, sir. I figure this will be our last day here."

"You've done a good job," Kenny complimented around a mouthful of sandwich. He waved his free hand to encompass the water treatment facility that covered several acres. "Not that anyone will ever see your handiwork—it smells too bad."

Mancil had gotten used to the odors of sewer water in various stages of treatment, and he didn't care if other people saw his accomplishment. This job would serve his purpose.

Kenny took a big gulp from a bottle of apple juice. Then he unwrapped his second sandwich. "How much longer before you'll be ready to head back? It's getting pretty cold out here."

"A couple more hours and we can pack it in," Mancil said, hoping that the job would actually be over sooner than this. He forced himself to eat and resisted the urge to check his watch. According to the research he'd done on oleander plants, Kenny, who already had a heart condition, should begin experiencing heart arrhythmia within a few minutes.

When Mancil noticed that the other prisoners were finished with their lunches, he abandoned his half-eaten sandwich and asked Kenny, "You want me to collect the trash?"

The guard nodded. "Make sure you get it all. I don't want no complaints from the sewer folks."

Mancil removed a garbage bag from the back of the van and walked around to each of his fellow prisoners. Once the trash was collected, Mancil asked the guard if he should return the cooler to the van.

Kenny rubbed his chest. "Leave it. I got a little indigestion, so I think I'll sit here on it for a while. You fellows go ahead and do what you need to do to finish up before I freeze to death."

Mancil closed up the garbage bag and waved for the other men to follow him.

As they walked, Isaac stepped up beside Mancil and said, "Don't feel too bad that this one is done. It turned out so good I bet the warden will have people standing in line to get our services."

Mancil didn't contradict his fellow prisoner, but he knew that one way or another, this was the last project he'd ever handle for Hardeman County Correctional Facility.

CHAPTER 4

Gray had the lead position, walking with experienced hikers through some of the Great Smoky Mountains National Park's more challenging terrain. The going was difficult and required total concentration, so there was very little small talk among the men who followed him. The sun was streaming through the thick foliage, dappling the path in front of him. The air was cool and snow remnants still clung to some of the lower limbs of the yellow trees where the first fragile blossoms were beginning to bud.

It was his favorite time of year, and Gray usually enjoyed watching winter yield to spring. But today he was too preoccupied with the possible ramifications of Lowell's secret trip to enjoy the annual metamorphosis.

If Lowell married, would his wife demand that Lowell work more regular hours? Would Lowell need more income to support a family? How would these changes impact the business? Would Lowell want to sell his interest in the tour guide company? Gray had some savings, but nothing close to what it would cost to buy Lowell out. He'd be forced to take on another partner or, even worse, lose the business all together.

Just as Gray thought he might go crazy with worry, they reached a clearing. He waited for the others to catch up and announced that they would stop for a break. His clients pulled out canteens and settled into friendly conversation. Gray moved a few yards away from the congenial group and used the opportunity to call Lowell on his company-owned satellite phone.

"Smoky Mountain Tours," Lowell answered promptly.

"Hey," Gray responded.

"Hey," Lowell returned. "How far have you made it?"

"We're on Charlies Bunion—about halfway in."

"Making good time." Lowell's tone was approving.

"What are you doing?" Gray asked.

"Getting all the paperwork in order for my trip," his partner responded vaguely.

"Have you checked the weather?"

"Of course," Lowell confirmed. "Clear and cold—perfect for hiking and camping."

Gray couldn't argue with this, but he had to add, "The National Weather Service is predicting record cold temperatures, and they might get freezing rain as far north as Chattanooga."

"But they said that right here we're gonna be fine."

"The National Weather Service *predicts* the weather—they don't *make* it," Gray reminded his friend. "The forecast is not a guarantee, and conditions can change without much warning."

Lowell laughed. "I know that. I've lived here all my life, remember?"

Gray felt silly for trying to instruct his friend—who knew more than Gray ever would about the park and its weather. "Sorry."

"You act like you don't trust me to take a group out on my own," Lowell teased.

"I trust you," Gray muttered. "But we usually know all the details of each other's trips so if there's trouble we can help out."

"There's not much to tell about this trip," Lowell replied. "We're driving in to the base of the Alum Cave Trail. Then we'll hike up to LeConte Lodge."

Gray frowned. "The lodge doesn't open until next Monday."

"They're letting me rent the dining hall for the weekend," Lowell told him. "Without food services, of course. I'll have to do the cooking."

"I'm surprised the lodge folks were willing to do that."

"They owe me a couple of favors, and my campers are novices. The dining hall at LeConte will be roughing it enough for them."

"Well," Gray said. "I guess you can't get into too much trouble there."

Lowell laughed. "Your confidence in me is heartwarming. And as much as I enjoy chatting with you, I've got to go to the airport to pick up my friends."

The Alcoa airport was nearly an hour's drive from their office, and making a pickup there was a major inconvenience. "I didn't know we'd started offering airport service."

"I don't plan for it to become a habit," Lowell said. "But these folks are special."

Gray sighed. "Obviously."

"I'll see you when I get back."

Gray heard Lowell disconnect and closed his own phone, feeling more curious and more excluded than he had before.

* * *

The minute the four women were settled on the airplane for the short flight to the McGhee-Tyson Airport in Alcoa, Tennessee, Alexa fell back asleep.

"You think she's taking too many pills?" Beth whispered to Lettie and Mary Margaret.

Lettie made a face. "Definitely—but you heard her. Until I take the Hippocratic Oath, she's not going to listen to me."

"And you should've seen her apartment," Mary Margaret interjected. "It looked like a garbage dump."

Little worry lines formed between Beth's eyes. "That's not like Alexa. She was always such a neat freak."

Lettie glanced at the woman snoring softly beside her. "No, she's not like herself at all."

"I wonder, why is Brian allowing it to go on?" Beth asked.

Lettie shrugged. "She said he's been out of town, so apparently he doesn't know how out of control things have gotten."

"If she's been taking the medicine long enough to get addicted to it, stopping won't be easy," Beth said. "It might not even be something she can do on her own. She might have to go to a hospital."

"While we're in the mountains we can try to talk her into getting treatment," Mary Margaret said with optimism.

"Or I could just throw away her pills," Lettie murmured.

Beth shook her head. "We can't make decisions for her."

Lettie stared at Alexa for a few seconds and then said, "If I were in her shape, I'd want you to make decisions for me."

* * *

As Eugenia took her cake out of the oven, she heard someone knocking on her back door. Since Cornelia Blackwood always came to the front door when she was on an errand for the Lord, Eugenia felt safe, but she peeked out the window to be sure. When she saw Winston Jones, the police chief of Haggerty, standing on her back stoop, she pulled the door open to let him in.

"I hope you aren't planning to stay long," she informed him immediately. "Because I'm trying to bake a cake for the grand opening at the senior center tonight and don't have time to entertain you."

Winston stepped back outside. "If you're participating in the contest I'd better stand out here. I've been asked to judge for the contest, and if I see your entry I won't be impartial."

Eugenia didn't know if seeing her cake would prejudice him in her favor or against her, and she didn't dare ask for a clarification. Instead she said, "Are you trying to find out where I'm going to attend church on Sunday?"

"No ma'am," he replied. "I'm here on official business."

Eugenia's eyes widened in surprise. "Official?"

"Yes, ma'am. Miss Cornelia Blackwood said she's been trying to reach you all day and you won't answer your phone or the door. She thought you might have fallen and broken your hip, so she asked me to come by and check on you."

Eugenia knew she'd been outmaneuvered by the Baptist preacher's wife. "Obviously I haven't broken my hip. Cornelia is just trying to smoke me out."

Winston removed his police hat and scratched his scalp. "Why does she need to smoke you out?"

"Because I won't talk to her."

Winston looked even more confused. "Why not?"

"Cornelia and Barbara Jean are competing for my attendance at church on Sunday. Until I decide which service I'll attend, I'm lying low."

Winston laughed. "You must feel pretty honored to have them fighting over you like that."

Eugenia kept her reply purposely vague. "I can't begin to tell you."

Winston descended the steps. "Well, I'd better go call Miss Cornelia and tell her you're okay. You want me to tell her you'll come to services at the Baptist church on Sunday?"

Eugenia shook her head impatiently. "I told you I don't know which church I'm going to."

Winston settled his hat securely onto his head. "But, if I *tell* Miss Cornelia you're coming to worship with the Baptists, she'll stop bothering you."

Eugenia considered this for a few seconds and then nodded. "And if I don't worship with the Baptists, it will be you who lied, not me."

* * *

When Lettie and her companions walked into the small baggage claim area of the McGhee-Tyson Airport in Alcoa, Tennessee, they found Lowell Brooks there waiting for them. Lowell was a big man with an open smile. His head was shaved, so he resembled a lumberjack version of Mr. Clean—minus the earring.

Lettie had never met Lowell and was predisposed to dislike him. Mary Margaret made introductions, and he greeted each woman in turn. Then he welcomed them effusively and offered to carry their luggage. By the time they reached his mud-splattered black Jeep, Lettie was starting to warm up to him in spite of herself.

"Sorry about the condition of my vehicle," he apologized as he opened the doors for them. "I meant to run it through a car wash, but I didn't have time."

"We don't mind," Mary Margaret assured him. "In fact, I like it."

Alexa put a hand to her mouth to cover a yawn. "Yes, there's something distinctly masculine about a dirty Jeep."

Lowell laughed. "In that case, I'll never wash it again."

"It is possible to take manliness too far," Beth warned.

Lowell winked at her. "I'll keep that in mind."

After an hour of riding in the Jeep, Lowell pulled off the road and parked in front of a modest-sized building made from split logs. A sign hanging from the roof proclaimed it to be the offices of Smoky Mountain Tours—owned and operated by Lowell Brooks and Lettie's ex-fiancé, Gray Grantland.

Lettie couldn't control a little shudder. Lowell noticed it and assumed she was reacting to the dropping temperature.

"Let's go inside for a few minutes," he suggested. He climbed out of the Jeep and led the way up the stone path. "You ladies might as well stay warm until I get our gear all packed."

The last thing Lettie wanted to do was go inside. For almost five years she had trained herself not to think about Gray. Being in his office would make that impossible, and she wasn't sure she was up to it. But she knew refusing to go inside would cause a fuss, so she followed the others.

"I can't believe how cold it is!" Beth cried as they all rushed inside. "Back home it's already spring."

Lowell closed the door behind them. "Spring comes a little later in the mountains."

"It's nice and warm in here," Mary Margaret pointed out.

Lowell checked the thermostat. "Yep, I can always tell when Gray has been here before me. I tell him he must have thin blood because he always turns up the heat."

Lettie saw Mary Margaret and Beth glance at her. Alexa was too drug dazed to wonder if Lettie found remarks about Gray unsettling.

Mary Margaret changed the subject by saying, "Your office is very nice."

"Modern," Beth agreed, rubbing her hand along the back of a small couch.

Lowell pointed to a counter in the corner that held a microwave and a small refrigerator. "That's the snack area. You ladies help yourselves."

This comment seemed to pull Alexa from her fog. "Do you have any bottled water? It's time for my next dose of medication."

"We've got water and juice and soft drinks," Lowell itemized.

"Quite a selection," Mary Margaret praised.

Beth walked over and opened the refrigerator. She handed a bottle of water to Alexa and then took a juice box for herself. "What can I get for the rest of you?"

"I'll take a Sprite," Mary Margaret said.

Lettie shook her head. "Nothing for me." Then she looked around the office. Two desks facing each other formed the business side of the room. On the walls there were several huge maps, a large calendar, and a bulletin board covered with official-looking notices. On the far side of the room was the snack area with the cozy little couch, arranged to give anyone sitting there a gorgeous view of the mountains.

Lowell walked over to one of the desks and turned on the computer. "I'm going to check the weather report real quick. If anyone's hungry, there are cookies and chips in the cupboard above the refrigerator."

Beth opened the cupboard and extracted a pack of cheese crackers. Mary Margaret walked over to look out the window, and Alexa flopped down on the couch.

"I think I'll rest here until we're ready to go." Alexa closed her eyes and pressed her cheek against the plaid fabric.

"What a beautiful view," Mary Margaret remarked.

Beth took a seat beside Alexa on the couch. "We could just stay here for the weekend."

Lowell laughed. "If you think this view is good, wait until you see the one from the lodge."

Lettie smiled. She had to admit that Lowell was pleasant. Once they got out of this place—which fairly screamed Gray's name—the weekend would probably be fun. She leaned against the wall by the door, trying to keep herself separated from the room as much as possible. Of their own accord, her eyes swung to the empty desk.

So this was where Gray sat day after day, helping to run the tour business. There were no pictures of a wife or girlfriend, and somehow the absence made Lettie feel better. On the pretext of looking at a map on the wall, she walked to the desk. She put her hand on the back of his chair and had the unreasonable desire to burst into tears.

Before she could make a complete idiot out of herself, Lowell turned off his computer and stood. "The weather report looks okay, but it's going to be a lot colder than I expected. So you ladies need additional gear." He pulled open the door to a closet and revealed a neat row of insulated clothing.

Alexa perked up at this announcement. She walked over and peered into the closet. "Do you have something in pink?"

"Sorry, but our selection is limited," Lowell apologized.

Alexa frowned as she fingered a pair of pants. "Brown isn't my best color."

Lowell laughed. "You ladies might not be the most fashionable hikers, but at least you won't be cold."

After everyone was dressed warmly enough to suit Lowell, he moved toward the door. "What do you say we head out to my *manly* Jeep and go camping?"

Mary Margaret was game. "I say let's go!"

With varying levels of enthusiasm, the women followed Lowell outside.

* * *

Mancil checked his watch with growing alarm. It had been two hours since Kenny had eaten the oleander leaves, but so far the guard had given no indication that he was in any real distress. Mancil had been so sure that the oleander leaves would work he hadn't bothered to devise a backup plan. But there was no way he was going back to Hardeman. If necessary, he would take Kenny's gun and incite a riot.

Mancil's thoughts were interrupted by the sound of Isaac yelling. Mancil looked up to see the other prisoner leaning over Kenny, who was now prone on the ground. Careful not to let his satisfaction show, Mancil trotted over to stand beside Isaac.

"This ain't good," Isaac said unnecessarily.

"What's the matter?" Mancil asked.

Kenny clutched at his chest. "It's my heart," the guard gasped. "Call for help."

Mancil reached down and removed the radio from Kenny's belt. "It won't turn on. I guess the battery is dead," he announced. And it was true—Mancil had made sure of that by switching out the batteries before they left that morning.

Kenny cursed once and then passed out.

"What are we going to do?" Isaac asked Mancil, his eyes wide with terror.

Mancil leaned down and fished the keys to the prison van from Kenny's pocket. "I'm going to drive into Bolivar and get help."

The other prisoners had now formed a concerned semicircle around the unconscious guard. "Shouldn't we load him in the van and take him to town?" one of them asked.

Mancil shook his head with certainty. "No, moving him might kill him." He took off toward the van, hoping to get away before anyone had time to stop him—and before anyone realized he had taken Kenny's wallet along with his keys. "I'll be back in a few minutes." Then he climbed into the van and stuck the key into the ignition. Five minutes later he was driving down the road in the prison van headed for Memphis and freedom.

* * *

Lettie stopped along the trail that led up to the LeConte Lodge and waited for Alexa. "Come on," she encouraged. "You're letting the others get too far ahead."

"I don't understand why we had to hike up to the lodge," Alexa grumbled.

"Because the road doesn't go that far," Lettie reminded her with dwindling patience. "But we're almost there."

"Thank goodness. This pack is killing me."

Lettie gritted her teeth to keep from snapping at the ungrateful woman. Lowell had purposely given Alexa a light load—which meant he had to carry the extra weight. They trudged together for another few yards into a stiff breeze until the LeConte Lodge came into view.

"We're here," Lettie said a little breathlessly. Then she studied their accommodations. The main building was moderate sized, and behind it were several small cabins. A split-rail fence lined the walkway that led to the lodge's large front porch

Alexa frowned. "It looks kind of run-down."

"It's not run-down," Lettie countered. "It's rustic."

By the time Alexa and Lettie climbed the steps of the lodge, the others were already inside.

"It's colder in here than it is outside," Alexa complained, rubbing her gloved hands together. "I hope the furnace isn't broken."

Lowell laughed. "There is no furnace—only propane space heaters and this fireplace. Once I get a fire going it will be comfortable, though. You ladies have a seat." He pointed to a couple of worn leather couches in front of the fireplace. "I'll get some wood from out back."

Alexa looked like she was ready to complain again, and Lettie didn't think she could stand it, so she shrugged off her backpack and followed Lowell outside. "I'll help."

Before they reached the woodpile, his cell phone rang. "Hello, Gray," he said.

Lettie's breath caught in her throat when she realized her former fiancé was on the other end of the line. To keep Lowell from noticing how badly her hands were trembling, she leaned down and picked up a couple of small logs.

"Yeah, we just got here a little while ago," Lowell was reporting. There was a pause, and then Lowell said, "I know my secrecy has been driving you crazy, and I guess I can tell you now. My mystery guest is Lettie Stewart."

Lettie was so astonished that she dropped a piece of wood and it barely missed her left foot. She looked up in time to see Lowell wink.

"You don't have to worry about us being up here without chaperones, though," Lowell continued outrageously. "We brought a few of her friends along—Beth, Mary Margaret, and Alexa. You might remember them—I think they were supposed to be bridesmaids at your wedding." Lowell laughed at Gray's response and said, "I didn't tell you sooner because I wanted to avoid a conversation like this, of course." Lowell listened for a minute. Then he added, "I don't know why you care. You said you were over her."

Lettie's cheeks burned with embarrassment as Lowell said, "Good. I'm glad we've got that settled. Although I have to say, I think you made a mistake when you let her go. She's even more beautiful now than she was in those pictures you showed me on the mission." Lowell was still smiling when he lowered the phone from his ear. "Gray hung up on me," he told her. "I hope you don't mind me needling him a little."

Lettie minded very much, but she wouldn't admit it. "I couldn't care less."

"It's funny," Lowell mused. "Gray said the same thing. But he sure *sounded* like he cared."

Lettie turned away. "I don't want to discuss Gray Grantland."

Lowell shrugged. "Okay then. Let's get this wood inside and start a fire before we all freeze to death."

* * *

Gray put his phone into his pocket and took several deep breaths in an effort to control his temper. He knew that he was unreasonably upset with Lowell and tried to convince himself that it was Lowell's lack of straightforwardness—not his unexpected relationship with Lettie Stewart—that bothered him. His eyes drifted over in the direction of the LeConte Lodge. This was the closest he had been to Lettie in years, but he couldn't enjoy the knowledge that she was nearby because she was there at the invitation of his best friend. He reached up and rubbed the ache in his chest, surprised that it still hurt so much after all these years.

* * *

Since the prison van would be easy to identify, Mancil had to use back roads to avoid detection. As a result, it was getting dark by the time he reached the outskirts of Memphis. It was also cold and starting to sleet—but he was enjoying this taste of real freedom too much to complain. His immediate needs were a change of clothes and a different vehicle. His minor needs were something to eat and a safe place where he could get a couple hours of sleep.

One of these minor needs was met when Mancil found a collection bin for a local charity called "The City of Hope—A Happy Place for Troubled Boys and Girls." He figured the troubled boys and girls wouldn't mind if he borrowed a few donated items. He parked the van so that it blocked the view of the box from the road—just in case a passerby got curious. Then he pulled out some boxes and stacked them on the ground beside the van.

His search through the discards was hampered by the weather and the fact that he didn't have a flashlight. But he finally found a pair of blue jeans, a long-sleeved T-shirt, a nylon jacket with a zip-out lining, and a well-worn Atlanta Braves baseball cap. He changed behind the van, then buried his prison coveralls under the clothing in one of the boxes and returned them all to the collection bin.

A few miles down the road he saw a Wal-Mart Supercenter. He drove two blocks past the store and parked the van at a body shop that had closed for the night. Then he walked back to the Wal-Mart. As he pushed his shopping cart down the food aisles, his mouth watered. There were so many things he hadn't eaten in years— doughnuts and chocolate milk and real Oreos—not the cheap imitations they served the inmates at Hardeman. But he used restraint and only bought a few sweets. Mostly he tried to stick with practical foods that would store well, like string cheese and beef jerky. He picked up a toothbrush and some toothpaste then swung by the pharmacy for a box of latex gloves. He got an atlas of the United States and then headed to the sporting goods department.

After he'd added a tent, sleeping bag, mess kit, and other camping essentials to his basket, he stopped at the gun counter and asked the clerk to take out a rifle and a couple of knives. While he was inspecting them, an old man stepped up beside him and said, "You a hunter?"

Mancil examined the man. He seemed harmless enough and didn't show any signs of recognition, so Mancil smiled. "Yeah."

The old man smiled back. "I used to love to hunt. You got kids?"

Mancil shook his head. "No."

"Me either, but I wish I did. My wife's dead now and it's lonely." He pointed at the rifle. "That's a pretty good piece—for the money anyway."

"You know a lot about guns?" Mancil asked.

"Oh yeah," the man replied. "I got a bunch of them." He held out an age-spotted hand. "Avery Ingle."

Mancil shook Avery's hand firmly. "What I really wish I had is a handgun—for protection, you know."

"Yeah," the old man agreed. "The criminals all have them, so I never leave home without one." He patted the pocket of his jacket, and Mancil could see the bulge of a revolver.

Mancil had never considered himself a lucky man—in fact most people would say his life had gone wrong from the very beginning. But at that moment he wondered if his luck had changed. "Yes sir. A handgun is a mighty good thing to have these days."

"Do you want to get that stuff?" the Wal-Mart associate asked, pointing at the array of weapons on the counter.

"Just the knives," Mancil said. "And these things, too."

The clerk looked annoyed as Mancil piled everything from his cart onto the counter, but he rang it all up. Then Mancil used some of the money he'd taken from Kenny Dobson's wallet to pay for his purchases.

Once the transaction was complete, he turned back to the old man. "It was nice meeting you."

"You too," Avery said with a smile. "Hope you enjoy your hunting trip."

"Thanks." After waving good-bye, Mancil left the store and stood in the shadows by the entrance. While he waited, he removed two of the latex gloves from the box he'd purchased and slipped them on. When Avery Ingle emerged, Mancil followed, careful to stay several yards behind him. When the old man stopped beside a late-model Altima and reached into his pocket for the keys, Mancil parked his cart and closed the distance between them.

"Avery!" he called out.

The old man looked up in surprise, but when he saw Mancil his face relaxed into a friendly grin. "Oh, it's you."

"I was wondering if you could tell me a good place to hunt around here."

Avery seemed flattered by the question. "Oh yeah, there are several great spots . . ."

Mancil's arm shot out and wrapped around Avery's neck. He jerked once and heard the old man's neck snap like a twig. After glancing around to make sure no one was watching, he removed the keys from Avery's lifeless fingers. He pressed the keyless entry, opened the back door, and shoved the body into the car.

He retrieved his grocery cart and put his purchases in the trunk. Then he circled the car and slid into the backseat beside the dead man. He searched Avery's pockets and removed the wallet and handgun. Mancil tucked the revolver into his belt and leafed through the impressive number of bills in the wallet. He now had another two hundred dollars in cash, plus a few credit cards to work with. Mancil removed Avery's driver's license and studied the address. Then he opened the newly purchased atlas and determined the quickest route from Wal-Mart to Avery's home.

Ten minutes later Mancil pulled up in front of a modest brick house on a quiet residential street. Flipping down the driver's side visor, he was pleased to see that his good luck was holding. Clipped to the underside of the visor was a remote control for the garage door. He pressed the button, and after glancing around to make sure his arrival hadn't attracted any attention, he eased the Altima into the garage. Once the car was parked, he pushed the button again and the heavy garage door rolled back into place. Then Mancil climbed out of the car, unlocked the door to the house, and slipped inside.

The house was neat and the furnishings old fashioned. As Mancil walked from room to room searching for valuables and making a mess, he allowed himself to wonder what it would be like to have a place like this to call home. Soon, he promised himself. But first things first.

There was a door leading from the kitchen down to a basement that Mancil decided would suit his purpose. He went back to the garage and retrieved Avery. The old man was surprisingly heavy, and, in spite of the cold, Mancil was sweating by the time he had the body arranged at the bottom of the basement stairs. Since Avery lived alone, it would be days before anyone missed him. And when his body was discovered, Mancil hoped the police would classify it as a robbery. It might be days, even weeks, before they made the connection between the old man's death and the escaped convict.

Mancil walked back upstairs and gathered the things he was 'stealing.' Then he put them in the trunk of Avery's car, moved the groceries to the front seat, and opened the garage door, shutting it behind him again after he pulled out. He waited until he was several miles from Avery's home—but still on the western side of Memphis—before switching license plates with a minivan.

Once he was driving east on I-40, Mancil reached into one of the Wal-Mart sacks and removed an Oreo. He popped it into his mouth and smiled. Yes, things were definitely looking up for him.

CHAPTER 5

In honor of the senior center's grand opening, Eugenia chose to wear one of the new pantsuits Annabelle had forced her to buy for their trip to Hawaii the previous fall. She pulled her white hair into a neat bun and dusted a little face powder across her nose. After dabbing on some light plum lipstick, she examined her reflection in the mirror mounted over her dresser. She smiled at herself, thinking she looked pretty good for an old woman.

There was a knock on the back door and Eugenia walked down to admit Polly. Her neighbor had a cake saver in one hand and an umbrella in the other. "I hope the rain doesn't keep people from coming tonight," Polly said as she put the umbrella down by the door. "The grand opening is all anyone has talked about for weeks."

"See what I mean?" Eugenia demanded. "Old people like us have nothing to look forward to, and grand openings at senior citizen centers just force us to face that fact."

"Oh, Eugenia," Polly said. "You're so funny."

"I'm not trying to be," Eugenia replied. "I'm completely serious." Then she pointed at the cake Polly was holding. "So you decided to go with the Italian cream cake?"

"Yes," Polly acknowledged as her eyes moved to the kitchen table. "Oh! And your red velvet cake looks fabulous! Did you find your mother's recipe card?"

Eugenia studied her friend for signs of guile or deceit, but didn't see either. "No," she finally said. "But I think I remembered the recipe."

"Knock, knock!" Derrick said from the back door. "Are you ladies ready?"

Eugenia picked up her cake. "As ready as I'll ever be. Let's get this over with."

The old armory was lit up like a Christmas tree, and in spite of the rain there were quite a few cars parked out front when they arrived. Derrick dropped Annabelle, Polly, and Eugenia off at the entrance to keep them dry. Then he drove down the street in search of a place to park.

The newspaper had reported that the armory had been "renovated" as a part of its conversion to Haggerty's new senior citizen center. But as Eugenia looked around, the only differences she could see were a coat of pink paint on the walls and a couple dozen card tables arranged around the large, drafty room.

"Oh look!" Polly pointed toward a far corner. "There's a piano!"

"That's so schoolchildren can come sing carols to us old folks at Christmastime," Eugenia told her.

Before Polly could respond, Winston Jones walked over and greeted them. "I can't look at your cakes," he said, "since Miss Sullivan invited me to judge the contest."

"I'll take them for you," Whit said as he stepped up beside them, and Eugenia thought he looked particularly handsome in a charcoal gray suit that contrasted nicely with his snow-white hair. He relieved both ladies of their cakes and then said to Eugenia, "You're looking lovely tonight."

"I was just thinking the same thing about you," Eugenia said with her usual candor.

He laughed. "Find a seat while I take these to the cake table. I'll come and sit with you later."

Pleased, Eugenia turned to Winston and whispered, "I haven't gotten any more calls or visits from Cornelia, so I assume she fell for your little trick."

Winston nodded. "Worked like a charm. In fact, Miss Cornelia was so happy when I told her you'd be worshiping with the Baptists on Sunday that I thought she was going to cry."

Eugenia felt a little guilty about misleading the preacher's wife since no decision about Sunday services had been made, but it served Cornelia right for being so pushy. "Let's go find someplace to sit." She led the way across the room and picked out a table close to the microphone.

"There's the refreshment table," Polly noticed immediately. "The paper said that several local businesses were donating food items."

Annabelle put her purse on one of the chairs at the table Eugenia had chosen and waved at Polly. "Let's go see what they've got." She turned to Eugenia. "Are you coming?"

Eugenia shook her head. "I'll stay here and save our seats." Eugenia regretted this decision a few minutes later when Brother Blackwood and Cornelia approached her.

"Eugenia!" the preacher's wife cried. Cornelia apparently equated homely with "highly spiritual" and therefore never wore makeup or put color on her hair. As a result she always looked to Eugenia like a character from the movie *Night of the Living Dead*. "We've been so worried about you!" Cornelia gave Eugenia a quick but firm hug.

"Yes, Winston told me when he came to see if I'd broken my hip."

"We were relieved to hear you were okay," Cornelia continued. Then she lowered her voice and added, "And thrilled that you'll be attending services with us on Sunday! I promised Winston I wouldn't tell a soul so it can be a surprise."

"Hmmm," Eugenia murmured vaguely. Later she'd blame the misunderstanding on her aging eardrums. Sometimes being old came in handy.

The others returned with plates full of appetizers and exchanged greetings with the Blackwoods. Then the preacher and his wife headed off in search of new souls to save.

Relieved, Eugenia asked Derrick, "What kind of cake did you make?"

"A German chocolate upside-down cake," he replied.

"He didn't have time to do anything fancy since you gave us such short notice," Annabelle added.

"I wonder who is judging the contest," Polly said with her mouth full of cucumber sandwich, "besides Winston, of course."

"The mayor, Brother Watty, and Brother Blackwood are also judges," Annabelle itemized. "And in case of a tie, Miss Sullivan will cast the deciding vote."

"How convenient," Eugenia murmured.

"How *smart*," Annabelle countered. "With a representative from law enforcement, local government, the Methodists, *and* the Baptists, nobody is going to dispute the fairness of the contest."

"There are some beautiful cakes," Derrick reported. "But in my opinion, the ones you ladies baked are the front-runners."

"Oh my." Polly blushed with pleasure as the mayor tapped on the microphone and called everyone to attention.

"Welcome!" The mayor's amplified voice reverberated throughout the room. "And now it's my pleasure to introduce our senior center's new activities director, Miss Charlotte Sullivan."

A woman stepped up beside the mayor and beamed at the crowd. She was in her late fifties or early sixties, thin, and well preserved. Even Eugenia had to admit that she was quite attractive. She was wearing a pair of jeans that would probably fit a ten-year-old, and a T-shirt that said "Haggerty Chamber of Commerce." Watching her, Eugenia felt old and overdressed. And she wondered why Whit had never offered her a chamber of commerce T-shirt.

Miss Sullivan tossed her glossy auburn hair and addressed the crowd. "Please, everyone, just call me Charlotte!" she invited.

"I'd love to call you, Charlotte!" an old man with a walker hollered from the back. "What's your number?"

Polite laughter rippled across the room.

Then Charlotte Sullivan said, "It's great to see so many of you here tonight, and I encourage all of you to come back regularly."

"We are so fortunate to have Miss Sullivan . . ." the mayor began.

The new director waved her finger and corrected, "Charlotte."

The mayor laughed. "We are so fortunate to have *Charlotte* running our center. I'd also like to recognize Whit Owens, who was instrumental in bringing her to Haggerty." The mayor looked around. "Whit, where are you?"

Whit stepped up beside the mayor. "I'm right here."

"Whit and the other members of our chamber of commerce recruited Charlotte and convinced our local businesses to pay her salary. Let's all give Whit a big hand."

There was a smattering of applause and Whit waved at the crowd.

Charlotte Sullivan flashed everyone another brilliant smile and pointed at the cake table. "These contest entries look absolutely delicious!"

"It won't be an easy job choosing a winner," Whit contributed, leaning close to her in order to speak into the microphone.

"There will be several awards given," Miss Sullivan said, "including best use of fruit, most original, and most nutritious. But the highest award is, of course, the Best All-Around." Miss Sullivan tried to lift a large trophy but faltered under its weight. Whit had to step in and help her. "Thank you, Whit," she said a little breathlessly. "The Best All-Around winner gets to keep this trophy until next year's contest."

"We hope that this will become an annual event for the senior center," Whit explained.

"What you really hope is that we'll all still be around next year!" the old man in the back called out.

"Well, that, too!" Whit agreed good-naturedly. "Now, while the judges taste the cakes, we're going to have some music and dancing. Ferrell Knight's here to call for us, and he's brought his family along to pick and grin."

The Knight family band filed in and quickly set up. Then they struck up a rousing rendition of "Rocky Top." While Eugenia watched in dismay, Whit held out his hand to Miss Sullivan. "May I have this dance?" he asked, and the whole room heard him, thanks to the microphone.

Charlotte Sullivan smiled. "I'd be honored."

Eugenia felt conspicuously alone while Whit and the senior center's new activities director scooted around the dance floor. She didn't know why it came as a surprise to her that Whit was enjoying Charlotte Sullivan's company so much. He had three ex-wives and all of them were very attractive women. Eugenia had to laugh at herself. An hour ago she felt like she looked pretty good for an old woman. Now she just felt like an old woman.

The first number ended, and Eugenia was pleased when Whit came over to their table. "Is everybody having a good time so far?" he asked. His cheeks were flushed and his eyes were shining.

"Everything's wonderful," Polly effused. "We saved you a seat."

"Thanks," he said, but he didn't sit down. "I'll try and come back later if Charlotte ever gets finished with me."

He waved to the group as a whole and then rushed off. Eugenia stared after him, thinking it was unlikely that Charlotte Sullivan *would* ever get finished with him.

"Is anyone sitting there?"

Eugenia turned to see George Ann Simmons standing behind the empty chair they'd been saving for Whit. She shook her head. "No."

George Ann pulled out the chair and settled herself at the table.

"So, what do you think of the senior center's new activities director?" Annabelle asked George Ann.

George Ann had an unattractive habit of lifting her chin slightly before she spoke. "Well, I think it's odd that she goes by 'Miss' Sullivan even though she's been married and widowed three times. And she's the only person I've ever met who brags about traveling more than you, Annabelle. She's been everywhere—Hawaii, Alaska, Hong Kong. Even Russia."

"I don't brag about anything," Annabelle defended herself.

Eugenia rolled her eyes. "Humph."

Annabelle ignored this and continued. "But traveling does cost a lot of money. I wonder how she affords that on a nurse's salary."

"That's Annabelle's way of letting us all know that she and Derrick are rich," Eugenia told the others.

Annabelle gave her sister a cross look. "For heaven's sake, Eugenia, that's not what I meant at all."

"If Charlotte has lost three husbands, maybe she travels to keep from being lonely," Polly suggested.

"Charlotte?" Eugenia objected to Polly's familiar form of address. "So now you *and* Whit are on a first name basis with this woman?"

"She asked us to call her Charlotte," Polly reminded them. "Didn't you hear her?"

Eugenia nodded. "I heard her."

"Or maybe she travels to meet men," Annabelle returned to the previous topic.

"Since all her husbands had at least one foot in the grave, it's more likely that she's meeting her matrimonial prospects at the nursing homes where she works," George Ann interjected. "Idella Babcock said Charlotte has been employed at nearly a dozen nursing homes or assisted living centers all across the country."

"Whit said she had a lot of experience," Eugenia remarked.

George Ann lifted her chin again. "My question is, why does she change jobs so often?"

"My question is, how does Idella know how many times Charlotte has been married and how many places she's worked at?" Annabelle asked.

"Whit put a folder on Idella's desk and told her someone from the chamber of commerce would pick it up tomorrow," George Ann replied. "Idella peeked inside and happened to see Miss Sullivan's application for employment."

Annabelle raised her eyebrows. "And during this brief 'peek,' Idella was able to read the woman's full personal and employment history?"

"I'm sure I don't know," George Ann responded coolly. "Idella was the one who peeked, not me."

Derrick cleared his throat and said, "I wonder which cake is going to win the contest?"

Polly fell for this obvious attempt to change the subject. "They all look so good. What kind of cake did you decide to make, George Ann?"

George Ann turned away from Annabelle and replied, "It was a hard choice since I have so many delicious recipes, but I finally decided on a Boston cream cake. What about you, Polly?"

"I made my Italian cream," Polly told her. "Derrick did a German chocolate upside-down cake, and Eugenia made her mother's red velvet cake."

George Ann gasped. "Eugenia! You only make your mother's red velvet cake on Christmas Eve!"

This remark annoyed Eugenia, partly because George Ann said it and mostly because it was true. "It's *traditional* that I only make red velvet cake on Christmas Eve," she conceded. "But it's not *illegal* for me to make it whenever I want to."

George Ann was unconvinced by this argument. "But it might be bad luck. Your mother always said . . ."

Eugenia cut her off. "I know what my mother said."

"What did your mother always say?" Derrick asked.

"That red velvet cake should only be baked on Christmas Eve," Eugenia provided reluctantly.

Derrick frowned. "Why?"

"Our mother was superstitious," Annabelle explained. "One Christmas Eve at the end of World War II, she baked a red velvet cake. As she finished icing the cake, my father walked through the door— home from the war. So from then on she baked a red velvet cake every Christmas Eve until she died—and on no other occasion. Eugenia, as the oldest daughter, took up the practice after her death. But Charlotte Sullivan made Eugenia break the long-standing family tradition."

"Charlotte Sullivan didn't make me do anything," Eugenia insisted. "I just wanted to win."

Before anyone could contradict her, Whit and Charlotte returned to the microphone. Whit waved for Ferrell and his family to be quiet and then said, "Charlotte has an announcement to make."

"The judges have tasted all the cakes," Charlotte informed those gathered. "They are now conferring to determine the winners in the various categories, and in the meantime, you are all welcome to help yourselves."

Polly jumped to her feet and rushed the cake table like a starving woman. "Would you like me to fix you a plate, Eugenia?" she called over her shoulder.

"No thanks," Eugenia replied. Her stomach was still turning from watching Whit laugh at something Charlotte had whispered in his ear.

Annabelle and Derrick stood and moved toward the cake table at a less frantic pace. When they returned a few minutes later, Polly was raving about the red velvet cake. "You're sure to win," she told Eugenia. "It's the best I've ever eaten."

"It's delicious," Derrick agreed.

"And you should take his opinion very seriously since he's an expert cook," Annabelle reminded them with a fond smile at her husband.

"It is good," George Ann said grudgingly. "Although I think my Boston cream cake turned out awfully well."

"It's delicious too," Polly confirmed with her mouth full. "So moist."

George Ann smiled at the compliment she had so openly solicited.

Charlotte tapped the microphone and announced that the judges were ready to make their presentations. Then the mayor stepped forward and acted as spokesman. Inez Thatcher won best use of fruit for her strawberry cake. George Ann's Boston cream cake was named the most original, and Lester Spivey's sugar-free cake won most nutritious.

As Lester was receiving his ribbon Eugenia whispered to the others seated at her table, "You notice they didn't mention how it *tasted*, just that it was nutritious."

"And now for the moment you've all been waiting for," the mayor continued, trying to build the suspense. "The Best All-Around category. Actually, we have two finalists and require a tie breaker." The mayor turned to the Baptist preacher. "Brother Blackwood, please present Charlotte with a sample of each contender's cake and allow her to taste them."

Brother Blackwood brought forward a tray containing two saucers. On one saucer was a slice of pound cake. On the other was a slice of red velvet cake. The entire table gasped in unison as they realized simultaneously that Whit and Eugenia had been pitted against each other.

Eugenia was watching Charlotte and thought she saw a little gleam in the other woman's eyes. The identities of the cooks were supposed to be kept secret, but everyone in Haggerty knew Eugenia made the best red velvet cake, and Whit was famous for pound cakes. It wouldn't have been difficult for her to find out which cake belonged to Whit.

Eugenia had to give her credit. Charlotte made a good show of analyzing a bite from each piece, but in the end she chose Whit's pound cake as the best. Then she acted amazed when she found out that Whit was the big winner. And, of course, she took advantage of the opportunity to throw her arms around his neck and give him a congratulatory kiss on the cheek.

"Man, if I'd known she was going to kiss the winner I would have brought a Little Debbie cake and entered that contest!" the old man with the walker called out.

There was more general laughter and Whit smiled. At this point, Eugenia decided she'd had enough. "Derrick, would you mind running me home?"

Annabelle frowned. "Already? It's barely seven o'clock."

"I know what time it is," Eugenia assured her sister.

"Are you going to pout because you didn't win?" Annabelle demanded.

"I'm not pouting," Eugenia replied. "I'm tired, and if Derrick won't take me, I'll call a taxi." This was an empty threat since the closest cab service was in Albany.

"I'll be glad to take you home," Derrick said. "Let me get your cake plate."

"Go ahead and get mine too, please," Polly requested.

Annabelle stood. "Well, if the rest of you are leaving, Derrick and I might as well go home too."

On the way out Eugenia made a point of congratulating Whit.

"I feel like this should belong to you." He pointed at his trophy.

"No, you earned it," Eugenia told him, and she meant it. "You made hundreds of pound cakes in order to perfect your recipe. I inherited my mother's recipe." Then Eugenia turned to Charlotte. "Tonight was an amazing success."

Charlotte nodded graciously. "Thank you for your support, Mrs. Atkins." Eugenia assumed that the use of "Mrs." was intended to put her firmly into the "elderly" category. "I hope you'll come back tomorrow night. We're going to play bingo, and there will be door prizes and everything."

Probably Polygrip and Geritol, Eugenia thought to herself. "I'll try," she said out loud.

"If you'll come we can share a bingo card," Whit offered with a charming smile.

Eugenia couldn't stop herself from feeling a little hope. Maybe she hadn't lost Whit to Charlotte after all. "I might take you up on that."

On the way home Polly said, "I'm sorry you didn't win, Eugenia. I thought your cake was the very best."

While she appreciated Polly's loyalty, Eugenia wanted to downplay the whole episode as much as possible. "Whit makes an excellent pound cake."

"His pound cakes are exceptionally good," Polly agreed. "But the most perfect pound cake in the world couldn't beat your mother's red velvet cake in a fair fight."

Polly could be a little ditzy, but when she was right, she was right. "It doesn't matter," Eugenia assured her. "I'll see you tomorrow."

Eugenia walked through her back door, and Lady greeted her enthusiastically. Eugenia fed the dog and then sat in one of her kitchen chairs and described the night's events while Lady ate.

"Maybe it's just me," Eugenia said as she finished her discourse. "But it doesn't seem natural for a woman to breeze into town and immediately put everyone under a spell." Eugenia looked down at the little dog. "Do you think I'm crazy?"

Lady barked and nuzzled Eugenia's ankle.

"Thank you for the vote of confidence. Since Charlotte Sullivan has been widowed three times, I can't help wondering if she's come to Haggerty in search of a new husband. And if so, it looks like Whit is her chosen candidate."

Lady barked again.

"It may be a silly waste of time, but I'm going to ask Kelsey to do a background check on Charlotte Sullivan. Wouldn't it be something if I found out that she has a criminal record! That would give the town something to talk about!"

Lady turned several excited circles.

"We can't get our hopes up, because Kelsey probably won't find a thing. But at this point I don't see what I have to lose."

* * *

As Lettie stood by the entrance to the LeConte Lodge and watched Lowell add logs to the fire, she tried to forget about the conversation she had overheard on the porch earlier. Gray was a part of her past. She hadn't allowed herself to think about him for years, and she would continue to resist the temptation.

Once the fire was blazing again, Lowell addressed the group.

"I've let you ladies rest for long enough. Now we're going to make stew for dinner. It's an old family recipe and I'll need everyone's help to make it turn out right."

Lettie glanced at Alexa, who was asleep on one of the couches. "You'd better hope it will turn out okay if you have *most* everyone's help."

"What's wrong with her?" Lowell asked softly.

It would be disloyal to tell him that she suspected Alexa was addicted to prescription drugs, so Lettie decided to sidestep the question. "Some medicine she's taking makes her groggy, but she'll be okay after a few days of breathing this invigorating mountain air."

Lowell filled his lungs and patted his chest. "It works for me. Now, will all my volunteers please assemble in the kitchen?"

Alexa slept soundly as the others were assigned to peel potatoes and carrots. There were several things that had been bothering Lettie, and while they worked, she took the opportunity to question Mary Margaret. "I can't figure out why you asked Lowell to be our guide on this trip. I didn't think the two of you had ever met."

"We hadn't," Mary Margaret confirmed, "until last Christmas Eve. Mother and I went to the mall to pick up a few last minute things, and we ran into Gray and Lowell. Mother insisted that they eat lunch with us, and I could tell that Gray *really* didn't want to, but you know how Mother is."

Lettie nodded. Trying to tell Sister McKenzie "no" was a waste of breath.

"During our meal Gray didn't eat a thing and barely said a word. But Lowell told us all about their tour business. As we were leaving he invited me to come to Tennessee for a guided tour. I knew he was just being polite and never expected me to take him up on it. But later, when I started planning the reunion, it seemed like the perfect solution."

"The fact that I'm the best tour guide in Tennessee also affected her decision," Lowell interjected.

"As did the fact that he told me he'd do it for free," Mary Margaret added.

Lowell shrugged. "I guess that might have had some bearing." He opened the bag of onions and said, "Okay ladies, I'm going to start peeling the onions, so prepare to see a grown man cry."

* * *

It was well after dark on Thursday night when Gray and his hikers reached their predetermined camping area on Eagle Creek Trail. Gray attended to his various guide duties and then helped to build a fire and make dinner. He even sat around the campfire with the others while they ate. But once the meal was over and the dishes washed, he excused himself and went to his tent.

Grateful for a few minutes of privacy, he stretched out on his sleeping bag and stared at the nylon dome above him. In some ways he was a very lucky man. He enjoyed hiking in the mountains and spending his days outdoors. The fact that he was able to make a good living doing the things he loved made him truly fortunate. And he couldn't imagine being anything but his own boss.

If he'd done things differently, he would be living in Atlanta now. He'd probably have a house in the suburbs with a monstrous mortgage. He would never even have time to go for walks much less get the chance to spend hours climbing mountain trails. But he would still have Lettie.

The ache returned to his chest as he shifted onto his side and closed his eyes, hoping that sleep might eventually come.

* * *

Mancil drove to the western edge of Memphis and stopped at a Chevron station. He filled the car with gas using Avery's credit card. Then he went inside and bought several candy bars, a bag of potato chips, and some more powdered doughnuts. He asked for a map of the United States and made sure that both the attendant and the security camera got a good look at his face.

"What's the best way to get from here to Little Rock?"

"West on Interstate 40," the man replied in a bored tone.

"Thanks." Mancil collected his purchases and walked out to the sedan.

Confident that he had laid down a false trail that the police wouldn't be able to ignore, he eased the Altima onto the I-40 entrance ramp and headed east.

* * *

Lettie was impressed with the dinner stew they had made under Lowell's direction. When the meal was over they all helped him clean up—even Alexa. Then the women settled on the couches in front of the fire, and Mary Margaret suggested they play their favorite game.

Lettie smiled. "We're too old for that."

"What kind of game?" Lowell asked as he joined them.

"When we were teenagers we had a sleepover every Friday night and we always played a game called Truth or Die," Mary Margaret explained.

Lowell's eyes widened. "The penalty for a lie was pretty steep!"

Beth laughed. "We never actually killed anyone."

Lettie shot a glance at Alexa. "Although we were tempted."

"How did it work?" Lowell wanted to know.

"We'd each take a turn and tell our deepest, darkest secret," Beth told him. "Then we voted on who had the best secret and the winner got a prize."

Alexa looked around the lodge. "I'd like to see you find a decent prize here."

Mary Margaret thought for a minute. "I have a Snickers in my backpack."

Beth shook her head. "I'm not spilling my secrets for a candy bar."

"Well, how about the winner gets my Snickers *and* doesn't have to do breakfast dishes tomorrow?" Mary Margaret sweetened the deal.

Beth nodded. "Now you're talking."

Alexa put her hand up to cover a yawn. "Sure, why not."

Lettie either had to consent or be the spoilsport. So reluctantly she said, "I guess I'll play along."

Mary Margaret pointed at Lowell. "Since you've never played before, we'll let you start."

"Oh thanks!" Lowell said. "Let's see, what secret do I have?"

"Remember, it's got to be deep and dark," Mary Margaret coached him. "Just a regular secret won't do."

Lowell thought for a few minutes. Then he smiled. "I have six older sisters, and when I was little they used to dress me up in their clothes."

Mary Margaret's eyes were huge as she asked, "Are you serious?"

Lowell nodded. "Unfortunately, I am completely serious."

Beth scrutinized him. "I'm trying to picture it."

"I had hair back then and they would put little bows around my head." He shuddered. "It was terrible."

Lettie couldn't help but laugh. "I'll bet you were a sight!"

"I was a sight—no question about it," Lowell agreed. "But if any of you tell my secret, I'll deny it to the death."

"That goes without saying," Alexa assured him.

Lettie added, "It's one of the few rules associated with Truth or Die."

Mary Margaret turned to Beth. "Okay, you're next."

"Why me?" Beth asked.

"Oldest to youngest," Mary Margaret replied.

Beth didn't put up a fight. "I'm pregnant and I haven't told anyone—not even Jack."

Alexa glanced up, but didn't comment.

"Congratulations!" Mary Margaret reached over to hug Beth. "Maybe it will be a girl so Chloe will finally have a sister."

"And if it's not a girl, hopefully it will be a boy," Lowell contributed.

Beth smiled. "Hopefully."

"Why didn't you tell Jack?" Lettie wanted to know. "Doesn't he want more children?"

Beth laughed. "He wants a *dozen* children—at least. But he worries so much, I was afraid that if he knew he'd make me bring a registered nurse and an ambulance up here with me—just in case."

Lowell grinned. "It would have been entertaining to see an ambulance try to make it up the hill to the lodge."

"Why would he want to send an ambulance?" Alexa asked. "I'm here, and I'm a nurse."

Lettie wanted to point out that since Alexa was under the influence of drugs, she was unlikely to be of any assistance in a medical emergency, but instead she just scowled at her.

"Well, that's going to be hard to top," Mary Margaret said. "How about you, Alexa?"

Alexa shook her head. "You're the next oldest."

"Okay," Mary Margaret agreed. "I don't mind sharing my deep, dark secret. But first I want to thank you all for coming on this trip. I know it was a sacrifice for everyone—but I think it will be a wonderful experience that we'll remember for the rest of our lives."

Alexa frowned. "If you ask me it's off to a slow start."

Lettie was formulating a reprimand when Mary Margaret smiled and said, "Remember, Alexa, tomorrow *is* another day!"

"Hey," Lettie objected. "That's my line."

"Frankly, my dear," Beth began, "I don't give . . ."

"Enough!" Mary Margaret cried. "We used to quote *Gone with the Wind* because Lettie's real name is Scarlett," she explained for Lowell's benefit.

"And it was an excuse to say a bad word," Alexa put in.

"You're the only one who actually *said* it," Beth reminded her. "The rest of us settled for 'darn.'"

Alexa sighed. "That's me, the bad girl."

"I didn't mean it that way," Beth said.

Alexa waved this aside. "Forget it. Quit stalling, Mary Margaret. What's your secret?"

Lettie held her breath, waiting for Mary Margaret to describe the struggle she'd had with cancer. Instead, she said, "I quit my job at the elementary school."

Nothing Mary Margaret could have said would have surprised Lettie more. Mary Margaret had always loved children. From the time they were teenagers all she'd talked about was teaching school and making bulletin boards and finger painting. Lettie saw the same astonishment she felt reflected on the faces of the other game participants. Even Lowell looked stunned.

"You're kidding." As usual Alexa voiced what everyone wanted to say but couldn't.

Mary Margaret shook her head. "No, I'm completely serious. I've spent my entire life in Tifton, and I finally decided it was time to see the world."

"What part of the world are you planning to examine first?" Beth asked with obvious skepticism.

"Washington DC," Mary Margaret informed them. "This summer I'll be teaching inner-city kids who are at risk due to economic factors. The pay is terrible and the only apartment I could afford is a dump, but at least I'll be trying to make a difference."

"Can't you make a difference closer to home?" Lettie asked.

"Where nicer apartments are available?" Alexa wanted to know.

"And what do your parents have to say about this?" Beth demanded.

Mary Margaret laughed. "One at a time, please. I guess I can make a difference anywhere, Lettie, but this summer I've chosen our nation's capital. I was exaggerating about the apartment. It's not that bad, and it's convenient to the school. And my parents aren't happy, but they are supportive."

"I'm impressed," Alexa said grudgingly. "I didn't think you had the nerve."

Mary Margaret frowned. "Thanks, I guess."

Lettie was still astounded by the whole thing. "You're going to Washington DC by yourself?"

Mary Margaret nodded.

"And you aren't going to be a schoolteacher?" Lettie pressed.

"I still want to teach," Mary Margaret clarified. "But I don't want to work for a school system anymore. In the fall I'm thinking about teaching an adult education class for Hispanics in Texas."

"Okay, who are you and where is our friend Mary Margaret?" Beth demanded.

Mary Margaret smiled. "It's really me. But a few months ago I reevaluated my life, and I didn't like what I saw. I'm through with letting time pass me by. After all, none of us are getting any younger."

"Thanks for that reminder," Alexa muttered.

Mary Margaret ignored this. "So I made a list of things I wanted to accomplish and started marking them off, one by one."

"What are some other things on your list?" Beth asked.

"To sail a boat, milk a cow, and kiss a man." Mary Margaret blushed. "That last one is kind of a long shot I know—but nothing ventured, nothing gained."

"Kissing is a cinch," Alexa assured her. "It's that cow you need to worry about."

"You can kiss me," Lowell volunteered. "In fact all of you can kiss me—there's plenty of me to go around!"

Mary Margaret laughed. "Thanks for the offer. I'll let you know if I decide to take you up on it."

Lettie wanted more details about Mary Margaret's lifestyle overhaul, but before she could ask, Mary Margaret challenged Alexa to divulge her deepest, darkest secret. Lettie hoped that Alexa might use this opportunity to discuss her growing dependence on pain pills. But instead Alexa said, "Brian left me. He wants a divorce."

Lettie couldn't control a gasp of shock and Alexa smiled bitterly.

"I know temple marriages are supposed to last forever. But then I never could get anything right."

"It was Brian who left, not you," Beth pointed out.

"I always thought Brian was such a nice guy!" Mary Margaret cried.

Lettie recovered enough to ask, "Do you still talk to him?"

"Not directly," Alexa replied. "His lawyer calls about once a week to remind me that we need to proceed with the divorce so that we can 'move on.' Whatever that means."

"Have you suggested counseling to Brian?" Beth asked.

"Suggested, demanded, begged," Alexa confirmed. "He says it's all a waste of time. He just wants out."

"Maybe he'll change his mind," Mary Margaret ventured.

Alexa shook her head. "He's not going to change his mind."

Mary Margaret reached over and put a hand on one of Alexa's. "I'm so sorry."

Lettie felt bad. "I had no idea."

"Is there anything we can do?" Beth offered.

"There isn't even anything I can do," Alexa said. "My life is hopeless."

"Never give up," Mary Margaret encouraged with sympathy in her eyes. "Tomorrow really is another day."

"Thanks for that *Gone with the Wind* wisdom," Alexa replied. "But I don't want to think about Brian or my failed marriage anymore right now. In fact, I don't want to think about *anything* right now."

"It's because you're taking too many of those pain pills," Lettie said.

Alexa scowled. "And thank you, once again, Dr. Lettie."

Lettie refused to back down. "I don't have to be a doctor to know that those pills have a bad effect on you."

"Brian's divorce request had a bad effect on me," Alexa corrected. "The pills just help me cope. And since you never even made it to marriage, let alone divorce, I don't think you're in a position to judge me."

"I'm not judging you," Lettie said. "I'm trying to help you." Then she stood. "I think we've heard enough secrets for one night. Let's go to bed."

"Oh no you don't!" Mary Margaret cried, grabbing Lettie's hand. "You're not leaving until you tell us your secret. And remember it has to be a deep, dark one."

"I don't have any secrets," Lettie brushed off Mary Margaret's request.

"Everyone has secrets," Lowell responded. "And it won't be fair if you don't share one."

Lettie tried to keep her voice casual. "I think I'll forfeit the candy bar and wash dishes in order to keep my secrets to myself."

"Coward," Alexa accused.

The accusation annoyed Lettie—especially since it was issued by someone who admitted to using drugs to hide from her problems. "I am not!" she denied. "But I can't think of anything. I don't have siblings, so I was spared any cross-dressing traumas. I'm not pregnant and I don't have a boyfriend. And as you so kindly pointed out, I've never been married and therefore don't have to worry about a divorce."

"Why haven't you married?" Lowell surprised her by asking.

"That's not much of a secret," Alexa said. "She never married because she's still in love with your partner, Gray Grantland."

Lettie's humiliation was so intense that words completely failed her.

"Alexa," Mary Margaret chided. "That was cruel."

Lettie pulled herself together and said firmly, "Not to mention stupid. I don't love Gray—I hate him."

Alexa burst out laughing. "And you're trying to give *me* advice? I've never seen a more classic case of self-denial in my life."

"Alexa," Beth cautioned. "I think you've said enough."

Alexa rounded on Beth. "You know it's true! Why should Lettie get off easy? I exposed my pain—she can too."

Mary Margaret stepped into the fray. "Everyone's supposed to have the opportunity to choose their own secret."

"It's just a game," Lowell reminded them.

Alexa wouldn't back down. "A game that requires the participants to be honest—and isn't the truth supposed to make us free?" She looked at Lettie, tears glistening in her eyes. "Don't you want to be free of Gray once and for all?"

Mary Margaret stood and captured Alexa's hands in her own. "You're going through a bad time now, but it's not right to take your hostility toward Brian out on Lettie. And you can't give up on your life. I know that eventually you'll find happiness again."

Alexa shook herself free of Mary Margaret's grasp. "Grow up, Mary Margaret. Face the fact that life stinks." She turned and addressed Lowell. "Where are we supposed to sleep? On the floor in front of the fire?"

After a quick glance at Mary Margaret, Lowell waved toward the kitchen. "There are a couple staff bedrooms back there that sleep two each. I figured you ladies can use them and I'll sleep here."

"That means you get the fire," Mary Margaret said in a teasing tone, and Lettie realized that she was letting everyone know that she wasn't upset with Alexa.

Lowell smiled. "The bedrooms have space heaters that should keep you pretty cozy until morning."

Alexa picked up her duffel bag and walked to the kitchen.

When they heard the bedroom door slam, Lettie said, "If I room with her—she won't live until morning."

"I'll stay with grumpy Alexa," Beth volunteered as she stood and stretched. "It can be my punishment for having the lamest secret."

Mary Margaret got up too. "Okay, but I need to talk to her first. She and I have unfinished business." With this remark, Mary Margaret followed Alexa into the back.

* * *

Mancil sat in the shadows and watched traffic move past the brick booth that divided the Great Smoky Mountains State Park's entrance and exit lanes. Business was slow, with only an occasional visitor leaving the park—which was a problem for Mancil. He'd been counting on lots of cars both coming and going so that the rangers inside the booth wouldn't be able to examine the occupants of each vehicle too closely. He considered circling around to use the park's service entrance—but that would take at least an hour and he hated to waste the time.

He was beginning to think that his luck had taken a turn for the worse when several vans with "World Victory Church Youth Ministry" emblazoned on the side pulled up to the booth. A large man emerged from the lead van waving his arms and hollering. Based on the man's numerous gestures toward the sky, Mancil assumed that he was complaining about the weather. Mancil waited until both rangers had left the booth and joined the screaming man. Then he eased Avery's car onto the road and drove past the booth without earning a glance from the rangers.

Smiling to himself, he reached into the convenience store sack on the seat beside him and pulled out the last doughnut. The road conditions continued to worsen, and soon he stopped smiling and eating so he could concentrate on the road. The car's tires lost traction frequently, making his progress slow and dangerous. He was again worrying that his luck might be turning bad when a fallen tree forced him to stop at the base of Hughes Ridge. Realizing that the decision about where to ditch the car had been made for him, Mancil loaded up what he could carry and headed into the woods.

He chose a camp spot about a half mile into the forest. It was far enough from the road that he wouldn't need to worry about being spotted but close enough to the car that he could get there quickly if necessary.

It was almost dawn by the time he had his tent set up. He wanted nothing more than to climb into his new sleeping bag and get some much needed rest. But he knew he had to get everything out of the car. It took him three trips to retrieve all his food and camping equipment.

Before returning to his camp, Mancil climbed into the car one last time. After he got the heater going full blast, he turned on the radio and found a newscaster describing his escape. The guard, Kenny, was dead. Mancil was sorry about that. Kenny had always been decent to Mancil and his fellow prisoners. But a great plan required great sacrifices.

The guy on the radio didn't mention the oleander leaves. Maybe they knew and weren't telling or maybe they thought Kenny really had a heart attack. Mancil didn't figure it made any difference. Either way, if he was caught he'd be in maximum security for the rest of his life. But every minute that he evaded recapture, his chances for permanent escape increased.

Mancil ate a piece of beef jerky and drank a bottle of water. Then he returned to his campsite and snuggled down into the sleeping bag and dreamed about his future. Once he got out west, he'd change his name and start a landscaping business. He'd keep it small to avoid drawing attention to himself. He'd buy a little house and even find a nice girl to spend the rest of his life with. *The rest of his life*—for the first time in years the words had a nice ring to them.

* * *

Alexa was face down on a bed in one of the staff bedrooms at the LeConte Lodge, fighting tears and feeling like a fool. *Crybaby,* she berated herself. *Why do you care what they think?*

Her thoughts were interrupted by a tentative knock on the door.

"Alexa?" Mary Margaret's muffled voice came through the wood.

After impatiently wiping the tears from her face, Alexa said, "Come in."

The door opened slowly and then Mary Margaret asked, "Are you asleep?"

Alexa turned to give the other woman an incredulous look. "Since I just spoke to you a few seconds ago, I guess not."

Mary Margaret ignored the sarcasm and smiled. "Good, because I have something I need to talk to you about."

"If it has anything to do with the medication that has been prescribed for me by my doctor, you're wasting your breath," Alexa said belligerently.

Mary Margaret held up a hand. "It doesn't have anything to do with you at all. It's about me."

Alexa laughed but it was a harsh, humorless sound. "If you need advice you'd better talk to Lettie or Beth. They're the ones with all the answers."

Mary Margaret shook her head. "No, you're the one I need to talk to."

Alexa was still suspicious, but she sat up on the bed and crossed her legs Indian style. "Go ahead then."

Mary Margaret perched herself on the edge of the other bed. "Last summer I was diagnosed with ovarian cancer."

This announcement shocked all the defensiveness out of Alexa. "That's why you're skinny and have short hair."

Mary Margaret nodded. "I had surgery and did six weeks of chemotherapy. I've been in remission now for several months."

Alexa was cautiously relieved. "Does Lettie know? And Beth?"

Mary Margaret nodded. "Yes. Beth has known for some time. I told Lettie just before the trip."

Alexa was disappointed. As usual, she was the last to find out.

"It's difficult to tell people," Mary Margaret continued. "They always get so upset, and I feel obligated to put on a brave face. For a few minutes I want to be honest."

Alexa dragged her eyes over to meet Mary Margaret's. "Okay."

"Facing death on a daily basis is utterly terrifying," she confessed. "And because I'm scared, I feel so guilty. It seems like if I had enough faith, I wouldn't be afraid."

Alexa didn't remember Mary Margaret ever asking her a spiritual question before and wanted to give the right answer, so she considered for a minute. Finally she said, "Being afraid doesn't mean you don't have faith. The Lord will bless you to get through this trial, but He may not cure you. Remember all those Primary lessons about prayer and how sometimes the answer is no?"

Mary Margaret nodded. "That concept was much easier to accept when I wasn't sick."

"Most gospel principles are that way—easy when we aren't facing a challenge, hard when we are."

Mary Margaret sighed. "Even if my cancer doesn't come back, I'll never be able to bear a child. I mind that—I mind it a lot."

"Before I knew that Brian wanted a divorce I'd started thinking it was time for us to have a family. I'd been thinking about names and how I wanted to decorate the nursery. I hurt as much for the children we'll never have as I do for the death of our marriage." Alexa smiled sadly. "So I think I understand a little of how you feel."

"Thank you," Mary Margaret whispered. "Pretending is such a burden."

"You don't have to pretend with me. Ever."

They sat in companionable silence for a few minutes, and finally Mary Margaret said, "So, if the cancer comes back, do you think I should repeat the treatments? Or should I just accept that my death is the Lord's will and enjoy the time I have left?"

"I had a patient once who was in the final stages of bone cancer," Alexa replied. "She'd spent two years going through every treatment imaginable trying to beat the disease. And after all the time and money and misery she'd invested, she still died. But I'll never forget what she told me that last night."

Mary Margaret leaned closer. "What did she say?"

"She said that if she had it to do over again she wouldn't change a thing. She'd suffer anything for the chance to live."

Mary Margaret wiped the tears that slipped from her eyes onto her cheeks.

"So that's my advice," Alexa said softly. "Fight until the end. Then if you die, you'll know it's the way the Lord wants things to be."

Mary Margaret pulled Alexa into a hug. "Thank you. I knew you'd give me an honest answer without sugarcoating it."

Alexa laughed gruffly. "Yeah, I'm always good for that."

"And you won't tell anyone that I'm really a big coward?"

Alexa made an *X* on her chest with one finger. "Cross my heart and hope to die. But you do have to promise me something."

"What?" Mary Margaret asked.

"You have to promise me that if your cancer does come back, you'll call me. I'll be your chemo partner. We'll get little matching scrub suits and wear them to your treatments."

"Are you serious?" Mary Margaret asked in wonder.

"Well, maybe not the matching outfit part—but I will go with you to your treatments."

"I believe that's the nicest thing you've ever said to me," Mary Margaret proclaimed. "Or anyone else for that matter."

Alexa smirked. "I told you—life stinks. But it stinks less if you have company."

Mary Margaret gave her a tremulous smile. "That was almost profound."

"You can quote me if you like," Alexa offered. "Now I'm going to bed. All this talk of death and dying has worn me out."

"Good idea. I'll see you in the morning." Mary Margaret stood and slipped out of the room.

* * *

Park Ranger Lamar Penny squinted through the windshield of his Land Rover in a near futile attempt to see the road in front of him. For hours he'd been inching his way along the winding, snow-covered roads without any assistance from the moon or stars. Now, as dawn approached, there was a little light, but it was still snowing and visibility wasn't significantly improved.

Cold and hungry, Lamar checked his watch. His shift should have ended an hour before, but he was still miles from the closest ranger station. He was feeling sorry for himself when a voice spoke from his radio.

"This is dispatch. Report please."

Dispatch was a beautiful redhead named Jill that Lamar had asked out several times during the six months he'd been working for the park services. On each occasion, she'd given him a polite smile and turned him down flat. Lamar brought his Rover to a stop and unclipped the radio from his belt. Then he pressed the TALK button and said, "Hey, dispatch."

"Your report please, Ranger Penny," Jill replied in a crisp, professional tone.

Lamar looked out the windshield into the fog and snow. "Not much to report. It's still snowing, I can't see a foot in front of my Rover, and the roads are getting slicker by the minute. What's up with this weather? I didn't see any mention of snow in the forecast."

"That's because it wasn't there," Jill in dispatch said. "National Weather Service missed the call. They've been apologizing like crazy. I kind of feel sorry for them."

Lamar didn't feel sorry for them. A more accurate forecast would have given the captain time to call him in before he got caught in this mess.

"What's your location?" Jill requested.

Lamar grimaced. He wasn't exactly sure where he was, but this wasn't something he wanted to admit to a girl he was trying to impress. So he said, "Near the bottom of Hughes Ridge," which he thought was close to the truth.

"The captain wants you to go over to the Greenbriar station. He's expecting some emergency calls from campers caught by surprise in the storm. We'll call you there if we need you."

Lamar was disappointed that he wouldn't be going back to the welcome center where Jill worked, but being inside the station at Greenbriar watching television and drinking hot coffee sure beat sitting in a cold Rover.

"Roger that," he said. Then he reclipped his radio to his belt and took the sheaf of laminated maps from the glove compartment. He found what he thought was his current location on the map. Next he found Greenbriar station and determined the shortest route between the two. Then he eased the Rover forward again in the nearly blinding storm.

Anxious to get to the station, he pushed the Rover as hard as he dared. The defroster couldn't keep up with the interior moisture, so Lamar leaned forward and rubbed the inside of the windshield. But since the windshield wipers were fighting a losing battle against the snow, this did little to improve the visibility.

He turned a curve at the base of Hughes Ridge and slammed on his brakes when he saw a late-model sedan blocking his path. The Land Rover went into a skid and hit the other vehicle broadside. The force of the impact threw Lamar forward against the steering wheel and his last conscious thought was, *I guess this is how it's going to end.*

CHAPTER 6

Eugenia woke up early on Friday morning after a restless night. Her dreams had been filled with images of Charlotte Sullivan smiling up at Whit while they danced. Lady interrupted her unhappy thoughts by begging to be taken outside.

Eugenia got out of bed and pulled on a housedress. Then she walked downstairs and followed Lady into the backyard. While the dog explored, Eugenia tried to decide why Whit's interest in Charlotte Sullivan had upset her so much. Either Whit meant more to her than she had realized or her subconscious was trying to tell her that Charlotte Sullivan posed a threat to him. Or maybe it was a little of both. She couldn't be sure.

Eugenia summoned Lady, and the little dog obediently followed her mistress into the house. Eugenia gave Lady some dog food. Then she picked up the phone and dialed Kelsey's number. "I'm sorry to call so early," she began the conversation with an apology. It was two hours earlier in Utah, where Kelsey lived.

"That's okay," the girl replied, but she sounded sleepy.

"I've got you a customer," Eugenia informed her.

"Who?" Kelsey asked.

"Me."

Kelsey laughed. "You?"

"Yes, we have a new woman in town and she seems suspicious to me."

Kelsey became all business. "Suspicious how? Like dangerous?"

"Well, I don't know for sure," Eugenia admitted. "All I know is that she has been widowed three times and has worked in a lot of nursing homes. She came to Haggerty and immediately latched onto one of our most eligible, elderly bachelors, Whit Owens."

"Your boyfriend?"

"I'm too old to have a *boyfriend*," Eugenia countered. "But Whit is a friend, and I'm a little worried about him. I want to be sure she's not a spider who has surveyed the available flies and determined that he's the plumpest and juiciest."

Kelsey laughed. "That's an interesting metaphor."

"You'd have to meet her to understand how accurate that description is. She's very attractive and seems to have an almost hypnotic effect on men. So, even though it might be silly, I'd like to have you check her out for me."

"I don't think it's silly at all," Kelsey assured her. "Even if I don't find anything, knowing you checked will give you peace of mind."

Eugenia felt better already. Kelsey was such a sensible girl.

"I'll run a background check and see what I come up with," Kelsey promised.

"Do I get an employee discount?" Eugenia asked.

Kelsey laughed again. "Definitely. Now, tell me what you know about her."

"Her name is Charlotte Sullivan, and she worked in LaGrange before she came here, but according to Whit's receptionist, she's been employed by nursing homes all across the country."

"That's good," Kelsey said. "Now what is her birth date?"

"I don't know."

"Then can you give me an estimate of how old she is?" Kelsey requested.

"Somewhere between fifty and seventy."

"Do you know where she was born?"

"No, I'm sorry I don't." Eugenia was surprised by how much information Kelsey needed just to find information on the woman.

"I don't suppose you have her Social Security number?"

"No," Eugenia admitted.

"Charlotte Sullivan isn't a terribly uncommon name." Kelsey's tone wasn't promising. "If I check the entire country for her without a specific birth date, I'll come up with hundreds of possibilities. Is there any way you can get more facts so I can narrow my search?"

Eugenia considered this. Whit would know quite a bit about Miss Sullivan, but Eugenia couldn't very well ask him to provide information for a background check. Idella Babcock had read the woman's employment application so she probably had the details Kelsey needed. But Idella didn't care for Eugenia and certainly wouldn't do her any favors. Then Eugenia remembered George Ann saying that Miss Sullivan's application was in a folder on Idella's desk, waiting to be picked up by someone from the chamber of commerce.

"I think I might have an idea," Eugenia told Kelsey. "I'll call you back in a little while."

Eugenia hung up the phone, collected her purse, and reached for Lady. "You'll have to come with me," she told Lady. "I hate to make you my partner in crime, but since Idella is allergic to you, my plan requires your presence."

Eugenia drove her old Buick to the town square and parked directly in front of Whit's office. Then she and Lady went inside.

"Good morning, Idella," Eugenia greeted cheerfully.

Idella looked up and when she saw the dog, she reached for a Kleenex from the box on her desk. "Why do you always have to bring that thing inside?" she complained.

"We won't stay long," Eugenia promised, her eyes perusing the top of Idella's desk for the folder that contained Charlotte Sullivan's employment application. "I came by to ask Whit if he'd be willing to donate twenty dollars to the Albany Humane Society."

Idella pressed the Kleenex to her nose as she sneezed. "Go on back and ask him."

"Oh no! I don't want to interrupt him while he's working."

"It's never bothered you before," Idella pointed out.

"I'm trying to be more considerate of his time during office hours," Eugenia claimed as her eyes spotted a plain manila folder on the corner of Idella's desk. "So maybe you could ask him for me—since you're his receptionist and all."

"I'll do it on one condition," Idella negotiated.

"What?"

"That you'll take that dog and leave!"

"I accept your terms," Eugenia said. Then she stood in front of Idella's desk expectantly.

"Well?" Idella prompted. "What are you waiting for?"

"Whit's answer."

"You want me to ask him *now?*" Idella demanded.

"Of course," Eugenia replied as if this were the most ridiculous question.

With an exasperated sigh, Idella reached for the phone.

"Don't call him!" Eugenia instructed the other woman, and Idella looked up sharply.

"Why not?"

"Because you need to ask him in person so you can get his donation—assuming he wants to contribute to such a worthy cause."

Idella shot Eugenia a hateful look and then stood. "I'll be right back," she said as she walked down the hallway toward Whit's office.

Eugenia put Lady on the floor and grabbed the folder. Inside she found what she was looking for—the application for employment filled out by Charlotte Sullivan. Eugenia scanned it quickly. Then she reached for a ballpoint pen on Idella's desk and wrote Miss Sullivan's Social Security number on the back of her left hand. She had just returned the folder to its original location when Idella returned, waving a twenty dollar bill.

"Why are you letting that dog run around, shedding hair all over my office?" Idella cried. "The last time it was here I had to go to my allergist and get a shot."

Eugenia did her best to look sheepish. "I'm so sorry, Idella." Eugenia took the money from the receptionist's hand. "And tell Whit the homeless animals of Albany thank him."

On the way home from Whit's office, Eugenia called Kelsey on her cell phone and recited the Social Security number imprinted on her age-spotted skin. Then she added the personal information she'd gleaned from the application during her quick perusal.

"Lastly, our Charlotte Sullivan was born in Dallas on May 12, but the year was conveniently left off."

Kelsey laughed. "This is plenty to get me started. I'll call back when I have something for you."

Eugenia closed her phone. "I've done all I can think of to do," she told Lady. "Now we'll have to see what happens."

* * *

Lettie shivered as she woke up in the LeConte Lodge on Friday morning. Despite the best efforts of the space heater, it was cold in the little staff bedroom. She looked across the room and saw that Mary Margaret's bed was empty. Feeling a little guilty, Lettie forced herself from the warm confines of the bed and dressed quickly while standing close to the heater.

With the intention of brushing her teeth and putting on some makeup, she took her cosmetic case into the tiny bathroom that separated the staff bedrooms. But when she glanced out the window, all thoughts of improving her appearance disappeared. There was nearly a foot of snow on the ground with more fat flakes falling from the low, dark clouds.

Lettie rushed into the dining hall where she found Mary Margaret and Lowell sitting on the couch in front of a roaring fire.

"Have you looked outside?" she demanded.

Mary Margaret confirmed that she had by commenting, "It's snowing!" Then she added, "Isn't it beautiful?"

"It's beautiful," Lettie agreed. "But it will make getting down this mountain extremely difficult."

"We're not planning to leave until Sunday and by then all this will be melted." Lowell pointed to a tray on the coffee table. "So why don't you grab a cup of hot chocolate and enjoy the view."

"The storm knocked the electricity out," Mary Margaret said. "But fortunately the stove and space heaters run on propane." She pointed to a Coleman lantern sitting on the long table. "And we have plenty of lanterns."

Lettie picked up a cup of hot chocolate and sat beside Mary Margaret on the couch. "I guess it's not that big of a deal," she conceded. "But how did this happen? The forecast called for *clear* and cold."

Lowell shrugged. "Apparently there was a shift in the jet stream during the night that blew the moisture from down south up here— which gave us an instant blizzard."

"Nobody's perfect," Mary Margaret said. "Not even the National Weather Service."

Beth walked in at this point. She walked to a window and said, "Please don't tell me that's snow."

Mary Margaret laughed. "Okay, I won't tell you."

"Don't worry," Lettie contributed. "Lowell says it will melt in time for us to leave on Sunday." She gestured toward the mugs. "Have some hot chocolate."

Beth took a mug and settled onto the couch across from them. "But what will we do up here if we're snowed in?"

"Outdoor activities are pretty much out—at least until the snow stops," Lowell said. "But we're safe and snug. We've got plenty of firewood and enough food to last us for a week."

"A week?" Beth whispered.

"We won't be here a week," Lowell promised. "I was trying to reassure you." He stood and rubbed his hands together. "And our first indoor activity can be to make breakfast. Any volunteers?"

Mary Margaret smiled. "We'll all help."

"I'll get Alexa," Beth offered as she turned and walked back toward the bedrooms. "I've got to get my cell phone anyway. If Jack sees this on the news, he'll panic."

After Beth was gone, Mary Margaret said, "Jack's so sweet."

"He's borderline obsessive if you ask me," Lettie said.

"I think it would be wonderful to have someone care about me so much." Mary Margaret's tone was a little wistful.

Beth returned a few minutes later with a sleepy Alexa in tow. Under Lowell's direction, they prepared eggs, bacon, and canned biscuits. Once everything was ready to eat, they gathered around one of the long tables in the dining hall.

"We did a great job," Lettie praised them all, herself included.

Beth took a bite of bacon. "It is delicious."

Alexa popped a couple of pills into her mouth and washed them down with a swig of orange juice. "I'm not really hungry," she said around a yawn. "I think I'll just go back to bed. Wake me up when the blizzard is over."

The others watched Alexa disappear. Then Mary Margaret asked Beth, "Did you get in touch with Jack?"

Beth nodded. "He wasn't thrilled that we're stuck up here, but I assured him we were in good hands."

"That's me!" Lowell wiped perspiration from his head with the sleeve of his shirt. "Is it getting hot in here?"

Lettie shook her head. "No, it's still chilly." She reached up and pressed a hand to Lowell's forehead. "You may be a little warm."

"You mean I have a fever?" he asked.

Lettie shrugged. "Could be—I'm not a nurse."

"I hope you're not getting sick," Mary Margaret said, her voice full of concern.

Lowell smiled at her. "I never get sick. I'll take a couple of aspirins and be as good as new."

* * *

Gray brushed several inches of snow from a log and sat down by the campfire.

"What about this weather?" Brad Mills, one of the hikers, commented. "I don't ever remember getting this much snow so late in the year—even up here in the mountains."

"Me either," Gray muttered. "It's going to make hiking a chore."

"Yeah," Brad agreed. "I talked to the other guys, and I think we'll abandon the hike and head back. Maybe we'll try it again in a few weeks if you have an open date."

Gray was surprised but relieved. "I'll work you in," he promised. "And I won't charge you full price."

Brad smiled. "Mighty decent of you."

Thirty minutes later they had broken camp and were headed down the mountainside.

* * *

When Park Ranger Lamar Penny opened his eyes, he wanted to weep with relief. He wasn't dead. He was, however, nearly frozen. He couldn't feel his feet or his hands, but everything he could feel hurt. There was a lot of blood on his shirt and he glanced in the rearview mirror. His reflection looked like something from a horror film. He was as pale as a ghost and had a gash in his forehead—which explained the blood.

He got a handkerchief from his pocket and pressed it against the still oozing wound. Then he tried to restart the Rover, but the engine wouldn't turn over. Cursing, he hit his right hand on the steering wheel. Then he screamed in agony as pain shot up his arm. Once he got his breath back, he probed the tender spot on his arm gently. Based on what he knew about first aid, it looked like his arm was broken.

With extreme reluctance, he removed his radio from his belt and called Jill in dispatch again.

"This is Penny," he said. "I've wrecked my Rover."

"Roger that," Jill said as calmly as if they were still discussing the weather. "Are you injured?"

"I'm okay, but the Rover won't start." Anxious to defend his driving abilities, Lamar added, "There was a car parked in the road, and I couldn't see it until it was too late."

"Was anyone in the other vehicle injured?" dispatch wanted to know.

Belatedly Lamar realized that he should have determined that before he called in. "I can't tell from here since it's already covered in snow. I'll check it out."

"Roger," Jill said. "I'll tell the captain and see if we can arrange for someone to come in and get you."

Embarrassed that he needed to be rescued, Lamar said, "Thanks." Then he returned his radio to his belt.

It took him a few shoves to get the door of the Rover open. Angry with himself and the driver of the other vehicle, he stepped gingerly out into the snow. Once he was sure both of his legs were sound and would hold him, he moved toward the car. He rubbed the snow from the windows and looked in. It was empty.

He unclipped the radio and told Jill, "Nobody here," as he walked around and kicked the snow from the back of the car. "It's a 2006 Altima."

"I'll need to run the license," Jill said.

While reciting the numbers, Lamar forgot about his broken arm and tried to use it. The pain was so intense he had to grab the side of the car for support. His arm was still throbbing when Jill's voice spoke from the radio.

"The car is registered to Mary Hooper from Memphis. She must be camping somewhere close by. Is her vehicle disabled?"

Lamar looked at the crumpled metal that used to be a nice car. "Yes. I'm pretty sure."

"Then she's stranded there as well. You'll need to find her and let her know that help is on the way."

Lamar ground his teeth in frustration. An hour ago he had been looking forward to coffee in the ranger station at Greenbriar. Now his Rover was wrecked, his head was cut, and his arm was broken. And if that wasn't enough—he was going to have to go looking through the woods for the stranded campers who had caused all his problems.

"I'll search the area," he muttered.

"Report in when you find her," Jill requested.

"I will." Lamar walked around the car and stared at the foreboding line of pine trees. He was trying to determine which direction to search in first when he saw the faint trail of footprints under the latest layer of snow. He knelt down for a closer look. Then he told dispatch, "There are some footprints—headed toward the woods. Based on the amount of snow they've collected I'd say they're only about an hour old."

"So maybe Ms. Hooper is camping nearby," Jill murmured. "In this storm she should have stayed in the car where she would be out of the wind and snow."

"It doesn't make much sense that she left the car," Lamar agreed. "But at least I have a trail to follow—if I hurry. It's going to be completely buried soon."

"Copy that," Jill confirmed.

Lamar followed the footsteps into the trees. His arm was killing him and his head was starting to ache. As if this wasn't enough, his efforts were further hampered by the driving snow and thick underbrush. He clinched his teeth to keep them from chattering and pressed further into the forest—hoping for some sign of Ms. Hooper. About a half mile in, he stepped into a clearing. Lamar took in the empty tent and the remnants of a small campfire. Then he spoke into the radio.

"I found a campsite, but it looks deserted. I'll keep looking for Ms. Hooper."

There were more footprints on the far side of the camp. He followed them to the edge of an abrupt drop off. With reluctance, he looked over into the gulley below. A body was sprawled at the base—the head at an odd angle from the neck.

"I've found someone," Lamar reported to Jill. "Face first on the ground. But it looks like a man."

"Roger that," Jill replied. "We contacted Ms. Hooper in Memphis. She's safe at home and doesn't even own an Altima."

Lamar frowned at the body several feet below him. "So somebody switched plates with her?"

"Yes. The number on the license plate that is now on her minivan is registered to a man named Avery Ingle, also of Memphis. We've tried to contact Mr. Ingle without success, so Memphis PD has a car on the way over to check on him."

Lamar's heart pounded. "Wasn't that escaped convict supposed to be in the Memphis area?"

There was a brief pause. Then Jill said, "Proceed with extreme caution, Lamar."

The ranger was so euphoric over Jill's use of his first name that he didn't even notice the additional bumps and bruises he received as he careened down the embankment. Once he reached the body he examined the snow-encrusted face. "It's that escaped convict from Hardeman!"

Jill's voice reflected the same excitement he felt. "You're sure?"

"Positive," Lamar confirmed. "I studied the bulletin before I left last night."

"And he's dead?" Jill asked.

"Definitely." Lamar stood and put some distance between himself and the corpse. "He must have come out here to use the bathroom and slipped and fallen off the ledge. Broke his neck. Can't have happened very long ago."

"I'll get the captain," dispatch offered.

Lamar stamped his feet in the snow, trying to get some circulation going in his lower extremities. *What a night,* he thought to himself. But at least the captain wouldn't be too mad about the Rover since he'd found an escaped convict. And Jill was acting friendly for the first time since he'd met her. This pleasant reverie was interrupted by the captain's voice.

"What you got there, Penny?"

Lamar repeated what he'd found.

"What's your condition?" the captain wanted to know.

"I've got a cut on my forehead, and I think my right arm is broken."

"I have a team on the way up to get you," the captain said. "There should be some emergency gear in the back of the Rover. Put on any additional clothing you can find and then wait in the Rover until the rescue team gets there."

The prospect of sitting in the frigid vehicle wasn't a pleasant one to Lamar, but at least help was on the way. "Yes sir."

"There's a chance that the team won't be able to make it to you because of the road and weather conditions," the captain continued. "Our backup plan will be for you to walk to LeConte Lodge. It's only a couple of miles from where you are the way the crow flies. You think you could make it?"

Lamar glanced at the blood on his shirt and his useless arm. Then he remembered that Jill was listening. "I'm sure I can."

"Keep your radio off to conserve the battery, but report in regularly. We should know in an hour if the rescue team is going to make it to your location."

"Yes sir." Lamar looked down at the body. "What about the convict?"

"Leave him there," the captain said. "When the rescue team gets there they can handle the removal."

Lamar was relieved that he was no longer responsible for the dead man.

"Dispatch again," Jill's familiar voice announced. "The captain said to give you the coordinates for LeConte, just in case. And he told me to remind you to use your compass. Everything looks different in the snow, and he doesn't want you getting lost."

Lamar knew it was only a precaution, but it seemed a little insulting anyway. "Give me the coordinates," he requested. Once he'd committed them to memory, he turned off his radio and began the difficult climb back up to the Rover.

He opened the hatchback and rummaged through the emergency supplies—no small feat with one arm. He found a disposable insulated blanket, which he wrapped gratefully around his shoulders. There was another pair of gloves that he pulled on over the pair he was already wearing. He found bottled water and a couple of MREs, but no compass. Reluctantly he accepted the possibility that his compass was at home. It didn't bother him too much—after all, he knew his way around the park. The captain had suggested it only as a precaution. So he closed the hatchback and walked around to the front of the mangled Rover.

* * *

The phone rang while Eugenia was addressing an envelope to the humane society in Albany. She picked up the receiver and held it between her cheek and shoulder as she inserted Whit's twenty dollar bill.

"Hello?"

It was Kelsey. "Hey, Miss Eugenia."

"That didn't take long." Eugenia licked the envelope and pressed it closed. "Do you have good news for me?"

"Well, it depends on what kind of news you were looking for," Kelsey answered. "There are no outstanding warrants on your Miss Sullivan, and she's never been arrested as far as I can tell. But she's been married *seven* times, not three."

"Seven!" Eugenia exclaimed.

"She lied," Kelsey sounded positive. "All of her husbands were elderly and all died within a year of marrying Charlotte."

Eugenia felt a little dizzy at this announcement and sat down quickly. "She *killed* them?"

"I didn't find any evidence of that," Kelsey said. "Apparently the only time she was accused of even contributing to anyone's death was six months ago in Sipsey, Georgia. Do you know where that is?"

"Yes, it's only about an hour's drive from here."

"She was engaged to marry an elderly gentleman named Myron Bell. When Mr. Bell passed away, his great-nephew, who is a registered nurse, told police that Miss Sullivan had poisoned his great-uncle. He also claimed that she had tricked the old man into giving her a lot of money."

"What did the police find out?"

"Nothing," Kelsey replied. "There was a brief investigation, but apparently not enough evidence. So the police closed the case."

"And Charlotte was free to go to another town and find her next victim." Eugenia thought of Whit and shuddered. "How did she kill Mr. Bell?"

"The great-nephew, Dean Lumpkin, claimed that she kept his uncle out late, exhausted him physically, and even encouraged him to discontinue medications that his doctor had prescribed. Then she gave him an overdose of a medicine called Vitality."

"I've never heard of it," Eugenia said.

"Me either."

"So the police didn't believe the great-nephew?"

"I don't know if they believed him or not," Kelsey said. "But there just wasn't any evidence to support his claims. It was the great-nephew's word against Charlotte's."

"So robbing from the nearly dead is a career for her," Eugenia murmured. "She must be rich by now."

"Her financial statement is impressive, but she spends a lot, too," Kelsey reported.

"George Ann said she's traveled all around the world."

"Yep, she's been about everywhere," Kelsey confirmed. "She also buys jewelry and designer clothes and has had cosmetic surgery several times."

"How much money has she 'earned' this way?"

"Over two million dollars," Kelsey said. "And in addition to her marry-for-money schemes, she has received thousands of dollars in *gifts* from men she didn't marry."

"What kind of gifts?"

"Cash, cars, property," Kelsey itemized. "Apparently if she meets a man with limited resources, she doesn't bother to marry him. She accepts gifts from him until he's broke. Then she moves on."

"That's horrible!" Eugenia was incensed.

"It is horrible, but it's not against the law unless you can prove that she killed the men. And since they're already old and sick when she marries them, proof will be hard to find."

"Whit must be her next victim," Eugenia said. "He has money, so she's probably planning to marry him, but he's not near death."

"Not yet," Kelsey replied grimly.

"What am I going to do?"

"The first thing I would do is tell Mr. Owens what we've found," Kelsey advised. "You know they say forewarned is fore-armed."

"Yes, of course I'll tell him."

"Then you could go and visit Mr. Bell's great-nephew. He might be able to give you more details than I was able to get from the police report."

"That's what I'll do. Thank you so much, Kelsey."

"You're welcome. Call me if you need anything else."

"I will," Eugenia promised. "Now, could you fax me a copy of your report?"

After ending her conversation with Kelsey, Eugenia sat by the computer and watched as each page of the report printed off. She read the information Kelsey had compiled on Charlotte Sullivan, and when she finished, she called Whit at his office.

Idella answered the phone.

"Hey, Idella," Eugenia said impatiently. "Let me speak to Whit, please."

"What happened to your vow not to bother him at work?"

"This is an emergency. Now hurry up."

"Well!" Idella replied. When elevator music started playing in Eugenia's ear she realized she'd been put on hold.

After what seemed like a very long wait, Whit's voice came on the line. "Eugenia? Idella says there's an emergency."

"It's a good thing I'm not bleeding to death," she responded. "Because by now I'd be dead. If I were you, I'd fire Idella."

Whit laughed. "I'm not going to fire Idella because she put you on hold. Now what do you need?"

"I'm not sure how to tell you this," she began hesitantly. "I know you're partly responsible for bringing Charlotte Sullivan to Haggerty, and I don't want you to feel that it's your fault."

"What's my fault?" Whit asked.

"That you've put all the single, elderly men in town at risk."

"Risk for what?" Whit sounded genuinely confused.

"Risk of being murdered!" Eugenia informed him.

"Eugenia, what are you talking about?" Now Whit sounded exasperated.

"Charlotte Sullivan has been married seven times—not three like she listed on her application for employment," Eugenia divulged in one breath. "All of her husbands were elderly, and they all died within a year of marrying her. In addition to the two million dollars she's inherited from all those deceased husbands, she's received thousands of dollars in *gifts* from men she didn't marry. Her most recent prospective husband was a man named Myron Bell who lived in Sipsey. He died before they could get married and his great-nephew is convinced that Charlotte killed him. She's a menace, Whit, and you've got to fire her so she'll leave town before someone here dies." Eugenia wanted to add, *most likely you,* but decided that restraint was called for.

An uncomfortable silence greeted Eugenia's impassioned revelation.

Finally she added, "I'm planning to go visit Mr. Bell's great-nephew, and I was hoping you'd come along with me so you can hear what he has to say."

Still, Whit didn't reply.

"Whit, did you hear what I just said?"

"I heard you," he confirmed. His voice was so cold she barely recognized it. "I won't ask how you gained access to information listed on Charlotte's employment application since your answer would very likely land you in jail. But I will say that I find this petty, gossiping behavior beneath you. I'm terribly disappointed."

Eugenia processed his words. He had chosen to completely ignore her warning. He had scolded her and even threatened her with *jail.* "So you won't go with me to Sipsey?" she confirmed.

"No, this afternoon I will be at the senior center helping Charlotte set up for tonight's bingo."

"I see," Eugenia replied. "I guess there's nothing left for me to say."

"Good-bye, Eugenia." The words had a terribly final tone. Then the line went dead.

"Well," Eugenia said to Lady as she hung up the phone. "Whit doesn't deserve my help. Maybe I should let Charlotte kill him. Then he'll be sorry."

Lady barked and Eugenia smiled.

"Yes, I'll be sorry too. So Whit will get my help whether he deserves it or not."

Wishing, not for the first time, that Mark was home, she reached for the telephone and dialed Jack Gamble's number. She had to talk to Jack's secretary, Roberta, for several minutes before she was finally put through to the state senator himself.

"Hello?" Jack sounded busy.

After taking a deep breath, Eugenia plunged in. She told Jack about the new senior center and Charlotte Sullivan's instant popularity with the town's elderly men. She admitted to reading Charlotte's employment application and hiring Kelsey to do a background check. She explained the results Kelsey came up with and described Whit's reaction. When she finished, she said, "So, what do you think?"

"Well, Whit was bluffing about putting you in jail," Jack assured her. "The worst thing you're guilty of is invasion of privacy, and since there were no witnesses, you can't be arrested."

"I never thought for a minute that Whit would have me put in jail!" Eugenia responded emphatically. "I meant what do you think about Charlotte Sullivan?"

"I think she's a very smart woman," Jack said. "She didn't marry all seven husbands in the same state, and she goes after men with relatively small estates—thereby decreasing her chances of attracting attention. And if she is killing these men, she's leaving no evidence behind."

Eugenia didn't want to hear about how smart Charlotte was. "But what can we do to protect Whit?"

"You've already warned him, and even if he doesn't completely believe you, subconsciously he'll be on guard."

"Can't I just take Kelsey's report to Winston and insist that he investigate?" Eugenia asked.

"Charlotte hasn't committed a crime in Haggerty," Jack pointed out. "At least not yet. So if you're going to appeal to the police, it would be wiser to try the ones in Sipsey. But the FBI would be more likely to take on a case like this since they have broader jurisdiction and more manpower. When Mark gets home you should show him what you have and see what he says."

"*If* Mark ever gets home," Eugenia muttered under her breath.

"I beg your pardon?"

"Nothing," Eugenia said. "Do you think I should talk to the nephew in Sipsey?"

"You might be able to collect more information that way, but you really shouldn't get too closely involved. And I'll warn you that cases like this are hard to prove. It would probably take a full confession to get a conviction."

Eugenia was discouraged by Jack's assessment. "A full confession?"

"Otherwise there would always be reasonable doubt that the old men died of natural causes."

"I see."

"Well, I'm sorry I couldn't be of more help." Jack was obviously trying to wrap up the conversation.

To be polite, Eugenia asked, "Is Beth having fun on her camping trip?"

She heard Jack sigh. "Actually I don't know if she's having any fun at all. She's snowed in at a remote lodge in the Smoky Mountains."

"Snowed in!" Eugenia repeated. "That's terrible! I saw a movie once where a group of people got snowed in and they ended up eating each other."

Jack laughed. "Beth and her friends have plenty of food, so hopefully they won't get that desperate."

"That's what the people in the movie thought too," Eugenia told him. "Then the next thing you know the food's gone and they're looking around trying to decide who would taste best. If I were you, I'd go up to the Smoky Mountains and get Beth before anything terrible happens."

There was a brief pause. Then Jack said, "I guess I could call and check on flights."

"It would be wise," Eugenia encouraged. "I'd offer to keep the children for you, but I've got to stop Charlotte Sullivan from killing Whit."

"I understand," Jack assured her. "I'll ask Beth's mother to come and stay until I can get back."

After Eugenia hung up the phone, she spoke to Lady. "This is going to be more trouble than I expected. I've a good mind to let Mr. Whit Owens cook in the pot he put on to boil. But I guess that wouldn't be the Christian thing to do."

Eugenia referred to the fax Kelsey sent and dialed the number for Mr. Bell's great-nephew, Dean Lumpkin. A man answered on the second ring and Eugenia identified herself. Then she asked if she could visit him to discuss Charlotte Sullivan.

"I've put that woman and her evil deeds behind me," he said. "I'd rather not dredge it all up again."

"Dean," Eugenia addressed him in her most persuasive voice. "Do you realize that until that woman is stopped, she'll keep killing elderly men?"

"I guess so," he mumbled.

"Do you want that on your conscience?"

"No ma'am."

"Then please allow me to come and see you this afternoon," Eugenia said. "I won't take much of your time."

Finally he surrendered. "I guess about one o'clock would be okay."

* * *

Jack sat in his office and stared at the telephone. He knew Miss Eugenia was prone to overreact, and he didn't seriously believe that Beth and her friends were going to become cannibals. But Miss Eugenia's comments had hit a raw nerve. He hated being separated from Beth, and he hated even more that she was trapped so that she couldn't leave if she needed or wanted to. He thought about calling Beth and talking to her about it, but he knew she'd just tell him not to worry. No, it would be better to make it a surprise when he showed up to rescue her—whether from a blizzard or just from missing her husband. Yes, she definitely needed rescuing.

He called the number Beth had left him for Smoky Mountain Tours and got an answering machine. He explained that he was coming and wanted to be taken up to the lodge once he arrived. He left his cell number and asked for a phone confirmation. Then he called the airport and reserved a seat on a plane leaving Albany in an hour. After throwing a change of clothes into a carry-on bag, he called Beth's mother and explained the situation. She promised to come immediately. He drafted Roberta as a temporary babysitter, said good-bye to his children, and headed for Albany.

When he arrived at the Delta counter, he was informed that the Alcoa airport was closed due to weather. The closest they could get him to the Great Smoky Mountains National Park was Chattanooga. There he could rent an all-terrain vehicle and drive to the office of the tour company—where hopefully someone would be waiting to take him up to the lodge where Beth was.

Jack felt better once he was on the plane. A man of action, he didn't like to sit back and wait for things to happen to him, or to those he loved. He figured that at worst he would spend the next few days at the lodge snowed in with Beth. And at best, he'd be able to convince her to leave with him. They could get a hotel room in Gatlinburg and spend a romantic weekend there before flying home.

He smiled as he leaned his head back against the airplane seat. Yes, this was the right thing to do. He was sure.

* * *

After breakfast Lettie gave Lowell a couple of aspirins, and by midmorning he claimed to be feeling better. He challenged the ladies to a game of Scrabble, and everyone except Alexa gathered around a card table near the fire.

"You don't want to play?" Lowell asked Alexa as she stood and stretched.

Alexa shook her head. "No, I'd rather sleep."

Lowell gave Lettie a questioning look.

Lettie shrugged and said, "She's afraid to play Scrabble with me since she knows I always win."

Alexa didn't rise to the challenge. Instead she yawned and headed for the bedrooms.

"So, you never lose at Scrabble?" Lowell asked Lettie.

"Never," Lettie confirmed.

"She's a walking dictionary," Beth warned. "By playing with her we're really only feeding her ego."

Lowell laughed. "Actually, I'm pretty good myself."

Lettie smiled. "Then at least you'll make it interesting." Lowell was better than pretty good, and Lettie was enjoying herself when he challenged a word she put on the board.

"There's no such word as *obtrude*," he said.

"Of course there is," Lettie replied. "It's the root word of *obtrusive*."

Lowell laughed. "You're making that up! I see how you always win at Scrabble! You play with people who never call your bluff."

Lettie narrowed her eyes at him. "Are you calling me a cheater?"

He held up his hands in surrender. "No! I'm just saying you're going to have to prove to me that *obtrude* is a word."

"Find me a dictionary," Lettie told him.

He produced a pocket version from the Scrabble box. "Apparently there have been disputes before." He handed the dictionary to Lettie.

She sifted through the pages and pointed out a word. "'Obtrude,'" Lettie quoted, "'to put forward unasked; to force.' Or in other words," she added, "to be *obtrusive!*"

Lowell smiled. "I yield to your superior knowledge."

Lettie accepted his capitulation graciously. "It was only a matter of time."

Lowell shivered and rubbed his hands up and down his upper arms. "Is it getting cold in here?"

"I'm comfortable," Mary Margaret said.

"Me too," Beth agreed.

"I'm warm," Lettie said. "But I'm glowing with victory, so maybe I don't count."

Lowell stood and moved closer to the fire. "I think my aspirin is wearing off."

"But you just took it an hour ago," Mary Margaret pointed out with a frown. "It can't be wearing off already."

He rubbed his midsection. "I'm feeling a little nauseated, too."

"It could be the flu," Beth said. "There's a lot of it going around."

"If I rest for a while I'll feel better." He glanced at the unoccupied couch.

Mary Margaret followed the direction of his gaze. "There are too many distractions out here," she said. "You can lie down on my bed."

Lettie nodded, "I think that's a good idea, Lowell. You'll be able to rest better back where it's quiet."

Lowell looked at the fire. "I'd better get some more wood first."

Lettie walked over and put a hand on his arm. Then she gently propelled him toward the kitchen. "I'll get the wood. You go to bed."

It took Lettie three trips outside to get enough wood to return the fire to blazing status. When she was finished, she collapsed on the couch.

"Whew!" she exclaimed. "Maybe I should have let Lowell get the wood."

Mary Margaret gave her an anxious smile. "Do you think one of us should go check on him?"

Lettie glanced at her watch. "He's only been resting for fifteen minutes. Why don't we wait a while?"

Mary Margaret nodded, but her eyes drifted toward the kitchen door, and Lettie could tell she was concerned about Lowell.

Beth stood. "I'm kind of hungry. I think I'll look through our food supply for a snack. Would the rest of you like something?"

"I'll have some of whatever you find," Lettie said.

Beth returned a few minutes later with Alexa in her wake. "Look who has risen from the nearly dead."

Alexa collapsed onto the couch beside Mary Margaret. "Ha, ha."

"This was all I could find snack-wise." Beth held a bag of semi-sweet chocolate chips out to Lettie.

Lettie stuck her hand into the bag and pulled out a few morsels. "Only people who are truly desperate for chocolate would resort to these."

"There's no shame in being desperate where chocolate is concerned," Beth said. Then she offered some to the others.

"No thanks," Mary Margaret declined.

Alexa didn't even bother to open her eyes. "No."

"It doesn't get much better than this," Beth murmured. "The company of friends, a cozy fire, handfuls of chocolate."

"Just like the sleepovers we used to have," Mary Margaret agreed.

"Except it was rarely cold enough for a fire," Lettie pointed out.

"And we never got snowed in," Alexa added.

Beth shook the nearly empty chocolate-chip bag. "And our mothers always provided better snacks." She pulled her cell phone from her pocket. "I guess I'd better call Jack and let him know we're still okay."

Lettie frowned. "You called him an hour ago."

"It's been a whole hour?" Beth asked in mock horror. "He's panicking for sure!"

Lettie shook her head in feigned disgust. "Happily married people make me sick."

A minute later, Beth said, "That's odd."

"What?" Mary Margaret asked.

"My call went straight to Jack's voice mail. His phone must be off." Beth was frowning at her phone.

"Maybe he's in a meeting where he doesn't want his phone to ring," Mary Margaret suggested.

Beth shook her head. "He just puts it on vibrate when he's in meetings. He wants to be sure I always have a way to contact him in case anything happens."

"Maybe the battery in his phone is dead," Mary Margaret tried again.

"He's fanatical about recharging his phone," Beth said. "And he even carries a spare battery in case of an emergency."

"Why don't you call your house phone?" Mary Margaret suggested.

Beth smiled sheepishly. "Of course, that's what I should do." Beth dialed again. Then after a few seconds, she closed her phone. "I got the answering machine."

"They're probably outside!" Mary Margaret said.

Beth nodded. "Probably."

Mary Margaret pulled an afghan up under her chin. "There, see? Nothing to worry about."

"I suggest you wait fifteen minutes and try Jack's cell phone again," Lettie recommended.

"I'll wait that long," Beth agreed. "And if he still doesn't answer, I'm calling the police."

"And you say *Jack* is obsessive?" Lettie teased.

Beth shook her head. "No, Jack isn't obsessive—he's possessive. And handsome and brilliant."

Lettie rolled her eyes. "Enough already."

"I worry all the time that he made a mistake when he married me because I'm none of the above." Beth laughed. "I should have used *that* secret last night when we were playing Truth or Die."

"I wouldn't worry about your lack of perfection or Jack's over-abundance of it," Lettie said.

"You're wonderful and Jack is lucky to have you," Mary Margaret agreed.

Beth bit her lip. "Jack is probably going to run for governor of Georgia next year."

"Ahhhh!" Mary Margaret screamed. "That's almost as exciting as the baby!"

Lettie nodded. "You should have used *that* secret in Truth or Die."

Beth gave her a weak smile. "I know I should be glad. It's a great honor and Jack would make a wonderful governor, but I absolutely hate politics. I hate the meetings and the dinners and the parties and the TV interviews and, well, there's not a single thing about it that I like."

Lettie raised an eyebrow. "I'm guessing you haven't told Jack about this either?"

Beth sighed. "How can I tell him? I don't want his marriage to me to be a limitation for him."

"Sacrificing your happiness for his might not be doing him a favor in the long run," Alexa said without opening her eyes. "Once he's elected and you're miserable, he'll have to live with you."

"For once I have to agree with Alexa." Lettie was only half teasing. "It's not fair of you to let Jack make a decision that important without giving him all the facts."

"For once I think you're *both* right," Beth said. "The minute I get home I'm going to tell Jack I *hate* the thought of him running for governor."

"And that you're going to have a baby," Mary Margaret prompted.

Beth laughed. "I'll tell him that first. Then he'll be in a good mood when I break the rest of the news."

Alexa opened one eye. "Are we playing Truth or Die again?"

Beth smiled. "Just an unofficial one-man version."

Alexa relaxed against the back of the couch. "Good, because I have no intention of divulging any more secrets—deep, dark, or otherwise."

CHAPTER 7

By midmorning on Friday, Eugenia had read Kelsey's report on Charlotte Sullivan from beginning to end three times. She was more convinced than ever that she needed to talk to Myron Bell's great-nephew, but the thought of driving all the way to Sipsey alone was daunting. Finally she called Winston and told him about Kelsey's findings.

"I'll admit that doesn't sound good," the police chief responded. "But unless she commits a crime here in Haggerty, I don't see what I can do."

"You can go with me to Sipsey," Eugenia told him. "I've got an appointment to talk to Mr. Bell's great-nephew at one o'clock this afternoon. He might have some information we could use to prosecute Charlotte Sullivan for Mr. Bell's death."

"If he had incriminating information, the Sipsey police would have already prosecuted her," Winston countered. "Driving to Sipsey is a waste of time."

"Well, old folks like me have nothing better to do," Eugenia replied heatedly. "So I think I'll go on just the same."

She heard Winston sigh. "Even though I think it's a wild goose chase, I'd take you if I wasn't on duty."

Eugenia was disappointed. Winston would have provided dependable transportation, and his presence might have encouraged Mr. Bell's great-nephew to be more cooperative.

"If you want to wait and go tomorrow I could take you then," Winston offered. "But I really wish you'd forget the whole thing. It's not wise for ladies like yourself to get involved with police matters."

"I've already got an appointment for today, but thank you anyway." Eugenia hung up the phone and addressed Lady. "If the police would handle their own matters then old women like me wouldn't have to get involved."

Left with no other reasonable recourse, Eugenia was forced to call Annabelle. "I need to go to Sipsey," she said when her sister answered. "Will you drive me?"

"Derrick and I have tickets to see a Czechoslovakian pianist play at the civic center this evening," Annabelle replied. "So I'd have to be back by about six."

"We'll be home well before then," Eugenia promised.

"Doesn't Sipsey have a big flea market?"

Eugenia had to think for a few seconds, but finally she said, "I think they do. Why?"

"Did you see those white wooden reindeer Cleo Ledbetter had in her front yard last Christmas?"

"Cleo's yard looked like a winter wonderland," Eugenia replied. "I don't remember any reindeer specifically, but it was hard to tell what she had amid all that other holiday clutter."

"They were beautiful—very simple and elegant."

"That doesn't sound like Cleo," Eugenia murmured.

"Nonetheless, she had some, and when I asked her where she got them she said a flea market. So I thought if we were in Sipsey we could stop by the flea market and check for some reindeer. This time of year they'd probably be discounted."

Eugenia shook her head. Everything with Annabelle had to be a compromise. "I'm meeting someone at one o'clock, but if you come and get me right now we should have time to stop by the flea market first."

"I'll pick you up in thirty minutes."

"And can you bring Derrick's little tape recorder?"

"His Dictaphone?" Annabelle asked.

"Yes," Eugenia confirmed. "This interview might be important and I don't want to count on my memory."

"That's wise since you can't remember a thing," Annabelle said and disconnected the call.

Eugenia hung up the phone and smiled at Lady. "Well, that worked out quite well."

* * *

Ranger Lamar Penny clutched the emergency blanket closer around him and turned on his radio.

"Penny reporting in," he said.

He was disappointed when a voice he didn't recognize replied, "What's your condition, Ranger Penny?"

"Cold, but otherwise okay," Lamar answered.

"I'm sorry to report that your rescue team had to turn back due to adverse weather conditions," the dispatcher informed him. "The captain would like for you to walk to the LeConte Lodge and stay there until another rescue can be attempted."

"Roger that," Lamar said without enthusiasm. Then he turned off his radio and climbed out of the Rover.

* * *

Eugenia was waiting at the end of her driveway when Annabelle arrived to pick her up for their trip to Sipsey.

"You're late," Eugenia said as she climbed into Annabelle's car.

"I am not." Annabelle disputed this allegation. "Now who is it you're meeting in Sipsey and why?"

"A man named Dean Lumpkin," Eugenia explained. "His great-uncle was killed, and I'm hoping he will help me prevent the next murder."

Annabelle laughed. "Well, that's a switch. You're usually forcing your way into the middle of a murder that has already taken place."

"Forcing my way," Eugenia repeated. "The very idea."

Annabelle glanced over at her sister. "Do you mind if I ask who you're trying to save?"

"Whit," Eugenia said. Then she proceeded to fill Annabelle in on all she had discovered about Charlotte Sullivan. "But when I told Whit about Kelsey's report, he got mad." Eugenia summed her story up. "He accused me of being a gossip and as good as ended our friendship."

"That's a shame," Annabelle said. "But what do you hope to accomplish by interviewing Mr. Bell's great-nephew? If Jack and Winston say there's no case against Charlotte, it seems like a waste of time to me."

"I'm going to record the conversation with Derrick's little tape machine. Then when I play the tape for Whit, surely he'll come to his senses."

"Don't count on that," Annabelle warned. "Men don't have much sense where beautiful women are concerned."

Eugenia decided to ignore this remark.

When they reached the outskirts of Sipsey, she pointed out her window. "There's the flea market."

Annabelle's eyes followed the direction of Eugenia's finger. Then she nodded. "And I think I see some reindeer."

An hour later they pulled up in front of Dean Lumpkin's house with four wooden reindeer sticking out of the trunk. Annabelle parked by the curb and asked, "Do you want me to wait in the car?"

"I do not," Eugenia returned. "I might eventually need you to testify about this conversation in a murder trial."

Annabelle rolled her eyes. "Heaven help us, Eugenia. I can't decide whether you suffer from a severe case of self-importance or if it's just the early onset of senile dementia."

"Humph," Eugenia responded. "We'll see who's demented. Now come on." Then she led the way up the sidewalk to Mr. Lumpkin's front door.

The owner responded promptly to her knock by pulling the door open about two inches. "Mrs. Atkins?" he asked cautiously.

"Yes," Eugenia addressed the eyeball that was regarding them. "And this is my sister, Mrs. Morgan."

The eye moved to Annabelle and then the door opened wider. "I'm Dean Lumpkin. Please come in."

The house was cluttered and in serious need of a deep cleaning. This didn't bother Eugenia since she wasn't much on housekeeping herself, but she saw Annabelle wrinkle her nose in disapproval.

Dean Lumpkin was a little older than Eugenia had expected—probably in his late thirties. He led them into a small den and waved toward a couch.

"Please have a seat," he said. Once Eugenia and Annabelle were settled, Dean sat down across from them in a recliner.

"We appreciate you taking the time to meet with us." Eugenia lifted the little tape recorder from her purse. "Would you mind if I record our conversation?"

"I don't mind," Dean consented.

"Maybe you could start by telling us a little about yourself and your great-uncle."

Dean took a deep breath and began. "About three years ago Uncle Myron had a stroke, and he wasn't expected to live long. His wife is dead, and they never had any children, so when he was ready to leave the hospital, his sister, my great-aunt Lavada, was told she should put him in a long-term care facility. But she knew he'd be more comfortable at home, so she asked me if I would take a leave of absence from my job at the hospital and assume responsibility for Uncle Myron until his death."

Eugenia was surprised that his aunt would make such a request. "That was asking a lot of you."

"Uncle Myron and I had always been close, and I'm a registered nurse with years of experience caring for the elderly," he explained. "Aunt Lavada was Uncle Myron's beneficiary, and she promised that in return for my nursing services, she'd deed this house over to me when he died. And in the meantime I could live here rent free."

Eugenia repented of the bad thoughts she'd had toward Dean's aunt. "Well, that wasn't such a bad deal for you, then."

"The house isn't worth all that much." Dean waved to encompass the shabby room. "But I knew Uncle Myron would receive better care from me than in a nursing home. In fact, I took such good care of him that he started to improve."

"But you continued to live here?" Eugenia asked.

Dean glanced at the tape recorder and spoke toward it. "Yes. Uncle Myron and I got along great until Charlotte Sullivan came into our lives."

"How did she meet your great-uncle?" Annabelle asked.

Dean sighed. "The city provides activities for seniors at our community center. Uncle Myron asked me to take him there for bingo on Monday nights."

That sounded familiar. "And Charlotte Sullivan worked at the community center?"

"Yes. Soon Uncle Myron started asking that I take him to the community center every night—not just on Mondays for bingo. I felt it was too much for him, but he insisted. So I called his doctor."

"What did the doctor say?" Eugenia asked.

"That a little socialization would be good for Uncle Myron. I wasn't convinced, so I called my Aunt Lavada."

Eugenia leaned forward. "What did she say?"

"She didn't want to interfere. So I took Uncle Myron to the community center every night. About a week later he told me he had a girlfriend named Charlotte, and he was taking her out to dinner after bingo. He said she would bring him home." Dean's pale skin turned pink. "And he said not to wait up because he might be late."

"And was he?" Eugenia asked.

"Yes. Over the next few weeks Uncle Myron 'dated' Charlotte Sullivan almost every night. And based on the time he got home, I have reason to believe that their relationship was improper." Dean's blush deepened.

Eugenia shot Annabelle a quick glance before asking, "Were these dates expensive?"

"Yes. Once Uncle Myron started dating Charlotte, I had to take him to the bank almost every day. And after a few weeks of staying up late every night, Uncle Myron started looking bad. I made an appointment for him with his doctor, but he refused to go. Then he said he wanted to buy a car so Charlotte wouldn't have to keep driving him around. I suggested a sensible used car, but he said Charlotte liked 4Runners."

Annabelle raised her eyebrows. "Pricey."

"Yes," Dean agreed. "One day I noticed it wasn't in the driveway. I asked him about it, and he said he'd given it to Charlotte."

"He *gave* her that brand-new vehicle?" Annabelle sounded appalled.

"Is that legal?" Eugenia demanded.

"Oh yes," Dean assured them. "She went with him to the courthouse and made sure the title was in her name. Then I started smelling alcohol on his breath when he came in from their dates. Since drinking was a direct violation of his doctor's orders, I was very concerned."

"I presume you talked to your uncle about it?" Eugenia asked.

"Of course, but he said a little drink now and then never hurt anyone."

Eugenia considered this. "I guess he was entitled to make that decision for himself, even if it was an unhealthy one."

"I would agree with you, except that I know Charlotte Sullivan was exercising undue influence on him," Dean replied. "She arranged for him to be in situations where he was almost *forced* to drink or look unmanly. Shortly after that, I caught him flushing his medication down the toilet. He told me Charlotte said only old men need to take so many pills. Then he showed me a bottle of an over-the-counter medication called Vitality. He said that Charlotte bought it for him and it was supposed to make him feel young again."

Annabelle frowned. "That was irresponsible of her to suggest that he discontinue his prescribed medications!"

"And encouraging him to take the other medicine without approval from his doctor is even worse!" Eugenia agreed. "But obviously keeping Mr. Bell in good health was not Charlotte's intention."

"Oh, of course not," Annabelle said.

"I called Aunt Lavada again." Dean sounded weary. "She was concerned but refused to have him declared incompetent."

"Which is what you felt needed to happen," Annabelle asked. "Yes."

"So your uncle continued to date Charlotte and buy her extravagant gifts?" Eugenia prompted.

Dean nodded. "Yes. Then one day, out of the blue, he announced that they were getting married. He showed me an expensive ring and said that Charlotte had picked it out herself."

"Charlotte had everything except the house?" Eugenia guessed.

"Yes. The only way she could get it was to marry Uncle Myron."

"Since he couldn't be declared incompetent," Eugenia murmured.

"Right," Dean replied.

Annabelle frowned. "But they never actually got married?"

"No," Dean said. "The night before the wedding, Charlotte took Uncle Myron out for a 'bachelor party.' They didn't get home until 3:30 the next morning. She had to help him inside and told me he'd had a little too much to drink. I thought it was interesting that she seemed stone sober."

"That is interesting," Eugenia agreed.

"I helped Uncle Myron dress for bed, but he couldn't seem to get comfortable and finally admitted that he was having chest pains. He had a heart attack before the ambulance could get here. At the hospital they discovered large quantities of alcohol and Vitality in his bloodstream."

Eugenia knew the rest of the story. "But the doctors at the hospital attributed your great-uncle's death to the heart attack, not the alcohol or Vitality."

"Yes. But I know that the stimulants and overexertion, combined with the fact that Uncle Myron wasn't taking his heart medication, killed him."

"So he died on what should have been his wedding day," Annabelle remarked.

"Bless his foolish old heart," Eugenia said.

"And I never saw Charlotte Sullivan again," Dean said with a grim smile.

Even after all she'd heard about Charlotte, Eugenia was shocked by this. "She didn't come to the funeral?"

"Nope. She just disappeared with Uncle Myron's 4Runner and that expensive ring."

"You told the police everything you've told us?" Eugenia asked.

"Of course," Dean said. "But there was no real evidence—just suspicious circumstances. Charlotte's fingerprints were on the bottle of Vitality, but I couldn't prove she had given him an overdose. In fact, I couldn't *prove* that Charlotte convinced Uncle Myron to do anything."

Eugenia was angry. "So the police decided to turn a blind eye?"

Dean spread his hands. "They said they didn't have a choice."

"A lawyer friend of mine thinks that the FBI might be willing to investigate her," Eugenia said. "It's clear from your story that Charlotte Sullivan takes jobs at nursing homes or senior citizen centers so that she can identify her next victim. She picks someone with fragile health and then pushes him to the edge—or over it. The FBI might be able to find evidence to prove it."

"In which case you might get the 4Runner and that ring back," Annabelle said hopefully.

Dean shook his head. "I'm sure she's sold the ring and spent all the money. I don't care about that anymore. In fact, I told my Aunt Lavada that I don't even want the house. I've put in some applications at several hospitals in Phoenix, and as soon as I get a job offer, I'm going to move. This place has too many bad memories now."

"Well, good luck to you," Eugenia said as she turned off the Dictaphone. Then she thanked him again for his time and waved for Annabelle to follow her out.

On the way home Eugenia asked Annabelle what she thought.

"Well, there's no question that Charlotte Sullivan is evil," Annabelle said slowly. "But she's good at what she does, and catching her is going to be tough. Since you know that Whit is her next intended victim, maybe you could just follow him around, acting like a jealous old girlfriend. Then when she moves in for the kill, you'll be there to save him."

Eugenia gave her sister a bland look. "First of all, I'm not going to act like anyone's jealous *old* girlfriend. And second, what if I fail to realize she's moving in for the *kill* until it's too late?"

"You're right," Annabelle admitted. "If you can't get Whit to listen to the tape, you'll have to send a copy of it to Charlotte. She'll leave Haggerty to save her own hide, and Whit will be safe."

"If she leaves Haggerty without being brought to justice, she'll go to another town and find some other unsuspecting old man!"

"You think you can save the whole world, Eugenia," Annabelle said. "But this time you may have to be satisfied with saving just one man."

* * *

Lettie was almost asleep on the couch when Mary Margaret said, "Did you hear that?"

Lettie yawned. "What?"

"I thought I heard a noise," Mary Margaret replied.

Lettie shook her head. "I didn't hear anything."

"Me either," Beth seconded.

"Shhhh!" Mary Margaret put a finger to her lips and they all listened closely. A few seconds later they heard a low moan.

"It's Lowell!" Mary Margaret cried. She sprang to her feet and ran toward the kitchen door with Lettie and Beth close behind her. When they reached the door to the bedroom Mary Margaret and Lettie had shared the night before, Beth knocked once. There was no response, so she pushed the door open.

Lowell was sprawled on the bed, turning his head from side to side and moaning. He didn't seem to be aware of their presence as Mary Margaret walked into the room and pressed a hand to his forehead.

"He's burning up with fever!" she reported.

Lettie stepped forward and put her hand beside Mary Margaret's. Lowell was very warm. She glanced up at Beth. "Would you try and wake Alexa up? Maybe she can figure out what's wrong with him."

Beth nodded and hurried back toward the dining hall.

A few minutes later Lettie watched Alexa follow Beth into the room, rubbing her eyes with the heels of her hands. It was an obvious attempt to wake herself from a drug-induced stupor, and Lettie fought a new wave of irritation toward her old friend. The four women had all experienced major disappointments since their high school days. She'd been dumped by her fiancé, Beth's fiancé had been killed on what was supposed to be their wedding day, and Mary Margaret was fighting cancer. Alexa's marital problems just didn't seem to warrant this fatalistic, I-have-nothing-to-live-for attitude.

So Lettie decided it was time to administer some tough love. She grabbed Alexa by the arm and pulled her into the corner, whispering through clenched teeth. "Lowell is sick, and I don't mean he has a stuffy nose. We need you to pull yourself together and examine him."

Alexa jerked away from Lettie's grasp. "First of all, I'm a nurse, not a doctor."

"You're all we've got," Lettie said, hoping how she felt about *that* didn't show.

"And I don't have the equipment to do a proper examination," Alexa continued.

"Do the best you can." Lettie stepped closer and lowered her voice again. "Keep in mind that we need Lowell to get us off this mountain. So returning him to good health is in *your* best interest."

Alexa brushed past Lettie with a scowl and walked over to the bed where Lowell was thrashing around. "Please do something to help him," Mary Margaret begged.

Alexa put two fingers to Lowell's neck. "His pulse is racing, and he's got a high fever. Without a thermometer it's impossible to determine exactly *how* high." She shot a rebellious glance at Lettie.

Lettie ignored the look and asked, "Give me an estimate."

"Around 104," Alexa answered sullenly. Then she turned to Mary Margaret. "Go get me some wet towels."

"Lowell's temperature is 104?" Mary Margaret whispered. "That's so high."

"Which is why I told you to go get me wet towels!" Alexa said. "Now hurry!"

As Mary Margaret scurried off to obey, Beth asked, "Is there anything I can do?"

"Keep Mary Margaret out of here," Alexa replied. "If she hovers over him he won't be able to breathe, and he's in bad enough shape without adding oxygen deprivation." Alexa lifted Lowell's shirt and gently manipulated his abdomen. Lowell screamed in anguish, and they heard Mary Margaret drop something in the kitchen.

Lowell opened his eyes. "What's wrong with me?" he demanded with his teeth clenched.

"Based on what little I have to go on," Alexa prefaced her remarks, "I'd say it's one of three things."

"And they are?" Lowell asked.

"It could be a kidney infection," Alexa said. "That would explain the high fever."

"I've had a kidney infection before and it never hurt like that." Lettie gestured toward Lowell.

"If they're bad enough an infection can be quite painful," Alexa assured her. "But I think that's the least likely possibility. It could be a kidney stone, which is excruciatingly painful, and if accompanied by an infection, that would explain the fever as well. If that's what he has I can give him some of my pain medication and he will eventually pass the stone."

"What's the third possibility?" Lowell asked.

"Acute appendicitis. If that's what you've got, my medicine will help dull the pain, but if you don't get help soon, your appendix could rupture." She looked up at Lettie. "Which under these conditions would probably be fatal."

Lowell closed his eyes as Mary Margaret appeared in the doorway. "Oh Lettie!" she cried. "You won't let him die, will you?"

"Of course not." Lettie took the wet towels from Mary Margaret's trembling hands and passed them to Alexa. "It may not be appendicitis," she continued in a soothing tone. "That's just one of the likely possibilities. Now you and Beth go back to the dining hall and sit by the fire. Alexa and I will take care of Lowell."

"I don't want to leave," Mary Margaret objected.

Lettie turned Mary Margaret around and pushed her gently out of the bedroom. "This room isn't big enough for all of us. I'll come give you a report on his condition soon."

Beth moved to follow Mary Margaret. When she reached the doorway she stopped and said to Lettie, "I'll get in touch with Jack one way or another. Maybe he can figure out a way to help us."

"What can he possibly do?" Lettie whispered.

Beth shrugged. "Jack's pretty resourceful."

Once Beth and Mary Margaret were gone, Lettie returned to Lowell's bedside, where Alexa was arranging the cool towels on their patient. They managed to get Lowell to swallow a couple of pain pills, but Alexa wasn't encouraging.

"I doubt if he'll be able to keep that down," she told Lettie. "And it's not sufficient for the amount of pain he's in anyway. We need to get him out of here. Fast."

Lettie nodded. "Okay. How?"

Alexa kept her eyes fixed on Lowell. "There's only one person who even knows where we are," she said slowly. "There's only one person who has a chance of making it up here through all the snow in time."

"Gray," Lowell whispered as if on cue.

"No!" Lettie cried.

"I'm sorry, Lettie," Alexa said with unusual gentleness. "But we don't have a choice."

Lettie's mind searched desperately for an alternative. "There has to be another way."

"Name one," Alexa challenged.

"We'll call the park rangers," Lettie proposed in desperation. "They have search and rescue teams that handle things like this."

Alexa shrugged. "I guess it's worth a try. But you'd better hurry. Lowell doesn't have much time."

Lettie went into the kitchen and removed the receiver from the phone mounted on the wall. There was no dial tone, so in frustration she returned to the bedroom.

"Can I use your cell phone?" she asked Alexa. "I haven't had service on mine since we got off the plane in Alcoa."

"You made me pack so fast I forgot to bring mine," Alexa replied. "Ask Beth."

Lettie walked through the kitchen and into the dining hall. Beth was sitting beside Mary Margaret on a couch.

"Beth, can I borrow your phone?"

"Is Lowell feeling better?" Mary Margaret asked as Beth pulled her phone from her pocket.

Lettie took the phone and turned back toward the kitchen. "Maybe a little."

She studied the list of emergency numbers posted on the wall beside the phone. She found the one for the ranger station and entered the number into Beth's cell phone.

"Busy," she muttered to herself as the staccato tone sounded repeatedly in her ear. Next she dialed 9-1-1. An operator answered promptly and Lettie explained the situation.

"We have power out and phone lines down all over the park," the operator informed Lettie. "In addition, many of the roads are impassible. I'll notify the ranger station by radio, but I don't know how soon they'll be able to respond." The operator disconnected abruptly, and Lettie closed Beth's phone, blinking in surprise. She had expected a more definite response.

"Well?" Alexa asked when Lettie returned to the bedroom.

"The emergency operator said she'd notify the park rangers."

"How soon can they get here?"

Lettie walked over and looked out the window at the snow. "She couldn't give me an estimate."

Alexa joined Lettie by the window. "Then we have to call Gray."

"I can't," Lettie said, her tone pleading.

"I know you don't want to see him again." Alexa sounded almost kind for a change. "But we're talking about Lowell's life here."

Lettie clasped her hands together and returned her gaze to the window. She stared at the snow and searched for another option. "Maybe the rangers will call back in a minute," she suggested. "We should give them some time . . ."

"Lettie, it's cruel to make Lowell suffer," Alexa said, and Lowell groaned, punctuating her remark.

Okay," Lettie whispered finally. "But I can't make the call."

"Go ask Beth to do it," Alexa said. "If you're lucky, her obsessive, possessive husband has already rented a helicopter to come save us."

Ignoring Alexa's sarcasm, Lettie said, "I'll be back in a few minutes." Then she walked to the dining hall.

Mary Margaret stood when she saw Lettie, but it was Beth who spoke. "How is he?"

"About the same," Lettie replied. "Mary Margaret, do you have a cell number for Gray?" Just saying the name made her shudder.

Mary Margaret shook her head. "No."

Lettie ignored the relief that flooded through her. Maybe there was another way.

"Why do you need Gray's cell number?" Mary Margaret asked.

"Alexa wants Lowell moved to a hospital, but because of the weather we don't know how long it will take for a park ranger to get here." Lettie returned Beth's cell phone to its rightful owner. "Have you been able to reach Jack?"

"Yes," Beth confirmed. "He's on his way here."

Lettie was surprised and extremely pleased. "Already?"

"He got worried about me being snowed in and caught a flight to Chattanooga this morning. He had his phone turned off while he was on the plane, and that's why I wasn't able to reach him earlier. He rented a car at the airport and is driving up. He should be at Lowell's office in less than an hour."

"Unfortunately Jack doesn't know how to get up here," Mary Margaret pointed out. "He'll need Gray's help."

Beth nodded. "He said he's been trying to reach Gray at the tour office, but no one's answering the phone."

"Their lines must be down too," Lettie guessed.

"But when Jack gets to the office with his cell phone, we'll have a way to communicate with Gray," Mary Margaret said.

Beth glanced at Lettie. "Then Gray can contact the park rangers and organize a rescue."

Lettie felt the tension ease from her shoulders. Maybe she wouldn't have to see him after all.

"Assuming Gray is at the office," Beth continued.

Mary Margaret and Lettie nodded. "Yes, assuming that."

* * *

Gray pulled his truck off the road in front of the Smoky Mountain Tours office and parked near the entrance. He pulled his pack out of the truck and slipped the straps over his shoulders. Then he walked up the stone path and unlocked the door. After stomping the snow off his boots, he stepped inside and flipped the light switch, but nothing happened. Gritting his teeth, Gray lifted the phone receiver to his ear. There was no dial tone.

"Great," he said to himself as he dropped the heavy pack on the floor beside his desk. He was cold, wet, and nearly out of his mind with unreasonable jealousy. The lack of electricity and phone service did nothing to improve his mood. Since he couldn't do anything else, he decided to sulk.

He sat down in his chair and stared across the room at Lowell's empty desk. Since the beginning of their cooperative venture, he and Lowell had been bachelor businessmen—able to dedicate all their time and energy to building up their company. Lettie too had dedicated herself to establishing a successful career. Years ago Gray had come to grips, intellectually anyway, with the fact that eventually both Lowell and Lettie would abandon their single, career-intensive lifestyles and get married. He just never dreamed that they'd marry each other.

Because of his business relationship with Lowell, he'd be forced to see Lettie on a regular basis. He'd have to attend the wedding and congratulate them when they had children. Gray's hand closed around a beautiful snow globe a customer had given him. Without thinking he drew back his hand and hurled it across the office.

The globe shattered, and glass fragments fell to the floor, leaving a trail of water and artificial snowflakes on the wall. Embarrassed by his outburst and thankful no one had been there to witness it, Gray got the broom and dustpan. Then he walked over to clean up his mess. As he deposited the remnants of what had once been a nice desk ornament into a trash can, Gray noticed a fax in the printer tray. He picked it up and scanned it quickly. It was a notification from the Tennessee State Police that a convict had escaped from the Hardeman County Correctional Facility.

The man's name was Mancil Bright, and he was serving a life sentence for first-degree murder. He had escaped from a work-release project after his guard suffered a heart attack. He had been tracked as far as Memphis, where authorities lost his trail. It was assumed that he was heading west, but since he was born in a small town right outside the Great Smoky Mountains National Park, there was the possibility that he had circled back. Therefore everyone in the area was being warned.

As Gray secured the fax to the bulletin board with a tack for future reference, the office door opened. He turned to see a man standing in the doorway. His unexpected visitor was of average height with longish dark brown hair and very blue eyes, which at the moment were regarding Gray with irritation.

"Can I help you?" Gray asked.

"I hope so," the man replied. "I'm Jack Gamble, and my wife is stranded up at some lodge with your partner."

Gray nodded. He'd dealt with a few unhappy customers before and knew that being agreeable was the best way to pacify them. "This snow caught a lot of people by surprise, but it's just a temporary inconvenience. They should be able to get down on Sunday as planned."

Jack Gamble shook his head. "That won't be soon enough. Beth, my wife, called and said that your partner is sick."

All thoughts of turning Jack into a satisfied customer left Gray's mind. "How sick?"

Jack shrugged. "One member of their group is a nurse, and she's narrowed his condition down to three possibilities, all of which require medical care and one of which could be fatal. So we've got to get them off that mountain right now."

Gray picked up his cell phone and dialed Lowell's number. "There's no answer," he told Jack. "He must have his phone off."

"You can call Beth's cell phone," Jack offered. Then he recited Beth's number, and Gray entered it into his phone. A few seconds later he heard her answer. "Beth? This is Gray Grantland."

"Gray!" Beth sounded happy to hear from him. "You *are* at the office."

"Yes." Gray glanced at Jack. "Your husband is here, and he says that Lowell is sick."

"Yes," Beth confirmed. "Alexa thinks it might be appendicitis. We called 9-1-1, and they're supposed to be notifying the park rangers, but we haven't heard back from them."

"I have the captain's cell number. I'll call him," Gray promised. "You all hold tight, and someone will be there as soon as possible." Gray disconnected the call and searched the numbers in his cell phone. When he found the one for Captain Woods, he pushed SEND.

The phone rang several times before finally connecting to Captain Woods's voice mail. Gray thought about leaving a message but realized he wouldn't be able to rest easy until he was sure help was on the way for his best friend. When he closed his phone, Jack, who had been staring out the window at the snow, glanced over at him. "No answer?"

"Voice mail," Gray confirmed. "I'm sure he's swamped with disgruntled campers caught in the storm. The National Weather Service really dropped the ball on this one, but people looking for someone to blame aren't going to think about that. They'll go straight to the park rangers. Captain Woods could be tied up for hours." He hit REDIAL and tried the captain's number again, but with the same result. On the third try he finally got through.

"Woods," the captain answered.

"Gray Grantland," Gray identified himself. "Lowell Brooks and four women he took on a hiking trip are stranded up at LeConte Lodge. I just found out that Lowell is sick."

"Yeah, I got word about that a few minutes ago," the captain told him.

"Do you have a search and rescue team on the way to bring him down?"

"We've really got our hands full here, Gray," the captain said. "People stranded everywhere. We're handling things in order of priority, and it could be a while before we can get a team up Mount LeConte."

Gray tried not to sound as impatient as he felt. "One of the women with Lowell is a nurse, and she thinks Lowell's condition might be fatal. So could you move him up to the top of your list?"

"I just got off the phone with the nurse," the captain replied. "She said Lowell might just have a kidney infection. I'm sorry, Gray, but I've got a family with small children lost on the east side of the park. If we don't get to them by dark, one of the little kids might freeze to death. I do have a ranger on his way to the lodge by foot, though. When he gets there he might be able to assist them."

"Can he bring Lowell down the mountain?" Gray asked.

"I doubt it," the captain replied. "His vehicle was completely disabled in a collision that also broke his arm, and the closest snow-mobile shed is several miles away at the base of Rainbow Falls Trail."

Gray tried not to sound as frustrated as he felt. "I understand that you have several crises and limited staff," he told the captain. "The husband of one of Lowell's stranded guests is here with me. We should be able to make it to the bottom of the Rainbow Falls Trail and get the snowmobiles. Then we'll go up and get Lowell ourselves."

After a brief pause, the captain said, "I'll agree on one condition. You'll have to write out a waiver."

Gray put the phone against his chest to cover the receiver. Then he whispered to Jack, "He wants us to sign a waiver. Can you believe that? Lowell may be dying up there and the captain is talking about waivers!"

Jack nodded. "Everyone is afraid of getting sued these days."

"What should we do?" Gray asked.

"Agree to anything," Jack told him. "It would never hold up in court anyway."

Gray smiled as he moved the phone back to his mouth. "Okay. We'll sign a waiver."

"Say that you release me and the park from liability and promise to pay for any damages. Then both of you sign it and leave it on your desk," the captain said. "I'll go by and pick it up if you kill yourselves."

Gray tried not to be insulted and started writing. Jack moved to stand behind him so he could read over his shoulder. "Anything else?" Gray asked

The captain missed the sarcasm. "That should do it. Do you know where the shed is?"

"I've seen it," Gray confirmed.

"Do you think you can make it that far in your truck?"

Gray continued writing. "If not, we'll go the rest of the way on foot."

"Since I don't have any way to get you a key, you'll have to break the lock off the shed," the captain continued. "The keys to the snowmobiles are in the first-aid kit mounted on the wall."

"Thanks," Gray said.

"But remember, if you wreck them, you buy them," Captain Woods warned.

"I understand," Gray assured him. Then he hung up and held his homemade waiver up for Jack to see. "What do you think?"

"Terrible," Jack said with a smile. "But like I said—it doesn't really matter."

Gray put the waiver on his desk and signed it, then handed Jack the pen. Jack added his signature, shaking his head and smiling. Then Gray asked him, "Can you drive a snowmobile?"

Jack nodded. "It's been a few years, but I'm sure it will come back to me."

"Like riding a bike," Gray predicted.

"Then let's go." Jack turned toward the door. "I know my wife will be glad to see me."

When he heard this remark, a knot of anxiety started to form in Gray's stomach. The woman who could have been his wife was also at LeConte Lodge. But unlike Jack, he didn't expect the woman he was thinking of to be excited to see him.

Both men walked outside, and Gray whistled when he saw the Hummer that Jack had driven up the mountain. "An H3." He ran his hand along the slick black paint. "I haven't even seen one of these yet."

"It drives great," Jack told him. "It's got a shorter wheelbase so it can fit into tight spaces, and they claim it will handle just about any terrain."

"I'm surprised that you found a rental agency that had one," Gray said as he continued to admire the SUV.

Jack smiled. "I didn't. The rental agent called the local Hummer dealership and arranged a test drive—for a fee, of course. Since you know the area, you'd better drive. Here, catch."

Gray caught the keys Jack tossed to him. "You want me to drive *this* to the snowmobile shed?"

"It has a better chance of making it than your truck," Jack said. "And I figure that will be a good test of its abilities."

"I can't argue with that, but I'm afraid we'll damage the paint."

Jack shrugged as he opened the front passenger door. "That's the least of our worries."

CHAPTER 8

After Annabelle dropped her off at home, Eugenia sat on her front porch and mulled the situation over for a while. She was completely convinced that Charlotte Sullivan meant Whit harm, but she didn't know how to stop her from succeeding. Eugenia was deep in thought when Polly called from the sidewalk.

"Hey, Eugenia!"

"Hey yourself! Would you like to come up and sit with Lady and me for a bit?" Eugenia invited.

"I'd love to." Polly climbed the steps and settled herself in the porch swing. "How was your trip to Sipsey?"

Eugenia frowned. "How did you know I went to Sipsey?"

"Violet Honeycutt told me when she stopped by to give me a recipe for the new fund-raising cookbook. She said Leita at the police station told her."

"And Winston told her." Eugenia was well aware of how fast news traveled in Haggerty, but she was still annoyed. Winston was a police officer and should be able to keep confidences.

"And Annabelle got herself some of those white wooden reindeer," Polly continued.

"Did Violet tell you that too?" Eugenia demanded.

"No, I saw them sticking out of Annabelle's trunk when she dropped you off," Polly explained. "I wouldn't mind having a few of those reindeer myself. I thought they looked mighty nice in Cleo's yard last Christmas."

Polly already had too many Christmas decorations, and the last thing she needed was a herd of wooden reindeer. To discourage her, Eugenia said, "I don't think wooden reindeer would blend very well with the rest of your decorations. You've got what I'd call a delicate balance."

"I guess you're right," Polly said, but she didn't sound convinced. "Have you decided where you'll be attending church services on Sunday? That's all Violet could talk about when she was here."

"No, I haven't decided," Eugenia snapped. "And if Violet and the rest of this town don't leave me alone about it, they're going to drive me to atheism."

Polly laughed. "I know you don't mean *that!*"

Anxious to change the subject, Eugenia said, "I got a box of handmade pralines from the flea market in Sipsey. Would you like one?"

"I'd love one," Polly replied with predictable enthusiasm.

Eugenia stood and opened the front door. "Well, come on in." She led the way to the kitchen and pointed at the box of pralines on the table.

Polly had the wrapper off and the box open in less than a minute. "Oh, these are good!" Polly proclaimed as she sat beside Eugenia. Then her eyes settled on Derrick's little tape recorder. "What's this?"

"It's called a Dictaphone, and I used it to record my conversation with the man I met in Sipsey."

Polly's eyes widened. "You went to Sipsey to meet a *man?*"

Eugenia waved this silly remark aside. "It wasn't a date! I met a young man named Dean Lumpkin, and he claims that Charlotte Sullivan killed his great-uncle!"

"Oh my." Polly reached for another piece of candy. "Can I listen to the tape?"

"I don't see why not." Eugenia rewound the tape and pressed play. By the time it was over, Polly was weeping, and the box of candy was empty.

"That poor old man! Why would Charlotte be so mean to him?"

"Because all she wanted was his money," Eugenia explained bluntly. "And that's what she's going to do to Whit if I can't hammer some sense into his thick old skull."

"She wants Whit's money too?" .

"Apparently so. She's had *seven* husbands, not three like she listed on her application for employment with the chamber of commerce," Eugenia informed her neighbor. "They all died and left their money to her, which I don't believe is a coincidence. Then there are lots of men like the great-uncle from Sipsey who didn't make it to the altar but still gave her most of their earthly possessions."

"What are you going to do, Eugenia?"

Eugenia frowned at the little tape recorder. "I'm going to try to get Whit to listen to this tape, although he might not even answer the phone when I call."

"Why wouldn't Whit answer your phone calls or listen to the tape if you ask him to?"

Eugenia remembered her last conversation with Whit. "We kind of had a fight about Charlotte," she said. "He thinks I'm being catty and jealous."

"I'll take it to him," Polly offered. "He might listen to it if I ask him to, since he's not having a fight with me."

Eugenia was moved by rare tenderness for her lifetime friend. "Thank you, but I couldn't ask you to do that. Besides, once Whit realized what it was he'd turn off the tape, and then he would be fighting with both of us." *Darn his fickle hide,* Eugenia added to herself.

Polly looked at the empty praline box. "I'm sorry I ate all your candy," she said. "I'm a nervous eater."

"It's okay," Eugenia assured her. "I don't really like them anyway. Annabelle made me buy the candy because she said it was rude for me to go to the flea market without making a purchase."

Polly traced the inside of the candy box with one of her plump fingers. "I wish we could think of a way to use this tape to make Charlotte leave Whit alone."

"Annabelle suggested I make a copy of the tape and mail it to Charlotte, hoping that would scare her off."

A look of horror settled on Polly's face. "Eugenia! If she recognizes your voice on that tape she might kill *you!*"

"I'm not afraid of Charlotte Sullivan!" Eugenia said.

"That's probably what all her husbands thought, just before she killed *them!*" Polly cried.

This gave Eugenia a moment's pause. "To be safe, I could put only the parts where Dean Lumpkin is talking on the copy I give to Charlotte."

"And what if she kills *him?*" Polly demanded.

Eugenia sighed. "I guess it won't work."

"You could write her a letter and tell her that you have a tape that incriminates her in a murder. You don't have to mention Mr. Bell, and you can sign it 'Anonymous.'"

"That's not a bad idea," she told Polly. "I could take it to her house tonight while she's making old folks play bingo at the senior center."

"You can leave it in her mailbox!" Polly suggested.

Eugenia shook her head. "That's illegal and, besides, she wouldn't see it until sometime tomorrow. I'll put it on her front door so she won't be able to miss it."

"Eugenia, you'd make such a good spy!" Polly complimented her. "And if the letter doesn't work, you could make her think Mr. Bell has come back from the grave to get revenge. I saw that on a television show once."

Eugenia raised both eyebrows. "We'll save that for a last resort."

"Are you going to write it now?" Polly asked. "I'd love to see what you say."

"No point in delaying." Eugenia found a piece of clean typing paper and a black ballpoint pen. Then she settled back down at the table and began to write.

Charlotte Sullivan—
I know what you did to Myron Bell and your seven husbands.

"That's a nice touch," Polly encouraged her. "It will show Charlotte that you know more about her than the information she provided on her employment application."

Eugenia glanced up. "I'm glad you approve." Then she returned her attention to the letter.

*I'm watching every move you make and if you know what's good
for you, you'll pack your blood money in your stolen 4Runner
and get out of town.*

"Oh, Eugenia!" Polly pulled the handkerchief from her neckline
and pressed it to her trembling lips. "I'm scared and I didn't do a
thing to Mr. Bell!"

Eugenia smiled as she signed *Anonymous* with a flourish along
the bottom of the letter. "Let's hope Miss Sullivan feels the same."

* * *

Gray drove the H3 up the steep mountain roads as quickly as he
dared. His concern for Lowell was tempered by the pure joy of
driving such a wonderful vehicle. In spite of the slippery, uneven
terrain, they had an amazingly smooth ride.

"Man, I'm going to have to get me one of these," Gray finally said.

"I'll bet the dealership in Chattanooga will have this particular
H3 marked down sometime next week," Jack predicted. "As long as
you don't mind a few scratches on the side."

"Don't remind me," Gray pleaded. "It's a desecration to scratch
up this vehicle."

Jack turned on the radio. "I think I'll see what they're saying
about the weather."

The forecast was disappointing. Subfreezing temperatures were
expected to continue for at least another twenty-four hours, and
more snow was possible in the higher elevations.

"The higher elevations—that's us," Gray told Jack.

The other man nodded. "I figured."

Then the newscaster announced that a convict who had escaped
the day before had been found dead in the Great Smoky Mountains
National Park, and Jack looked over at Gray in alarm. "There's an
escaped convict here in the park?" he demanded.

Gray nodded. "There *was* one, I guess. I saw a fax at the office
warning that he might have been headed here."

They returned their attention to the radio.

Mancil Bright has been incarcerated at Hardeman County Correctional Facility for the past seven years following his conviction for the brutal murder of his stepfather and subsequent shooting of three police officers. Because of an exemplary conduct record in prison, Bright was allowed to join a landscaping work crew at the water treatment plant in nearby Bolivar. Late on Thursday afternoon, Bright poisoned the guard responsible for the work crew and escaped in a prison van. He drove to Memphis, where he murdered and robbed an elderly man named Avery Ingle. It was assumed that he was headed west, but early this morning a park ranger found his body in the Great Smoky Mountains National Park. Officials say they are relieved by this fortunate turn of events. "Mancil Bright was a very dangerous man," said the warden at Hardeman County Correctional. "He's not the kind of man we want loose on our streets."

Jack was looking a little pale when the newscaster changed to a report on the unrest in the Middle East. "I was worried enough about Beth," he said. "I'm glad they got him."

"Yeah," Gray agreed. "Me too."

"How much further?" Jack asked.

"A couple of miles. The Rainbow Falls Trail isn't the quickest way to the lodge, but that's where the snowmobiles are, so that's the way we'll go."

The H3 drove so smoothly, even over the uneven terrain, that they arrived at the snowmobile shed sooner than Gray expected. He had to slam on the brakes and skidded to a halt in front of the metal building. They climbed out of the Hummer, and Gray saw the sturdy padlock that held the doors closed.

"I got so excited about the Hummer I forgot to bring a crowbar," he told Jack. "Captain Woods told me to break the lock off."

"There's probably one in the Hummer somewhere," Jack said, and he was correct. A quick search of the spare tire compartment yielded a shiny new crowbar. Gray threaded it through the top of the padlock and levered it against a metal door. With minimal effort, the lock snapped. Gray pushed the doors back and they walked into the shed.

"The keys are supposed to be back here." He led the way to the back wall where the first-aid kit was mounted and rummaged through it until he found the keys. "I'll back the snowmobiles out and then I'll give you a quick refresher course."

Jack agreed with a nod. Ten minutes later they were riding the snowmobiles up a narrow path. Gray took the lead, but kept Jack in sight by using his mirrors. Jack slipped and slid occasionally, but he seemed to have control of the vehicle, so Gray concentrated on driving toward the LeConte Lodge.

* * *

Lettie paced nervously around the dining hall. She was anxious for help to arrive for Lowell's sake, but she dreaded it, too, since help meant Gray. While she conceded that denial was not the healthiest way to deal with problems, it had worked well for her up to this point. After that harrowing afternoon at the Circle of Love Bridal Shoppe, she had put Gray out of her mind and refused to look back.

Lettie had built a good life for herself. It might not have been the life she'd hoped for, but it was a good one. She knew, however, that seeing Gray again might upset the balance of her universe—or at least make denial more difficult. Finally she started to feel dizzy. So she suspended her pacing circuit and walked to the back bedroom to check on Lowell.

"How's he doing?" she asked when she reached the doorway.

Alexa and Mary Margaret both looked up.

"He's resting quietly right now," Alexa said. "But that could change at any second."

Lettie frowned in frustration. "Surely someone will be here soon."

"Let's hope so," Alexa said grimly.

When Lettie returned to the dining hall to resume her pacing, Beth was sitting on the couch, eating a sandwich. "Would you like me to make you one?" she offered.

"No thanks," Lettie replied. Then she turned her ear toward the window. "Do you hear something?"

Beth put her sandwich down and joined Lettie. They listened intently for a few seconds.

"Motors," Beth whispered.

"They're coming," Lettie agreed, relief overpowering dread—temporarily at least.

Beth wiped tears from her eyes. "Jack's obsessive nature may be annoying sometimes, but if I'm in trouble, I know he'll help me."

Lettie smiled. "Somebody's always got your back."

Beth nodded. "Lettie, about Gray . . ."

Lettie shook her head. "I don't want to talk about that now."

"We don't have to talk about it," Beth replied grimly. "But I have a feeling you're going to be thinking about it." She pointed out the window as two snowmobiles came to a stop in front of the lodge.

Lettie stared out the window as Mary Margaret came running in from the back. "Are they here?"

"They are," Lettie confirmed. The men climbed off of the snowmobiles, and Lettie's eyes moved automatically to Gray's familiar form. His face was pink from the cold and his hair was a windblown mess. She was so affected by the sight of him that she had to remind herself to breathe. He glanced toward the lodge, and Lettie took a step away from the window. She pressed a hand to her pounding heart. This was going to be even worse than she had thought.

The front door opened and Lettie turned to see Beth and Mary Margaret rush outside. Beth ran down the stairs and launched herself into Jack's arms. Feeling like a voyeur, Lettie forced her gaze back to Gray. Mary Margaret had him by the hand and was trying to pull him toward the lodge. In his defense, Gray didn't seem any more anxious to be there than Lettie was to have him.

With a sigh of resignation, Lettie squared her shoulders and walked into the back bedroom to help Alexa prepare the patient for transport.

* * *

Ranger Lamar Penny looked up at the sky, hoping for a break in the clouds so he could determine from the position of the sun which direction he was heading. The sun was still completely hidden, but for his effort he got snowflakes in his eyes. Lamar leaned against the trunk of a tree to rest for a few minutes. He'd been walking for several hours. If he had been going the right way, he would have reached LeConte Lodge by now. It was time to admit defeat and ask for help.

He pressed the TALK button on his radio and said, "Penny checking in."

"What's your position, Ranger Penny?" Jill's daytime replacement asked.

"I don't know," he reported dully. "I need you to check the GPS and figure out my coordinates. Then give me directions to LeConte Lodge."

There was a brief, disapproving silence, and then dispatch said, "I'm making the request. Please stand by."

Lamar would have laughed if he'd had the energy. That's what he would do, all right. Stand by.

He nearly dozed off before dispatch returned.

"Ranger Penny, you're two miles off course," dispatch informed him. "Haven't you been following your compass?"

Lamar wasn't the least bit interested in impressing this woman, so he said, "I couldn't find it."

"Well, you need to head east. Can you see the row of power lines?"

Lamar shielded his eyes from the falling snow and searched the horizon. "Yes."

"Go toward the power lines," dispatch instructed him. "Once you reach them, follow them. You'll be at the base of Mount LeConte. From there you just have to go up."

"Thanks," Lamar said. Then he turned off the radio, pushed away from the tree, and headed east toward the power lines.

* * *

"Come on in," Mary Margaret insisted as she drew Gray toward the porch that fronted the lodge.

Gray glanced over his shoulder at Jack and Beth. "I'll wait for them," he said, trying to delay the moment of truth for as long as possible.

But Mary Margaret was determined. "Beth!" she called out, interrupting a tender embrace between the married couple. "We need Jack to help get Lowell onto a snowmobile."

Beth nodded and led her husband up the stairs and into the lodge.

Mary Margaret resumed her tugging on Gray's hand. "Please, Gray," she begged.

Surrendering himself to certain doom, he allowed Mary Margaret to guide him inside.

Once they were in the dining hall, Gray looked around. Lettie was nowhere in sight and he felt himself relax slightly.

"Lowell is back here," Mary Margaret told him.

He followed her through the kitchen to the doorway of a small staff bedroom. The first thing he saw was Lowell lying motionless on the narrow bed. Then his eyes seemed to move of their own volition to the far corner of the room where Lettie stood.

Her face was leaner, her eyes more solemn, and the honey-blonde hair that used to hang to her waist now barely brushed her shoulders. Lowell was right—five years had made her lovelier. He forced himself to meet her gaze, and the concern for Lowell he saw in her eyes confirmed his worst fears.

"Gray," Alexa said, forcing his attention back to Lowell, his partner and Lettie's future husband. "I'll need you and Jack to carry him out to the snowmobile."

Gray nodded. "Is he in pain?"

"I've given him some medication, which seems to be working for the moment. But you'll need to strap him in very well because if the pain returns during the trip down the mountain he might start thrashing around, and we don't want him to fall off."

"What will I do if he's in that much pain?" Gray asked in alarm.

"You'll keep going," Alexa told him. "The pain won't kill him, but delaying his arrival at a hospital might."

"Okay, I'll get Jack . . ."

"I'm here." Jack spoke from behind him.

The men walked into the room and Lettie slipped out.

With Gray and Jack helping lift the unresponsive man, Alexa was able to get Lowell into a parka. Once she was satisfied, she nodded. "Okay. Take him out."

Gray put his hands under Lowell's shoulders and Jack got him at the knees. They carried him outside, and then Gray held him up while Jack ran and drove one of the snowmobiles right up to the porch steps. Lowell opened his eyes as Gray was strapping him in.

"I'm sick," he rasped.

Gray decided to keep things light. "Yeah, but I'm here to save your hide—as usual."

Lowell managed a smile. "Thanks, man. Someday maybe I can return the favor."

"Maybe," Gray said, but he knew this was unlikely since the minute Lowell got well, Gray planned to tell him he wanted to sell his interest in the business and get as far away from the happy couple as possible.

Gray was double-checking the straps when Jack stepped up beside him and said, "We have a problem."

Gray rubbed his temple. "What now?"

"I'm not leaving Beth up here," Jack said simply.

"I wouldn't expect you to," Gray replied. "After all, you've invested a brand-new Hummer in this rescue. She can ride on the back of your snowmobile."

Jack pointed over his shoulder where Mary Margaret was standing with Beth. Both women were dressed for travel and had their bags in their hands. "And Mary Margaret says she has to go to the hospital with Lowell. In fact, she's insistent."

Gray frowned as Mary Margaret approached them.

"I'm sorry, Gray," Mary Margaret said. "But this whole thing is my fault. None of us would even be here if it weren't for me. So I absolutely have to go with Lowell and make sure he's all right."

"*I'll* make sure he's all right," Gray responded. It was getting late, and going down the mountain in the dark was going to be more difficult than getting up it in the daylight had been. The sooner they left, the better, and Mary Margaret was costing them time.

"I also have to make sure that Lettie and Alexa are okay. Surely you don't plan to leave three defenseless women up here overnight?"

Gray was losing patience. "What?"

"If you and Jack both leave, we won't have anyone to protect us," Mary Margaret said. "But if I go down with Lowell, you can stay and bring the others down when the snow melts."

Gray finally understood what she was proposing and shook his head. "I can't stay here."

"Actually, I think you are obligated to stay, both morally and legally," Mary Margaret continued with a tenacity that seemed completely foreign to her gentle nature. "You are Lowell's partner and he contracted this trip. Since he can't fulfill his responsibilities, they fall to you."

Gray was trying to formulate a response when Jack spoke. "Legally speaking, she's right," he told Gray. "And I can't argue with the moral issue either. Leaving three women here alone would be irresponsible. Up to this point they've had a strong, experienced man to help them, and look how things have turned out."

"There's a park ranger on his way," Gray whispered. "He can help the others get down."

"I thought the captain said the ranger was injured," Jack reminded him unnecessarily. "He may not be able to get himself down without assistance."

"Then I'll come back." Gray searched frantically for a solution that wouldn't leave him here to face the mistakes of his past.

"The snowmobiles only hold two people," Jack pointed out. "You'd have to make three trips in the dark to get all the women down, and during the second trip, you'd be leaving someone up here all alone."

Finally Alexa said, "If you don't get this settled soon, you'll have one less person to worry about."

"Please, Gray," Mary Margaret begged. "You have to stay."

Gray sighed in resignation. "Can you drive a snowmobile?" he asked, and Mary Margaret shook her head.

"I can," Beth volunteered. Then she held up a hand to stop Jack's inevitable objection. "I'll follow you and we'll be fine."

"Beth," Jack tried.

"We're out of choices and we're wasting time." Beth was firm.

Jack didn't look happy, but he nodded.

"Okay, Mary Margaret, you ride with Beth," Gray said.

Jack pressed a kiss to Beth's forehead and said, "You'd better be careful."

"I will," she promised. Then Jack settled into the seat in front of Lowell, and Beth and Mary Margaret followed Gray over to the other snowmobile.

Gray supervised while the women took their places and situated their bags. When he handed her the key, Beth whispered, "Now show me how to drive this thing."

"You lied about being able to drive a snowmobile?" Gray hissed.

She gave him a disapproving look. "I said I *could* drive one—not that I ever had."

Gray knew they didn't have time for another argument, and the snowmobile was fairly easy to maneuver, so he showed her the start button. Then he explained the basics of steering and how to brake. When he was finished she smiled up at him.

"That should do," she said. "See you when the snow melts."

Gray jogged up to the first snowmobile and spoke to Jack. "Beth's a little rusty on her driving skills, so keep an eye on her."

Jack nodded. "You can be sure I will."

Gray handed Lowell's satellite phone to Jack. "This is Lowell's. I've got one just like it so you can reach me even if you get into spots where your regular cell phone doesn't have service."

Jack put the phone in the pocket of his parka.

"You should be able to follow our tracks back out, but the phone has GPS if you need it. Captain Woods's cell phone number is in the phone. Here are your keys for the Hummer and Lowell's keys so you can get into the office. There's also a key to my truck on his ring. If you can't find the snowmobile shed, go straight back to the office and take my truck to the hospital."

Jack added the keys to the phone in his pocket.

"The satellite phone is a little complicated," Gray said. "Do you want me to show you how to use it?"

Jack smiled. "I'll figure it out. Try not to worry. We'll be in touch." Then he started his snowmobile and Beth did the same. Seconds later they were out of sight.

Gray considered staying where he was—figuring that freezing to death might be preferable to what awaited him inside. But finally he gathered his courage and climbed the stairs. He needn't have worried. When he walked into the dining hall, Alexa informed him that Lettie was changing the sheets on Lowell's sickbed.

"And I'm going to take a nap, so you're on your own," Alexa added with a yawn.

After Alexa was gone, he stoked the fire and called Captain Woods at the ranger office. "I'll get the snowmobiles gassed up and put back in the shed as soon as I can," Gray promised.

"That's fine and I'm glad you got there safely," the captain said, sounding a little distracted. "Has my ranger made it yet?"

"Not yet."

"I'd appreciate it if you'll let me know as soon as he arrives. And keep me posted on Lowell's condition."

"I will," Gray promised.

After disconnecting the call with Captain Woods, Gray made a few more phone calls, including one to Lowell's mother. He also cancelled the trips Lowell had scheduled for the next week. Once this was accomplished, he tested all the propane lanterns to be sure they would be in working condition when the sunlight faded completely. Then he zipped up his parka and went outside to chop more firewood.

* * *

It had been dark for almost an hour by the time Jack and the others reached the snowmobile shed. The Hummer was a welcome sight, looking substantial and comfortable to them after hours of being exposed to the elements. Jack stopped in front of the Hummer and waited for Beth to pull up alongside him. He pushed back the visor of his helmet and she did the same.

"Are you okay?"

She nodded. "Cold."

"Once we get in the Hummer you'll warm up," Jack promised.

They climbed off the snowmobiles and Jack pocketed the keys for both vehicles. Then he said to Beth, "I'm going to need your help to move Lowell." He handed the keys to the Hummer to Mary Margaret. "Open the back door for us, please. Beth and I will carry him."

Mary Margaret hurried to the Hummer and inserted the key. "Is he okay?" She glanced over her shoulder at Lowell.

"He'll be better when we get him to a hospital," Jack responded evasively. "Climb in the backseat and we'll hand him up to you."

Mary Margaret scrambled into the Hummer, and Jack loosened the straps that held Lowell to the snowmobile.

"If you'll get his feet, I'll get his shoulders," Jack told Beth.

Lowell opened his eyes and regarded Jack with misery.

"You're hurting again?" Jack whispered and Lowell nodded. "We'll be as gentle as we can," he promised. Then he slipped his arms under Lowell's shoulders and lifted while Beth grabbed the big man's feet. Lowell clenched his teeth against the pain.

Jack staggered under Lowell's weight and with Beth's help half carried, half dragged him the short distance to the Hummer. Then they all pulled and pushed until Lowell was stretched out on the backseat. Lowell moaned softly, and Mary Margaret cradled his head in her lap.

Breathing hard, Jack opened the front passenger door for Beth. Once she was settled inside, he walked around the vehicle as quickly as the deep snow would allow. Jack climbed in under the wheel and turned the key that Mary Margaret had inserted in the ignition.

"Okay, we're on our way," he said.

"What about the snowmobiles?" Beth asked. "Shouldn't you put them in the shed?"

"I'll come back and move them later," Jack replied. "Right now we've got to get Lowell to a hospital." He backed up the Hummer and circled around the snowmobiles. Then he turned down the mountain road. "Beth, you and Mary Margaret put on your seat belts. This ride could be a little rough."

Beth reached out and ran a hand along the sleek dashboard of the Hummer. "This is very nice."

"I'm glad you like it, because I'm thinking about buying one," Jack told her, and he was only half kidding.

She smiled. "You'll probably have to buy this one when the rental company sees all the scratches in the shiny new paint."

He acknowledged this with a nod. "You're probably right."

Jack fought to keep the H3 on the road as they slipped and slid down the mountain. When they reached the park exit, Jack stopped to ask directions to the nearest hospital. The ranger on duty pointed the way and even said he'd call the hospital to let them know they were coming.

* * *

Eugenia locked the back door behind her as she left her house at 7:45 on Friday evening. On the way to her car, Eugenia clutched the envelope containing the letter she'd written. Soon Miss Charlotte Sullivan would be continuing her search for her next soon-to-be-late husband in another unfortunate town. And Whit would be safe.

On her way to Charlotte's rental house, Eugenia drove past the old armory. There were a lot of cars parked outside, indicating that the senior center was gaining popularity with the town's older citizens. Eugenia saw Whit's Lexus parked close to the entrance, which probably meant that he had arrived early to help Charlotte prepare for the evening's event, just as he'd said he would.

Pushing negative thoughts about Whit from her mind, Eugenia drove to the town square and turned left on Cypress Court. She followed the road several blocks down and then turned onto Sycamore Street. She parked in the shadows of an old oak tree a few houses down from Charlotte's.

She waited until she was sure there were no neighbors outside. Then she got out of the car and carried the envelope up to Charlotte's front door. Anxious to make sure she wasn't recognized, Eugenia was careful to stay out of the circle of light created by the electric hurricane lantern mounted on the house.

Eugenia opened the screen door and wedged the envelope between the door and the frame. Once she was sure it was secure, she closed the screen and hurried back to her car. There, she slumped down as far as her arthritic bones would allow and began her surveillance.

CHAPTER 9

Lettie stayed in the small bedroom at the lodge until she began to feel claustrophobic. Finally, angry with herself for allowing Gray Grantland to control her in even a small way, she walked into the kitchen. She could hear Gray and Alexa talking in the dining hall and tried hard to ignore them as she struck a match and lit the propane lantern on the counter. Then she searched through the cupboards to see what they could have for dinner.

Her cooking skills were limited, so she removed a bag of pasta and a jar of alfredo sauce. Lettie put a pot of water on the stove, and once it was boiling she added the pasta. While the noodles were cooking she made a salad. As she chopped the vegetables she occasionally heard Alexa laugh from the other room. Attacking the lettuce with a vengeance, she wondered what in the world Gray was saying that was so amusing.

Once the pasta was cooked, she drained the water and added the sauce. She put the finished product on the table beside her salad. She added a loaf of bread, several bottles of water, and some individual serving packets of salad dressing to the assortment. Then she stacked plates and eating utensils on one end of the table and dished herself a portion of everything.

"Dinner's ready," she announced to no one in particular when she walked into the dining hall. "Help yourselves." She carried her food over to a chair by the window and settled down to eat.

Not bad, she thought to herself as she tasted the pasta. In fact, she was enjoying her meal until Alexa and Gray returned from the kitchen. They sat together like buddies at one end of the long table. Lettie's appetite disappeared, and she put her plate on the windowsill and stared out at the snow. Gray's cell phone rang, and Lettie listened carefully to his side of the conversation. She had already determined that Lowell was safely at a hospital before Gray made the announcement.

"That's a relief," Alexa said. "Have they decided what's wrong with him yet? I'm curious to see if my diagnosis was correct."

"Jack said appendicitis," Gray told her.

"I knew it!" Alexa claimed. "I'm good!"

Lettie could have pointed out that Alexa had waffled between three different diagnoses, but she preferred to stay out of their conversation.

"They're preparing Lowell for surgery now," Gray continued. "Jack said he'd call back when it's over."

Lettie heard a chair scrape against the wooden floor, and Gray offered to take Alexa's dishes into the kitchen.

"I'll take mine," Alexa volunteered with a rare burst of energy.

Once they were gone, Lettie willed herself to relax. Slowly the tension left her neck and shoulders. She heard water running and Alexa laughing. Apparently they were cleaning up the kitchen. Lettie was glad that this task wouldn't fall to her, but she refused to feel any gratitude toward Gray. Cleaning up was the very *least* he could do.

She looked out at the moonlight reflecting off of the snow and had the creepiest feeling that someone was out there, watching her. She shuddered as Gray and Alexa returned to the dining hall. Alexa sat down on the couch in front of the fire, but Gray walked up behind Lettie. She stared at his reflection in the window glass and he stared back. She thought of the phrase "so close and yet so far away." The words described their situation perfectly.

Finally he said, "Thanks for making dinner. It was delicious."

She nodded. "You're welcome."

He looked as uncomfortable as she felt. "This lodge is too small for us to avoid each other. Maybe we can put the past behind us until we get out of here."

"I've already put the past behind me," she assured him.

He took a step backward. "That's good, then. And I'll handle breakfast in the morning."

She nodded again, hoping he'd just go away and leave her alone. Apparently he sensed her feelings because he joined Alexa on the couch.

Lettie was spooked and didn't want to sit by the drafty window where she was clearly visible to anyone outside. But joining Gray and Alexa in a friendly chat was unthinkable. She could go back to her tiny bedroom and stare at the walls, but that plan didn't have much appeal either. Before she was forced to make a decision, there was a knock on the door, followed immediately by a heavy thump.

"Who could that be?" Alexa demanded.

Gray stood and moved toward the door. "Captain Woods told me hours ago that a park ranger was coming here by foot. It must be him."

Lettie took a few steps forward as Gray pulled the door open to expose a figure lying in a heap on the porch. Gray knelt down and felt for a pulse. "He's alive."

"Did he pass out?" Alexa asked as she joined him on the other side of the prone man.

Gray nodded. "It could be hypothermia. He's been out in the cold for hours."

Alexa frowned. "The question is *why* has he been wandering around in the cold?"

"The captain said he wrecked his truck, and the lodge must have been the closest place he could get to on foot," Gray replied. "Now we'd better get him inside before he freezes to death."

Alexa helped Gray drag the man inside, and Lettie rushed over to close the door behind them, feeling greatly relieved. It must have been the ranger she had sensed earlier. By the time she had secured the locks, their unexpected guest was stretched out on one of the couches, and Alexa was struggling with the buttons of his coat.

"Let me give you a hand with that," Gray offered. Lettie watched from a few feet away as they peeled off the coat, exposing a khaki uniform shirt with a dark red stain down the front.

The man started to shiver, and Alexa headed for the kitchen. "I'm going to get some blankets. Gray, you and Lettie push the couch closer to the fire."

Lettie was startled by this command and not very happy about her sudden inclusion in their little team.

Gray waited until Alexa was out of hearing range. Then he said, "I can do it myself."

"Nonsense." Lettie grasped her end of the couch and strained against the weight as they eased it forward. Then she picked up the ranger's coat and hung it on a hook by the fireplace to dry out.

Alexa returned, and Gray helped her tuck the blankets around the unconscious man.

Finally, Lettie became concerned about his shaking. "Is that shivering normal?"

"Yes," Alexa said. "It's the body's way of generating heat."

Gray looked worried too. "How long before he comes around?"

"That depends on why he's unconscious," Alexa replied. "If he passed out from exhaustion or hypothermia, he should rouse soon. If he bumped his head when he fell, it could take longer." She brushed the ranger's hair back from his forehead, revealing a small gash. "Or maybe it's a combination of the two. From the looks of the blood on his shirt, this head injury happened a few hours ago."

Lettie gasped, and Alexa turned to her. "Don't worry, it doesn't look too deep. But will you heat up some canned soup? Once he wakes up we're going to need to feed him something warm and easy to digest."

Lettie went to the kitchen and found a can of chicken noodle soup. She was in no hurry to rejoin Gray and Alexa, so she took her time warming it in a small saucepan. Then she put the soup in a bowl and carried it into the dining hall. By the time she got there, the ranger was sitting up, drinking a bottle of water. When the water was gone, he collapsed against the couch. "Thank you!" he said with a gasp. "You folks have saved my life."

"That might be overstating the situation a little," Gray demurred.

"In my condition I wouldn't have been able to build a fire for myself," the ranger insisted. "So even though I made it this far, I'd have frozen to death."

"Why were you out in this weather?" Alexa asked.

"I was on patrol when I came around a corner and slammed into a car that was parked in the middle of the road." He paused for a deep breath before continuing. "That's how I hurt my head and broke my arm. Then I found the escaped convict—dead at the bottom of a cliff."

"Convict?" Lettie and Alexa said in unison.

"A guy named Mancil Bright escaped from a prison in western Tennessee yesterday," Gray explained. "Jack and I heard on the radio when we were driving up that his body had been found."

The ranger nodded. "That was me that found him."

"Well, good for you," Alexa told him with a smile.

"It's bad enough being trapped up here without an escaped convict on the loose!" Lettie agreed.

Alexa held her hands out for the bowl of soup. "Let me see if I can convince my patient to eat a few bites."

Lettie relinquished the bowl of soup to Alexa and took a seat on the other couch.

With Alexa's help, the young man managed several spoonfuls of the soup and his shivering decreased. "Very good," Alexa praised his efforts. "Now you can tell us your heroic story."

"The story isn't all that heroic," the ranger said modestly.

"Well then tell us your name," Alexa suggested.

"Penny." The man pointed at the name tag pinned to his shirt. "Lamar Penny."

After introductions were made, Alexa sat on the coffee table directly in front of their guest. "Okay, *now* tell us how you captured the convict."

"The car I hit was the one he'd stolen in Memphis." The ranger blushed. "Slick roads."

"The weather did get bad fast," Alexa said.

"The car was empty, so I went looking for the owner. Instead, I found the convict at the bottom of a cliff with a broken neck. Apparently he stepped off the edge in the dark."

"Where is he now?" Alexa asked.

"The captain told me to leave him there," Ranger Penny said. "I felt kind of bad, but . . ."

"Since he was already dead, leaving him there was the sensible thing to do," Gray said.

Ranger Penny seemed relieved. "The captain sent a rescue team after me, but they had to turn back. So he told me to come here until the weather clears, but I got lost."

"Well, you found us and now you're going to be fine." Alexa was obviously enjoying Ranger Penny and his account.

"Did you hurt your head when you hit the car?" Lettie asked.

"It's just a little cut," Ranger Penny downplayed his injury.

"A little cut that bleeds that much definitely needs to be cleaned," Alexa said, eyeing the blood on his shirt. She looked up at Gray. "Is there a first-aid kit here?"

He nodded. "I'll get it."

"And if you hit your head you could have a concussion," Alexa told the ranger. "That might be the reason you passed out on the front porch, so I'll have to watch you closely."

Ranger Penny gave her an adoring smile. "Thank you."

Gray returned with a professional-looking first-aid kit, and Alexa tended to the cut on the ranger's forehead. "You were lucky," she told Ranger Penny. "It isn't too deep."

Once she had finished cleaning and bandaging his head, the ranger leaned back against the couch and closed his eyes. "I lost my radio somewhere in the woods," he said. "Could one of you call the captain and let him know I made it?"

Alexa tucked the quilt more securely around his neck. "You try and rest. Gray will call your captain."

* * *

Jack sat beside Beth in the waiting area at the hospital, staring at the clock. When the surgeon had taken Lowell back to remove his appendix, he had said they should be finished by eight. It was now almost nine and Jack was starting to get worried. Mary Margaret had succumbed to exhaustion and was asleep on the plastic couch across from them. Finally Lowell's satellite phone rang, startling Beth and waking Mary Margaret.

"Who is it?" Mary Margaret asked, looking disoriented.

Jack pulled the phone from his coat pocket and stared at the numbers lined up on the screen. "I don't know," he said, "but I'm hoping it's Gray." He pressed ACCEPT.

"Jack?"

"Hello, Gray."

"How is Lowell?"

"He's still in surgery but should be coming out any minute." Jack decided not to mention the fact that the operation was taking longer than the doctor had predicted.

"You'll call me as soon as he's out of surgery?"

"I will," Jack promised. "How are things up there?"

"Okay I guess," Gray replied. "I just checked the forecast, and the National Weather Service is predicting another night of freezing temperatures, so the snow won't melt anytime soon."

"That's too bad," Jack commiserated.

"Yeah, well, at least we're safe and warm," Gray said, but he sounded disappointed. Jack heard a beep on the line and then Gray's voice cut back in. "Great," he said, now sounding exasperated. "The battery is low on my phone. I'm going to need to preserve it as much as possible. Could you make a call for me?"

"Sure," Jack agreed.

"That park ranger finally made it and we need to let Captain Woods know," Gray told him.

"I'll tell him," Jack promised.

"I'm going to keep my phone turned off to conserve the battery," Gray said. "So I guess you won't be able to call me about Lowell. I'll just check back with you in a little while."

* * *

Gray put more wood on the fire and then watched Ranger Penny sleep.

"Is he going to be okay?" he finally asked Alexa.

She nodded. "He warmed up quickly and that's a good sign. I couldn't tell about his arm. When I tried to examine it he screamed in pain, so I just taped it in place to keep it still and we'll let a doctor check it out later. And that cut on his head really is just a scratch."

"There's a lot of blood on his shirt," Gray pointed out.

Alexa shrugged. "Head wounds bleed." She stretched and turned to Lettie. "I'm about to wake him up. Is there any more of that soup?"

Lettie stood and moved toward the kitchen. "I can check."

Gray felt obligated to follow her and offer his assistance.

Lettie was staring at the cupboards when he walked in. She glanced over her shoulder and said, "There's no more chicken noodle. I've never eaten green pea or bean with bacon, but they sound equally awful."

"Given a choice, I'd take the bean with bacon," he said.

"We'll go with that glowing recommendation." Lettie removed a can from the cupboard, and Gray rinsed out the saucepan she'd used to heat up the chicken noodle. She made a face as she opened the can and poured it into the pan. "I hope it tastes better than it smells."

Gray smiled. "It has to."

They stood side by side and watched the soup heat up—not quite together, but not as far apart as they'd been when he first arrived.

"The ranger is awake. Do you have his soup ready?" Alexa asked from the doorway.

"I'm heating up bean and bacon paste," Lettie replied. "And if he doesn't like that we've got canned green goo."

Alexa frowned. "I guess it doesn't matter how it tastes as long as it's warm and nutritious."

Lettie turned off the flame under the saucepan and poured some of the soup into a bowl. "Well, it's warm anyway."

"Thanks," Alexa took the bowl and headed back into the dining hall.

Gray waited for Lettie to precede him and then followed.

* * *

Eugenia dozed off several times while waiting for Charlotte to return home. By eleven o'clock she was beginning to wonder if the woman's relationship with Whit had already progressed to the point of dates at nightclubs that lasted into the wee hours of the morning. Then she saw a new black 4Runner turn onto Sycamore Street. The vehicle pulled to a stop in front of Charlotte's house, and the senior center's new director climbed out.

Eugenia grimaced when she saw Charlotte's outfit—a shimmery silver number that accentuated her plastic-surgery–enhanced figure. As Charlotte climbed her porch stairs and pulled back the screen door, Eugenia squinted, hoping to see her reaction when she found the letter, but the angle was wrong. A wedge of light escaped from the house as Charlotte opened the door and disappeared inside.

Eugenia remained where she was for a few minutes—just in case Charlotte looked out her window and recognized her driving away. Finally she started her car and drove slowly down the street. She didn't turn on her headlights and remained slouched in her seat until she was two blocks away. Then she sat up straight, turned on her lights, and headed for home, confident in the knowledge that she had protected Whit from the evil Charlotte Sullivan.

* * *

"Are you in pain?" Alexa asked the ranger after he finished his second bowl of soup.

"Yes," he replied. "My head hurts and my arm is killing me."

"I have some medicine, but it will make you sleepy," Alexa warned.

Ranger Penny nodded. "I could probably use the rest."

"The medication is in my purse in the bedroom," Alexa told him. "I'll be right back."

Once in the bedroom she removed the prescription bottle from her purse. She shook two tablets into her palm and tried not to worry about her dwindling supply. There were only six pills left in her bottle, but they'd be leaving in a couple of days and she'd be able to get more. In the meantime, she'd cut back on her own dosage so she could share with the wounded ranger.

Gray was coming in with more firewood when she gave the medication to Ranger Penny. He popped both pills into his mouth and swallowed without the aid of any water. "Nice trick," she complimented him.

He smiled. "That's the first thing they teach you in ranger school."

Gray piled the wood by the fireplace and said, "Well, it finally stopped snowing. But I'm going to get one more load just to be sure we have enough to get us through the night."

Alexa nodded in approval. "We need to keep my patient warm."

Ranger Penny swung his legs over the side of the couch and placed his feet on the floor. "Is there a bathroom I can use?"

Alexa stood and moved to his side. "Of course. It's just through the kitchen." She put a hand on his elbow, but he was able to stand on his own. She led him to the bathroom and then asked, "Can you handle this alone or should we wait for Gray to come back?"

"I'll be fine," he assured her.

Alexa hated to leave him but didn't want to invade his privacy, so she went back to the dining hall just in time to see Lettie get up and walk over to the window. Alexa watched her stare outside for a few moments and then asked with a grin, "See anything interesting out there?"

Lettie blushed and stepped away from the window. "No."

Alexa raised an eyebrow. "Are you sure? Gray looks pretty interesting to me—not to mention gorgeous."

Lettie shook her head. "I've been down that road before."

"It might be worth a second try," Alexa suggested.

Before Lettie could reply, Ranger Penny spoke from the doorway. "Do you folks have any coffee?"

"There's some instant coffee in the cupboard," Lettie replied.

"But you don't want any coffee made by Mormons," Alexa assured him.

"Mormons?" the ranger repeated in obvious confusion.

"Lettie and I are both Mormons, and we don't drink coffee. So we've never learned how to make it. I tried once and nearly killed a coworker."

Ranger Penny smiled. "If you'll show me the jar of coffee and a pan where I can heat water, I'll make my own."

"And I'll follow you around in case you collapse." Alexa turned to Lettie. "Where is the coffee?"

"In the cupboard over the stove," Lettie replied. Then her eyes drifted back to the window.

Alexa walked to the kitchen and opened the cupboard above the stove. The coffee was right where Lettie had said it would be.

"Why don't Mormons drink coffee?" Ranger Penny wanted to know.

Alexa shrugged. "It's part of a health commandment. We don't drink coffee or tea or smoke tobacco or drink alcohol or take drugs." Alexa thought about the pain medicine she'd been abusing for the past month. "Unless it's medication prescribed by a doctor."

The ranger pointed at a can of Carnation Hot Cocoa Mix. "Can you have hot chocolate?"

She nodded. "Yes."

"Then why don't we make that instead of coffee so everyone can have some?"

"That's thoughtful of you." She removed the can of hot chocolate mix and put it on the counter. Then she reached behind him and got four mugs.

"What can I do to help?" he asked.

She glanced at his injured arm that she'd taped securely to his shirt. "Why don't you put a couple of scoops of hot chocolate mix in each mug while I heat the water?"

She handed him four spoons from the silverware drawer. Then she got out a saucepan and filled it with water while the ranger performed his task with diligence. When the water was boiling she carried it over and poured some into each mug. Then she emptied the leftover water into the sink, and Ranger Penny stirred the hot chocolate vigorously.

"Is there a tray we could use to carry this?" he asked.

"Somewhere," Alexa confirmed. "Mary Margaret and Lowell used one this morning." She only had to search a few cupboards before she found the tray she'd seen earlier. When she placed it on the counter, Ranger Penny put three of the four mugs on it one at a time, using his good arm. Once he was done, he lifted the last mug to his lips.

"Not as good as coffee," he said. "But not bad."

Alexa smiled and carried the tray into the dining hall.

Gray had just walked in from outside and gratefully accepted his cup of hot chocolate. "It's freezing outside." He took a couple of sips. Then he said to the ranger, "You must be feeling better."

"I am," Ranger Penny replied. "In fact, I'm feeling good enough to feel guilty about sitting around here when I should be out attending to my duties."

"With a bum arm you probably wouldn't be able to do much anyway," Gray pointed out.

"True," the ranger agreed as Alexa delivered a mug of hot chocolate to Lettie.

"Thanks," Lettie said.

Alexa removed the last mug from the tray and brought it to her lips. It was very hot, so she blew on it before taking a sip. Finally this became tedious, and she decided to let it cool. She set her mug on the coffee table and asked, "Well, what are we going to do for entertainment tonight? Anyone up for another game of Truth or Die?"

All color drained from Lettie's face and Alexa regretted her teasing words. "I'm kidding!" she promised.

Lettie didn't seem reassured. "I think I'm going to go lie down."

"Please stay," Alexa begged. "We won't play any games, but maybe Ranger Penny will tell us what it's like to be a park ranger. That sounds exciting."

"I'd love to hear your experiences another time," Lettie said politely to the ranger. "But tonight I'm too tired."

Ranger Penny nodded. "I understand completely."

"How are we going to handle sleeping arrangements?" Lettie asked.

"I figure you and Alexa can share one bedroom, and Ranger Penny and I will take the other one."

The ranger shook his head. "Actually, I'd rather stay by the fire. I'm fine with sleeping on the couch."

Alexa nodded her agreement. "And I have to stay with my patient. I've given him some strong pain medication that will make him drowsy, and since he might have a concussion, I'll need to wake him up regularly. We'll just stay here on the couches."

"I can sleep out here and wake him up," Gray offered.

"I'm sure I'll be okay," Ranger Penny tried.

"I'm the nurse and I can't transfer responsibility for my patient. So I'm going to stay up tonight." She turned to Gray. "You're welcome to stay with me and share the couch. Or you can take the other bedroom."

He smiled. "I guess I'll take the other bedroom."

"I'm in the one on the left of the bathroom," Lettie told him.

Alexa stood. "And my things are in the one on the right, but I'll come move them into Lettie's room."

Gray put up a hand to cover a yawn. "I think I'll go on to bed then." He stood and followed the women into the kitchen. "But if you need me, come get me."

"I will," Alexa promised. Once her things were moved to Lettie's room, she returned to the dining hall and settled down on the couch across from the ranger. "Now, tell me all about being a park ranger."

* * *

The phone was ringing when Eugenia returned from her letter delivery at Charlotte Sullivan's house. She seriously considered not answering it, which was a total departure from her normal practices. According to her mother's version of Southern etiquette, not answering the phone was as bad as not answering the door. Eugenia figured she'd broken one rule that day so she might as well break another.

Finally it was curiosity that made her pick up the phone, and she was glad she had. Kate's sister, Kelsey, was on the other end of the line.

"I declare, I was afraid you were another over-zealous church member calling to invite me to services on Sunday!"

Kelsey laughed. "No, I just wanted to find out what Mark said about Charlotte Sullivan."

"I decided not to bother Mark about that until he comes home," Eugenia replied. "He's so busy learning how to run the FBI and all."

"But I thought you were concerned about Mr. Owens's safety."

"I am," Eugenia confirmed. "And I've developed a little plan of my own. I've even consulted with a lawyer, Mr. Jack Gamble here in Haggerty. He's also a member of the Mormon Church."

"That's good," Kelsey said. "Because you wouldn't want to interfere with an ongoing investigation or taint any evidence that could eventually be used to convict Miss Sullivan."

Eugenia was sure that no investigation of Charlotte and her evil ways was under way and wasn't likely to be in the near future. And since her plan to get rid of Charlotte didn't involve a court case, she wasn't worried about tainting evidence. But to Kelsey she just said, "Thank you for that good advice, dear."

* * *

Alexa was floating in the worry-free state her pain medication always provided. But for the first time, the sensation wasn't pleasant. She felt uneasy and tried to fight the lethargy that she usually embraced. Instinctively she knew that she needed to wake up.

Finally she succeeded in opening one eye about halfway. Dazed and disoriented, she struggled to remember where she was and why. After a few seconds her memory returned. She was in the mountains on Mary Margaret's ill-fated reunion trip. She was supposed to be watching the injured ranger, but apparently she had fallen asleep. Her eye shifted to the other couch and found it empty.

With an effort she pushed herself into a semisitting position and managed to get both eyes partially open. A movement in the kitchen caught her eye, and she squinted enough to see Ranger Penny standing in front of the counter. Inexplicably, he was filling a backpack with canned goods from the cupboard. The medical tape she had so carefully wrapped around his arm to hold it in place was torn and hanging from the ranger's uniform shirt. And he didn't appear to be having any trouble at all using the arm that had been causing him so much pain earlier.

Alexa watched the ranger walk into the dining hall and cross the room to retrieve his coat from the hook by the fire.

"Ranger Penny?" Alexa whispered in confusion.

The ranger seemed surprised to see her awake. "I was trying to be quiet," he told her. "I didn't want to disturb you."

She rubbed her eyes and managed to get them completely open. "What are you doing?"

"I can't sit here when I know there are people stranded all over the park," he said. "Now that I'm warmed up and have my bearings, I'm going to walk to the nearest ranger station."

"Why don't you wait until the snow melts?" Alexa asked. "Or at least until it gets light?"

"By then the crisis will be over and they won't even need me," the ranger pointed out.

Alexa stared at the blood stain on the ranger's shirt, trying to process all the information through her muddled brain. "Did you tell your captain what you intend to do?"

Ranger Penny nodded. "I borrowed Gray's phone and called in. The captain was okay with it."

Alexa stretched her legs and wiggled her toes. "Well, if you're determined to go, I'll wake Gray and get him to go with you."

"No!" Ranger Penny declined her offer more sharply than seemed necessary. Then he smiled to soften his words. "He was sleeping soundly when I borrowed his phone, and I don't want to disturb him. Besides, I can't risk anyone else's safety."

She pointed at the hand holding the backpack. "You're using your right arm."

The ranger stretched out his fingers and then clenched them into a fist, flexing the arm for her inspection. "Yes. It's not hurting much anymore."

"That's amazing," she managed around a yawn. "A few hours ago just a little touch had you screaming."

"I guess that medicine you gave me helped," the ranger said. "Or maybe my elbow was just dislocated and worked itself back into joint. Anyway, I'm much better."

Alexa swung her legs over the side of the couch and stood. "I'd better get you a couple more pills to take with you in case it starts hurting again."

"I think I'll be okay," he said.

She waved this aside. "It's always best to be prepared."

The ranger stepped in front of her. "I don't want to have to go through this same argument with the others, so be careful not to wake them up."

Alexa nodded and moved around him. She walked through the kitchen and stopped by the bathroom to revive herself by splashing some cold water on her face. When she came out of the bathroom the ranger was standing near the door and followed her as she moved quietly into Lettie's bedroom. Her duffel bag and purse were on the bed where she had left them earlier. She picked them up and carried them into the kitchen.

Alexa placed her things on the counter and removed the prescription bottle from her purse. She twisted off the lid and stared at the empty bottle in disbelief. Earlier, when she had gotten two for the ranger, there had been six tablets left in the bottle. Now they were gone.

She looked back toward the bedroom. Did Lettie steal the pills in order to force her stop taking the medication? She squared her shoulders in preparation for a confrontation with her friend, but the ranger put a hand on her arm, redirecting her attention back to him.

"I took your pills," he said.

Alexa frowned at him in confusion. "You took eight pills?"

He shook his head. "I took them out of your purse, but I didn't *take* them," he clarified. "I dissolved them in the hot chocolate—all the cups except mine."

Alexa stared at him, struggling against the effects of the medication. "Why?"

"So I could leave without having to go through any explanations," he answered. "I knew you and your friends would try to stop me." He gave her a disapproving look. "I guess you didn't drink enough of your hot chocolate."

Alexa glanced down at the prescription bottle in her palm and blinked, realizing that she'd forgotten to take her usual two pills before bed last night. "I guess not." If she hadn't been so preoccupied with her patient, she might have taken a lethal dose of Lortab and never woken up. It was a sobering thought. She looked back at the man in front of her. "How did you know you weren't giving us a dangerous dosage?"

"I know about drugs," he replied. "It would have taken a lot more than eight pills to kill all three of you." He led the way into the dining hall.

She stopped abruptly. "Wait a minute. You didn't take the two pills I gave you last night? You added them to the hot chocolate too?"

He nodded and her eyes dropped to his right arm. "Then what happened to all the pain you were experiencing earlier?"

His fingers wrapped tightly around her wrist and he pulled her farther into the dining hall. He stopped beside the table where he had left the backpack full of food and swung it up onto his shoulder. "You ask too many questions."

Her mind was racing. There was so much blood on his shirt— more than was reasonable based on the small cut on his forehead. His arm was not broken—in fact it wasn't bothering him at all. She looked at the hand that held hers in a viselike grip. The cuff of his shirt hung several inches lower than it should. The shirt was too big, she realized. Then she dragged her eyes up to meet his. "You're not Ranger Penny, are you?"

"No," he confirmed.

"Then who are you?" she whispered.

"My name is Mancil Bright."

"Mancil Bright," she repeated. "You're the convict that's supposed to be *dead?*"

He shrugged in acknowledgment. "I planned to leave you all here asleep so that I'd be long gone before anyone noticed. Now you've ruined that plan."

"You're not going to kill us, are you?" Alexa asked.

He shook his head, and she felt faint with relief.

"No, I want the feds to forget about me. A bloodbath here in the mountains would just make them look harder."

His matter-of-fact tone while discussing mass murder chilled Alexa. "Just leave," she suggested. "I won't even wake the others! I'll sit here on the couch, and by the time Gray recovers from his drugged sleep you'll be long gone."

He shook his head. "I wouldn't trust anybody with my life, especially not a complete stranger."

She searched for another option. "You could tie me up."

"That won't work," he dismissed the idea. "Too risky. You'll have to come with me."

Alexa had never felt such pure terror before. Being with an escaped convict inside the warm lodge with Lettie and Gray nearby was frightening. But being alone with him in the woods was unimaginable. "Please, no," she begged.

"Believe me, I don't want to take you along, but since you didn't drink your hot chocolate, I don't have a choice," he said grimly. "My survival depends on me making good time, so you'll either keep up or freeze to death."

"I'll keep up," she said, hoping she could.

"And if you don't cooperate, I can always shoot you."

She nodded that she understood the dynamics of their relationship.

He pointed toward the coat closet. "Get on some warm gear. I've wasted too much time as it is."

When she was ready to go he held the door open for her and she slipped out into the night. As the cold air enveloped her she asked, "Did you kill the real Ranger Penny?"

"What do you think?" he replied.

She closed her eyes briefly and prayed for strength. Then she stepped off the porch and walked toward the woods with the convict close behind her. She took slim comfort from the fact that every step they took away from the lodge improved Lettie's and Gray's chances of survival. For the past month she had been looking for a purpose in what was left of her miserable life. Maybe she'd finally found one.

* * *

By the time Lettie woke up on Saturday morning, the sun was shining through the small window of her bedroom at the lodge. She checked her watch and saw that it was already ten o'clock. Amazed that boredom and misery had combined to make her sleep so long and hard, she stood and stretched. As she did so, her stomach growled, reminding her that she hadn't eaten much over the past couple of days. Hoping there was more than green pea soup for breakfast, she pulled fresh clothes from her duffel bag and went into the small bathroom.

Once she had sponge-bathed and dressed, Lettie looked around the kitchen. No breakfast awaited her, so she ventured into the dining hall and was surprised to find it empty. The fire had died out, so the room was uncomfortably cold. She was immediately irritated with Gray. It seemed like the least he could do was keep the fire going.

She crossed the room to poke at the blackened wood, hoping she would be able to locate a surviving spark. When she reached the fireplace and saw that both couches were empty, she frowned. It was possible that Gray had gone outside to collect wood so he could restart the fire, but it didn't make sense that Ranger Penny would go outside to help with a broken arm and a head injury. And where was Alexa?

Mildly alarmed now, Lettie walked over to the coat closet where they had stowed their backpacks and coats when they arrived on Thursday. Alexa's coat and ski pants were gone. Lettie's eyes swung back to the hook beside the fireplace where she'd hung Ranger Penny's coat to dry the night before. It was gone too.

With effort, she controlled the panic that welled inside her. There had to be a logical explanation. After crossing the room, she opened the front door and called outside. "Alexa! Ranger Penny!" There was no response, so she hurried through the dining hall and into the kitchen.

Lettie stopped in front of the door to the bedroom Beth and Alexa had shared the first night and stared at the scarred wood for a few seconds. If Gray was not inside that bedroom, then she was here all alone. If he was in the bedroom, the two of them were stranded together. She wasn't sure which would be worse.

Rallying her courage, Lettie lifted her hand and knocked on the door. There was no answer and her question was answered. Being alone was definitely worse than being with Gray.

She reached for the doorknob, and it turned easily under her hand. She pushed the door open and stepped inside.

Gray was asleep on one of the narrow beds. He was lying on his back, wearing the same insulated ski pants and thermal shirt from the day before. The blanket was tangled around him, his sock-covered feet were hanging off the end of the bed, and he was snoring softy. Given this opportunity to see without being seen, for a minute all Lettie could do was stare. He looked so helpless and warm and . . .

Lettie shook her head, forcing her thoughts from dangerous paths. Then she stepped up beside the bed. "Gray!"

His eyes flew open in surprise and confusion. When they focused on her, he whispered, "Lettie?" as if she was the last person he expected to see.

"You have to wake up!" she told him. "We're at the LeConte Lodge, remember?"

Gray pushed himself into a sitting position and ran his fingers through his unruly hair. "I remember now."

"Alexa and Ranger Penny are gone," she told him urgently.

Gray held up a hand. "Whoa, start over. Alexa and the ranger are *gone?*"

Lettie nodded. "I can't find them, and their coats are missing."

"Maybe they just went for a walk," Gray suggested.

Lettie gave him an incredulous look. "We couldn't even keep Alexa awake long enough to play a game of Scrabble, and the ranger is injured. Besides," she admitted, "I called for them, and they didn't answer."

"I guess a walk isn't a logical explanation." Gray swung his legs over the side of the bed and checked his watch. "It's after ten o'clock."

Lettie was irritated by this remark. "What does the time have to do with anything?"

"I never sleep in."

"We stayed up late," Lettie said impatiently. "That's why we slept in."

He pulled on the other boot and reached for his parka. "I stay up late a lot."

"Could we discuss your sleeping habits later?" Lettie couldn't hide her frustration. "We need to decide what to do."

Gray pushed his arms into his parka one at a time. "Maybe the ranger decided he was well enough to walk to a ranger station. If so, we'll have to hope he was right."

"What about Alexa?" Lettie asked. "Why would she go with him?"

"She seemed to take her responsibility as his nurse pretty seriously last night," Gray pointed out. "If he was determined to go she must have felt she had to go too."

Lettie shook her head. "That's not like Alexa. I know she seemed all selfless and dedicated to her patient last night, but really she's very self-centered, and she's definitely not an outdoorsy sort of person. I can't see her going for a walk in the woods ever—but especially not when it's dark and snowing." Lettie frowned. "And if they had decided to walk to a ranger station, why didn't Alexa wake us and share this plan or at least leave us a little note?"

Gray shrugged. "Let's go outside and see if we can find them."

He stood, overwhelming the small space with his size. She stepped back, but the room was too small for her to put an adequate amount of distance between them.

Their eyes met, and Lettie couldn't breathe for a few seconds. She finally managed to say, "I'll help you."

He nodded solemnly.

Lettie hurried into the dining hall and grabbed her coat out of the closet. Gray was waiting for her at the front entrance, and she joined him, still buttoning her parka. He stepped out onto the porch and put a hand up to shield his eyes. He called out several times, but his words just echoed back.

"I told you," Lettie said as she stepped out beside him.

"I had to try," he replied. Then he studied the snow-covered clearing between the LeConte Lodge and the woods that surrounded it. She followed the direction of his gaze. There was a series of footprints leading from the lodge entrance into the woods ahead of them.

"Is that the way they left?" Lettie asked, pointing at the broken snow.

"Yes," he confirmed. "And the way Ranger Penny approached the lodge last night." He pointed toward the stack of firewood. "Those prints going back and forth from the woodpile are mine."

Lettie rubbed her hand up her arms. "Speaking of which, the fire is out."

Gray nodded absently as he transferred his gaze to a set of footprints that led up close to one of the lodge windows. He walked over and knelt down for a closer look.

Reluctantly, Lettie followed him. "What's the matter?"

"These prints belong to just one person, and they are coming in toward the lodge from the woods." He glanced up at the window. "They stop here about ten feet away and then turn and go back to the woods."

She shivered more from fear than from cold. "Last night, I got the feeling someone was watching me at that window. It was just before Ranger Penny arrived, so I assumed it was him."

Gray pointed at the unbroken snow between the prints and the entrance. "If he looked in the window and saw us, why didn't he just cross over and walk to the entrance instead of walking back into the woods?"

Lettie shrugged. "I don't know, and I don't see how it's going to help us find Alexa and the ranger."

Gray stood and dusted snow from his hands. "I guess you're right." He stared at the prints for a few more seconds and then turned toward the lodge. "Let's talk about this inside where it's warmer."

She followed him into the lodge, but once they were in the dining hall, she pointed out that coming inside had been a waste of time. "Without a fire the room is so cold I can see my breath."

"At least we're out of the wind," Gray said as he searched closets, cupboards, and a little utility room behind the kitchen.

Finally she asked, "What are you looking for?"

"Things that are missing," he replied.

"Like what?"

"A tent, a sleeping bag, food, a backpack."

"Alexa and the ranger took them?"

Gray nodded. "Which pretty much rules out the nature-walk theory."

"So they're walking to the ranger station?"

"I guess," Gray agreed, although he didn't look completely comfortable with the conclusion. "I can't think of any other reason they would have taken camping gear."

Lettie's eyes settled on the kitchen counter. "There's Alexa's purse." She walked over and quickly looked through the contents. "Her prescription bottle is empty—so she took her supply of medication with her."

"She might have taken them to give to the ranger for his arm," Gray said.

Lettie didn't argue the possibility, but she knew how dependent Alexa was on those pills. "Alexa is not thinking clearly." She glanced out the window at the snow-covered landscape. "Obviously." Then she turned to Gray. "So now what?"

"We're going to call the ranger station and tell them that we think Ranger Penny and Alexa are on the way to Greenbriar. That way if they don't arrive soon, the rangers can go look for them," Gray said as he pulled his satellite phone from a pocket of his coat. He pressed a few buttons and then frowned.

"What's wrong now?" Lettie asked in exasperation.

"The battery is dead. It was low yesterday, so I turned it off to conserve the battery. Or I thought I did . . ." He looked over at her. "Do you have a cell phone?"

"Yes," she responded. "But I can't get service up here."

"Great," he muttered.

"You have a fancy phone like that and no charger?" she asked, pointing at the phone in his hand.

"I have a charger," Gray corrected. "But when Jack came to the office yesterday, we left in such a rush that I didn't think to bring it with me. I wasn't planning on being up here so long."

Lettie rubbed her temple where a headache was forming. "So what if Ranger Penny and Alexa are lost? Or what if he's passed out and she can't move him? Are we just going to let them freeze to death?"

Gray looked annoyed and said, "I'll think of something."

"Well, you'd better hurry." Lettie took a deep breath and commanded herself to remain calm. Then a thought occurred to her. "Where is Lowell's phone?"

"I gave it to Jack," Gray said.

She was appalled by this. "They had phones!"

"But I wasn't sure they'd be able to get service in all parts of the park," Gray explained. "So I gave them Lowell's satellite phone."

"Which left us with *no* phone!"

"At the time I didn't realize mine was dead or that a wounded park ranger would decide to walk through the woods with your friend," he defended himself.

This remark only served to infuriate her more. "You have to plan for the unexpected! It's what responsible business owners do!"

"I had my phone," Gray bit out. "And this was Lowell's trip, not mine. If you want to yell at someone, yell at him."

"I will," Lette assured him. "The first chance I get." She dragged her eyes from his and began to pace in front of the cold fireplace, as much to keep warm as to facilitate constructive meditation. Finally the pacing paid off. She turned back to him and said, "Since this was Lowell's trip, maybe he packed his charger."

Gray smiled and her heart pounded. "Let's find out."

They walked to the closet where the gear was stowed, and Gray searched Lowell's backpack. "Here it is!" he said triumphantly as he pulled the charger from the pack.

Lettie's relief was so intense that if he'd been anyone but Gray, she would have kissed him. "Hurry and plug it in so you can make a call to the ranger station."

Gray gave her a bland look. "I know who to call." He pulled his phone from his coat pocket and moved toward the wall outlet. Then he stopped suddenly. "The electricity's out," he said. "We can't charge the phone here."

Lettie collapsed into a chair. "Now what?"

"The charger has an adapter that can be plugged into the lighter in a car. I'll take my phone down to Lowell's Jeep and call the ranger station from there."

"That means walking over a mile through the snow," Lettie clarified.

Gray put the phone and the charger into his coat pocket. "Unless you've got a better idea?"

"I used up my good idea when I thought of Lowell's charger, so I guess we'll have to go with your less-than-good idea."

He started buttoning his parka. "I'll be back as soon as I can."

Lettie pulled on her gloves. "You're not leaving me here alone!"

"It's freezing outside," he reminded her. "And Lowell's Jeep is over a mile away."

Lettie nodded grimly. "I know."

"I can move faster on my own," Gray added to his list of objections.

"I'll try not to hold you back too much," she muttered.

He sighed, apparently giving up the fight. "Did you wear ski pants on the way up here?"

"Yes."

"I'll wait while you get them on," he said with an impatient look toward the door.

When she was dressed in her cold weather gear, he examined her critically for a few seconds. Then he leaned over and cinched the strings around the hood of her parka. "Keep this tight," he told her. "You can lose a lot of body heat through your head if you don't keep it properly covered."

She nodded, hoping that the heat rising in her cheeks was from her irritation at his assumption that she was an imbecile and not a result of his glancing touch.

Gray emptied Lowell's backpack and refilled it with bottles of water and a blanket that looked like it had once belonged to a horse. Then he stood and hooked the straps of the pack over his shoulders. "Let's go."

With deep trepidation, Lettie followed him out of the lodge and into the woods.

The hike across the snow-covered ground was harder than she had expected, and she wanted to cry with joy when Lowell's Jeep finally came into view. Gray opened the passenger door and she climbed in—trying to keep her teeth from chattering. He walked around, slid under the wheel, and plugged the charger in. Then he turned on the phone, but nothing happened.

"The battery might be weak after sitting here in the cold," he said. "Lowell keeps a spare key under here somewhere." He reached under the seat and a moment later he held up the key. He inserted it into the ignition and turned it, but the Jeep didn't start. He slammed the heel of his hand against the steering wheel in a rare show of anger.

"The Jeep's battery is dead *too?*" Lettie guessed.

"Probably," Gray admitted. "I'll check under the hood and see if I can find a loose cable or something. You wait here."

Gray opened his door and climbed out of the Jeep. Lettie did the same and met him at the front.

He seemed annoyed when he saw her. "I thought I told you to stay inside."

She raised an eyebrow. "First of all, you don't *tell* me what to do. And second, it's warmer out here than it is in that frozen Jeep."

She noticed that his jaw was clenched again as he handed her the worthless phone. "Will you hold this?"

"As long as you're not *telling* me to hold it," she agreed conditionally.

He shot her an impatient look before opening the hood. He examined the battery connections and the cables for a few minutes. Finally he stepped back. "I can't fix it."

Fatigue and hunger and old resentments overwhelmed Lettie and she lashed out at him. "I'd like to know exactly what it is you *can* do! You can't plan ahead, you can't remember to charge your phone, you can't fix a car." She waved at the Jeep. "Do you ever even take it in for routine maintenance?"

"This is Lowell's Jeep, not mine," he began, but she cut him off.

"If you'd stayed in college instead of dropping out to play tour guide in the woods . . ."

"Lettie," he interrupted sharply.

"Don't you 'Lettie' me!" she yelled. "How could you have been so stupid?"

"Stupid?" he repeated.

"That's the best word I can think of to describe a tour guide who leaves without charging his phone and has no backup plan for emergencies!"

"I've already explained that." Now he was as mad as she was.

"I'm tired of listening to your excuses," she fumed. "You're supposed to be a *professional.* You take people's lives into your hands when you bring them up here. And because of your irresponsible behavior, Alexa is probably going to die!"

"Alexa is probably already at the Greenbriar Ranger Station drinking hot chocolate and flirting with the park rangers," Gray yelled back.

Lettie swiped at the tears that spilled out of her eyes onto her cheeks. What she really wanted to say was, "You broke my heart and somehow you should have to pay," but instead she settled for, "You just wanted to impress Jack with your fancy satellite phone. That's why you gave Lowell's phone to him even though he and Beth *both* had phones that worked!"

"That's not true!" Gray denied the accusation.

"Well, here's what I think about you and your fancy, worthless phone!" Lettie hurled Gray's phone across the road and over an embankment. She expected this vengeful action to give her some satisfaction, but all she felt was empty and sad.

Gray watched in speechless horror as the phone that had cost him nearly a thousand dollars sailed through the air and into the ravine across the road. He ran to the guard rail and looked over the edge. All he could see were rocks and debris covered with snow. He flexed his hands several times until the urge to strangle Lettie passed. Then he turned back to face her.

"Why did you throw my phone into that gulley?" he asked through clenched teeth.

"Because it's worthless," she replied, but the anger she had displayed a minute before was gone. "What's the point of carrying around a phone that won't work?"

"I don't plan to be in these woods away from a charger forever," Gray told her. "And even though I couldn't use the phone to call anyone, it had GPS. That means it could be used to help locate us if we get lost while we're out looking for your friend and the ranger."

Lettie frowned. "I thought you said Alexa was probably at the Greenbriar station."

"We can't be sure," Gray replied grimly. "And since we can't call anyone to check on them, we'll have to follow their tracks."

She looked mildly repentant, but Gray figured this was probably just because she now realized her rash behavior had put her in danger—not because she'd cost him an expensive phone.

"If I climb over the ledge maybe I can find it," she offered half-heartedly.

"Or maybe you'll break your neck, which will give me more problems instead of less," he said. Then he took pity on her. "Don't worry about the GPS. I won't get lost."

With one last remorseful look toward the ravine, Lettie asked, "How far will we have to go?"

Gray gazed out at the trees that surrounded them. "The Greenbriar station is only about two miles from the lodge."

Lettie's expression brightened. "That doesn't sound too bad."

"Well, it's pretty bad," Gray informed her. "Before we can even head out after Alexa, we have to go back to the lodge and pick up their trail. Otherwise if they're lost, we won't find them. So that adds another mile to our trip. And with all this snow *three* miles will take us several hours. In case we don't find them and make it to the Greenbriar station by dark, we'd better take some of the emergency supplies from the back of Lowell's Jeep."

He walked behind the disabled vehicle. Lettie followed him and watched as he opened the hatch. He pulled out two tents, a first-aid kit, two backpacks, a flashlight, and some MREs. He stacked the supplies on the snow and then began putting things into the backpacks.

Lettie peered into the Jeep. "You had all that stuff just in case of an emergency?"

He reached into the Jeep again, and she was very close to him. He breathed in the smell of her shampoo and whispered, "It's one of the few responsible decisions we made."

Lettie cleared her throat and stepped back. "That does sound pretty responsible," she allowed with a ghost of a smile. "However, I suggest that in the future you keep a backup phone with your emergency gear."

Gray nodded. "I'll buy a couple as soon as I get back." He put a light load in a small pack for Lettie and handed it to her. Then he put everything else is his pack and strapped it on his back. "So, are you ready?"

"As ready as I'll ever be," she murmured.

He reached into the Jeep and pulled Lowell's gun out of the glove compartment. When he glanced up, Lettie was regarding him with wide eyes.

"What is that for?" she asked.

"Emergencies," he responded vaguely. Then he headed back toward the woods, and she fell into step behind him.

CHAPTER 10

On Saturday morning Eugenia waited until ten o'clock before driving down Sycamore Street to find out how successful her plan had been. She hoped to see Mr. Bell's 4Runner pulling away from Charlotte's rental house with a U-Haul trailer attached to the back. However, she knew it might take Charlotte a few days to get all her things together, so she prepared herself to find only signs of a move in the near future. Maybe a few boxes stacked on the porch, or a For Rent sign in the yard.

But when Eugenia reached Charlotte's address, all was quiet, and the 4Runner was parked right where Charlotte had left it the night before. Wondering if the woman knew how to read, Eugenia returned home.

Polly was watering the hanging ferns on her porch when Eugenia pulled up. "Good morning!" Polly put down her watering can and joined Eugenia on the driveway.

"I don't know if I think it's a good morning or not," Eugenia replied as she led the way through her back door and into the kitchen. "Charlotte Sullivan hasn't budged."

"You gave her your letter?" Polly confirmed.

Eugenia nodded. "Yes, I delivered it myself last night. I even sat in my car and watched her house until she got back from the senior center so I'd know for sure she got it."

"Well, I don't know what to make of that," Polly said. "I certainly wouldn't stay in a town where someone knew I was a murderer."

Eugenia picked up a plate of fresh tea cakes and put them on the table. "Have one," she invited.

Polly picked out a cookie and took a bite. "Oh, these are delicious," Polly complimented. "Very moist."

"Thank you," Eugenia returned absently.

"Did you actually see Charlotte?" Polly asked, reaching for a second tea cake.

"No," Eugenia replied. "But her car is parked in front of her house."

"Maybe the letter scared her so bad that she packed a bag and took a bus out of town."

As much as this suggestion appealed to Eugenia, she doubted it was true. "I'll just have to wait until tonight when I can go to the senior center and see for myself."

"I could go over to her house right now," Polly offered.

"That's kind of you, Polly, but the whole point of writing an anonymous letter was to keep our identities secret."

"I wouldn't have to ask about the letter," Polly said. "I could pretend like I was stopping by to invite her to church tomorrow. I might even be able to see inside her house and tell if she's packing boxes."

"Hmmm," Eugenia considered this. "That's not a bad idea. Goodness knows there have been a lot of church invitations issued around here lately."

"I'll go right now," Polly offered. "I'll tell Charlotte that I'm visiting all the new folks in town this morning. And I won't be lying because there aren't any other new people in town besides her!"

"Okay," Eugenia agreed. "I'll drive you to the end of Cypress, and then you can walk around the corner and up to her door."

Eugenia parked her old Buick behind Vivian May's hedges and watched as Polly walked up to Charlotte's house. Her nemesis answered the door and invited Polly inside. Eugenia waited anxiously, her cell phone handy so she could call Winston if she heard Polly screaming. A few minutes later Polly emerged from the house. Charlotte stepped out on the porch and waved good-bye. Eugenia slumped further down in her seat to keep Charlotte from seeing her.

When Polly slipped in through the passenger door, Eugenia drove down Cypress and turned back toward town. "Well?" she said to Polly. "Did it look like she was packing to leave?"

"Oh no! She said she loves Haggerty and plans on staying here a long time," Polly reported. "And I saw the letter! It was on top of her television for all the world to see. I asked her if it was a love letter. Wasn't that clever?"

"Very," Eugenia replied. "What did she say?"

"She said, 'In a manner of speaking,'" Polly quoted. "Don't you think that was an odd thing to say?"

"I think everything about Charlotte Sullivan is odd," Eugenia muttered.

"I can't believe she's going to stay here, knowing her secret is out," Polly said.

"She's going to stay because she knows we don't have any proof," Eugenia said bitterly. "There's nothing illegal about marrying old men and inheriting their money when they die as long as they die of natural causes. And since Whit is determined to take her word over mine . . ."

"You'll just need to find proof that she killed them," Polly said. "Even a lawyer like Whit can't ignore cold hard evidence."

"Jack said a full confession is all that will convict her in a court of law."

"But she'll never confess!" Polly sounded sure.

"Not on purpose," Eugenia said as they parked in her driveway. "But what if I took Derrick's little tape recorder and hid it in my purse. Then if I could convince her to tell me about Mr. Bell . . ."

"Do you really think she'd confess to a crime?" Polly asked.

Eugenia shrugged. "She might. I don't pose any danger to her since she thinks I don't have any proof."

Polly wrinkled her forehead in dismay. "But Eugenia, you *don't* have any proof."

"I will when she admits everything and I have it on tape!"

Polly clapped her plump hands together. "Oh, you are so smart! What excuse could you use for setting up a meeting with Charlotte?"

"I haven't thought of a good excuse yet," Eugenia admitted.

"You could say you want to talk to her about the new senior center."

Eugenia shook her head. "No, it will have to be a more compelling reason than that." She remembered Annabelle's suggestion that she pose as Whit's old girlfriend and smiled. "I'll say that I need to talk to her about Whit. That should intrigue her."

"Where will you ask her to meet you?"

"It can't be anywhere public like a restaurant since that might inhibit her desire to confess," Eugenia thought out loud. "It will have to be some place where she feels completely secure so she won't be suspicious."

"How about the senior citizen center?" Polly suggested.

Eugenia nodded. "That's perfect. I'll call and ask if she'll meet with me tonight at the senior center after all the activities are over. To break the ice I'll tell her that Whit is all I have and beg her to step aside." Eugenia grimaced as she spoke. It was difficult enough to say such humiliating words when Polly was her only audience. And she knew saying them to Charlotte was going to be much worse.

"Do you think she will?" Polly asked.

"Will what?"

"Step aside," Polly clarified.

"Of course not." Eugenia was sure about this. "But the more pitiful I seem, the bigger my advantage because she'll underestimate me."

"Will you tell her that you spoke to Mr. Bell's nephew and wrote the anonymous letter?"

Eugenia nodded. "I don't see any way around that."

"What if she grabs you by the neck and tries to strangle you?" Polly asked in alarm.

Eugenia smiled. "I should be able to ward her off. After all, I'm twice her size."

"You're right. If she decides to kill you, she'll probably use a more subtle method—like poison."

Eugenia gave Polly a bland look. "That's a comfort."

The sarcasm was lost on Polly. "I know!" she cried with enthusiasm. "I'll sit out in your car while you're talking to Charlotte so I can be your witness!"

Eugenia laughed. "I declare, Polly, you're full of surprises today."

"So you'll let me go?"

"I'd be grateful to have your support."

"Oh, my." Polly pulled the lace handkerchief from the neckline of her dress. "I feel just like a real detective!"

* * *

It seemed to Lettie like they had been walking for hours by the time they reached the clearing in front of the LeConte Lodge again. She stared longingly at the only shelter for miles, imagining how good it would feel to be sitting in front of a blazing fire.

Gray must have noticed the direction of her gaze because he said, "I wish we had time to go up to the lodge and thaw out, but they've already got a big head start on us."

Lettie nodded as she fell into step behind him. "Even a hot bowl of green pea soup sounds pretty good to me at the moment."

He smiled over his shoulder. "I'm glad to see that you've still got your sense of humor."

Her sense of humor *and* the feeling in her extremities were gone by the time he stopped for lunch. "You look half frozen," he told her.

"Only half?" she replied. "Then I'm hiding my misery well."

He helped her take off her pack and set it on the ground. "We're making pretty good time, so I think we can invest a few minutes in building a small fire."

She was sure there had to be a catch. "You're not going to make me collect buffalo chips first are you?"

He laughed. "If you find any buffalo chips, we're certainly not going to burn them! I don't know if there were ever any buffalo here, but I'm sure there haven't been any in a couple hundred years. So buffalo chips found here would belong in a museum."

She raised an eyebrow. "So you're saying I don't have to look for any."

He laughed again. "That's what I'm saying. Have a seat on your pack."

He used his boot to scrape snow and the underlying dead leaves from a spot of ground. Then he pulled a small square piece of presswood out of his pack and struck a match. He put the match on the wood and it ignited.

Lettie stared at the tiny blaze "You weren't kidding when you said we were going to have a *small* fire."

"This is just the starter," he explained. "I'll look around for some dry wood." He moved toward the woods. "Or buffalo chips."

She rolled her eyes as he walked away.

He returned a few minutes later with a handful of sticks. He piled the sticks on his starter fire. "They don't teach you how to do that in college," he pointed out. "Lucky for you I do have a few practical skills."

"Yes, lucky me," she muttered.

"While you get warm we'll have lunch. You can choose from several delicious MREs."

"What are MREs?" Lettie forced herself to ask.

"Meals Ready to Eat," Gray replied. "They aren't known for being tasty, but they'll keep us from starving."

She held her hands out to absorb the minimal heat coming from the pile of burning sticks. "Great."

He opened his backpack and pulled out two packets. He pulled the top off one and offered it to Lettie. She surveyed the prepackaged food, but didn't recognize anything.

"What is it?" she asked.

He pointed at the various sections. "This is chili with macaroni, these are wheat crackers, and this is pound cake." He lifted the tray closer to his nose and sniffed a yellowish substance. "I think this might be squash, but I can't guarantee it."

"I can't eat that," she said with a shudder. "It's disgusting."

"It's the best you're going to find out here," he told her. "If you don't eat you won't have the strength to walk. And if you can't walk, we'll never find Alexa."

With a sigh, Lettie held out her hand. "Give me the other one. It can't be worse than chili with macaroni."

She squatted close to the fire while she ate what the package proclaimed to be a veggie burger. It wasn't good, but it did fill her stomach. There were also a little section of applesauce that tasted better and a pack of saltine crackers that were almost delicious.

Gray put a bite of the yellow substance from his MRE into his mouth. He analyzed it for a few seconds before nodding. "Definitely squash."

"Ugh," Lettie responded.

After she was finished eating, Gray collected all their garbage. Then she watched in astonishment as he put the garbage bag into his pack.

"You're taking the trash with us?" she asked.

He glanced up from his task. "You're not much of a camper, are you?"

She shook her head.

"There's no garbage pickup out here, so all *responsible* people take their trash with them."

Lettie nodded. "And we both know how big you are on responsibility."

He laughed. "Exactly. Now I've got to douse this fire."

Lettie looked down at the black sticks. "That shouldn't take long."

She dropped her nose down into the top of her coat and breathed the slightly warmer air as she watched him smother the little fire with snow. Then he stamped it thoroughly and checked to be sure all the embers were cold and wet.

When he was satisfied that the fire was completely out, he pulled on his pack. "I hate to say this, but we've got to go."

She stood and Gray helped her to get her pack back on. "I'm sorry that I threw your phone over that cliff," she forced herself to say. "I'll pay to replace it."

"That's okay," Gray replied generously. "The dealer will probably give me a good price when he finds out that I need two more for emergencies."

"When you negotiate your deal on the new phones, I have only one suggestion."

He raised an eyebrow, waiting for her to continue.

"Be sure and get extra batteries."

He smiled. "I definitely will."

She smiled back automatically before she could stop herself.

* * *

Jack and Beth spent the night at the Best Western near Gatlinburg. They were awakened a little before noon on Saturday morning by Jack's cell phone. He reached for it after giving Beth a reassuring smile. She didn't smile back but watched anxiously, as if expecting bad news of one kind or another.

"This is Jack."

"Brother Gamble?" a female voice responded. "This is Kelsey Pearce. My sister is Kate Iverson."

"Yes, Kate's mentioned you several times." To Beth, he mouthed, "It's Kate Iverson's sister, Kelsey." He then pulled Beth's head against his shoulder as he continued the conversation. "What can I do for you?"

"Miss Eugenia told me that you were providing legal advice on the case she's trying to build against Charlotte Sullivan, and I just wanted to touch base with you to be sure all the evidence is collected legally. I'd hate for Miss Sullivan to get off on a technicality."

For a few seconds Jack was too surprised to reply. Finally he said, "Miss Eugenia did tell me about Charlotte Sullivan, but I definitely didn't agree to provide legal advice." He stopped. "Not officially, anyway," he amended. "I'm a state senator and can't be involved in a criminal case, since that would be a conflict of interest."

"Oh," Kelsey sounded surprised as well. "I'm sorry for disturbing you then."

Jack stifled a yawn. "You didn't disturb me," he lied. "And in my *unofficial* opinion the FBI should look into Miss Sullivan and her marriage-for-money schemes. But that's something you'll need to talk to Mark about."

"Actually I think I'll just leave it to Miss Eugenia," Kelsey replied. "Thanks again."

After Jack disconnected the call, Beth asked, "What did Kate's sister want?"

Jack slid down so that his face was right beside hers. "There's this woman who just moved to Haggerty named Charlotte Sullivan. Miss Eugenia called me about her yesterday. Apparently she travels around the country looking for old men she can marry. When they die she inherits their assets."

"Why is Miss Eugenia involved?" Beth asked.

"Because Charlotte Sullivan's newest victim is Miss Eugenia's boyfriend, Whit Owens. And besides, Miss Eugenia thinks the woman kills her husbands so she can inherit more quickly."

Beth gasped. "Well, that is a reason to worry!"

"I advised Miss Eugenia to talk to Mark Iverson about it when he gets back from Atlanta. Kelsey has compiled a report of Miss Sullivan's misdeeds and had the mistaken impression that I was going to give the FBI legal advice on the case."

Beth smiled. "That's Miss Eugenia's wishful thinking."

"Well, it's not happening," he assured her. Then he opened his phone again. "I'm going to call the hospital and get a report on Lowell."

Jack talked to Mary Margaret, who said Lowell was improving and they didn't need to rush about getting back to the hospital. "Well, that's good news," he said as he closed his phone. "If we don't have to hurry to the hospital, we can enjoy a leisurely lunch here in the room and then watch some television. I've lost touch with what's going on in the world."

Beth reached for the room service menu and handed it to him. "Call and order lunch before you get involved in world events so I don't starve to death while you worry about problems you can't solve."

Jack ordered lunch, and when the tray arrived, Beth studied it critically.

"Don't you see anything that looks good to you?" he asked as he used the remote to turn off the television.

"Everything looks fine," she replied, but he noticed that she only put a few pieces of fruit on her plate.

"Aren't you going to eat?" she asked.

"Definitely." He stretched his arms above his head and yawned.

Beth popped a plump strawberry into her mouth. "What's the weather forecast?"

"Continued cold today, but a warming trend tomorrow," Jack told her.

Beth sighed. "Lettie and the others won't be coming down the mountain today then."

"Maybe tomorrow," Jack tried to sound hopeful. He walked over to the room service tray and put some of everything onto a plate.

When they were finished eating, Jack collected the plates and stacked them on the tray. Then he said, "I guess we'd better get cleaned up and go back to the hospital."

"I guess," Beth replied, fidgeting with her plastic fork.

"I'm going to take a shower." Jack zipped open his overnight case and pulled out some clean clothes.

"Wait," Beth requested, and he looked up in surprise. "Come over here for a minute," she requested.

He put down his clothes and sat beside her on the edge of the bed. "You want to take your shower first?"

"No."

She took both of his hands in hers, and his heart started to pound. "Is there something wrong?"

"No," she repeated. "But there is something I need to tell you."

She had his undivided attention. "It's not bad news, I hope."

"Actually, it's kind of good news and bad news," she said. "Which would you like first?"

"Definitely the bad news."

She took a deep breath and said, "I hate the idea of you getting *more* involved in politics."

He relaxed. "Is that all? If the governor thing is a problem for you, I'll tell Mr. Fuller not to nominate me. I don't know why I ever let him talk me into running for public office in the first place."

Beth didn't look relieved. "I appreciate that, but it's not fair for me to limit you. If you really want to pursue a career in politics . . ."

"What I really want is to spend more time with you and the kids," Jack assured her. "I feel obligated to do what I can to make the world a better place. But there are other ways to do that besides politics." He leaned down until their noses were touching. "Now it's time for the good news."

She put her hands on both sides of his face and looked into his eyes. He waited and finally she said, "I'm going to have another baby."

Words failed him, so he pulled her against his chest and stroked her hair. Unbidden, memories of the day he found out he was going to be a father for the first time came to his mind. His first wife, Monique, didn't want to go through with the pregnancy and said she wasn't even sure that the baby was his. Under those circumstances, he couldn't enjoy the prospect of parenthood. But now he was glad that he'd had that painful experience, since it gave him perspective and made him appreciate Beth more.

"I'm so thankful that this new child will have you for a father."

"Sometimes I feel so inadequate," he whispered into her hair.

"You're a great husband and father."

"I want to be," he said earnestly.

"You are wonderful, if a little obsessive," she added.

"I won't deny it." His heart felt lighter than it had in years. He knew his happy mood was mostly a result of the baby news. But he had to admit that the thought of being free of his political responsibilities was also appealing. "When my senate term expires maybe we can sell our house in Haggerty and move to an iceberg in Alaska," he said wistfully. "Nobody would bother us there."

She laughed. "I can see it now. We'll have a huge igloo with a twelve-foot security fence made from blocks of ice and topped with sharp icicles."

He frowned at her. "Are you making fun of me?"

"Just a little," she admitted. "On an iceberg all we'd have to worry about is the kids freezing to death or falling off into the sub-zero water. And, of course, you'd have to deliver the new baby since there wouldn't be any doctors . . ."

"Whoa!" he held up both hands. "I surrender. We won't move to Alaska."

She kissed him. "Good. I've had enough cold weather to last me a while. But I have been thinking about something." She looked away as if she was embarrassed. "I didn't mention it because it didn't seem like a possibility, but if you're really considering a career change . . ."

"What?" Jack demanded.

"Well, I was talking to my father a couple of weeks ago, and he was telling me about this boys' ranch that Cole Brackner has started." She glanced up at him. "You remember Cole? You met him and his wife Sydney at my parents' house last Christmas."

He nodded. "I remember them. He's nice and she's kind of a smart aleck."

"You *do* remember them," she praised him with a smile. "Anyway, Cole's family used to own a huge farm, but after his mother died he had to sell most of it to give his sisters their inheritance. The developer who bought the land went bankrupt and the land is on the market again. Cole would like to buy it and expand his boys' ranch, but in order to do that he'd need an investor."

"Are you suggesting that we give Cole Brackner money to buy land for his ranch?"

She shrugged. "You could do that. It's certainly a worthwhile cause."

"But . . ." he prompted.

"But it would be even better if you became more like a partner. You could use all your contacts to help raise the money Cole needs. And you could use your administrative skills to run the business side of the ranch while Cole handles the farming end of things. Imagine the fun you'd have making sure all the boys' houses were well built, installing state-of-the-art security systems and miles of safe chain-link fencing."

Jack chose to ignore her teasing and asked, "Would we build a house for ourselves near the ranch property?"

"We could." Beth sat up, obviously warming to the topic. "We'd be the only farmhouse in Georgia with a security fence. And to help the house blend in with the farming community, we could use pitchforks along the top instead of barbed wire. Or maybe . . ."

Jack smiled. "Okay, I get the idea. What makes you think that Cole Brackner would welcome my involvement in his boys' ranch expansion?"

"Because my father said Cole had mentioned you to him specifically."

Jack considered it for a few seconds and then nodded. "I'll give it some thought."

"Really?" she seemed pleased.

"Really."

She leaned over and kissed him. "I can't believe it."

He pulled her close. "Kiss me again and there's no telling what I'll agree to."

She laughed and slid off the bed. "I won't take unfair advantage of you." She opened her suitcase. "But I will take the first shower, since you offered."

He leaned back against the hotel pillows. "It's a good thing you don't take advantage of people."

She nodded. "And *you* can take advantage of this free time to check on the kids. It's been at least fifteen minutes since your last call."

* * *

It was midafternoon before Mancil stopped for lunch. Alexa collapsed onto the ground and watched as he dug some energy bars out of his pack. He extended one to her and she ate it gratefully.

Anxious to extend the break, Alexa asked, "How long had you been in prison before you . . . left?"

"Six years," he replied.

"Was it terrible?"

He glanced up. "It was pretty bad."

"How did you stand it?"

"Everybody dealt with prison life in different ways. Some guys turned to drugs, others to exercise, some to violence. Me, I chose gardening."

"Gardening?" Alexa asked in surprise.

"Yeah. My mom always grew vegetables when I was a kid, and she taught me the basics, but I found out I have kind of a talent for it. I've done lots of gardens all over western Tennessee."

She was impressed. "You must be very good at it."

He nodded. "I am."

She hated to make him angry, now that they were being friendly, but she felt that she had to ask, "Why were you in prison?"

"I killed my stepfather," Mancil replied without emotion.

Alexa swallowed hard. "Why?"

Mancil didn't answer right away, and Alexa realized that he might not want to talk about this.

"That is, if you don't mind telling me," she added.

Mancil shrugged. "I don't mind. My stepfather was an okay guy most of the time—dumb, but harmless. I learned early, though, to stay out of his way when he'd been drinking. One day I came home in the middle of one of his drinking binges. He wouldn't stop hitting me, so I shot him."

Alexa pulled her legs up so she could rest her chin on her knees. "That sounds like self-defense to me."

"Yeah," he agreed.

"Then why did you have to go to prison?"

"Because I also shot three cops. When one died the next day, my fate was sealed."

This was unfathomable to Alexa. "Why did you shoot at the police?"

"I'd been in trouble with the cops before and didn't have any reason to trust them or to think they'd believe me. My stepfather was lying there dead, and I figured my only hope was to shoot my way out."

"Surely you realized that eventually you were going to have to give yourself up."

He shook his head. "No, I never remember thinking that. I was just a stupid kid."

"And the judge didn't take that into account?"

"He did," Mancil replied. "That's why I didn't get a death sentence."

"Oh," Alexa whispered.

He stood and slung the backpack over his shoulder. "Enough talking. We've got to get going."

* * *

Jack was relieved to find Lowell recuperating nicely when he and Beth finally arrived at the hospital on Saturday afternoon. Lowell was in a small private room and Mary Margaret was sitting in a chair by his bed.

"How are you both today?" Beth asked.

"Some of us are better than others," Mary Margaret said with a quick look at Lowell.

"I'm doing much better," he assured them. "They were able to do laparoscopic surgery, so I only have a tiny, unimpressive incision."

Beth smiled. "Impressive is overrated."

Lowell rubbed his bald head. "I agree."

"Sorry about that rough snowmobile ride," Jack apologized. "But we were trying to get you here as quickly as possible."

"Don't apologize," Lowell said. "I understand that I owe you my life."

"Gray helped a little," Jack said with a smile. "And speaking of Gray, how are things up at the lodge this morning?"

A little line of worry formed between Mary Margaret's eyes. "We don't know. He still hasn't called."

Jack frowned. "You can't call him?" The others looked back at him and then he remembered. "Oh yeah, he turned his phone off. But why wouldn't he call to at least tell us they're okay?"

Lowell shrugged and then winced. Holding his hand against his side, he said, "I'm hoping it's just that his battery is dead. He mentioned yesterday that it was low."

"The weather report is bad for today," Jack reported. "It will be at least another day before they can get down."

"Yeah, that's what I figure," Lowell agreed.

Mary Margaret smiled. "I wanted to arrange for Gray and Lettie to spend some time together so they could work out their differences, but I couldn't because I promised Lettie. Now it looks like the snowstorm and Lowell's illness have provided that opportunity after all."

"Why did you want to get them together?" Jack asked.

"I told you that they used to be engaged," Beth reminded Jack. "And it didn't end friendly."

"Which was my fault," Lowell accepted responsibility. "I'm the one who came up with the idea for our tour business, and Lettie strongly opposed it."

"Your business seems to be doing well," Jack remarked. "So it must have been a pretty good idea."

"Yes," Lowell agreed. "But Gray paid a high price."

"Lettie?" Jack guessed.

Beth nodded. "She hasn't spoken to him since the day they broke up almost five years ago. Maybe Mary Margaret is right. This forced togetherness will be good for them."

"I hope so," Mary Margaret said. "I'm convinced that they still love each other but are both too proud to make the first move."

"Rekindling their love might be asking for too much," Beth remarked. "I'd be satisfied if she'd just quit acting like she hates him."

"That would be a step in the right direction," Mary Margaret agreed. Then she leaned toward Beth and whispered, "Did you tell him about, well, you know?"

"About the baby?" Beth asked, and Mary Margaret nodded. "Yes, I told him."

Lowell smiled at Jack. "Beth was afraid you'd insist that we take an ambulance on our trip if you knew about the baby. And I have to say, that ambulance would have come in handy later."

Jack nodded. "Everyone always accuses me of overreacting, but I maintain it's impossible to overreact. It's called being well prepared."

Beth shook her head. "You're hopeless."

"I won't argue with that," Jack allowed. "Speaking of which, I haven't called the kids in almost an hour." He pulled out his cell phone. "If you'll excuse me?"

"Of course," Lowell said with a smile.

Jack walked over into the corner of the room and dialed his home number. Roberta answered promptly. "Jack Gamble's office."

"Hey Roberta," he greeted. "What are you doing there on a Saturday?"

"I'm providing babysitting backup for your mother-in-law and I'm charging you triple time," Roberta replied with typical flippancy. "So, did you rescue Beth?"

Jack considered telling his secretary that a rescue *had* been necessary, but decided that would just extend their conversation. "Beth is safely down from the frozen mountain," he confirmed. "But a friend of hers is in the hospital here, which will delay our departure. I'm test-driving a Hummer, and since I inflicted some minor damage on it while driving through the mountains, I'm probably going to have to buy it and drive it home instead of flying. So it will be Monday night or even Tuesday morning before we get back."

"That's fine with me," Roberta returned. "Things are much calmer here when you're gone."

Jack decided to ignore this. "So the kids are okay?"

"The kids are fine," Roberta assured him. "Beth's mother may need therapy."

Jack decided to ignore this as well. "In your spare, highly paid time, please cancel my appointments for next week."

"The whole week?" Roberta confirmed.

"Yes, just to be on the safe side."

"Will do," she promised.

As Jack hung up the phone, a man wearing the green uniform of the National Park Service walked through the door.

"How are you feeling, Lowell?" the man asked.

"I've been better, Captain," Lowell answered. "But I've definitely been worse. Let me introduce you to my friends." Lowell worked his way around the room. "Captain Woods, meet Mary Margaret McKenzie and Beth and Jack Gamble."

The captain nodded to each of the women before transferring his gaze to Jack. Then he surprised Jack by saying, "Mr. Gamble is the man I'm here to see."

"You're here to see me?" Jack asked.

"Yes, I spoke with you yesterday. You reported that Gray Grantland and some others were stranded at LeConte Lodge and had Ranger Lamar Penny with them?"

"Yes," Jack confirmed. "Gray said the ranger had a few minor injuries but should be fine until the weather clears enough for them to make it down the mountain."

Captain Woods frowned. "Unfortunately, your friends might not be fine. Yesterday Ranger Penny found the body of an escaped convict at the base of Hughes Ridge. We couldn't pick him up because of the weather, so I told Penny to walk to the lodge on Mount LeConte."

"Gray said he arrived late last night," Jack confirmed.

The captain didn't seem reassured by this. "I was finally able to get a team on snowmobiles in to Hughes Ridge a little while ago, and they said there's no body at the base of the embankment."

"That doesn't make sense," Lowell said. "Where's the body Ranger Penny saw?"

The captain pulled at the collar of his uniform shirt in obvious discomfort. "I can only assume that my ranger made a mistake about Bright being mortally wounded."

"A mistake?" Mary Margaret whispered. "The convict wasn't really dead?"

Captain Woods shook his head. "I think Bright pretended to be dead so that the manhunt for him would be called off."

"Was it?" Beth asked.

"Yes. It was a good ploy."

"Do you think the convict poses a danger to our friends?" Mary Margaret asked.

"Yes," the captain confirmed. "The LeConte Lodge is the only shelter in the area, and it's where I would expect the convict to head. I've tried to call Gray's cell phone to warn him, but I don't get an answer. I was hoping you had some other way of getting in touch with him."

Lowell and Jack both shook their heads. "We don't," Lowell said. "Gray's battery was low yesterday, so by now it must be dead."

"Or maybe Mancil Bright is already at LeConte and won't allow him to answer the phone," the captain said.

"I guess that's also a possibility," Jack admitted with a quick glance at Beth and Mary Margaret.

"Does Gray's cell phone have GPS?" the captain wanted to know.

"It does," Lowell replied.

"That might come in handy." The captain started toward the door. "You keep trying to call Gray by phone. If you're able to get through, warn him about Bright and tell him that I've got a team on the way up there with a couple of U.S. Marshals."

Lowell nodded. "We'll keep trying."

The captain disappeared out the door, and the occupants of the hospital room regarded each other in mutual despair.

* * *

Eugenia was sitting by the phone, trying to get up the courage to call Charlotte Sullivan and set up their showdown meeting, when the phone rang. Eugenia jumped and Lady barked.

"I declare we're as nervous as ninnies," Eugenia said to the little dog. Then she picked up the phone. "Hello?"

"Eugenia? This is Norma Yates, and I was calling to invite you to services at the Methodist church on Sunday. We understand that you don't like Brother Watty." Norma's tone was disapproving. "But I thought you'd like to know that for the one-day revival on Sunday we're having a guest preacher."

"I've already heard about the guest preacher," Eugenia replied. "And I like Brother Watty just fine. But I'm not sure where I'll be attending on Sunday."

"If you want to *prove* that you're not mad at Brother Watty, you should attend services with us," Norma suggested slyly.

At this point, Eugenia lost patience with the woman. "I'm not trying to prove anything, and I'm tired of this silly contest. Where I go to church is nobody's business but the Lord's."

"Well!" Norma replied. "You don't have to get huffy."

"And everyone in town doesn't have to keep calling me." Eugenia hung up the phone without saying good-bye. "A guest preacher," Eugenia said to Lady. "This religious fervor has gotten out of control."

Lady barked in agreement, and Eugenia had to smile.

"Okay, now I'm going to call Charlotte Sullivan. Wish me luck."

Lady barked again and Eugenia reached for the phone.

When Charlotte answered, Eugenia forced herself to sound feeble as she said, "Charlotte, this is Eugenia Atkins."

"Yes, Mrs. Atkins," Charlotte replied. "We missed you at the senior center last night."

"I've been a little busy," Eugenia said. *Trying to keep you from killing anyone else,* she thought to herself. "I have a favor to ask."

There was a brief pause before Charlotte said, "I'll be glad to help you if I can."

"It's a private matter that I don't want to discuss on the phone," Eugenia told her.

"Well, come to the senior center tonight," Charlotte suggested. "We can talk while we watch folks karaoke."

"I'd rather talk when there are no other people around," Eugenia requested. Then, thinking of the little tape recorder that she'd have in her purse, she added, "When it's nice and quiet."

There was an even longer pause this time. Finally Charlotte said, "Everyone should be gone from the center by 9:30. Why don't you come then?"

"That would be mighty convenient." Eugenia cleared her throat and forced herself to say, "Thank you."

"You're welcome," Charlotte replied.

Eugenia hung up the phone and looked at Lady. "Well, there's no turning back now."

* * *

Lettie had lost all sense of time while they walked through the woods, aware only of her misery and the need to keep moving so she wouldn't turn into a block of ice. She didn't even realize that Gray had stopped until she ran into him. He steadied her by putting both of his hands on her shoulders. She resisted the urge to throw herself against his chest and weep.

He gave her a sympathetic smile. "I know you're cold and tired. I've been out with experienced hikers who couldn't keep up the pace we've set this afternoon. You can be proud of yourself."

"Thanks," she managed with frozen lips.

"We'll rest here for a few minutes and then press on for a couple more hours until we can't see where we're going."

Lettie looked up at the sky and prayed for darkness. It wasn't that she didn't care about Alexa and the ranger, but she wasn't sure she wanted to exchange her life for theirs. And the way she felt, death could not be far away.

"Are you going to make another little fire?" she asked.

Gray shook his head. "I'd better conserve our last fire starter in case we need it later. I can set up a propane burner and heat some water for hot chocolate, though."

She tried to smile, but her face was so stiff it barely moved.

Once Gray had the hot chocolate ready he gave Lettie hers in a metal cup. She held it with both hands and sipped, savoring the warmth as much as the sweet taste. Then Gray handed her a granola bar.

"I found this in the bottom of the MRE bag and thought it might be more appealing to you than another veggie burger."

Tears stung her eyes at the sight of real food. She took it from him and said, "Thank you."

He smiled. "You're welcome."

By the time she'd finished her granola bar and her hot chocolate, her mouth was thawed, and she was feeling generous toward Gray. So she said, "It looks like your tour business has worked out pretty well."

Gray nodded. "We stay busy. How about you? My mom said you work for a high-powered investment firm in Tifton."

"They're going to make me a junior partner," Lettie told him lightly. "Which means I'm historical—the first woman ever to have the privilege at their firm."

Gray whistled, and she was impressed that he had that much control of his facial muscles. "That's quite an honor."

She shrugged. "So they tell me."

He raised his eyebrows. "But you don't think so?"

"I used to think so. I'm not sure anymore." She took a sip of hot chocolate and then continued. "Mary Margaret has been sick, but she didn't tell me because I was too busy."

"That was her decision," he pointed out.

"A decision that she based on the fact that whenever she invited me to lunch or a movie, I couldn't spare the time," Lettie admitted bitterly. "I'm going to be the first woman partner at Tatum and Trent, but I'm a failure as a friend."

He smiled. "You're pretty hard on yourself."

She acknowledged this with a little nod. "When the shoe fits . . ."

"You came on this trip, so obviously you've decided to make time for your friends."

"Even if it kills me." She looked around. "Which it might."

His eyes dropped to his cup of hot chocolate as he asked, "Assuming you survive this trip, when will you be able to carve out enough time to marry Lowell?"

"What?" Lettie asked in surprise.

"It's okay, I've figured out your little secret," Gray said. "You don't have to pretend anymore."

Lettie felt stupid, but all she could do was repeat the word. "Pretend?"

"I knew he had a girlfriend," Gray continued. "But I'll admit I was surprised to find out it was you."

If she'd had the energy, Lettie would have laughed hysterically at this ridiculous remark. "I'm not Lowell's girlfriend," she assured him. "I'm not anyone's girlfriend." She regretted this last part immediately, but it was too late to recall the words. And Gray didn't even seem to hear them.

"Then who has Lowell been talking to?"

"Mary Margaret was the one who set up the trip, so I guess it was her."

Gray looked embarrassed when he said, "I wonder why Lowell led me to believe he was interested in you?"

Lettie shrugged. "It makes no sense to me."

"He probably did it just to see if it would bother me," Gray said after a few moments of contemplation.

"And did it?" she couldn't help but ask.

He dragged his eyes up to meet hers. "Yes."

Lettie turned away before he could read too much in her eyes. "What about you? Are you anyone's boyfriend? Or husband?" she forced herself to add.

He shook his head. "No."

His eyes were the passionate brown she used to love so much. Unable to bear the intensity of his gaze, she stood. "We should probably get going," she said, and she meant it. Trudging through a foot of snow was more comfortable and much safer than staring into Gray's eyes.

He stood as well. He cleaned out the mugs with snow, stowed their supplies, and slung his pack up onto his back. Then he knelt down and examined the trail of footprints they were following.

"Is something the matter?" she asked.

Gray frowned. "I'm not sure. I wish Lowell was here. He could tell us everything about these footprints—even the shoe sizes. I'm not nearly that good, but even I can tell that they aren't headed to the Greenbriar station."

Lettie stared at the snow path. "Where are they going?"

He shrugged. "If I didn't know better, I'd say they were headed for the service entrance out on Highway 321."

"But you do know better," Lettie pointed out wearily. "It doesn't make any sense for Alexa and the ranger to be leaving the park through a back entrance instead of going to the nearest ranger station."

"No," Gray agreed. "That doesn't make any sense. Unless they're lost and just following any trail."

He stood and helped Lettie put on her backpack. Then he waved toward the footprints in the snow. "Ladies first."

She knew he was kindly allowing her to set the pace, and if he hadn't ruined her life, she could have almost liked him.

* * *

The phone rang on the table beside Lowell's hospital bed, waking him up.

"Would you like me to get that?" Jack offered, and Lowell nodded.

It was Captain Woods. After Jack identified himself, the captain said, "The GPS signal for Gray's cell phone is close to the Alum Cave Trail entrance, but it's not moving."

Jack relayed this information to the others.

"Tell Captain Woods that I left my Jeep at the entrance to the Alum Cave Trail," Lowell told Jack. "Maybe they left the lodge and went to the Jeep."

"I heard him," the captain said, saving Jack the trouble of repeating Lowell's comments.

"But if they did that, then why aren't they driving down the mountain?" Jack asked.

"The roads are still too bad," Captain Woods predicted.

"So they're sitting in the Jeep?" Beth asked.

"They could be resting before they start back up to the lodge," Mary Margaret suggested.

Jack could think of another, much worse scenario. Maybe the convict had decided to leave the lodge and had forced the others to go with him. Once they reached the Jeep, he might have shot them and then driven off. But there was no reason to share this possibility with the others.

"My men will check out the Jeep on the way up to the lodge," Captain Woods said. "And tell Lowell to stand by. He knows the terrain of the park better than anyone, and we might need his advice."

"He's standing by," Jack confirmed. Then he looked at Lowell lying on the bed. "Well, sort of."

"I'll keep you posted," the captain promised.

Jack glanced at the others and said, "We would appreciate that."

"How long will it take them to get to the entrance of the trail?" Mary Margaret asked after Jack hung up the phone.

"At least an hour," Lowell replied.

Mary Margaret wrung her hands. "I'll be so glad when this is all over."

Jack nodded. "We all will."

* * *

Lettie stared at the footprints in front of her and continued to walk. She had reached the point where she was too tired to hold back the tears, and they froze on her eyelashes. When it started to get dark, her mood improved a little because she knew that the end was near. Then snow began to fall, and she turned to look at Gray.

He didn't seem to be in much better shape than she was, and this heartened her even more. "How much farther are we going to go tonight?"

He pointed to a small clearing up ahead. "We'll camp there."

Lettie followed him to the spot he'd selected and collapsed on a tree stump while he opened his pack. Rationally she knew that she should help him. He had carried most of the weight in his pack to spare her, and he barely knew Alexa, so this effort to save her life was also for Lettie's benefit. But she was too overwhelmed with exhaustion to feel sorry for anyone else. So she watched in silence as he assembled two small tents.

"No fire?" she asked with chattering teeth.

He shook his head. "No." He took a little canister from his pack. "This is a catalytic heater." He turned it on and put it inside one of the tents. "It won't make the interior exactly warm, but it will raise the temperature by twenty or thirty degrees, which will help."

Lettie shivered as Gray set up his little burner and heated some more water for another round of hot chocolate. While Lettie sipped hers, he held an MRE tray over the heat. When she was finished with her hot chocolate, he opened the tray and handed it to her.

"This still may not be good, but at least it will be warm."

"Is it chili and macaroni or veggie burger?" she asked.

He glanced at the wrapper. "This one says chicken a la king."

Lettie controlled a shudder and ate the food without trying to distinguish between courses. Gray squatted beside her, and they ate in companionable silence. When they were finished, Gray cleaned up and then told Lettie to get inside the first tent while he removed two rolled-up sleeping bags from the frame of his backpack.

Lettie stooped down to enter the tent. "Why is this thing so short?"

"A shorter tent means less air to warm," he answered. Through the small opening he spread the horse blanket from the lodge out on the bottom of the tent and then handed her a sleeping bag. "Spread this out."

Gray held onto one end while she unrolled it. The sleeping bag looked like a sarcophagus—which she considered appropriate.

"Now take off your coat, your ski pants, and your boots," he said from the doorway.

"I'm not taking *anything* off!" she protested. "It's freezing in here!"

"The only way to be warm inside your sleeping bag is to take the coat and ski pants off first. They have snow on them, and when it starts to melt you'll get wet. Your sweatpants underneath should be dry."

Reluctantly she accepted the wisdom of this and unbuttoned her coat. She put it next to the tent door where Gray was still supervising and then untied her boots.

"Socks too," he insisted. "Spread them out over your boots so they can dry."

She obeyed, her hands trembling from the cold.

"Now get into your sleeping bag."

He watched until she was inside the sleeping bag with the drawstring pulled tight so that only a small circle of her face remained exposed.

"I feel like a mummy," she told him.

"That's the general idea," he said as he zipped her tent closed. "If you need anything during the night, just call me. I'm only a few feet away."

She closed her eyes, savoring the warmth provided by the sleeping bag and the comfort of knowing that Gray was nearby. Tears gathered in her eyes and at first she thought she was crying out of sheer happiness since, for the first time in hours, she wasn't freezing. But finally she realized that she was crying for what could have been. If not for Gray's selfishness, she would have been able to enjoy the comfort of his presence every day for the past five years.

"I hate you," she whispered.

"I know," he responded softly from the tent next door.

* * *

Beth and Jack were leaving the hospital for the night when the phone by Lowell's bed rang. Beth paused in the doorway as Lowell reached over and picked it up. "Lowell Brooks," he answered. Then he told them, "It's Captain Woods."

Beth walked over beside the bed and listened carefully to Lowell's side of the conversation. From what she could tell, the park service team had reached the entrance to the trail. The Jeep was there, but Gray and the others weren't.

Lowell requested that the captain keep them informed and then he hung up the phone.

"Gray and the others aren't at the Jeep?" Beth asked, and Lowell nodded in confirmation.

"What about the GPS?" Jack asked.

Lowell wouldn't meet their eyes as he said, "The signal is coming from the bottom of a ravine near where the Jeep is parked. It's too dark to see if anyone is down there."

Beth watched the color drain from Mary Margaret's face. "The captain thinks the convict pushed Gray into the ravine?"

"That's where the signal is coming from," Lowell said.

Beth searched frantically for another explanation. "What if someone threw his phone down there?"

Jack frowned. "Why would anyone do that?"

"I don't know," Beth admitted with a sigh.

"Maybe Gray threw it in the ravine since it had a dead battery," Mary Margaret suggested, "To keep from having to carry it."

Lowell shook his head. "The GPS feature was one of the reasons Gray wanted to get these phones. He would have kept it with him if he could, even if the battery was dead."

A feeling of dread started to form inside Beth. Suddenly she was sure that all was not well with her friends. She looked up at Jack and saw the same concern in his eyes.

"The captain's team is headed on up to the lodge," Lowell said. "He will give us more details as soon as they're available."

"We won't leave until the captain calls back," Jack decided. "Would anyone like a snack from the vending machines?"

Beth wasn't hungry, but knew she needed to eat, so she nodded.

Jack took Beth's hand and pulled her to the door. "We'll be back soon," he promised.

* * *

Alexa didn't have to be compelled to follow Mancil Bright as they continued their headlong journey through the woods. It was dark and cold, and she had no idea where she was. Her only hope of survival was to stay close to him, so any thoughts of escape had been abandoned hours before.

Her fingers and toes ached from exposure to the freezing temperatures, and every muscle burned with overexertion. But she found that the pain was almost a pleasant thing. She felt alive and worthwhile for the first time in over a month. If nothing else, she was helping to protect her friends.

Without warning, Mancil turned off the path they'd been following and led her up into the trees. They made slow progress through the thick underbrush until Mancil found a spot he apparently considered acceptable for camping.

After building a small fire, he told her to dish up some soup while he assembled the tent. She held the cans over the flickering flame for a few minutes before scraping the paste into the blue-speckled camping mugs Mancil provided. They finished their tasks at about the same time and huddled near the fire to eat.

Alexa ate a bowl of cold soup as fast as she could get it into her mouth. When she licked the last drop from her spoon, she started to laugh.

"What's so funny?" Mancil asked suspiciously.

"I've always hated soup," she told him. "But tonight it was delicious—even cold and unreconstituted."

He shrugged. "I guess even delicious is relative."

She studied him through narrowed eyes. "You're pretty smart."

"What did you think—all convicts are dumb?"

Actually, that was exactly what she had thought, and Alexa was embarrassed. "Sorry."

Mancil collected their dishes and put them in a corner. "It's okay. That's a common misconception. Actually there are a lot of educational opportunities in prison and most inmates take advantage of them. The classes are free and they look good on parole applications."

He stood. "Now we'd better get some rest. We'll have to be moving again tomorrow before dawn." He handed her the sleeping bag that had been attached to his pack. "You can have this. Take it into the tent and try to stay warm."

She was already inside the relatively cozy confines of the tiny tent before she realized that there was only one tent and one sleeping bag. "How are you going to protect yourself from the elements?"

"I'll dig myself a little burrow, and I've got these blankets." He held up what looked like aluminum foil covered in plastic wrap.

"Do those really work?"

He nodded. "They're insulated."

He was making a sacrifice for her—which seemed like a strange thing for a convicted murderer—and she didn't know what to say.

He assembled a small shovel and began digging an angled hole in the snowbank. "Zip up the tent so you can conserve body heat," he instructed.

She reached for the zipper, but just before she closed the barrier between them she said, "Thanks."

He glanced up from his snow burrow and nodded. "You're welcome."

Alexa snuggled down into the sleeping bag and tried not to feel guilty about Mancil. After a few minutes the digging stopped and she called to him, "Are you sure you're going to be warm enough out there?"

"No," he replied. "But I'll survive."

"It's funny," she continued. "I'm exhausted but not sleepy. I feel nervous and jittery."

"Probably because you're coming off your meds," he said, and Alexa heard him slide into his snow cave.

Since she'd taken her last pill early that morning, she knew that was most likely the case. "I guess so."

"Why do you take so many pills?"

"My husband wants a divorce," she said. "He won't return my phone calls or meet with a marriage counselor or anything. He just wants out."

"Did he hit you?" Mancil wanted to know.

Alexa frowned. "Of course not. He just left."

"Be glad he didn't hit you," Mancil advised her from his cave. "My mom wasn't so lucky."

She thought about this for a few seconds and then asked, "Is that why you killed your stepfather?"

She heard him exhale. "Yeah. I knew he knocked her around sometimes, but I'd never seen it until that day. I got between them and he started working me over pretty good. It wasn't any worse than the other times, and I knew I could take it. But then my mom tried to stop him and he turned on her again."

"And you couldn't take that?" Alexa guessed.

"No," he confirmed. "I knew where the old man kept his rifle. I got it and shot him. Then I kept shooting until I ran out of shells."

Alexa stared at the top of the tent and thought about Mancil Bright. He was a killer with little conscience and no regret for the crimes he'd committed. But he was intelligent, and given a fair chance in life, he might be able to succeed. Besides, he'd shown her more kindness in the past few hours than her husband had in months. Conflicted and exhausted, Alexa blinked back tears and fell asleep.

* * *

Jack and Beth returned from the hospital's vending machines with an assortment of snack foods and had just finished eating in solemn silence when the phone rang. Lowell answered it and had a brief conversation. Then he reported, "The team made it to the lodge, but there's no one there."

Jack thought about the GPS signal at the bottom of the ravine. This news could be very bad indeed.

"They left the lodge?" Mary Margaret cried in alarm.

Lowell nodded. "The tracks they left in the snow lead into the woods, headed north. The team is going to follow the tracks on the assumption that Gray, Lettie, and Alexa are all hostages of the convict."

Jack frowned. "That's a lot of hostages to keep track of."

Lowell nodded, but didn't comment.

"What are you saying, Jack?" Beth demanded.

"I'm saying that if I were a criminal and needed a hostage to ensure that I didn't get captured, I wouldn't want three, especially if one of them was a man in good physical shape who knew his way around the park."

"There are a hundred different situations where they would easily be able to overpower him," Lowell agreed.

"That's good, then," Mary Margaret said. "Maybe they've already gotten away from him."

"Maybe," Jack's tone was noncommittal.

"Mary Margaret," Lowell said. "The convict would realize that taking so many hostages—especially Gray—was a bad idea,"

Tears spilled over onto Mary Margaret's pale cheeks. "You think he killed Gray?"

"I think that's a possibility we all need to be prepared for," Lowell confirmed grimly.

* * *

Mancil Bright huddled under the insulated emergency blankets in his snow cave and thought about the woman sleeping in the tent a few feet from him. She was very beautiful and completely worn out. He had hoped to reach the park's service entrance before dark, but she had slowed him down considerably.

The smart thing to do would be to leave her there. Someone would probably find her before she froze or starved to death—but if not, well, sacrifices sometimes had to be made.

He willed himself to get up, but his body rebelled. Finally he closed his eyes. It wasn't something he had to decide right now. He'd rest for a couple of hours and then do what had to be done.

CHAPTER 11

Eugenia sat at the kitchen table, nervously drumming her fingers on the red Formica surface. She wasn't exactly scared of Charlotte Sullivan, but it would be a big relief to have their confrontation over with. At 9:15 PM Polly knocked on the back door.

"Are you ready to go?" Eugenia asked.

"Oh yes," Polly assured her. "It's the most exciting thing I've done in years!"

Eugenia resisted the urge to roll her eyes as she checked on Lady, who was sound asleep in the little dog bed. Then Eugenia put on a sweater, picked up her purse, and led Polly out to the old Buick.

There were only two cars at the senior center when she arrived—the black 4Runner and Whit's Lexus. Eugenia parked two blocks down and assumed her slumped surveillance position. Polly copied her and they sat in silence for a few minutes.

Finally Charlotte and Whit walked out of the senior center. They embraced briefly and Eugenia was pretty sure he kissed her, but it was hard to be sure from her less-than-perfect vantage point.

"He should be ashamed of himself!" Polly hissed, pretty much confirming the kiss.

Whit descended the stairs of the old armory with a decided spring to his step and climbed into his car. Charlotte waved to him before returning inside the building.

Feeling a little nauseated, Eugenia reached into her purse and turned on Derrick's tape recorder. "Showtime," she whispered as she handed Polly her cell phone. "If I'm not back by ten o'clock, call Winston."

Polly nodded. "You promise you'll be careful?"

"I promise," Eugenia assured her. Then she squared her old shoulders and walked up to Haggerty's new senior center.

Charlotte was straightening the chairs when Eugenia walked in.

"I want everything to be nice and neat when we get here on Monday," she said cheerfully.

Eugenia turned to close the door and then crossed the room to stand beside Charlotte. "Thank you for seeing me tonight."

"You're welcome," Charlotte replied graciously. "Please have a seat."

Charlotte settled herself into a chair at the closest card table. Eugenia sat opposite Charlotte and placed her purse, containing the Dictaphone, on the table right in front of her. She hoped this would enable the little recorder to pick up their conversation.

"Now, what can I do for you?" Charlotte asked.

"It's a little embarrassing," Eugenia began. "And I'm sure you weren't aware of it, but before you came to Haggerty, Whit Owens and I had been dating for a couple of months."

Charlotte's eyebrows rose is astonishment. "You and Whit?"

Eugenia hadn't thought she could like Charlotte less, but she had been wrong. "Yes. Whit and my husband, Charles, were friends in high school, so we've known each other almost all our lives."

"You and Whit are the same *age?*" Charlotte seemed even more surprised to hear this.

Eugenia controlled her annoyance and nodded. "After my husband died a few years ago, I was so lonely. In fact, I wasn't sure life was worth living. Then Whit moved back to town, and I've found happiness again." Eugenia knew she was pouring it on a little thick, but she wanted to be sure she established herself as completely pathetic.

Charlotte pursed her lips. "Oh, I see. We have an awkward little love triangle."

Normally Eugenia would have objected to the use of the word *love* to describe her relationship with Whit, since they were just close friends. But in order to encourage Charlotte's cooperation, she settled for, "Something like that." Then she moved to the first phase of her trap.

"You're quite attractive and considerably younger than I am. You could have your pick of any man in Haggerty." *Although that's not saying much,* Eugenia thought to herself. "My options are more limited. So I've come to ask you to reject Whit's advances. If he thinks he doesn't have a chance with you, maybe he'll be satisfied with me."

Charlotte looked at her beautifully manicured hands for a minute and really did seem to be considering Eugenia's appeal. But when Charlotte raised her eyes, Eugenia could tell that she was amused by the request.

"I'm sorry about your husband's death and the loneliness you face during your twilight years," Charlotte said. "But I think it's selfish of you to ask both Whit and me to ignore our feelings for each other. Why is your happiness more important than ours?"

This response was about what Eugenia had expected. So she moved smoothly to phase two.

"Well, actually, my lonely twilight years aren't the only reason I'm asking you to leave Whit alone," Eugenia said. "I know about Mr. Bell in Sipsey."

Charlotte's eyebrows rose. "*You* sent the letter? I never would have thought you'd have the nerve!"

Eugenia ignored this latest insult. "Yes, I wrote the letter after a very informative visit with Dean Lumpkin."

Charlotte laughed, apparently unconcerned. "Well, what do you know about that? I assumed it was from the bitter nephew."

Eugenia leaned forward and initiated phase three—where she moved in for the kill. "I know that you convinced Mr. Bell to stop taking his prescribed medication. Then you gave him a stimulant called Vitality and made sure that he overexerted his bad heart."

"I convinced Myron to *live,*" Charlotte countered. "He only had a short time left, whether he stayed in bed or went dancing. Instead of spending his final days as an invalid, taking handfuls of pills and shuffling around that dreary little house, I helped him to leave this earth in style!"

"Then you admit that you gave him the stimulant and encouraged him to stop taking his heart medication?" Eugenia demanded.

"It's not illegal to give someone an opinion," Charlotte replied. "I told Myron that I didn't think taking so many pills every day was good for him. He made the decision to stop. And the Vitality is harmless—otherwise it wouldn't be for sale in every pharmacy across the country."

"It might be safe for some people, but not for old men with heart conditions."

Charlotte dismissed this with a wave of her hand. "Myron only took a couple. I think the effect is mostly psychological. If you give an old man a pill and tell him it's going to make him feel younger, it works because he wants it to."

"Mr. Bell took the pills just to please you!" Eugenia pointed out. "And then you asked him to buy you expensive gifts and give you money."

"If you love someone, it's natural that you would want to give them gifts," Charlotte replied. "I told Myron that it wasn't necessary to give me anything, but he insisted. And since it seemed to make him so happy, I accepted them. Again, nothing illegal about that."

"You are a cold, heartless woman who preys on lonely, elderly men," Eugenia accused. "However, I believe that you do usually try to keep from actually breaking the law. After all, why take the risk of killing an old man when you can just encourage him to kill himself? But with Mr. Bell you went too far and gave him an overdose of Vitality."

Charlotte laughed. "You think you're so smart."

Eugenia pressed on. "The question I have is why? Did he figure out that you were using him? Did he want his 4Runner back?"

"I hate to burst your bubble," Charlotte said, although she didn't sound a bit sorry. "But I didn't kill Myron."

"Humph!" Eugenia expressed her disbelief.

Charlotte leaned forward so that her mouth was right above Eugenia's purse. "If I was going to kill him I would have had the sense to wait until *after* we were married so I would have inherited that old house. It was the only asset he had left."

Eugenia had met a few murderers, but never before had she met someone this cold-blooded about their crimes. Eugenia pressed a hand to her heart and prayed for the courage to finish what she had begun. "If you didn't kill Mr. Bell, then who did?"

"The only person who benefited from the fact that Myron died *before* our marriage was his great-nephew."

"Dean?" Eugenia gasped.

"I did buy a bottle of Vitality for Myron, and I know he took a few because I saw him. But then he got worried about their effect on his heart, so one day we stopped by his regular drug store and asked the pharmacist about them. He discouraged Myron from taking Vitality, so he stopped."

"And you didn't pressure him?"

"Of course not," Charlotte scoffed. "After the pharmacist had told him they were dangerous? That would have been foolish on my part. Once I was a part of his life, Myron wanted very much to *live!*"

Eugenia wanted to argue, but Charlotte's words resounded with a sickening sort of truth.

"But Dean didn't know about our consultation with the pharmacist," Charlotte continued. "So he chose the wrong thing to overdose Myron with. He should have used the heart medication. It would have been just as lethal and much less suspicious."

Eugenia remembered the tape recorder and tried to do what she could to salvage her multiphase plan to save Whit. "Maybe you didn't kill Myron Bell," she acknowledged, hoping the woman would feel safe and drop her guard. "But you did contribute to his early death. And what I find particularly suspicious is that you've been widowed *seven* times."

"Yes, I noticed that you've been a busy little snoop."

"I hired a professional investigator to check you out," Eugenia said. "And I've given a copy of the report to the FBI." This was mostly true. She'd put a copy on the desk in Mark's office at his house—which he would see if he ever came home. "So you'd better get out of town quick, before the FBI comes to arrest you."

"No one is going to try to arrest me," Charlotte replied. But the confidence she'd displayed earlier was gone. Apparently Eugenia's mention of the FBI had done the trick.

"There's one more thing I want to know," Eugenia said. "Why Whit? You usually choose men with one foot in the grave. Whit is as healthy as a seventy-seven-year-old man has any right to be."

"I'm tired of feeble old men," Charlotte said. "And Whit's got enough money that I figured we could spend several happy years traveling and enjoying life together."

"Until he gets sick or infirm," Eugenia said. "Then you'd have to put him out of his misery."

Charlotte stood. "This conversation is at an end, and I'll ask you to leave at once."

Eugenia collected her purse and moved toward the door.

"And let this be a warning," Charlotte continued.

Eugenia turned back to face the woman.

"If you come near me again, to deliver a slanderous letter or harass me in any other way, I'll call the police."

Eugenia didn't bother to respond to this ridiculous threat. Imagine, a murderer calling the police to report *her!* She calmly opened the door of the new Haggerty senior center and walked out. Then, just for the fun of it, she slammed the door.

* * *

It was after ten o'clock when Jack and Beth arrived back at their room at the Best Western on Saturday night. Jack pulled off his coat and threw the keys to the Hummer on the dresser. Then he sat on the edge of the bed and sighed.

"I feel so helpless sitting around waiting to see if they can find the others," he told Beth. "Maybe I should have gone with the rangers to look for them."

She wrapped her arms around his neck. "You're used to being able to fix things, and I know it's hard to accept that even you have your limitations."

Jack raised an eyebrow. "I have limitations?"

She nodded. "A few—like you don't know anything about camping or the park. You wouldn't be much help to the rangers and, in fact, you'd probably just be in the way."

"Was that supposed to make me feel better?"

She smiled. "Yes. You did the right thing by staying here. The park rangers will find them."

"It's so cold," Jack shivered. "I can't imagine sleeping outside in this weather."

"Stop thinking of all the negatives or you'll drive yourself crazy."

"I guess you're right," Jack murmured against her hair.

"Let's try to get some sleep and hopefully by morning the convict will be captured and our friends will be headed home."

Jack's cell phone rang and he pulled it out. "Hello?"

"Jack? This is Annabelle Morgan. I'm sorry to call so late."

"It's okay," Jack assured her.

"I just have to ask if you really think it's a good idea for Eugenia to try and trick a woman who's killed several men into confessing all her crimes?"

Jack frowned. "I definitely *don't* think that's a good idea."

"Well, I called Eugenia's cell phone a few minutes ago, and Polly Kirby answered. She said you told Eugenia the only way to convict Charlotte Sullivan was to get her to make a full confession. So Polly's sitting in Eugenia's car out in front of the new senior center. Eugenia is inside, with Derrick's Dictaphone hidden in her purse, trying to get Charlotte Sullivan to confess to multiple murders!"

"I remember having a conversation with Miss Eugenia about the Sullivan woman," Jack said, rubbing his temples in an effort to concentrate. "And I did say that it would take a full confession to convict her, but I didn't mean that Miss Eugenia should try and get one!"

"Well, that's exactly what she's doing," Annabelle reported.

"Call Winston Jones immediately and have him go to the senior citizen center," Jack advised. "If half of the things I've heard about Charlotte Sullivan are true, Miss Eugenia could be in real danger."

"I'll call Winston," Annabelle promised.

"Call me back when you're sure Miss Eugenia is okay," Jack requested as Annabelle disconnected.

Jack closed his phone and faced Beth's questioning look. He explained the situation. Then he muttered, "As if we don't have enough to worry about."

* * *

Eugenia stepped outside the senior center just as a Haggerty police car came around the corner with tires squealing and lights flashing. Arnold was behind the wheel, and Winston was in the passenger seat. Winston jumped out before the car came to a full stop and ran across the street.

"Miss Eugenia?" he yelled.

Eugenia met the police chief by the curb and demanded, "Winston, why are you and Arnold speeding around town wasting the taxpayers' tire tread?"

"I came here to save your life!" he informed her breathlessly.

"The very idea," Eugenia scoffed. "As you can see, I'm not in need of a rescue."

Winston removed his police hat and scratched his head. "Miss Annabelle just called the station and said you were about to get murdered at the senior center."

"What she should have said is that there is a murderer in the senior center," Eugenia corrected. "Or a murderess, Miss Charlotte Sullivan."

"Now, Miss Eugenia," Winston said. "You can't go around making accusations when you don't have any proof."

"As it turns out, I now have in my possession a tape that incriminates her in not one, but *two* murders," she informed Winston. "I'm going to have Derrick make a copy of it tomorrow. Then I'll give the original to Mark to go along with a comprehensive report compiled by Kate's sister, Kelsey. Hopefully the FBI will be more conscientious than our local law enforcement has been in bringing Charlotte Sullivan to justice."

"Now wait, that's not fair." Winston tried to defend himself and all other local law enforcement officers, but Eugenia waved his excuses aside.

"The Sipsey police didn't investigate the death of Mr. Bell sufficiently, and you have refused to take her presence in Haggerty seriously. So I have been forced to handle the investigation myself."

"I don't appreciate being called incompetent," Winston returned heatedly, "Especially when I just rushed over here to save your life."

"I do thank you for the thought, even though it was completely unnecessary," Eugenia told him. "And I don't think you're incompetent. Everyone is entitled to an occasional mistake."

"It wasn't my mistake!" Winston said. "Miss Annabelle told me to come."

"Then we'll blame her," Eugenia decided. "Now go on back to the police station. Somebody might be calling in an actual emergency."

Winston put his hat back on and walked toward the squad car, muttering under his breath. He climbed into his squad car and then he and Arnold drove off at a normal speed.

"Oh, that was so exciting," Polly said when Eugenia sat behind the wheel of the old Buick. "When I saw you come out of the senior center and Winston came flying up to save you, I half expected Charlotte to come running out with a knife!"

"Charlotte may be mean, but she's not stupid. She kills people subtly and only for financial gain. She has no reason to kill me."

"You're not exactly poor," Polly pointed out.

"I'm not exactly an eligible bachelor either!" Eugenia started her car and headed toward Maple Street.

"I wish I'd brought my camera," Polly said wistfully. "No one is ever going to believe this."

"Everyone probably heard it," Eugenia replied. "I declare, I don't understand Winston, making a scene like that in the middle of the night."

"I guess that was partly my fault," Polly admitted. "Annabelle called you on your little cell phone, and when I told her what you were doing, she was very upset."

As if on cue, Eugenia's cell phone started ringing.

"It's Annabelle," Polly reported.

Eugenia frowned. "Hand it to me." She pressed the little phone to her ear. "Annabelle, why do you always have to overreact? If Winston had gotten there a few minutes sooner he would have ruined my chances of getting Charlotte Sullivan's confession on tape."

"Okay, Eugenia," Annabelle said. "Next time I'll wait until you're *dead* before I call the police!"

Eugenia closed the phone and handed it back to Polly.

"So, did you get Charlotte to confess?" Polly asked.

"Not exactly," Eugenia replied. "Charlotte says she didn't kill Mr. Bell and, unfortunately, I believe her."

Polly looked confused. "But if Charlotte didn't kill Mr. Bell, who did?"

"Dean Lumpkin."

"The great-nephew?" Polly said with a gasp.

Eugenia nodded. "I'm going to call the Sipsey police first thing in the morning and advise them to reopen their case. I'll send them a copy of my tape if necessary."

"But how are you going to get Charlotte to leave town now?"

Eugenia shrugged. "She may not have killed Mr. Bell, but I'll bet she helped send some of her husbands into the next life. She acted nervous when I told her I'd given Kelsey's report to the FBI, so I expect Charlotte will soon be moving on to another unsuspecting town."

"I'm sorry you weren't able to trap her," Polly said as Eugenia pulled to the curb in front of her house. "I know that meant a lot to you."

"As long as she leaves Haggerty, Whit should be safe," Eugenia said. "That's the main thing."

"And when Mark gets home maybe he'll catch Charlotte."

"Maybe," Eugenia agreed.

Eugenia watched until Polly was safely inside her house. Then she drove down to her own driveway, careful not to look at the Iversons' dark and lonesome house. Whether it was her conversation with Charlotte or just knowing that Dean Lumpkin had killed his own great-uncle, she felt a little unnerved. She briefly considered going to spend the night with Annabelle, but that would be a victory of sorts for Charlotte. Telling herself that she was way too old to be intimidated, Eugenia climbed out of the car. She unlocked her back door and was greeted by Lady.

"Have you missed me, girl?" she asked, and the little dog barked hysterically. "Let me get you a little snack and then I'll tell you all about my meeting with Charlotte Sullivan."

Eugenia gave Lady some of her specially formulated food, and when the little dog was finished eating, Eugenia picked her up and sat in one of the chairs at her kitchen table. Then she gave her a full account of the night's events.

In conclusion she said, "So, while my plan wasn't a complete success, I do think it served my purpose. Since Charlotte Sullivan will leave Haggerty, Whit won't be dying anytime soon. And when Mark gets home, Miss Sullivan might find herself in the middle of an FBI investigation. It will be up to the Sipsey police to decide whether or not Dean Lumpkin is prosecuted. But after they hear my little tape, I think they'll at least consider it."

The phone rang and Eugenia reached for it automatically. It was Annabelle.

"I want you to know that I've caught you in a lie!"

Eugenia was too tired and discouraged to fight with Annabelle. "What lie?"

"I called Jack Gamble, and he said he never told you to get a confession from Charlotte Sullivan. He just told you that a confession was the only way to convict the woman!"

Eugenia stifled a yawn. "Okay."

"And now I've got to call him back so he can quit worrying about you." Annabelle sighed. "Sometimes you don't use good judgment, Eugenia."

"Can we argue about my lack of judgment some other time?" Eugenia requested wearily. "I've had a long day."

"As long as you promise me that you won't seek out any more killers," Annabelle relented.

Eugenia had to smile. "I promise—at least for tonight. And it was nice of you to send Winston to check on me," she added. "Silly, but nice."

Annabelle sighed. "Good night, Sherlock."

"Good night yourself." Eugenia hung up the phone and put Lady on the floor. "Are you ready to go outside one last time before bed?"

Lady answered by running to the back door. Eugenia laughed and followed her.

* * *

Jack had just dozed off when his cell phone rang. He used the remote to turn off the hotel television and answered the phone, trying not to sound groggy.

"Jack? It's Annabelle Morgan again. I hope I didn't wake you."

Jack rubbed his eyes and pushed himself up into a semisitting position. "Is Miss Eugenia okay?"

"She's fine," Annabelle reported. "I sent Winston over to the senior center, as you suggested, but she insists she was never in any danger from Miss Sullivan."

"Murderers quite often hide their intentions from their victims," Jack replied dryly. "So Miss Eugenia may have been in danger without knowing it. And now that Miss Eugenia has shown Charlotte Sullivan her hand, so to speak, she needs to be extremely careful."

"I'll tell her, but Eugenia doesn't listen very well."

"I know, I've met her," Jack replied.

"I'm sorry to impose, but would you mind calling to tell her?" Annabelle requested. "She might listen to you."

Jack decided the situation would be resolved more quickly if he agreed. "I'll call her," he promised. He ended the call with Annabelle and dialed Miss Eugenia's number. He let it ring ten times before disconnecting.

Beth raised up on an elbow and asked, "No answer?"

"No." Jack tried to hide his concern.

"Don't worry," Beth said. "She's probably taking Lady for a walk or something. You can call again in a little while."

"If I can go ahead and issue my warning now, I'll be done with it and I can go back to sleep."

Beth sat up. "How are you going to issue a warning if Miss Eugenia won't answer her phone?"

He scrolled down the names in his phone book until he found the number he wanted. "I'm going to pass the buck." The phone rang twice before it was picked up on the other end. "Winston?" Jack said. "I need you to do me a favor."

"Something wrong with your kids?" the police chief asked.

"No," Jack assured him. "But I'm a little worried about Miss Eugenia and this Charlotte Sullivan woman. I promised Annabelle that I would warn Miss Eugenia to be particularly careful, but when I tried Miss Eugenia's number she didn't answer her phone. Would you mind driving over there? Maybe you can talk some sense into her."

"Trying to talk sense into Miss Eugenia is a waste of time," Winston replied.

"That's probably true, but I feel partially responsible since I gave her the idea about getting a confession. It would give me enormous peace of mind if you'd go by."

"You'll owe me one," Winston warned.

"I already owe you several," Jack responded with a smile. "Add it to my tab."

"Okay," Winston agreed. "I'll be leaving for home in a little while, and I'll drive by Miss Eugenia's house on the way. I hope she'll have had time to get to sleep by then so I can disturb her."

Jack laughed. "Beg her to stay away from Charlotte Sullivan until I get back. Then I promise I'll do whatever I can to get the woman drawn and quartered if that's what Eugenia wants."

"I'll tell her," Winston said.

"Thanks." Jack closed the phone with a sense of satisfaction. "That's taken care of."

Beth yawned. "Yes, but now we're awake."

He pulled her into his arms. "This would be a good time to discuss baby names."

"We have months before we'll need a name," she pointed out.

"You know how I like to plan ahead." He kissed her gently. "If it's a girl we could name her Joyce after my mother, or Nancy after yours." He kissed her again. "Then there's always Nancy Joyce or Joyce Nancy."

"Those names sound awful together!" Beth objected.

"I have a grandmother named Ethel," he suggested. "We could use that."

She shook her head. "We should wait to discuss names until you're more rested."

"You're right. We'll save that for later and spend our time kissing."

Before Beth could respond Jack's cell phone rang again. Frowning, he reached over and picked it up.

"Hello?"

"Jack? It's Lowell."

Jack was instantly alert. "Is there some news?"

"Captain Woods just called and said that his team has had to abandon the search for tonight. They'll start again at first light."

"Keep me posted," Jack requested.

"I will."

Jack closed his phone. "Talk about killing a romantic mood," he muttered.

Beth put her arms around him in a comforting hug. He stroked her hair and reached for the remote. "Since we're wide awake now, we might as well catch up on world events."

* * *

Eugenia was watching Lady run around the yard when she heard her phone ringing. "I'll be right back," she told the little dog. She went into the house and reached for the phone just as the ringing stopped. Momentarily she regretted that she'd never gotten the caller identification machine that Annabelle had been after her to buy. The device had always seemed like a silly waste of money. After all, if someone wanted to talk to you and didn't reach you on the first try, they would call back later. But when you missed a call late at night it would be nice to see who called.

Eugenia waited for a few minutes by the phone hoping it would ring again, but it didn't. Finally she went to the back door and called for Lady to come in. Lady was never disobedient, so she was surprised when the little dog didn't appear immediately. Eugenia walked down the porch steps and into the backyard. "Lady!"

A figure emerged from the shadows, startling a little scream from Eugenia.

"Hello, Mrs. Atkins," Dean Lumpkin said. He had Lady in his arms.

The little dog whimpered and Eugenia held out her hands. "Hello, Dean. I must say this is a strange time to be calling on folks. Now give me my dog. She's nervous around strangers."

"I'd like to hold her for a few more minutes," he said politely. "I like dogs."

Annoyed by his response, Eugenia demanded, "Why are you in my backyard at this hour of the night?"

"I needed to talk to you," he replied. "Do you mind if I come in?"

Eugenia knew that allowing him to come inside her house was unwise. However, while he didn't seem to be hurting Lady, there was a veiled threat in his words. She didn't see another option, so she nodded and led the way up the back steps.

He followed her through the back porch and into the kitchen. There she waved for him to take a seat. Her eyes strayed longingly to the telephone as she sat across from him. "Now, what is so urgent?"

"I know that you talked to Charlotte Sullivan this evening and that you taped the interview."

Eugenia was startled by his words. "How in the world would you know that?"

"I followed you home yesterday when you left Sipsey. I heard you set up the appointment with Charlotte, and I listened to your conversation from my car."

Eugenia was more curious than frightened. "How were you able to do that?"

He seemed pleased by the question. "I have a device that picks up sound waves from window glass."

"I declare," Eugenia whispered. "I didn't even know there was such a thing." She thought about Derrick's Dictaphone in her purse and realized how amateurish her own recording attempts had been.

"Mine is a relatively cheap model," Dean told her. "But it works great."

"Then you know Charlotte accused you of killing your great-uncle," Eugenia began carefully. If she could convince him that she hadn't taken Charlotte seriously, maybe he would put Lady down and leave them alone. "Of course, I'm sure she just said that you gave your great-uncle an overdose of Vitality to deflect suspicion from herself."

Dean shook his head. "No, it's true. I'm sorry I wasn't completely honest with you."

Eugenia couldn't think of anything to say, so she waited for him to continue.

"Uncle Myron came in that last night drunk. He told me that I had to be out of the house as soon as they got back from their honeymoon because Charlotte didn't like me."

Eugenia wanted to keep him calm. "I can see how that would have been upsetting."

Dean went on as if he hadn't heard her. "When I was putting him to bed Uncle Myron grabbed his chest. His eyes rolled back in his head and he stopped breathing. I've seen a few massive heart attacks, so I knew what had happened and I knew there was nothing that could be done for him. I sat there by Uncle Myron's bed thinking about the way Charlotte had stolen his dignity and his money and his new 4Runner. I was sad that Uncle Myron was dead, but I was glad that he'd died before she could get the house, too."

"Then you didn't kill him," Eugenia said, trying to follow his story in spite of the pounding of her own old heart. "He died of a heart attack just like the doctors at the hospital said."

"No, Charlotte killed him," Dean corrected, "by convincing him not to take his heart medication and to live a riotous lifestyle. But while I was sitting there I thought of a way to stop Charlotte. I knew she'd given Uncle Myron that bottle of Vitality. I hoped her fingerprints were on it, but if not I figured there would be a record somewhere of her making the purchase. So I crushed the pills left in the bottle and mixed them with water. Then I helped him drink it."

Eugenia was skeptical. "How can a dead man drink?"

"The same way an unconscious one can, and I've dealt with lots of them," Dean replied. "I lifted his head and poured small amounts of the liquid into the back of his throat. I massaged his neck until the medicine moved down his esophagus and into his stomach. Then I called the ambulance."

"And you hoped that the police would think Charlotte killed him?"

"Yes. When the paramedics came, I gave them the empty Vitality bottle and told them that I thought Charlotte had put an overdose in his drinks while they were celebrating."

"But the doctors at the hospital ignored the Vitality and listed your great-uncle's cause of death as a heart attack?"

"Yes. They found high levels of Vitality in his system, along with a large amount of alcohol, but they ignored both."

"So your plan didn't work?"

Dean shrugged. "The police said they investigated Charlotte, but I don't think they tried very hard. She probably charmed them."

"That's a possibility," Eugenia acknowledged. "Especially if the Sipsey police force is predominantly male."

"It is," Dean said. "When you called I thought there was still hope. If you could convince the FBI to investigate Charlotte they might get her for attempted murder, at least."

"Of your great-uncle," Eugenia confirmed. "The one person we're sure she *didn't* kill?"

"What difference does it make?" Dean asked. "We know she killed other people and will kill more if we let her."

Eugenia knew his logic was terribly flawed, but she understood his desire to stop Charlotte. "So it's good that I have Charlotte's confession on tape," she ventured. "Now the FBI will have to investigate."

"No," Dean contradicted her. "It's not good at all. Your tape will draw negative attention to me instead of her."

"If you gave the Vitality to your great-uncle after he was already dead, then you didn't kill him," Eugenia said. "It still may be a crime, but I doubt they'll send you to jail for it. You can explain it all to the police like you have to me."

"They may not believe me, and it will be hard to prove," Dean pointed out.

There was some question of his innocence in Eugenia's mind as well, but she certainly wasn't going to tell this volatile young man about her doubts.

"And if the newspapers get the story they might twist it around so that I look guilty," Dean continued. "I can't let anyone find out."

Eugenia crossed her fingers under the table and said, "I promise not to tell anyone what you did."

He was holding Lady a little too tightly, and the dog whimpered again. "You've already told that old lady who lives next door about the tape, and your sister knows about the appointment with Charlotte at the senior center."

"My neighbor can't remember things for more than a few minutes, and my sister never believes a word I say," Eugenia said to protect Polly and Annabelle.

Dean ignored this. "You told the police chief too, and you've even talked to a senator about it! Before long everyone will know and a rumor like that could ruin me! I work with old people," he reminded her. "What kind of nursing home will hire me if they think I did something unethical to Uncle Myron?"

"I'm sure if you explain the circumstances," Eugenia tried, but Dean was too upset to listen.

"And if my Aunt Lavada finds out, she'll be mad. She might even take back Uncle Myron's house. I earned that house," Dean said. "I deserve it. Why should my aunt or some cousin get it when they didn't do anything to help Uncle Myron?"

"They'll understand," Eugenia tried.

"They won't!" Dean was becoming more agitated. "I regret giving Uncle Myron the pills now. I see that it was foolish. But you don't know what it's like to watch Charlotte Sullivan destroy someone you love. I wanted her to pay!"

Actually, Eugenia had an idea what Dean had experienced. Just thinking about Whit in Charlotte's clutches had been enough to drive her to drastic measures. "I do understand a little of what you felt," she told him. "But I can't condone what you did. You should have called an ambulance the second your great-uncle started having chest pains, and you never should have given him Vitality after he was dead—even in an effort to bring Charlotte to justice."

"I'm not asking you to condone my actions," Dean said. "But I am asking you to help me protect my reputation."

Eugenia recrossed her fingers. "I've already told you that I'll keep your secret."

"I'm afraid that's not good enough. I want you to give me that tape," Dean said softly.

Eugenia was disappointed by this request. It was very important to her that Whit hear the tape—partly because she wanted to be sure he stayed away from Charlotte, but partly because she wanted to be sure he knew she'd been right all along.

"I need to play it for my friend, Whit Owens," she told Dean. "He's Charlotte's latest victim, and I don't know of any other way to convince him that she's just after his money. I'm sure he won't tell anyone what she says on the tape. It would be too humiliating for him."

Dean shook his head. "I can't allow you to do that. The tape incriminates me more than it does Charlotte, and I can't risk anyone hearing it, especially not a lawyer. You'll have to hope that you've scared Charlotte off."

Lady wiggled in Dean's arms, reminding Eugenia that he was in the power position. So she stood and walked over to the counter where she'd put her purse. She reached inside, popped open the Dictaphone, and extracted the tape.

"Thank you," he said after she handed it to him, as if she were giving it to him willingly.

"Now can I have my dog?"

"Not quite yet. There's one more thing I need you to do." He slipped his hand into the pocket of his jacket and removed a small prescription bottle.

"You're going to kill me, too?" Eugenia whispered.

"Oh, no!" Dean seemed insulted by this accusation. "I'm not like Charlotte, killing defenseless old people. But like we discussed already, you've told others about the tape. The only way to protect my reputation is to ruin your credibility. So I need you to seem confused for the next few days. That way no one will believe the things you've said."

"That pill will make me crazy?" Eugenia asked, trying to mask her horror.

"Not crazy, really. You'll be forgetful and disoriented," Dean explained. The effects only last for a couple of days. Then you'll be back to normal and everyone will think you just went through a little bad spell."

Eugenia stared at the pill. She had no reason to trust him. For all she knew, he might have killed his own great-uncle. And even if he was telling the truth, while the effects of the pill might be temporary, the effect on her standing in the community would be permanent. Right now her opinion was respected. After a "bad spell" like the one Dean described, she would be relegated to "senile" in the minds of her friends, and they'd always be watching for her next episode.

However, Dean was holding Lady and although he hadn't said so, she knew that he was not going to release the dog until she took the pill.

"I don't need to take a pill to act confused," Eugenia said. "I'll gladly act foolish for a few days. If I say some crazy things voluntarily, it will accomplish the same thing."

"It won't be as effective." Dean dismissed the idea. "And you might slip and say something lucid, which would ruin the whole plan."

Eugenia glanced at Lady and said, "Okay. I'll take the pill if you promise to leave afterward."

"That's a deal." He stood and moved to the sink. "Where do you keep your cups?"

"The cupboard to your right." She stared at the pill on the table. When she was a child she used to be able to hide pills in the side of her mouth. That skill was a little rusty, but she would give it a try. And if that plan failed, she knew that Kate kept syrup of ipecac in her kitchen. As soon as Dean left, she'd hurry over and take some. Hopefully she'd get the medicine out of her system before it had time to affect her.

Dean interrupted her thoughts by placing a plastic juice cup in front of her. "Here you go."

She picked up the cup and tried to keep her hand from trembling. Dean gave her the pill and watched as she put it into her mouth. She moved it into the space between her cheek and gum. Then she sipped the water.

"Drink it all," Dean encouraged. "We don't want that pill getting lodged in your throat."

Eugenia drank the rest of the water and put down the cup.

"Now, I'll help you upstairs to bed and once you're asleep, I'll slip out the back. You won't hear from me again—unless I find out that you've been telling anyone about Uncle Myron."

"I won't do that," she assured him, and this time she didn't even bother to cross her fingers. Lying to a person who had just drugged you could not be considered a sin. She reached out and plucked a tissue from a box she kept on the table by the stairs and faked a sneeze. In the process she expelled what was left of the pill from her mouth.

"Bless you," Dean said kindly as she wadded up the tissue and put it into the trash can by the table. Then she hurried to the stairs and started to climb. The sooner she convinced Dean she was asleep, the sooner he'd leave and she could get that ipecac.

When they reached her bedroom, Dean suggested that she change into a nightgown so she'd be more comfortable. "Don't be embarrassed," he said. "I am a nurse, after all."

"I don't want to change," Eugenia replied.

He shrugged. "It will reinforce the idea that you're confused if you go to bed in your clothes." He pointed at the bed and Eugenia stretched out. Lady started to whine and Dean stroked her head absently. "That's good. Now we'll wait for the medicine to take effect."

Eugenia closed her eyes and tried to take slow, steady breaths, hoping he would think she was falling asleep.

"If you think that you fooled me by spitting out that pill, you're wrong," he said softly. "I anticipated that and dissolved two pills in the water you drank."

Eugenia's eyes flew open and she saw him smiling.

"I don't blame you. It's what I would have done myself," he told her. "But it's too late now. And if you're thinking about waiting until I leave to call someone, you can forget about that too. I'll probably spend most of the night here watching you sleep."

Eugenia realized she'd been completely duped. She considered screaming, but concern for Lady stopped her. Besides, with the Iversons out of town, no one was close enough to hear. She thought of all the times she'd gotten mad at Polly for spying on her. Too bad Polly chose tonight to be derelict in her busybody duties.

Dean smoothed the hair back from her forehead in a gentle gesture. "Don't fight the medicine. Just accept it."

Something about the tone of his voice made her wonder if he'd given her enough medication to kill her. She thought about Charles and how long it had been since she'd seen him. Maybe death wouldn't be such a bad thing. With resignation, she closed her eyes and relaxed against the pillow.

Then she thought about the Iversons, who would be returning from Atlanta soon. And Lady, and that ungrateful Whit Owens, and Annabelle. They all needed her. She couldn't just give up and let Dean Lumpkin kill her. She was resisting the fog that threatened to overtake her mind and searching for a plan when she heard Winston's voice at the bottom of the stairs.

"Miss Eugenia?" he called. "Where are you?"

Her eyes flew open and she cried, "Up here!"

Dean leaned close and whispered, "Your little dog's life depends on how you act while the policeman is here."

Seconds later Winston appeared in the doorway of her bedroom. He took in Dean, sitting in a chair by the bed holding Lady. Then his eyes moved to Eugenia. "Is everything okay?"

Eugenia's head felt fuzzy and her eyelids were heavy, but for Lady's sake she managed a small nod as Dean put a finger to his lips and motioned for Winston to be quiet.

"Shhhh," Dean admonished. "Miss Eugenia has a headache. She's taken some medication and is feeling a little better now, but the medicine is making her sleepy."

Winston was better at giving orders than taking them, and Eugenia could tell that he was annoyed with Dean. "Who are you?"

"My name is Dean Lumpkin." Dean extended his free hand to Winston.

After a brief hesitation, Winston shook it. "Winston Jones."

Dean smiled. "Oh yes, the overly conscientious police chief. Miss Eugenia and I were just discussing your heroic rescue attempt at the senior center tonight. We both had quite a laugh."

Dean's tone was snide and Eugenia saw Winston's face darken with humiliation. "Is that so?"

Dean stroked Lady's head. "You should know by now that Miss Eugenia can take care of herself."

"I've never had any doubt about that," Winston said. Then he asked, "And what brings you to Haggerty?"

"Miss Eugenia and I are working together to try and prove that Charlotte Sullivan is a murderer," Dean claimed cunningly.

Winston's expression changed to irritated. "Yeah, I've heard all about that."

Eugenia knew she needed to alert Winston that she and Lady were both in trouble, but she could barely hold her eyes open. Coming up with a clever signal for Winston was way beyond her capabilities.

"I plan to stay here until I'm sure Miss Eugenia is okay." Dean waved toward the bed. "Headaches can be a symptom of something worse. I'm a registered nurse and my specialty is geriatrics, so I know these things."

"Oh, well, that's handy," Winston said. Then he leaned down and spoke to Lady, "Hey girl!"

The little dog whimpered in response.

"Can I hold her?" Winston asked. "She's crazy about me."

"I promised Miss Eugenia that I'd keep her right here where she can see her," Dean replied smoothly. "It comforts her."

Winston nodded. "Well, okay, if you've got things under control, I'll let myself out."

"Okay," Dean replied.

"Sorry to have bothered you."

"No problem," Dean assured him.

Winston turned toward the door, and Eugenia felt a terrible sense of loss. All hope would leave with the police chief. Winston paused before he crossed into the hallway. "You think I should call a doctor or something?"

Dean shook his head. "I'm keeping a close eye on her. I'll be sure to call the paramedics if I think she needs further medical attention."

Winston raised a hand up to the brim of his hat. "Good evening, then."

Dean waited until the sound of Winston's retreating footsteps ended with the slamming of the front door. Then he leaned over her and said, "Well, that was a close call. It's a good thing for your little dog here that the local police chief is an imbecile."

Eugenia wanted to be offended for Winston, but she was finding it increasingly difficult to think about anything but the darkness that was clouding her consciousness.

"It will all be over soon," Dean was continuing from what seemed like a great distance.

The effort was just too much. She couldn't fight the medicine anymore. Eugenia sent Lady a silent apology with her eyes and allowed her lids to fall. Right before her lids closed completely, she caught a quick movement by the door. Using all her strength, she dragged her eyes open in time to see Winston rush inside the room, followed closely by Whit Owens.

Dean must have heard Winston's approach because he turned as Winston reached him. Dean looked at the window and then back at Winston, apparently unsure whether to run or fight. Winston made that decision for both of them by wrapping his arms around Dean. Whit removed Lady from Dean's grasp as the two men grappled. Dean was no match for Winston's superior strength and size, but Dean put up a good fight.

Winston finally subdued Dean, but two lamps and one antique vase were broken in the process. While Winston snapped handcuffs on Dean's wrists, Whit rushed to Eugenia's bedside.

"Lady's fine," he said.

She heard Winston say, "Call an ambulance!"

"Ipecac," she whispered with numb lips.

Winston leaned over her. "What?"

"Ipecac in Kate's kitchen cupboard by the phone," Eugenia repeated. As she lost consciousness, Eugenia thought what a shame it was that Polly had missed Winston manhandling Dean Lumpkin.

CHAPTER 12

When Eugenia woke up she was in a hospital room. She felt terrible, but she knew her name, so she was reasonably sure that Dean's medication hadn't taken full effect. She was looking for the button to call a nurse when Winston walked in.

"Oh, good, you're awake," he said. "You might be a little nauseated. The emergency room doctor said I gave you too much ipecac. But it sure did the trick. You threw up for an hour."

Eugenia frowned. "It tells you the normal dosage right on the bottle." Her mouth didn't fully cooperate, so her words were a little slurred.

"I didn't have time to read all that tiny print," Winston defended himself. "For all I knew that Lumpkin guy had given you poison! I just poured as much as I could down your throat."

"I'm not complaining," Eugenia assured him. "You saved me, and I can't begin to thank you enough."

Winston smiled. "You sound funny."

"My facial muscles aren't working right," Eugenia explained, annoyed by her temporary infirmity.

"The doctor also said that the medicine that kook from Sipsey gave you might make you feel confused."

Eugenia nodded. "That's why he gave it to me. He wanted me to act crazy for a few days, like I was having a spell of senility, so that no one would believe that I ever really had a tape of my conversation with Charlotte Sullivan."

"I got the tape," Winston informed her. "And I played it for Whit."

"That's good," Eugenia said. Then she tried to frown. "Why did you come by my house to check on me last night?"

Winston scooted a chair up close to her bed and sat down. "Jack Gamble called from Tennessee and asked me to go by because you weren't answering the phone. And I'll admit that I wasn't in a big hurry to see you again after the way you blessed me out at the senior center."

"I'm sorry about that," Eugenia apologized.

Winston waved this aside. "That was nothing. Anyway, I was kind of taking my time when Miss Polly called, babbling about Lumpkin killing his uncle and some other crazy stuff—I'll admit I didn't really pay much attention to her."

Eugenia did her best to smile.

"When I knocked and you didn't answer, I was worried. Then when I saw you had this possible murderer in your bedroom, I was dumbfounded. You wouldn't have inconvenienced a visitor by asking him to stay with you during a headache. You'd have had him call Annabelle or Miss Polly."

Eugenia nodded with approval. "That would have been the sensible thing to do."

"Besides," Winston continued, "I'd never seen you so quiet."

Eugenia didn't want to spoil her good mood, so she decided to ignore this comment.

"I knew something was up but decided it would be best to make him think I was leaving so I could sneak up on him," Winston said. "When I opened your front door I saw Whit standing there with a pound cake."

"I wonder why he decided to bring me a peace offering before he heard Charlotte Sullivan's taped confession," Eugenia muttered.

Winston shrugged. "I don't know about that, but I was sure glad to see him. I told him what was going on, and he put down his pound cake and came upstairs with me."

"Thank goodness Polly called and made you suspicious of Dean," Eugenia murmured. "She may be a kleptomaniac, but she does keep a close eye on things."

Winston looked surprised. "Kleptomaniac?"

"She's been stealing recipe cards, but after what she's done for me tonight I'll let her keep them. It's the least I can do to thank her for helping you save my life."

"Miss Polly's in the waiting room," Winston told her. "So you can deliver your thank-you in person. Annabelle and Derrick are there too. And Whit."

Eugenia frowned. She didn't know how she felt about Whit after the events of the past few days and wasn't sure she was up to dealing with him in her semidrugged state.

"He rode with me in my squad car to the hospital. That's when I played the little tape of your conversation with Charlotte Sullivan for him."

"What did Whit think about the tape?"

"He was horrified that he had misjudged Charlotte. And you."

"What will happen to her? Charlotte, I mean."

"She left town," Winston reported.

"That's good for us," Eugenia said. "But bad for the next town."

Winston shrugged. "Maybe the FBI will investigate her."

"What about Dean Lumpkin?"

"He's in one of our jail cells right now, but the Sipsey police are coming to get him tomorrow."

"I think he's insane," Eugenia said. "He should be in an institution, not jail."

"That's for a judge to decide." Winston didn't sound sympathetic. "Are you ready to see your visitors?"

Eugenia sighed. "As ready as I'll ever be."

"I'll go get them." Winston walked out into the hallway, and it couldn't have been more than a minute later when Polly, Annabelle, and Derrick rushed in.

"Oh Eugenia!" Polly cried. "You've been through such an ordeal!"

"But from what Winston has told us, you handled it with courage and ingenuity," Derrick added as Whit slipped into the room. Rather than come up to crowd around her bed as the others had, Whit chose a position in a corner of the room. Eugenia knew he was unsure of the reception he'd get from her. She decided to let him stew for a while.

"What I don't understand is how you keep getting yourself into these situations," Annabelle contributed. "You're going to be the death of me."

"Thank you for your help, Polly," Eugenia began. "And for your kind assessment of my conduct, Derrick." Then she turned to her sister. "And I'm sorry to be such a bother to you."

"You aren't a bother," Annabelle assured her. "But you are a constant source of worry for me. I'm afraid that one day a murderer is going to get lucky and best you."

Eugenia smiled. "You know I've always had an overactive sense of curiosity."

"Heaven help me, if I know *anything*, I know *that!*" Annabelle agreed.

"How are you feeling?" Derrick asked.

"You must be starving!" Polly added. "The doctor said Winston gave you enough ipecac to expel your stomach contents several times over!"

"I'm not hungry at the moment," Eugenia told Polly. "But I'm sure I will be soon. When are they going to let me leave here?"

"They want to keep you for a few more hours," Annabelle said. "You know they have to be careful with *elderly* patients."

Eugenia gave her sister a smirk. "You don't have to remind me of my age. I'm feeling every minute of it right now."

"I was just kidding," Annabelle said. "About the elderly part, anyway. The hospital is keeping you for a while. I'll come back in a few hours with a change of clothes and your toiletry items."

"Thank you," Eugenia said.

"And I'll have a big breakfast ready for you when you get home," Polly offered.

Eugenia smiled. "I'll be looking forward to that. Now, if you'll all give me a few minutes to speak to Whit." The others turned and saw Whit standing in the corner. "Alone."

"Oh, of course." Polly's hands fluttered up and removed the handkerchief from the neckline of her dress. "I really should get home. It's way past my normal bedtime."

"We'll see you in the morning," Derrick promised as he followed Polly and Annabelle out of the room.

"I'm going to stay for a while," Winston told her. "So if you need anything, tell the nurse to call me."

Eugenia blinked back tears. Good old Winston. "Thank you," she whispered, knowing the words were inadequate.

He smiled and turned to Whit. "She's all yours." Then he walked into the hall.

Whit moved forward. "I hardly know what to say." He paused to clear his throat. "I was such a faithless friend, yet you risked your life to protect me."

"That's because I understand the meaning of friendship," she said. "And I was immune to Charlotte Sullivan's charms."

"I feel like such a fool."

"You were a fool," she agreed. "But you're not the first old man to have his head turned by Charlotte's pretty face."

"I'm sorry that I have a tendency to be shallow. It was something all my wives complained about."

For the first time Eugenia felt an odd kinship with Whit's ex-wives. But instead of mentioning this, she said, "It's often difficult to put a value on things you can't see."

"Charles recognized your worth from the beginning and never wavered."

Eugenia remembered the moment a few hours before when she had thought she might be reunited with Charles, and tears clouded her vision. "Yes," she agreed.

He hung his head. "I don't deserve a friend like you."

Whit was no Charles Atkins, that was for sure, but she still cared about him. "That's true," she said. "But you've got my friendship just the same."

"How can I ever thank you?"

"When I'm feeling a little better, you can take me out for a nice dinner. But right now, you can go on home. I need to get some rest."

Whit leaned forward and patted her left hand. "Sleep well," he said. And then he was gone.

* * *

Gray opened his eyes and looked around his small tent. It was still dark, but even without checking his watch he knew dawn wasn't far away. He thought about Lettie, sleeping peacefully in the tent beside his. It would be nice to give her a little more rest, but Alexa and the ranger were out there somewhere in the park and might need help. So with a sigh he unzipped his sleeping bag and sat up to put his snow gear back on.

When he stepped outside his tent he was pleasantly surprised to see that the temperature was warmer than it had been when they went to sleep. He pulled his backpack out of his tent and set up the propane burner. After heating some water for hot chocolate, he dug through the MREs to find one that he thought Lettie would dislike the least.

When the food was warm, he opened her tent and crawled inside. She was curled on her side, sound asleep. He was tempted to watch her for a few minutes but was afraid she would wake up and catch him. She already had enough grievances against him, so he reached out and shook her gently. "Come on, Lettie," he said. "We've got to get going."

She murmured something unintelligible and thrust her arms outside the confines of her sleeping bag, but her eyes remained shut.

Gray leaned close and tried again, "Lettie, wake up."

A hand reached toward him. Her fingers brushed his cheek and then moved over to trace the edges of his mouth. "Gray," she whispered.

"Lettie," he returned.

Her hand circled behind his neck, and she pulled him forward until their lips touched in a tender kiss.

Everything was perfect until her eyes flew open, and she stared at him in horror. "I'm s-s-sorry," she stammered as she backed away from him inside the small confines of the tent. "I didn't mean, or at least I thought . . ." She paused and took a deep breath. "I thought I was dreaming—and now it's turned into a nightmare."

He smiled. "I can't argue with you there. The only good news is that I have your breakfast ready." He moved to the tent door. "And since you thought you were dreaming, that very nice kiss didn't count."

"Didn't count?" Lettie repeated, her cheeks pink with embarrassment.

"It wasn't real," he explained. "So don't worry about it." He left the tent and returned to the propane stove where their breakfasts were waiting. She joined him there a few minutes later, wearing her snow gear.

He held up the tray. "Here's your breakfast."

"Let me guess," she muttered. "*Scrambled* chili and macaroni?"

"It's oatmeal," he told her. "And I warmed it up a little."

She stared at the unappetizing paste. "I appreciate your effort, but I don't like oatmeal under the best of circumstances." She looked around. "And our circumstances are far from the best."

"It will give you energy," he said. "You need to eat it."

"No more granola bars?"

He shook his head. "Sorry."

She took the container and scooped up a bite of oatmeal into her mouth.

"If you eat it all, I'll give you a mug of hot chocolate," Gray offered.

"That's incentive enough." Lettie finished her oatmeal quickly, and Gray produced a mug. "Is it going to snow again?" she asked him.

"No," Gray replied. "In fact, the temperature is above freezing, and the skies are clear. Once the sun comes up, the snow will start to melt."

Lettie seemed encouraged. "That sounds good."

"We won't be as cold," Gray agreed. "But as the snow melts it's going to make it hard to follow the trail." Gray frowned at the mention of the footprints Alexa and the ranger were leaving in the snow.

"Especially since we don't know where they're going," Lettie added. "We don't even know if *they* know where they're going."

He decided it was time to share his worst fears with her even if they eventually proved to be groundless. That way he couldn't be accused of holding out on her. "That set of prints leading up to the window at the lodge is still bothering me," he told her. "It makes sense that anyone stranded in the park by the weather would come to the lodge. What doesn't make sense is that they would get there and see us inside with a warm fire and food and then walk back into the woods."

Lettie was frowning in concentration. "No, that doesn't make sense. Why would someone do that?"

"The only reason I can think of is that they didn't want anyone to know they were in the park."

"And they were willing to freeze to death in the woods to keep their presence a secret?" Lettie asked incredulously.

This was the hard part. "Only someone who's in trouble with the law would risk his life to protect his identity. Like the convict that Ranger Penny thought he found dead at the bottom of that cliff."

"You think the convict isn't really dead?" Lettie whispered.

"The ranger looked young, and he only has a few months of experience. It probably wouldn't be too hard to fool him. And it makes sense for a convict to head for the service entrance instead of the Greenbriar station," Gray shared his concern.

"So the convict is with Alexa and the ranger?" Lettie cried.

Gray shrugged. "It's possible. The convict might have waited in the woods by the lodge until he thought we were asleep and then sneaked in to get supplies."

"But Alexa and the ranger were on the couches," Lettie realized.

Gray nodded. "An unpleasant surprise."

"So he made them go with him?" Lettie asked.

"That's the theory that I can't seem to get out of my mind," Gray said. "From the window the convict wouldn't have been able to see us all. He probably didn't know we were in the back."

"And Alexa and the ranger kept quiet to protect us."

"And in the hope that we'd rescue them," Gray added with certainty.

"We're trying," Lettie said.

"If I'd had any idea that I was taking you into danger, I would have gone straight to the Greenbriar station instead of following the tracks," Gray told her. "But it's too late for that now. I wanted you to know that the situation may be more dangerous than we originally thought."

"Thanks, I guess." Lettie drank the last sip of her hot chocolate and extended the mug to Gray. "That was delicious."

He took the mug and gave her a quick smile. "I'm glad. Now if you'll give me your sleeping bag I'll roll it up for you."

Lettie retrieved her sleeping bag from her tent and passed it over to Gray. As he started dismantling her tent she told him, "I need to use the bathroom.".

He pulled a little bag from his backpack. "Here's the latrine kit. I'll wait here."

She took the kit. "I was happier when I didn't know there was such a thing." Then she stepped out as the first rays of sunlight broke through the trees.

* * *

Beth woke up early on Sunday morning after a restless night. By the time she finished with her shower, Jack was awake too, so they agreed to get ready and head to the hospital.

"The snow is melting," Beth pointed out as they walked through the hotel parking lot. "That's got to be a good thing."

"It should help the rescue efforts," Jack agreed. He took her hand and led her toward the Hummer. "We need to pass hospital duty over to someone else soon."

"Jack!" Beth was appalled. "We can't desert Lowell!"

He opened the passenger door for her. "Lowell seems like a nice guy and I want him to recover completely. And I really hope Gray and the others come out of this alive, but we've got to get back to our kids and our lives."

"The kids are fine," Beth said. "We talk to them every couple of hours."

"Well, if we're gone much longer, Miss Eugenia might overpower Roberta and your mother and move in. Then our lives will be *ruined*."

"Now that is a cause for concern," she acknowledged. "But seriously." She waited until he was looking at her before she continued.
"I'm not leaving until this is settled."

He sighed. "It was worth a try."

They stopped at an IHOP for breakfast and as soon as their
order was delivered, Jack's cell phone rang. He walked outside to
answer it. Beth forced herself to eat her egg-white omelet and drink
her orange juice. Then she prayed that it would all settle well on her
sensitive stomach. Just when she decided she couldn't handle
another bite, Jack returned.

"That was Annabelle," he said as he sat down across from her.
"We don't need to worry about Miss Eugenia moving into our
house. She's in the hospital."

Beth put down her fork. "What happened?"

"She was drugged by the great-nephew of the man she thinks
killed that Myron Bell in Sipsey."

Beth shook her head in alarm. "I thought Charlotte Sullivan was
the person trying to kill her!"

Jack sighed. "I thought so too. But apparently Miss Eugenia
managed to run into *another* murderer."

"Is she okay?"

"Fine," Jack said around a mouthful of grits. "They're releasing
her this morning."

"Did the nephew really kill his great-uncle?"

Jack shrugged. "I don't know, and honestly I don't care. I wish I'd
never answered the phone when she called asking for my legal advice."

"Jack," Beth reprimanded him mildly. "She's an old woman and
she needed help."

"Well, she twisted what I said into a plan to trap a murderer and
ended up in the hospital! If she's going to ask for my advice, she
should follow it instead of changing it to suit her purposes."

Beth couldn't think of an argument. "You're right. I don't know
what she was thinking. But I'm glad she's okay."

"She's more than okay—she's a hero. The guy who tried to
drug her is in jail, and the woman she claims is murdering old

men for their money is probably going to be the center of an FBI investigation."

Beth laughed. "Miss Eugenia is a force to be reckoned with."

"I guess I'd better try to stay on her good side," Jack muttered.

"It would be wise," Beth concurred. "Now eat your breakfast so we can go check on Lowell and Mary Margaret."

* * *

The patient was waiting for the doctor to come and release him when Jack and Beth arrived at the hospital.

"So, what did the doctor have to say?" Beth asked.

"He hasn't been by yet," Lowell replied with a decided edge to his voice.

Jack pointed out the window where water was dripping from the trees as the snow melted. "The weather's improving dramatically," he said. "Have you heard anything from Captain Woods?"

Lowell nodded. "He called at daybreak and said the team was headed into the woods, following the footprints in the snow. The captain said the trail was trampled—indicating that several people had walked it but not necessarily at the same time."

"Does that mean they're all alive and hostages?" Beth asked.

Lowell shrugged. "I don't know."

There was a knock on the hospital room door and Beth looked up, expecting to see the tardy doctor. But Captain Woods was standing in the doorway, holding a roll that resembled white wrapping paper.

"I need your help," he said.

"What's happened?" Lowell asked.

"The trail is disappearing thanks to the warmer temperatures and bright sunshine." The captain walked over to Lowell's bed and handed him one of the rolls. It was a detailed map of the Great Smoky Mountains National Park. "I've sent up dirt bikes for my team to use instead of snowmobiles. Now we need to determine which way Bright is headed." He spread the map across Lowell's lap and pointed to a spot on the far left edge. "It looks like he's headed toward the service entrance near Davenport Gap."

"That makes sense," Lowell agreed.

The captain nodded. "It's not busy, which will reduce his chances of being detected. And once he gets out on Highway 321 he can hitch a ride and be on his way to Knoxville or Chattanooga or any city in the United States for that matter. The question is, what trail will he take?"

Lowell studied the map for a minute. "If I was an escaped felon I wouldn't use any trail." He traced a faint line. "I'd keep to the woods of Brushy Mountain until I made it to Little Pigeon River. Then he'll only have a few yards of open space to cross in order to get to the exit."

The captain nodded. "That's the way I'll send the rescue team, and I'll have another group waiting at the service entrance."

"He may not use the gate," Lowell warned.

"We're prepared for that," the captain assured him.

"Lowell said there were several footprints on the path your men were following until the snow started to melt," Jack remarked. "Does that mean all the hostages are still alive?"

"My men haven't found any bodies or signs of struggle, so we're cautiously optimistic," the captain replied.

"What now?" Lowell asked.

"We're back to waiting." The captain rolled up his map and moved toward the door. "I'll call when we know something."

* * *

After an hour of walking, Lettie and Gray found the remnants of a campfire. Gray reached down and touched a piece of charred wood.

"It's still warm, so they can't be too far ahead."

"And obviously the convict isn't a responsible camper like you if he left warm wood."

Gray nodded as he kicked snow up onto the wood and stamped it firmly.

Lettie pushed the hood of her parka back. With the sun shining on her she was almost too warm. "Can we stop for a water break?" she asked.

Gray shook his head. "No, we need to press our advantage."

She bit back a complaint and fell into step behind him as he slipped back into the trees. She moved up close behind him and said, "The snow has melted too much for you to follow their footprints. So how do you know which way to go?"

"Even though most of the snow is gone, they are still leaving a trail."

Lettie looked down at the pine-straw–littered ground, which was distinguished in no way she could see from the rest of the forest. "This is a *trail?*"

Gray nodded. "One only an experienced and responsible tour guide like myself would recognize."

"I'm impressed," Lettie admitted, "by your experience more than your responsibility."

He smiled. "Besides, I know where he's going. So that makes it easier."

"And if you're wrong?"

"I'm not." Gray sounded certain. "He's going to the service entrance."

Lettie decided to trust him—mostly because her options were severely limited. They walked in silence for a while, and she was about to ask again for a water break when he put up his hand for her to stop. She froze in place as he turned around and leaned very close.

"I think I heard something," he whispered.

They inched forward, and then Lettie heard something too. She touched Gray's arm and mouthed, "It sounds like someone moaning."

He nodded. "You stay here."

She shook her head. "No way."

With a look of annoyed resignation, he pressed on through the woods. They moved with synchronized stealth. When Gray took a step, Lettie took a step. When he stopped, she stopped. Soon they found the source of the moaning. There was a man lying on the snow a couple of feet off what Gray claimed was the "trail." Gray knelt down and Lettie crept up beside him. Together they studied the man.

He was curled in a near-fetal position, presumably to ward off the cold. There was an ugly gash on his forehead, and he had his right arm tucked inside his coat in a Napoleon-like manner.

"He looks harmless," she whispered to Gray.

"Just in case he's not, I'll check on him alone. If he shoots me, you run."

Lettie rolled her eyes. "There's a great plan."

He ignored her sarcasm and walked over to the injured man. Keeping a safe distance, he asked, "Who are you?"

"Water, please," the man rasped.

"Could you hand me a bottle of water from my pack?" Gray asked.

Lettie unzipped the pack he'd left on the ground and tossed one of the few full bottles to him. He twisted off the top and handed it to the man before restating his question, "What's your name?"

"Park Ranger Lamar Penny," the man claimed weakly.

Lettie was so shocked that she charged up to them without any concern for safety. "But if he's Ranger Penny," she said to Gray, "then the man who came to the lodge is really . . ."

"The convict," Gray finished for her. "I always thought there was too much blood on his shirt."

"What?" Lettie asked for clarification.

"Never mind," Gray replied.

The ranger took another sip of water and then said, "The captain told me to leave him, but I felt bad. Decided to go back and move the body to the campsite if I could. Approached without caution—rookie mistake." He paused for a breath. "He had a gun, made me give him my uniform shirt. I tried to back away and he shot me." The real Ranger Penny pointed at a big hole in the pocket of his down jacket. "Couldn't find my compass, but it was here. Saved my life."

"And since then you've been following him?" Gray asked.

"Yes," the ranger confirmed. "Too weak to approach, just kept them in my sights."

"You came to the lodge?"

The ranger nodded. "LeConte, like the captain told me. Slow because of injuries. Bright was already there. Left with a woman."

"That's my friend Alexa," Lettie said. "She's his hostage."

The ranger shook his head. "Not a hostage. Been following them ever since and haven't seen any coercion."

"That's impossible!" Lettie objected. "Alexa wouldn't go with him if she wasn't a hostage!"

"She's with the convict of her own free will?" Gray asked the ranger.

The ranger shrugged. "Looked that way to me."

Lettie wanted to point out all the errors in this line of thinking, but Gray spoke first. "It doesn't matter why she's with him. Either way we need to catch up with them before they reach the service entrance." He shrugged out of his backpack and pulled off one of the sleeping bags. "I'm afraid we're going to have to leave you here," he told the ranger. "But we'll get you warm and give you some food and water."

The ranger nodded.

Lettie helped wrap the sleeping bag around Ranger Penny. Then Gray gave him another water bottle and an MRE. "We'll send help as soon as possible," Gray promised.

"Don't worry about me," the ranger replied. "Get Bright."

"We'll get him," Gray said. Then he turned to Lettie. "I don't guess I could convince you to stay here with Ranger Penny?"

"I don't guess you could," she replied.

"Our packs will slow us down, so we'll leave them here." He lifted hers off and placed it beside his on the ground, then moved forward, and she followed right behind him.

CHAPTER 13

In spite of the warmer weather, Alexa was shivering uncontrollably. The tremors had started early that morning and had grown steadily worse through the day. By the time they reached a little clearing on the edge of the woods she was barely able to stand.

Mancil crossed the small open space and stopped just inside the tree line. Leaning forward, he stared into the distance. Alexa hugged herself to reduce the shaking and followed the direction of his gaze. He was looking at a metal gate blocking a small road a few yards away.

"This is the service entrance," he said without taking his eyes off the gate.

"This is where you plan to leave the park?" she asked.

He nodded.

Alexa squinted into the glaring sunlight and studied the gate, hoping to see what Mancil found so interesting. But she couldn't find anything remarkable and didn't have the energy to keep trying. She dropped to the ground and pulled her knees up under her chin.

"You're sick." She looked up to see Mancil watching her instead of the gate.

"Yes." She wiped perspiration from her forehead. How was it possible for her to be cold and hot at the same time?

"Withdrawals won't kill you," he said. "The worst will be behind you soon."

She attempted a laugh. "I'll try to remember that while I'm shaking into little pieces."

He ignored the joke. "The gate looks clear, but that won't last long. I need to go now."

She was filled with despair at the thought. "You're going to leave me?"

"I should have done it a long time ago."

Their eyes met. In his gaze she saw the same regret she felt. "But you didn't."

He shook his head. "No."

"There's goodness in you," she managed to say. "I wish I could help you."

He stooped down in front of her. "No one can help me. And don't trust that goodness you think you see. I've killed before, and I'll do it again if I have to."

She was overcome with sadness, and tears leaked out of the corners of her eyes. In contrast with his harsh words, he reached over and gently wiped them away. "As soon as I can get to a phone I'll call the ranger station and tell them where to find you." He removed one of the insulated blankets from his pack and wrapped it around her shoulders.

She clutched the blanket and asked, "Won't you need this?"

"You need it worse," he replied. He was very close, and if she hadn't been shaking so much she'd have hugged him.

"So this is good-bye?" she forced herself to say.

He nodded, but before he could respond, they heard a noise behind them. Alexa looked up as Gray and Lettie stepped into the clearing.

* * *

Lettie followed closely behind Gray as he moved into the open and pointed the gun at the convict. "Put your hands up!" he yelled.

Rather than obey, Mancil Bright spun around with a gun of his own trained on them. Gray knocked Lettie to the ground and landed beside her, effectively shielding her with his own body just as the convict fired. Lettie barely had time to process the fact that she and Gray were both uninjured before she saw that Bright was standing over them. "Throw your gun over there," he told Gray, using his own gun to motion toward some underbrush several feet away.

Alexa came to stand beside Bright, and Lettie did a quick visual examination of her friend. "You look terrible," she told Alexa.

Alexa ignored this. "Do what he says, and he won't hurt you," she encouraged through chattering teeth.

Lettie was shocked and hurt. "Are you really helping him?"

Alexa didn't respond to this question and spoke to Gray again. "Please, Gray."

"I said throw your gun," Bright instructed with less diplomacy. "Now."

Gray hesitated and Bright grabbed Alexa. He pressed his gun to her temple and said, "If you don't drop your gun, I'll shoot her."

Left with little choice, Gray tossed his gun off to the side.

Bright stepped over and kicked it into the underbrush. "You two stand up and come here," he commanded.

"Please don't hurt them," Alexa said.

The convict didn't make any promises. Instead he removed a roll of duct tape from his backpack and waved for Gray to approach him. "You first."

Reluctantly, Gray walked toward the gunman.

"Turn around," Bright said. "And remember that if you try anything, I'll shoot your girlfriend first."

Lettie's eyes met Gray's. They were the warm brown color she loved so much, and tears stung her eyes. Gray was prepared to sacrifice himself to save her if necessary.

Bright handed the tape to Alexa. "Use this to secure his hands behind his back," he instructed.

"Don't do it, Alexa," Lettie begged.

Alexa gave her an annoyed look. "I have to do it," she said. "Otherwise he'll shoot you."

It took Alexa longer to secure Gray than normal because of her constant shaking. When Alexa finished with Gray's hands, Bright told her to wind the tape around Gray's shoulders as well. Alexa concentrated on her task and didn't seem to feel bad about cooperating with the convict.

"Now do her hands." Bright pointed at Lettie with his gun.

When Alexa approached her, Lettie asked, "Are you sick?"

The other woman nodded. "Withdrawals from the pain medicine."

"And why are you helping him?" Lettie hissed.

"Because I think I can keep him from killing you," Alexa whispered back.

"He's dangerous," Lettie returned softly. "He might kill *you!*"

Alexa shrugged indifferently. "We both know how valuable my life is."

"Enough talking," Bright said. "Alexa, tape their mouths."

"Please, Alexa, don't do this," Lettie tried again.

"Shut up!" Bright commanded. He took the tape from Alexa's trembling fingers and pressed a piece firmly against Lettie's mouth. He silenced Gray in the same way and examined them both. "That should do." He moved to the edge of the trees. After observing for a few seconds, he turned back to Alexa. "We have company," he said.

Lettie and Gray exchanged a hopeful look.

"That changes everything," Bright continued.

"What will you do?" Alexa asked.

"I'll need a hostage to get past the cops at the gate. You can stay here and I'll take her." He indicated toward Lettie with his head.

Lettie barely had time to process this unpleasant turn of events before Gray lunged toward Bright. With his arms tied behind his back, he wasn't much of a threat. Bright sidestepped him easily. Gray tried to regain his balance, but his forward motion propelled him to the ground. He hit hard, and Lettie winced.

Slowly, Bright turned to face Gray where he lay curled on his side a few yards away. "Well, you've just signed your own death warrant," Bright said. "I knew I should have shot you right off, but I didn't want to upset Alexa. I'll correct that mistake right now."

He raised his gun, and Lettie screamed against the thick tape that sealed her mouth. She staggered forward a few steps, but Alexa got there first. She stood almost within arm's reach of the convict, putting herself between Gray and the gun.

Lettie felt useless just standing there watching. She had to find a way to help them, but didn't know what she could do. She couldn't even remember which edge of the clearing Bright had kicked the gun toward, and even if she found it, without the use of her hands she wouldn't even be able to pick it up. Finally she decided all she could do was run into Bright. Maybe she'd be lucky, and he'd drop the gun before he had a chance to shoot Alexa or Gray.

Lettie staggered forward but the footing was bad and without her arms for balance she fell to the ground herself. Bright didn't even give her a glance, but Gray's eyes moved to hers. Then they stared at each other in frustration as Alexa tried to reason with the convict.

"I can't let you shoot him," Alexa told Bright.

"I'll do what I have to do to stay alive," the convict replied. "I told you not to trust your naive assessment of my character."

"You won't kill me," she said with certainty. "You're not a bad person."

Lettie watched in horrified suspense, waiting to see what Bright would do.

Finally he exhaled audibly. "You're right and wrong. I won't kill you, but I am a bad person."

He shoved Alexa backward, and she fell beside Gray. Then Bright reached down and hauled Lettie to her feet. "You two just sit there nice and quiet. If you don't cause any trouble I'll drop her off a few miles down the road."

As Bright was dragging her toward the tree line, Lettie looked back at Gray and tried to convey her feelings. She wasn't sure if she'd been successful or not, when she saw tears pool in his eyes.

Then a voice called from across the clearing. "Bright!"

They all turned to see Ranger Penny holding Gray's gun.

"Put down your gun," the ranger commanded.

"I'm not going back to prison," Bright whispered. Then he released Lettie and started to run. Ranger Penny's bullet caught Mancil Bright in the upper back, and Lettie watched in horror as the convict fell to the ground.

Ranger Penny stumbled forward as several rangers jumped the gate and ran toward them. The first one to arrive stood over the escaped convict, his gun pointed threateningly. If Lettie hadn't been so scared she would have been annoyed since this was obviously unnecessary. Mancil Bright's lifeless eyes were staring at the clear blue sky above them.

Soon the clearing was teeming with rangers and other uniformed men. One of the rangers knelt beside Lettie and helped her to sit up. "Are you okay?" he asked, and she nodded. "This is going to hurt," he warned her. She braced herself against the inevitable pain as the ranger grabbed the edge of the tape that covered her mouth. Tears sprang to her eyes as he ripped the tape off, but thankfully she was able to control a scream.

"Sorry," the ranger apologized.

"It's okay," she said.

He reached behind her and started unwinding the tape that bound her hands. She looked across the few feet that separated them and saw that Gray was already on his feet, rubbing his wrists. He was talking to another ranger, and although Lettie couldn't hear what they were saying, she assumed he was explaining what had happened.

The ranger finally succeeded in freeing her hands, and Lettie thanked him before hurrying over to Alexa, who was now kneeling on the ground beside Mancil Bright.

As Lettie pulled Alexa into her arms, she heard Gray say, "Ranger Penny needs medical attention."

The ranger who had untaped Lettie said, "We've called for a medivac helicopter. It should be here soon."

Alexa whimpered. "I killed him."

"No," Lettie corrected her gently. "The ranger shot him, not you."

Alexa shook her head, refusing to be comforted. "If he'd left me yesterday, he would have made it to freedom. But he didn't think I could survive on my own so he kept me with him and now he's dead." Alexa rocked back and forth. "It's all my fault."

Lettie couldn't consider the convict's death a bad thing, but she didn't say so in an effort to keep from upsetting Alexa more. "Try not to worry. You're not thinking clearly because of that pain medication. Everything will be clearer in a couple of days."

"That's not true!" Alexa denied. "I haven't taken any pills for over a day now. Mancil put most of them in the hot chocolate."

Gray squatted down beside them. "Of course. That's why we slept in so late."

Lettie gave him a worried look as Alexa continued.

"So the medicine wasn't clouding my ability to think. I knew that Mancil was really a good person and that he didn't want to hurt anyone. He could have killed us all at the lodge, but he took me as a hostage instead. And he treated me well. Don't you see?"

Lettie nodded. "I see that you were very brave."

Alexa shook her head. This wasn't the response she wanted. "No, about Mancil. He didn't belong in prison." She glanced over at the convict lying on the ground a few yards away. "He never had a chance."

Lettie was still struggling to find an appropriate response when a man wearing a U.S. Marshal uniform walked up to them and cleared his throat. "My name is McHale."

Lettie briefly introduced herself, Alexa, and Gray.

Marshal McHale said, "We'll need to get statements from all of you."

Lettie stood and pulled Alexa to her feet. "We'll be glad to give you statements, but right now Alexa needs to be taken to a hospital. Maybe we can come by later on this evening."

Marshal McHale looked uncomfortable as he said, "My instructions are to bring Ms. Whitstone directly to the station."

"But she's sick, as you can plainly see," Lettie pointed out.

"According to Ranger Penny, she was aiding and abetting the convict," the marshal explained apologetically.

"That's ridiculous. Alexa saved our lives!" Lettie waved a hand to include Gray.

Gray tried to help by saying, "It may have appeared that Ms. Whitstone was cooperating with the convict, but there were extenuating circumstances."

"I'm sure it's just a misunderstanding," the marshal said. "But until we get it straightened out, she has to come with me. I promise that we'll get her medical attention."

"I want to go with her," Lettie said, keeping one arm firmly around Alexa.

The marshal shook his head again. "Sorry, but we can't allow the participants in an event to consult before they've been questioned. That helps to prevent erroneous statements."

Lettie processed this remark and then narrowed her eyes at the marshal. "Are you saying that you think I'll try to convince Ms. Whitstone to be less than truthful when she gives her statement?"

The marshal blushed. "No ma'am. I'm not saying that at all. It's just regulations is all. You can go to our headquarters in Bryson City, but you won't be allowed to see her until after she's given her statement. The only person who will have access to her for a while is the district attorney and her lawyer."

Lettie digested this information. Then she looked at Gray. "I need to talk to Jack Gamble, fast."

Gray borrowed a phone from one of the rangers, and Lettie moved over into the woods where she could talk in relative privacy. Then she called Jack. Once she had assured him that everyone was unhurt, Lettie explained Alexa's precarious legal situation. "Alexa became the convict's hostage to save me and Gray," Lettie told him. "But her actions are being misconstrued as illegal and, well, she needs a lawyer. Quick. She's been abusing prescription drugs for weeks and is in withdrawal. I think she needs to be in a hospital, but they're taking her to the U.S. Marshals office in Bryson City, and they won't even let me go with her."

"I'll call the office in Bryson City and demand that she be brought here to Blount County Hospital where I can protect her rights," Jack replied.

"Thank you," Lettie said. Then, after glancing around to be sure that no one could hear her, she added, "Mostly she needs to be protected from herself. She's all confused and feels guilty about contributing to the convict's death, so there's no telling what she'll say or admit to."

"Don't worry," Jack comforted her. "We'll make sure that nothing she divulges during the ride here is admissible in court."

Lettie was horrified. "You think she'll have to go to *court?*"

"It's possible," Jack confirmed. "We'll play it safe with her unofficial confessions, just in case."

"Okay," Lettie said. "Thanks, Jack."

"Let the marshals bring her in," he said. "I'll take care of her."

Lettie closed the phone and gave it back to Gray as Marshal McHale approached them again. He addressed Lettie, "I've just gotten word that Ms. Whitstone is to be taken to Blount County Hospital." He turned to Alexa. "It's time to go now, ma'am."

Alexa turned frightened eyes to Lettie.

"Jack and Beth are waiting for you at the hospital," Lettie told her. "Remember, you need to be very *quiet* on the way there."

"Okay," Alexa replied. Then she walked docilely beside the marshal to one of the SUVs.

Lettie swiped at tears as she watched Alexa climb into one of the vehicles. "I feel like I'm abandoning her."

"Jack will take care of her."

Lettie took a deep breath. "Yes."

Lettie and Gray stood side by side and watched as the helicopter landed in the road on the other side of the service entrance. Ranger Penny was assisted to the helicopter by some of his fellow rangers. Once the helicopter was gone, Mancil Bright's body was loaded into one of the SUVs. After the vehicle sped away a ranger walked over and said, "I need to get your statements." He pointed at Lettie. "You first."

Lettie recounted the events of the past twenty-four hours as accurately as possible. Then she sat on a tree stump while the ranger interviewed Gray. Once the statements were complete, the ranger said, "I'm headed out. Would you like me to take you somewhere?"

Gray put a hand on her arm. "You go on to the marshals office or the hospital or wherever you want to go. I need to head back to the lodge and clean up or they'll never let us use it again."

Lettie couldn't bear the thought of parting from Gray so abruptly. So she said, "Since there's nothing I can do for Alexa or the ranger, I'll go back to the lodge with you. You'll be able to get done twice as fast with my help, and I know you're anxious to see Lowell."

Gray smiled. "I won't refuse an extra pair of hands." Then he turned to the ranger. "Do you have a spare vehicle we can use?"

"We've got a dirt bike," the ranger replied.

Gray nodded. "We'll take it."

Lettie followed Gray to one of the park service's trucks and watched as the motorcycle was unloaded. Then Gray swung a leg over the seat and waved for Lettie to join him. Lettie climbed on and wrapped her arms around his waist. As she leaned her cheek against his back she realized that at some point over the past twenty-four hours she had completely lost her aversion to touching him. Then they lurched forward, and it took all her concentration to stay on the back of the fishtailing dirt bike.

* * *

When Jack closed his phone, Beth, Lowell, and Mary Margaret were all regarding him anxiously.

"Well?" Beth prompted.

"Based on what little Gray and Lettie were able to tell me and the few additional details I got from Captain Woods, it seems that the convict didn't take all of them as hostages. Bright came to the lodge, pretending to be the ranger. Sometime during the night he and Alexa left. Lettie says she went willingly, but only to keep him from killing them all. Gray and Lettie didn't wake up until midmorning on Saturday, thanks to a heavy dose of Alexa's prescription medication the convict put in their hot chocolate."

"Poor Alexa!" Mary Margaret whispered.

Jack frowned. "Yes, and Alexa's problems are far from over. She's going through drug withdrawals, and it seems that the real Ranger Penny was following her and Bright. Based on his account, the authorities think that she was Bright's accomplice."

"That's ridiculous," Lowell scoffed.

Jack nodded. "I agree, and I don't think it will be hard to prove her innocence. But the important thing is to try to keep her from incriminating herself. She's on her way to the hospital, so I'm going to go down and wait for her at the emergency entrance."

Beth stood. "I'm going too." She glanced at Mary Margaret. "Will you and Lowell be okay here?"

"Of course," Mary Margaret assured her. "You go to Alexa."

"Gray and Lettie are going back to the lodge to collect the gear and clean up," Jack told Lowell. "Call if you need us."

"Don't worry about me," Lowell said. "The only thing I'm likely to die from in this hospital is boredom."

* * *

Lettie was surprised by the tenderness she felt when she saw the LeConte Lodge come into view. After all she'd been through, it seemed like a beacon of civilization—proof that comfort and safety still existed in the world.

Her entire body ached and she'd had enough death-defying experiences over the past hour to last her a lifetime. Gray parked near the entrance and waited until Lettie had climbed off before lowering the bike to the ground. Then he led the way inside.

Once they were in the dining hall, Lettie looked around at the now-familiar room. "I don't mind helping you clean up," she told Gray. "But I have to have a shower first."

He nodded. "I could use one myself. You go ahead."

Lettie went into the back bedroom and dug through her pack. She removed clean clothing and headed for the tiny bathroom. She turned the space heater on high and took a quick shower.

When she was dry and dressed in fresh clothes, Lettie packed her and Alexa's bags and carried them into the dining hall, where she found Gray sweeping ashes from the fireplace.

"The bathroom is all yours," she told him. Then she held out her hand for the broom. "I'll take over cleanup duty."

He smiled as he passed the broom to her. "I'll relinquish it gladly."

"Don't take too long in the shower," she said. "My cooperation does have limits."

"I'll hurry," he promised. Then he walked into the kitchen.

She had finished sweeping the fireplace and was washing the dishes by the time he emerged from the bathroom. His hair was damp and curling softly at the ends, and she was getting used to his little beard.

Lettie pulled her gaze away from him and looked out the kitchen window. The snow was melting in earnest now, and patches of soggy brown grass dotted the landscape. Soon she and Gray were going to walk out of this lodge, and their brief encounter would be over. She would go back to her life and he would go back to his. It might be years before they saw each other again—if they ever did.

The not-knowing was unacceptable, so she put her hands on the counter to brace herself and then demanded, "Why?"

He looked up sharply. "Why what?"

"I have to know," she told him. "For five years I thought you didn't love me, but after this morning . . ." Her voice trailed off as she thought about those few moments between dreams and reality when they had kissed. "Anyway, I know you still have feelings for me. So why did you ruin our lives?"

He walked over and put his hands beside hers, palms down, on the counter.

"I never said I didn't love you," he responded softly. "I never even said I didn't want to marry you."

This outrageous claim infuriated Lettie. "Yes you did!" she shot back. "That was the worst day of my life and I think I remember what happened!"

"It wasn't my *best* day either," Gray returned. "And my memories are very clear. I told you I needed some time."

"I'd already been waiting for you for two years. How much time did you expect me to give you?" She was angry now and that was an emotion she felt comfortable with.

"I'm not sure," he said. "A few months maybe."

"And why was it that you waited until after all the invitations had been sent out to tell me you needed this extra time?"

"Because I thought I could do it," he said. "I thought I could conform to your idea of happiness. But then, at that moment, I just couldn't!"

"So it had to be your way or no way at all!" she said louder than she intended.

He leaned toward her. "No, it had to be *your* way or no way."

She frowned. "I didn't call off the wedding."

"Why did we have to get married so soon after I got home from my mission?" he asked. "And why did we have to live in a condo in downtown Atlanta? Why did I have to go to college and get a degree in finance so I could bore myself to death for the rest of my life? Because that's the way you wanted it, that's why."

Lettie's confidence in her position as the injured party faltered a little. "I thought it was what you wanted too."

"I don't know why you thought that. You certainly never *asked* me."

"I talked to your mother and my mother and in my letters . . ."

"You told me," Gray repeated with annoying smugness. "You and our mothers decided things, and then you all told me how it was going to be. No one ever asked. By the time I got off the plane from my mission the whole thing was already planned. All you needed was a groom to plug in at the last minute. And that's when I finally became important."

"That's not true," Lettie objected. "I asked your opinion about the color of my bridesmaid dresses and which entrée we should serve at the wedding luncheon."

Gray waved this aside. "That was just fine-tuning of decisions that had already been made."

"Your feelings were hurt that you hadn't been given the opportunity to decide what size napkins we should order or which photographer to use?" Lettie recapped. "So that day in the bridal shop—that was a tantrum?"

"I felt railroaded!"

"Into marrying me!" Lettie shrieked. "Now that's a fate worse than death!"

Gray ran his fingers through his hair and took a deep breath. "I wanted to marry you," he insisted. "But I wanted to do it on my own terms. I didn't want our parents planning everything. I wanted it to be about *us*."

For the first time in five years Lettie realized that she did have to accept some of the blame for what happened. "I was young," she said. "And thoughtless."

Gray stared at her for a minute. Then he said, "Thank you for that."

She tried to shrug off what they both knew was a major concession on her part. "I want to be fair."

"It wasn't only the huge, over-the-top wedding that bothered me," Gray told her softly. "I really did want to give the business with Lowell a chance."

"So it all came down to a choice between the business or me, and you chose the business?" Even after five years it hurt to say the words.

"No, it came down to whether or not we loved each other enough to make a marriage work," he said softly. "I know I handled things badly at the bridal shop that day. But afterward I called you a hundred times, and you wouldn't take my calls. I came to your apartment, and you wouldn't answer the door."

"It was childish to refuse your calls," Lettie admitted, and this time it was easier.

"That's when I realized that if we couldn't work through our first big problem, we had no business getting married."

Lettie gave him a skeptical look. "Problem? You think calling off our wedding three days before it was to take place is a 'problem'?"

"It was a big problem," he acknowledged. "I know my timing stunk and I've apologized for that—over and over," Gray reminded her. "But the truth is that life is full of *huge* problems, Lettie. People lose their jobs and have car wrecks. Children get sick and sometimes they die. A marriage relationship has to be strong enough to withstand any and all of that. Ours wasn't."

"Your part of our relationship wasn't strong enough," she corrected. "That's why I lost in the contest with your hiking business!"

"You chose the wedding over me!" he countered. "If you'd really cared about me you would have taken my calls and we would have worked things out."

Lettie couldn't think of a response to this. For five years, her anger and a sure knowledge that Gray had ruined her life had been all that kept her going. If she had to readjust her thinking—give up her anger—how would she make it through a single day?

Finally Gray pushed away from the counter and walked over to the window. "I'm sorry. I didn't mean to say any of that."

"I forced the issue," she said. "I asked and you answered."

"I guess it doesn't change anything."

"It doesn't change what happened," she agreed. "But at least we have a better understanding of why."

"For what it's worth," he said, "if I had it to do over again, I'd do things differently."

She held her breath as he continued.

"I'd keep my mouth shut and go through with the wedding of the century. I'd get a degree in finance and take a boring job at an investment firm and buy a house in the suburbs. And right now I'd be your husband."

Lettie held onto the counter for support. "Oh Gray," was all she could manage.

"But we can't go back," he pointed out. "The hurt we've inflicted on each other and the regret and the lost years are things we'll have to deal with. We've established that we still have feelings for each other, and before we get back into the real world we need to decide where we go from here."

"I don't know," she told him honestly. "If our relationship wasn't strong enough five years ago, maybe it never will be."

He walked over and stood beside her, close but not quite touching. "There's only one way to find out."

"And what is that?" She stared at his expressive mouth, expecting a kiss.

"We'll have to get to know each other again," was his mildly disappointing reply.

"But we live in different states," she reminded him.

"We can talk on the phone," he proposed. "Then, if that works out well, you could come here and visit."

"And to be fair, you could come to Georgia."

"Fifty-fifty," he agreed. "Both of us making decisions together."

She smiled. "I guess we could give it a try."

"Since you happen to be in town, maybe we could go out to dinner tonight."

"Let's see," she pretended to consider. "Your partner is hospitalized, and I have a friend who is, at this very moment, probably confessing to every unsolved crime from the Lindberg kidnapping on. I don't see any reason why we shouldn't take time out for a nice dinner!"

"Okay," he conceded. "Tonight won't work. But soon."

"Soon." She looked up at him. Five years ago he had been the love of her life. After the horrible scene in the bridal shop, she had considered him her greatest enemy. Now, they were wary friends with the prospect of becoming more in the future. All in all, she decided she couldn't consider the past few days a total loss.

Once the lodge was clean, they gathered up their belongings and walked out into the sunshine.

"It's hard to believe that yesterday we were snowed in," Lettie remarked.

"It is," he agreed as he swung his leg over the seat of the dirt bike. Lettie started to climb on behind him, but Gray held up a hand to stop her. "Just one more thing."

She braced herself. "What?"

"I was wondering." He reached out and traced his finger along her cheek. "Before we leave this pleasant, peaceful spot . . . can I kiss you?"

Her head bobbed up and down of its own accord.

"I'd better warn you, though," he whispered. "This time it counts."

Rather than respond, Lettie leaned in and pressed her lips to his.

CHAPTER 14

Gray drove the dirt bike back to the tour office. The electricity and phone service had been restored so he was able to call Lowell at the hospital. After a brief conversation he hung up and reported to Lettie.

"Lowell is fine and will probably be released tomorrow. Jack and Beth are in the emergency room with Alexa. She's invoked her right to remain silent until she has an attorney present—so you can quit worrying about her being convicted of anything."

Lettie rolled her eyes. "That's a relief."

He pointed to the little snack area. "There are cookies and chips in the cupboard."

Lettie rubbed her stomach. "I was hoping for something a little more substantial."

"The only restaurant between here and the ranger station where we need to return the dirt bike is a Dairy Queen."

Lettie nodded. "Sounds delicious."

Gray led the way outside and opened the passenger door of his truck for Lettie. Then he loaded the dirt bike in the back and climbed in behind the wheel. It only took a few minutes for them to reach the Dairy Queen, and Gray ordered for them both.

When Lettie bit into the huge hamburger, she closed her eyes and said, "This is the best food I've ever eaten in my life."

Gray laughed. "After two days of eating MREs *anything* would taste good."

Lettie wiped a glob of mayonnaise from her chin. "True."

The small parking lot in front of the ranger station was full of vehicles, so Gray had to double-park his truck. "We won't be here long," he offered as an excuse.

The interior of the station was more crowded than the parking lot, but when Captain Woods saw Gray, he waved them back to his office. Once they were all inside, the captain closed his office door.

Gray pulled out a chair for Lettie and once she was seated, he leaned on the back. "You've got quite a bit of company," Gray remarked.

"More than I know what to do with," the captain agreed. "I've got four different law enforcement agencies claiming jurisdiction on the case, and the FBI's on the way to demand a piece of the action. And that's not to mention a hundred complaints from visitors who were trapped by the storm and need someone to blame. We'll probably be deflecting lawsuits for the next ten years." The captain dropped heavily into his swivel chair. "I may decide to retire early."

Gray laughed at this empty threat and then said, "I've got the dirt bike we borrowed in the back of my truck."

The captain reached for his phone. "I'll have someone get it." After the assignment was made, the captain returned his attention to them. "So what can I do for you folks now?"

Lettie scooted forward onto the edge of her chair. "First we wanted to check on Ranger Penny."

The captain leaned his elbows on his desk. "He's going to be fine."

"That's good." Lettie sounded relieved. Then she asked, "Is there anything you can do to prevent charges from being filed against Alexa Whitstone?"

"I just got off the phone with the U.S. Marshals office in Bryson City," the captain replied. "Apparently Jack Gamble has worked out a deal with all the involved parties. Your friend will have to be admitted to the psych ward at Blount County for a couple of weeks and get some drug counseling, but that's the extent of it."

"Oh, that's such good news," Lettie said.

"Yes," Captain Woods agreed. "You've all been through a difficult experience, but it will all be over soon."

Lettie considered this and then said, "Alexa said Mancil Bright was kind to her while she was his hostage. She insisted that she could see goodness in him. But he killed that prison guard and the old man in Memphis. How can a person be so decent in some ways and so heartless in others?"

"Bright was abused as a child and never got much of a chance in life. Maybe if his home situation had been different he would have grown up to be a regular person." The captain shrugged. "Maybe not. But I'm glad he treated your friend well."

Lettie nodded. "Me too."

Gray stood. "We've taken up enough of your time," he said. "We'll either be at the tour office or the hospital if you need us."

The captain nodded. "We'll call if we need you."

Gray opened the door and waited for Lettie to precede him out into the melee.

*   *   *

Beth had just dozed off in one of the uncomfortable hospital chairs when Jack's cell phone rang. She opened her eyes as he answered it.

"Oh hey, Miss Eugenia," he said with a meaningful look at Beth. She smiled.

"Yes, ma'am," Jack said. "We're all fine, and we'll be headed back home soon."

There was a pause before Jack added, "I'm glad you're out of the hospital and I appreciate your offer to move into our house and help with Chloe and Hank, but I think Beth's mother and Roberta can handle things until we get home. And I hope you learned your lesson about dealing with criminals."

There was a long pause. Finally Jack said, "Yes, ma'am," and closed the phone.

"Well?" Beth asked.

Jack frowned. "She didn't learn her lesson."

Beth laughed. "You know that saying about teaching old dogs new tricks."

"Miss Eugenia gives that saying a whole new dimension."

A nurse approached them. "Mr. Gamble?"

Jack stood. "That's me."

"We've got Ms. Whitstone admitted and now her doctor would like to speak to you."

"Great," Jack muttered under his breath. Then he followed the nurse down the hall.

* * *

When Lettie and Gray walked into Lowell's hospital room, Mary Margaret jumped from her chair to greet them. She gave Lettie a hug and asked, "Are you okay?"

"Gray's been torturing me with horrible food for two days, but otherwise I'm fine."

Mary Margaret's eyes moved to Gray. She didn't sense any of the animosity that had been present between the two of them at the lodge. "I'm surprised at you, Gray," she said. "I always thought you were a gentleman."

"I gave her first choice of MRE," he defended himself.

Lettie seemed only too happy to expound on the subject. "He let me pick between chili macaroni and chicken a la king! It's a miracle I didn't starve to death, not to mention freeze—he also made me walk miles through ten feet of snow!"

"Ten feet *might* be an exaggeration," Gray objected mildly.

Mary Margaret laughed. "In spite of your recent trial, I have to say you seem to be in good spirits."

Lettie acknowledged this with a smile. "What can I say? I'm a trooper."

Gray walked over to stand beside the bed and addressed Lowell. "You look like garbage."

"Then I look better than you," Lowell returned.

Lettie turned to Mary Margaret and shrugged. "I don't really get male bonding, but I think they're expressing love and concern for each other."

"Actually, I'm just stating the facts," Gray corrected as the phone rang.

"That's probably a reporter wanting to get the details of your ordeal," Gray predicted with a smile at Lowell.

Lowell groaned and Mary Margaret took pity on him. "Do you want me to get it?" she asked.

Lowell nodded. "Please."

She picked up the receiver and said, "This is Mary Margaret McKenzie."

"Mary Margaret," Jack Gamble's voice replied. "We've got Alexa admitted to the hospital and her parents are on the way."

"I'm glad that they are finally getting involved," Mary Margaret said. "Can we visit her?"

"Not for the first forty-eight hours."

"Do you know how long she'll have to stay there?"

"At least a week," Jack answered.

Mary Margaret sighed. "So are you and Beth headed back to Georgia?"

"Yes, we're climbing into our slightly weather-damaged Hummer as we speak."

"Tell Beth I said hi and be careful."

"I will," Jack promised. Then he disconnected the call.

Mary Margaret replaced the receiver and spoke to her audience. "It was Jack," she told them unnecessarily. "Alexa's been admitted and will have to stay for at least a week."

"Hopefully it will do Alexa some good," Lettie added.

"Hopefully," Lowell agreed.

"This reunion trip wasn't exactly a success in the traditional sense," Lettie remarked. "But I think you did accomplish what you set out to do. We're friends again."

Mary Margaret nodded. "We're there for each other."

"That reminds me." Lowell waved for Mary Margaret to come closer. "There's something I need to give you."

Mary Margaret stepped up to his bedside and Lowell leaned forward. Then he pressed a quick kiss to her cheek. "You've now been kissed by a man. Mark it off the list."

Lettie let out a small scream, but Mary Margaret just laughed. "I will." Then she turned to Lettie. "I guess that means we'll be flying home tomorrow by ourselves."

"I guess so," Lettie agreed, but she wasn't looking forward to leaving. "I can't say I've had fun," she said. "But I'll admit that I'm kind of sorry to go." She smiled at Gray and her cheeks turned pink.

Lowell caught Mary Margaret's hand in his. "I was a terrible host during your stay here, and I want to make it up to you. Would you be willing to come back—after I've had time to heal up—and let me show you the sights around Gatlinburg?"

If any other man had posed this question, Mary Margaret would have been tongue-tied with embarrassment. But for some reason she was comfortable with Lowell. "I think that sounds like a lot of fun."

Lowell seemed encouraged by her answer. "And this summer I might take a trip to the Georgia coastline. I'd have to drive right through Tifton, so maybe we could get together."

Mary Margaret squeezed his fingers. "Sure."

"Gray has promised to take me out to dinner," Lettie remarked. "And I figure he owes me at least that much after all those horrible MREs. So we can double."

"Double *date?*" Lowell looked from Lettie to Gray. Then he turned to Mary Margaret. "Can you call a doctor in here quick? My ears must be deceiving me!"

"You heard right," Gray told him. "Lettie and I have called a truce."

"I've accepted that Gray wasn't completely to blame for our breakup," Lettie added. "Mostly, but not completely."

Mary Margaret nodded in solemn agreement. "I told you it was bad luck to let Gray see you in your wedding dress. It was all downhill from there."

* * *

Beth snuggled down in the front passenger seat of the H3 as Jack maneuvered the vehicle through the sparse traffic in Gatlinburg. Once they were headed toward Chattanooga and the Hummer dealership where payment arrangements would be made, she closed her eyes.

A few minutes later Jack surprised her by saying, "I talked to Cole Brackner."

She opened her eyes. "You did?"

Jack nodded but kept his gaze safely focused on the road. "I explained that I was committed to the state senate until my term ends next January, so at this point I can only work for the boys' ranch part-time. But we can go ahead and buy the additional property and set up some fund-raisers—maybe even hire an architect to design the new houses we'll want to build."

Beth didn't know whether to laugh or cry. "You're really going to do it?"

"I really am."

"What if you miss politics?"

"I can still be actively involved in the political process," Jack said. "I'll just stay behind the scenes instead of in the spotlight." He risked a glance at her. "I wasn't successful in saving the world through new legislation. Maybe I'll do better if I concentrate on one boy at a time."

Beth smiled. "And I can work by your side instead of cringing in the background."

"Is that how it's been for you?" he asked, and she could hear the regret in his voice.

"Not all the time," she tempered her statement. "But I'll be much more comfortable with orphaned boys than I was with self-important politicians."

He reached over and stroked her cheek. "I'm sorry."

"Don't be." She caught his hand and pressed his fingers to her lips. Then she murmured, "I knew what I was getting into when I married the great Jack Gamble. But I'll admit that I'm excited about this change of direction." She laced her fingers through his and twisted in the seat so she could face him. "So, what's our first step?"

Jack disengaged his hand from hers and returned it to the steering wheel. "First, I'll call Mr. Fuller and tell him to find another candidate for governor. And while I have him on the phone I'll mention that I won't be running for reelection. Then I guess I should buy a cowboy hat—since I'm going to be a gentleman rancher."

Beth dissolved into laughter. "The boys are going to love you!"

* * *

As Eugenia mixed up a fresh batch of tea cakes to replace the ones Polly had eaten, her conversation with Jack kept running through her mind. "Learned my lesson," she said to Lady. "The very idea! That Jack Gamble has a lot of nerve."

The phone rang and Eugenia answered it promptly. It was Cornelia Blackwood.

"I hope you're feeling better," the preacher's wife greeted.

"I'm fine," Eugenia said for the hundredth time. Her phone had been ringing all morning with calls from gossip seekers disguised as well-wishers.

"I can't believe how brave you were, standing up to a murderer like that," Cornelia went on.

"I'm not sure Dean Lumpkin is a murderer," Eugenia replied impatiently. "He's a disturbed young man who needs professional help."

"What a Christian attitude!" Cornelia praised. "And that reminds me of the wonderful sermon Brother Blackwood preached this morning. It was about loving one another, as Jesus encouraged His disciples to do."

Eugenia had hoped that her hospitalization and subsequent inability to attend any church services that morning would put an end to the religious competition. But apparently that was not the case. "That sounds interesting."

"And since the preacher confides in me." Cornelia paused to giggle, and Eugenia rolled her eyes. "I happen to know that tonight, Brother Blackwood is going to honor you and your service to the community!"

Now this was a new twist on the "get-Eugenia-to-church" attempts, and Eugenia wondered how long it would take Brother Watty and the Methodists to come up with a commendation of their own. "That's awfully nice," she told Cornelia.

"I knew you'd want to know so you could make plans to be there," Cornelia added.

"I don't think I'll be sufficiently recovered from my ordeal with Mr. Lumpkin to attend any church services tonight. But please tell Brother Blackwood how much I appreciate the tribute."

"Well." Cornelia sounded disappointed. "I'll save you a seat at the front in case you feel better."

"Thank you," Eugenia said. "And please thank your congregation in my behalf."

As Eugenia hung up the phone, there was a knock on the back door.

"If this is the Methodists I'm moving in with Annabelle," she whispered to Lady.

The little dog barked and followed her to the door. When Eugenia opened the door she was pleased to see Whit Owens on her back steps.

"Hey Whit," she greeted as Lady ran out into the yard.

"I hope I'm not disturbing you," he said. "But I wanted to check and see how you're feeling."

She walked out and down the stairs to stand beside him. "I'm feeling pretty good. My only complaints are occasional dizziness and a sore right arm."

Whit frowned. "Did Dean Lumpkin do something to your arm?"

"No, that's from answering the phone too many times. I declare, everybody in Haggerty has called me at least once."

Whit laughed. "To get the juicy details of your ordeal?"

"No, Polly's already provided everyone with more details than they could possibly want to know," Eugenia replied. "I think folks are mostly calling to see if the medicine Dean Lumpkin gave me succeeded in making me crazy."

"Which it didn't."

"Not much anyway," Eugenia agreed. "And they want to invite me to their church services tonight, of course. Since this is their last chance to get me there this weekend."

"Of course," Whit said with a smile. "The religious zealots!"

Eugenia had to laugh. "I know most of them mean well, but I can only be in one place at a time."

"I've heard that the Baptists are dedicating their entire evening sermon to you."

Eugenia rolled her eyes. "And the Methodists have brought in a guest preacher since they think I don't like Brother Watty."

Whit frowned. "Who could dislike Brother Watty?"

"That's a good question," Eugenia said.

"So, which congregation are you going to choose?"

Eugenia gave him a narrow look. "You too?"

He shook his head. "I don't have a stake in your decision—I'm just curious."

"Since I don't want to hurt anyone's feelings, I'm going to stay home tonight and recuperate."

Whit nodded. "Very judicious."

She walked out into the yard and picked up Lady. "You don't think I'm a coward?"

Whit laughed. "That's one thing no one could ever accuse you of!"

"I'll take that as a compliment."

"You should," Whit assured her. They walked around the back-yard for a few minutes and finally Whit cleared his throat. "I was wondering," he began. "Well, since you're staying in tonight, would it be, or, I mean, could I . . ."

"What is it, Whit?" Eugenia prompted.

"Could I make you dinner?" he blurted.

Eugenia watched him squirm for a few seconds before saying, "Of course. Have you ever known me to turn down a free meal?"

Whit beamed at her. "I'll come back at six o'clock if that's convenient."

"That's perfect," Eugenia said absently as her attention focused on a silver van that was turning down Maple. Eugenia blinked, thinking that Dean Lumpkin's medication was finally kicking in, causing her to hallucinate. Then Kate waved to her from the passenger seat, and Eugenia knew the van wasn't a figment of her imagination.

As tears blurred her vision, she whispered, "They're home."

Whit followed the direction of her gaze and smiled. "It sure looks that way. Let me hold Lady while you go and greet them."

The van pulled into the Iversons' driveway and parked in its regular spot.

After Eugenia had hugged all the members of the Iverson family, she said, "I thought you were never coming back." She fixed an annoyed look at Mark. "How long could it possibly take to train you to be an FBI supervisor?"

Mark smiled. "I guess I'm a slow learner."

"We've got a present for you!" Emily announced.

"Emily! We were going to wait until Easter," Kate scolded mildly.

"Sorry," Emily said, but she didn't seem repentant. "Can we give it to her now?"

"Is it Easter?" little Charles asked in confusion.

Kate laughed. "It's not Easter, but I guess we can go ahead and give Miss Eugenia her present since the beans have already been spilled."

"What beans?" Emily asked.

"I hate beans," Charles assured them all.

Kate rolled her eyes and reached inside the van. A few seconds later she pulled out a frame and handed it to Eugenia. Underneath the glass, showcased by a combination of color-coordinated mats, was the recipe card for red velvet cake written personally by Eugenia's mother.

"That recipe card is such a treasure," Kate explained. "It worried me that you didn't have it protected in any way. So I took it with me to Atlanta and had it framed."

Eugenia stared at the familiar card, unable to speak.

"I wanted to do the recipe card Annabelle has for boiled custard too, so I got Derrick to sneak it out of her recipe box."

Eugenia shook her head. "*You* took our recipe cards."

"I know I should have told you," Kate admitted. "But I wanted it to be a surprise, and I knew you wouldn't need yours until next Christmas Eve, since that's the only time you make red velvet cake. And surely Annabelle has the recipe for boiled custard memorized by now!"

Eugenia started laughing. "I owe Polly a huge apology!"

Kate frowned. "Why?"

"Because I thought *she* took the recipe cards, and I've been calling her a kleptomaniac for days!"

"Poor Miss Polly," Kate said.

"That's not all she's been doing," Whit interjected. "She's also caught at least one murderer, maybe two."

Kate's eyes widened and Mark said, "Why doesn't that surprise me?"

"Whether it surprises you or not, it's going to involve you," Eugenia informed him. "I put the information on the desk in your office."

Mark sighed. "Yep, we're home all right."

Kate laughed. "And it feels wonderful!"

"I can't wait to tell you all that has been going on," Eugenia said. "The Baptists and Methodists have been competing for my Sabbath day attendance, and I didn't know which one to choose, since I didn't want to hurt anyone's feelings."

Mark frowned. "Since when are you worried about hurting people's feelings?"

Eugenia ignored him. "So I'm staying home all day!"

Whit laughed. "In spite of the fact that the Baptist service this evening is a tribute to Eugenia and her courage."

"So they'll be singing your praises without the guest of honor?" Mark clarified.

Eugenia waved this aside. "It will be good practice for my funeral. Now hurry and get unpacked and then come over so I can tell you everything that has happened since you left. Whit's making dinner."

"I'll be back at six," Whit promised, heading for his car.

Kate watched him leave and then said, "We haven't been gone all that long. How much could have happened?"

Eugenia shook her head. "You'll be amazed."

* * *

Lettie took a bite of the Hershey bar Gray had gotten for her from the vending machine and said, "I hope you don't think this is going to count as taking me out to dinner."

He smiled. "No, I have several ideas about where I'd like to take you for our first official date, and none of them involves hospitals or vending machines."

She was pleased by this answer. "Good. I'm not crazy about either one." She polished off the candy and tossed the wrapper into a nearby trash can.

Then Gray took both of her hands in his and leaned close. "I want to talk to you about something important."

"Okay," she agreed, although her heart was pounding so hard she doubted she'd be able to hear a word he said.

His fingers stroked hers and she smiled. She knew him so well. He was trying to find the right words to express his feelings. If only he'd known that the warm brown color of his eyes was already speaking volumes.

"When you get back to your life being a historical investment person, you're going to be busy," he began.

She nodded. "That's true. You'll be busy for the next few weeks too, since Lowell is out of commission."

"Yes," he agreed. "And you might even get so busy that you think you don't have time for me in your life. You might decide that you can't come back here for our big date."

Lettie wanted to reassure him. "The past few days have taught me to make time for my friends."

He shook his head. "Sometimes life gets in the way. So I want to give you something to help you remain committed to our new friendship."

"What?" Lettie asked breathlessly.

"I love you," he whispered. Then he leaned forward and pressed his lips to hers. It was the sweetest kiss they'd ever shared, full of not only love, but also forgiveness and understanding. It ended abruptly when they heard someone whistle.

Lettie's eyes flew open and she saw Mary Margaret and Lowell standing a few feet away.

"Now that's what I call a truce," Lowell said reverently.

HAGGERTY HOSPITALITY

MOTHER'S RED VELVET CAKE

2 Tbsp unsweetened cocoa powder
1 1/2 cups sugar
2 oz. red food coloring
2 eggs
1 cup buttermilk
2 1/2 cups all-purpose flour, sifted
1 tsp salt
1 1/2 tsp baking soda
1 tsp vanilla extract
1 tsp white vinegar
1/2 cup shortening

Grease two 9-inch round cake pans. Preheat oven to 350°F. Make a paste of cocoa and food coloring. Set aside. Combine buttermilk, salt, and vanilla. Set aside. In a large bowl, cream together shortening and sugar until light and fluffy. Beat in eggs one at a time, then add cocoa mixture and stir. Beat in buttermilk mixture alternately with flour, mixing just until incorporated. Stir together baking soda and vinegar, then gently fold into cake batter. Pour batter into prepared pans. Bake for 30 minutes, or until a toothpick inserted into the center of the cake comes out clean. Allow to cool completely before frosting.

Icing:

1 cup milk
1 cup butter
5 Tbsp all-purpose flour
1 tsp vanilla extract
1 cup sugar

In a saucepan, combine milk and flour. Cook over low heat, stirring constantly, until mixture thickens. Set aside to cool completely. Cream together butter, sugar, and vanilla until light and fluffy, then stir in the cooled milk and flour mixture, beating until icing reaches spreading consistency.

Refrigerate cake until time to serve.

MOTHER'S BOILED CUSTARD

1 quart whole milk
1/2 Tbsp vanilla extract
4 eggs, well beaten
1 1/2 cups sugar

Put eggs and sugar in a blender and mix well. Add as much of the milk as you can, and mix again. Then pour mixture and additional milk into a double boiler. Cook on high until the water in the double boiler is hot, then reduce heat to medium. Stir constantly until custard thickens enough to coat the spoon. Pour custard into a mixing bowl and beat with mixer on low until slightly cooled. Add vanilla. Refrigerate.

MISS POLLY'S ITALIAN CREAM CAKE

1/2 cup margarine
1 cup buttermilk
1/2 cup vegetable shortening
1 tsp vanilla extract
2 cups sugar
7-oz. can Angel Flake coconut
5 egg yolks
1 cup chopped pecans
2 cups flour
5 egg whites (stiffly beaten)
1 tsp baking soda

Grease and flour three 9-inch round cake pans. Preheat oven to 350°F. Cream together shortening and margarine. Add sugar and beat until smooth. Add egg yolks and beat well. Combine flour and soda and add to creamed mixture, alternating with buttermilk. Stir in vanilla, coconut, and nuts. Fold in egg whites. Pour batter into pans. Bake for 25 minutes. Cool and frost with icing.

Icing:

8-oz. pkg cream cheese
1 tsp vanilla extract
1/4 cup margarine
1/2 cup chopped nuts
1 box confectioners' sugar

Beat cream cheese and margarine until smooth. Add sugar and mix well. Add vanilla and beat until smooth. Spread between cake layers and sprinkle with nuts before stacking. Then frost sides and top of cake. Top with remaining nuts.

MISS GEORGE ANN'S BOSTON CREAM CAKE

1 milk chocolate cake mix
3 eggs
2 large vanilla instant pudding mixes
1 tsp vanilla extract
12-oz. tub Cool Whip
1/3 cup vegetable oil
6 cups cold milk
1 1/4 cups water

Mix cake according to package directions. Bake in a 9x13-inch pan. While cake is baking, mix 1 package vanilla pudding using 4 cups of milk (1 cup more than directions call for). When cake is done but still hot, poke holes in it with a straw. Then pour pudding mixture over cake. Refrigerate until cool. Mix one package vanilla pudding with 2 cups of milk (1 cup less than directions call for). Add vanilla and Cool Whip. Mix well. Spread over cooled cake. Keep refrigerated until time to serve.

DERRICK MORGAN'S GERMAN CHOCOLATE UPSIDE-DOWN CAKE

1 cup shredded coconut
8-oz. pkg cream cheese, softened
1 cup chopped pecans
16-oz. box confectioners' sugar
1 German chocolate cake mix
1 stick margarine

Preheat oven to 350°F. Lightly grease a 9x13-inch pan. Combine coconut and chopped pecans and spread on bottom of pan. Prepare cake mix according to package directions. Pour cake batter into pan (over coconut/pecan mixture) and set aside. Combine margarine and cream cheese in a saucepan and heat on medium-low until melted enough to stir in confectioners' sugar. Mix well. Spoon this mixture over cake batter. Bake for 40 minutes. Cool before cutting.

WHIT OWENS'S PERFECT POUND CAKE (back by popular demand)

    3 sticks butter
    8-oz. pkg cream cheese
    3 cups sugar
    6 eggs
    3 cups cake flour
    1/4 tsp salt
    2 tsp vanilla extract

Soften cream cheese and butter, then cream together. Add sugar and mix well (about 5 minutes). Add eggs one at a time, mixing well after each addition. Add salt and vanilla, then add flour 1 cup at a time and mix sparingly (just until blended). Pour into greased and floured pound cake pan and bake at 350°F for 1 hour and 15 minutes.

ABOUT THE AUTHOR

BETSY BRANNON GREEN currently lives in Bessemer, Alabama, which is a suburb of Birmingham. She has been married to her husband, Butch, for twenty-five years, and they have eight children. She loves to read—when she can find the time—and watch sporting events—if they involve her children. She is the Young Women president in the Bessemer Ward. Although born in Salt Lake City, Betsy has spent most of her life in the South, and her writing has been strongly influenced by the Southern hospitality she has experienced there. Her first book, *Hearts in Hiding,* was published in 2001, followed by *Never Look Back* (2002), *Until Proven Guilty* (2002), *Don't Close Your Eyes* (2003), *Above Suspicion* (2003), *Foul Play* (2004), *Silenced* (2004), *Copycat* (2005), *Poison* (2005), *Double Cross* (2006).

If you would like to be updated on Betsy's newest releases or correspond with her, please send an e-mail to info@covenant-lds.com, or visit her website at http://betsybrannongreen.net. You may also write to her in care of Covenant Communications, P.O. Box 416, American Fork, UT 84003-0416.